Diamond
Geezer

A crime thriller novel by

Sandra Prior

This paperback edition 2014

1

First published in Great Britain by JJD Publishers 2014

Sandra Prior asserts the moral right to be identified as the author of this work

A catalogue record for this book is available from the British Library

ISBN 978-0-9574442-4-9

Dedication

Diamond Geezer is dedicated to my brother, Johnnie Prior.

Johnnie wasn't just my brother; he was my friend. He was always there when I needed him, and he always gave me plenty of time and understanding. In fact, no one could understand my craziness like he did!

Johnnie taught me one of the most important purposes of life -- to show love and receive it. It's something he learned from our Mum and Dad. Sadly, my parents, Johnnie and my sister Shirley are not here with me today. Not a day goes by that I don't miss them. Johnnie and Shirley were both real characters whose memories I will carry with me forever.

So, Johnnie, here's to you! You will be in my heart for a lifetime, and you will always be my Diamond Geezer.

Acknowledgements

A big, big, "thank you" to Wendy Hearn, who has been there since day one. Ever since I wrote the first sentence of Dangerous, she has given me endless support. Wendy has always believed in me and my dreams -- and she has helped me believe in myself. She has become a friend and confidant who has listened to all of my rants, raves, moans, and groans. Without Wendy, I don't think I would have made it this far. She has always been energetic, positive, and encouraging about my writing, and every time we get off the phone, I have a smile on my face. I am grateful for her passion, dedication and support, and I can never thank her enough.

Don McNab-Stark - Don saw my manuscript and believed in it. Working with him has been a pleasure, and I will be forever grateful for his invaluable feedback and suggestions. I can't thank him enough for his insight, his inspiration, and his unflagging guidance -- and I can't wait to work with him on my next book!

For

My children: Jemma, Jade, Mark and Reece and my grandchildren Jaime, Johnnie, Darcey and Arabella. My greatest achievements.

To my readers:

I am nothing without you. Whether you've encouraged me on Facebook, followed my progress on Twitter, or taken the time to visit me at a book signing, you have given me more encouragement than you will ever know. This book is my gift to you!

"Whether we fall by ambition, blood, or lust, like diamonds we are cut with our own dust."

John Webster

Charlie and Samantha

Heads turned as the woman ordered herself a drink at the bar. Strikingly attractive in a figure hugging red dress and black high heels, her dark, lustrous hair fell on her slender neck. She was tall, at least five feet eight, but it was her eyes that were her most distinguishing feature. Big and brown, set above high cheekbones, they swept the room, taking everything in.

The man next to her hurriedly offered her his stool, which she accepted, but when he tried to make small talk she studiously ignored him. Instead, she drew deeply on her cigarette, scanned the bar and dance floor as though looking for someone.

She looked outwardly calm, but anyone paying close attention would spot the tension in her as she slipped her heel from her stiletto shoe and jiggled it up and down impatiently.

Suddenly her demeanour changed. She had spotted her target. She stubbed out her cigarette, rose to her feet, smoothed out her dress and glided out onto the dance floor.

Charlie Taylor loved being the centre of attention. Since his brother Bobby had died, he'd been putting himself about much more, muscling in on Mickey's territory, daring anyone to challenge him. He was a big man, over six feet tall and built like a brick shit house, with short, curly brown hair and a face like a pit bull. But the women didn't seem to care about his looks – they liked the hint of menace in his face, the way he threw money at them, even seemed to tolerate his sudden, violent changes of mood.

The girl he was dancing with was a typical Dagenham Slapper – that's what he called them. Lots of make-up, tits, no common sense. Thick as shit but good at opening their legs and giving a decent blow job. She knew who Charlie was, but she didn't care. If he hadn't drunk too much, he'd take her out back of the hotel later on, give her a seeing to, slap her around a bit, send her on her way with fifty quid in her pocket. Everyone happy, no questions asked. Occasionally he'd go a little too far, break a nose or something, and one of them would complain, but it was amazing what a few hundred quid could do. And if they didn't bite on that, well, the threat of violence, a visit to their family, would soon shut them up.

Charlie pulled the slapper close – what the fuck was her name? – ground his hips into her. He'd had a skinful, but he could still feel himself getting hard as she wiggled against him. He slobbered on her neck, squeezed her bum, but then suddenly stopped when he saw the woman in the red dress. The only person standing still in the mass of moving bodies, she had a presence that demanded attention. Charlie stopped dancing, gazed at the woman. There was no doubt, she was staring straight at him.

He could see his minders on the edge of the dance floor, on alert, wondering who she was. He waved them off, shoved the nameless slapper away from him, and returned his arrogant gaze to the woman in the red dress. 'Fuck me, you're a bit of alright, darling', he said, moving towards her.

The girl he had been with looked back and forth between them. 'Who the fuck is she?' she protested, pulling at Charlie's arm.

'Out of your league,' oozed Charlie as he stepped closer to the beautiful woman, held out his hand.

The slapper didn't give up. 'What the fuck you playing at? You're wiv me!'

Charlie turned, laughed in her face. 'Not anymore.'

The girl grabbed at his arm, he turned and pushed her away. 'Fuck off, you dirty slag!' he snarled. She stumbled on her high heels, fell flat on her arse. She started to climb to her feet, but before she could get close to Charlie, his minders had scooped her up, dragged her off the dance floor, pushed fifty quid in her hand. She glared back at Charlie and the woman in the red dress, then shoved the money inside her bra and staggered off to the ladies' room. 'Fucking wanker!' she muttered as she tottered away.

The woman held her hand out to Charlie. 'I'm Samantha.'

As Charlie reached forward to shake her hand, she leaned in close to him, so close that he could smell her perfume, whispered in his ear, 'Do you believe in fate?' Her voice was deep, husky.

He shrugged, noncommittal, but she could see the desire in his face, his beady eyes taking in her curves as he pulled her close, ground his hips against her in time to the music.

His breath was hot on her neck. 'Tell me what you're wearing under there.'

'Red French knickers, silk,' she replied huskily, her lips brushing against his cheek. 'Do you like the feel of silk on your face?'

He gurgled in anticipation.

'I've got a room here,' she whispered. 'Would

you like to join me for a nightcap?' she added, playing up the sex in her voice.

His hands slid down her dress, squeezed her. 'Come on then darlin', what the fuck are we waiting for?'

They walked out of the bar into the lobby. She pressed the lift button, the doors opened immediately and they stepped inside; for a second their eyes met, hers cool and appraising, Charlie's hot, full of lust.

She grinned at him as she pulled him into the lift. It was a smile soft and sweet with an alluring mixture of shyness and seduction. No sooner had the doors closed than he was all over her, his hands groping, his tongue jammed into her mouth. She leaned back against the wall of the lift, forced there by the weight of his body, let him squeeze and grope her.

Out of the lift, she led him to her room, his eyes and hands all over her.

As soon as the door was open they were at it again, kissing their way to the bed, twisting awkwardly as she undid his shirt. She felt his hands go to her knickers. 'Leave them,' she said hoarsely as she ripped open his flies, and then began licking his chest with her sinuous tongue.

Charlie was in no mood to wait. He liked to be in control, liked to make women do what he wanted when he wanted it. He pushed her to her knees. 'That's where you belong!' He dropped his trousers, pulled his pants down, and forced her hot mouth down onto his cock. 'That's what you want, isn't it, you dirty whore?' he growled, forcing her head up and down.

He tilted his head back, breathing hard, feeling the ecstasy rise, then suddenly froze – something cold had been jammed against his bollocks.

He looked down as Samantha looked up, his cock still in her mouth. The cold metal of the .45 shoved into his crotch turned him instantly soft.

Samantha smiled as she spat him out. 'Not so fucking hard now are you?' She flicked at his softening cock with her long, red fingernails. 'Doesn't look like you're up for it anymore.'

Charlie glared at her, tried to keep the fear out of his voice. 'Who the fuck sent you?'

She slowly stood up, running the gun across his fat belly as she rose. 'You're one sick perverted cunt, aren't you?' She scowled. 'Normally I loathe that word, hardly use it, but that's the only real way to describe you.'

Charlie felt himself starting to sweat. He had to wrest control back from this psychotic bitch before things got completely out of hand. 'Whatever they're paying you, I'll double it!' he blustered.

Samantha remained coolness personified. 'No one's paying me. The only one who's going to be paying anything tonight is you!'

She dropped a bag on the bed. The gun was jammed up underneath his jaw. She slid it up across his cheek, almost seductively, then suddenly forced into his mouth.

He gagged as the gun jammed against his tongue.

Again, that sweet smile. 'What was it you said? Oh, I remember – "That's what you want, isn't it, you dirty whore?" She shoved the gun in and out of his mouth, forcing him to suck it the same way he had been forcing her to suck him just minutes before.

Suddenly she pulled the gun out, whipped him across the face with it, sending him sprawling across the bed.

He landed face down, blood flowing from his nose, temporarily stunned – Samantha jumped on his back, straddled him. Click, click. He was handcuffed to the headboard.

'Do you know how difficult it was finding a room with a proper wooden headboard,' she said conversationally as she climbed off, handcuffed his feet to the foot of the bed.

Blinking, still slightly dazed, Charlie twisted his neck to look up at her, his old bluster starting to reassert itself. 'Who the fuck are you?'

Samantha smiled. 'Judge, jury and executioner.'

'When I get out of here I will find you and fuck you to death,' he snarled. 'You fucking hear me?'

Samantha nodded and laughed 'Oh I hear you, prick, and you're really beginning to piss me off. I've had quite enough of it.'

She reached up under her dress, peeled off her silk stockings, left leg first, then the right. 'You're lucky I'm in a good mood tonight. I'm going to make this easy for you.' She wriggled seductively out of her red, silk French knickers, knelt on the bed next to him. 'Remember I asked you if you liked the feel of silk on your face, and you drooled something disgusting at me?'

Before he could respond she wadded her knickers up into a ball, grabbed him by the hair, yanked his head back and jammed the knickers into his mouth. He started to gag, but she was relentless, cramming them in until his mouth was bulging. Then she pulled a roll of gaffer tape from her bag, slapped a strip of it across his mouth to hold the knickers in.

She pressed her face close to his, dropped her voice to a whisper. 'You should be thanking me, cunt. What I really wanted to do with you was lock you in a room full of all the women you have abused and destroyed.' She caressed the side of his face with the gun. 'We would strip you naked, slap your cock on a table, then one at a time batter your dick with a baseball bat. Then crush your fingers, one at a time. Next your toes.' She sat up. 'I'd imagine the pain would be indescribable? Then we'd smash your knees and elbows, for the pure joy of seeing you screaming for mercy, begging for it all to stop, wishing you were dead so that it would all end. That would be lovely, wouldn't it?'

Charlie stared up at her with bulging eyes, his face red as he struggled for breath, sweat pouring down his swollen cheeks.

'But instead, we're going to have to make do with this.' Samantha reached into the bag, pulled out an enormous black dildo. She turned it on – it began vibrating as she slid it across his face, down his back, stroked it between his cheeks.

His eyes bulged even wider, he squirmed, shook his head, tried to say something, anything, to scream, to break free.

Samantha looked down the length of his pale, bloated body, the cheeks of his arse quivering as he strained to look up at her. 'You're just one dirty perverted cunt, Charlie Taylor, a bully who gets pleasure from hurting women and children.' She smiled coldly, positioned the dildo. 'And now it's payback time!'

Charlie's body writhed in agony as she thrust, but no sound escaped his choking throat…

DC Evans

DC Evans walked into the noisy briefing room, a grim humourless smile fixed on his tired face. He had to quieten them down, he could hear the predictable joking and jeering at Charlie Taylor's expense from outside in the corridor. 'OK, OK, enough of that now. I know some of you call this justice, but we have sexual assault, male rape and murder on our hands.'

The room gradually quietened down.

'So,' Evans continued, 'what have any of you learnt from the witnesses?'

'Nothing that we didn't already know about Charlie Taylor, sir.' It was Davis, a young detective with a scrubbed face and short ginger hair who answered him. Jesus, thought Evans, my kids are older than him.

'He has been described as overtly sexual and aggressive towards women,' continued Davis. 'His wife has been in Accident and Emergency several times with various injuries; broken ribs, black eyes, the usual domestic abuse stuff. All accidental of course. On the QT, her friends said she regularly got a good hiding from him, but she was too scared to leave him. Apparently the only time her friends saw her smile was when Charlie Taylor was in prison.'

A cold smile went round the briefing room. 'Mrs Taylor and her children are also on Social Services' at risk register. They were placed in a safe house three months before Charlie Taylor's release from prison.' Davis snapped his notebook shut.

'Nothing new there,' murmured Evans. 'What about you, Ralph?'

Ralph Bloom was an old time cop. Shit, he was even older than Evans! Bloom met Evans' hopeful gaze. 'We talked with his friends, they all say that prior to his death they had been out drinking all night. Charlie Taylor had had a lot to drink and definitely left the night club with a very attractive woman, which friends said was nothing unusual or out of the ordinary.' He glanced round the room at the other officers. 'Word is that Taylor didn't give a toss that he had a wife and a kid indoors, Mr Taylor was never short of a bit of skirt on his arm. Bar staff and the doorman also confirmed this was a regular occurrence, when he left the night club he usually left with a woman on his arm.' He paused. 'Oh, and everyone questioned said Charlie Taylor was definitely not homosexual.'

'Not voluntarily,' sniggered someone.

Evans quieted them with a sharp glance. 'And the woman he left the bar with last night?'

'No one had seen her in the club before,' confirmed Bloom. 'She was a bit of a head turner, so they noticed her. Definitely not a regular.'

Evans nodded, turned to Clifton. Clifton had inspected the room where Charlie's body had been found. 'Does that match what you found at the crime scene?'

Clifton shrugged. 'Yes and no.' Clifton was never one to give a straight answer where a confusing one would do.

'What do you mean?' sighed Evans.

'Well, Charlie Taylor was a big, powerful man with a fearsome reputation. But he was found naked, bound to the bed by handcuffs on his wrists and ankles. Anal sex had taken place, yet there were no other signs of struggle in the room, nothing disturbed or knocked over.'

'And the cause of death?'

'Coroner says asphyxiation, silk underwear rammed deep in his throat.' Clifton looked round the room. 'But he wouldn't have lasted long even if he hadn't choked. He had severe internal bleeding from the rape.'

'And what about the rest of the room?'

Clifton sighed. 'It's the absence of anything that's strange. No robbery had taken place; his wallet was still in his pocket, full. His gold jewellery was still on him.'

Evans nodded. 'So we have to assume that it was either consensual or the woman had a partner?'

Clifton was tall, skinny, his face almost cadaverous. He looked around at everyone. 'Or both?'

Evans scowled, not understanding what he meant.

Clifton continued. 'Think about it. If Taylor was confronted by two men, his first reaction would be to fight. He always had his entourage in tow so if he did get in trouble they were there to protect him. Not that he needed any protection, he could look after himself.'

'But not if it was a woman?' suggested Evans.

'Right. The woman seduces him, somehow gets him handcuffed to the bed, then the man comes in after he's immobilised.'

Evans thought for a moment, his leg swinging as he perched on the edge of the table. 'Did you talk to the psych?'

Clifton nodded, opened his notebook. 'He said we could be looking for a couple.' He read carefully, quoting: 'A dominant-submissive team possibly in their early twenties. A heterosexual male, submissive in everyday life except with his female partner, to her he becomes dominant. The woman might appear to be apprehensive, timid, reclusive, with a problem with authority, socially awkward, not very assertive. This couple would target males who think women are their right.'

Evans rolls his eyes. 'Where do they get that stuff?'

Clifton shrugged his narrow shoulders. 'It fits though. He said that she would lure the victim back to the room, seduce him then tie him up, then once he's subdued her partner arrives.'

'That would explain the rape,' said Evans.

Clifton nodded. 'Right. He said it was about the power and dominance of the act itself. The victim has to be a male with aggressive sexual tendencies. The killer treats his victim the way he himself usually treats women.'

Evans looked around the room at the dubious faces. 'So there you have it. According to the expert, we are looking for a team. A woman who lures and seduces them and a man who rapes and murders him.' He rubbed his hand across his brow as he took a mouthful of his coffee. 'What the fuck happened to good old fashioned crooks?'

'They get fucked to death up the arse by a vibrator,' called a voice from the back of the room. A ripple of laughter greeted the comment.

'Very funny,' moaned Evans. He glared at them all. 'So which one of you wants to go tell this to Mickey Taylor?'

The room fell suddenly silent, everyone suddenly looking down at their shoes.

Evans nodded slowly. 'That's what I thought. Bunch of fucking pussies!'

DC Evans looked around uneasily. He hated putting himself at risk, coming into the heart of the Taylor's territory. But he had to look Mickey in the eye, had to see his reaction when he told him the news, had to know if Mickey knew anything about his uncle's death.

Evans had known Mickey for many years, since he was a little kid, glaring up at Evans when he came knocking at the door looking for Bobby. It was Evans who had been assigned to the case when Bobby Taylor was murdered. No one had ever been caught on that one, not even a peep. Evans was convinced the family knew who had done it, but whoever it was, they certainly weren't about to let on.

Evans had had a few cups of tea with Mrs Taylor and her brood of kids over the years. Lizzie often put a tot of whiskey in his cuppa, to keep him warm she would say to him. Evans thought about her husband, he was an evil bastard, was Bobby Taylor, a notorious east London gangster who made his name on the streets. Taylor had begun his career as a money lender, the word was that he would crucify those who didn't pay their debts, nail them to doors and floors. After his death, his son Mickey Taylor had stepped into his father's shoes.

Since then Mickey had often been in Evans' interview room over at Barking Police Station. Evans always made sure to treat Mickey fairly – he was a crook, and a vicious bastard, of that there was no doubt, but he wasn't a scum bag, didn't deal dope, in fact he hated drugs as much as Evans did. Having Mickey around kept a lid on the worst excesses of the Dagenham underworld – Evans was smart enough to know that without Mickey around things could be a lot worse.

But when you wanted to find Mickey Taylor, that wasn't easy. His family and friends were all suspicious of the police, all denied knowledge of his whereabouts. But after a bit of arm twisting and a couple of greased palms, Mickey had DCI Evans' phone number.

Mickey sat at the bar in the Cross Keys, looked at the phone number for a moment before grabbing the phone from behind the bar and dialling. He didn't want to talk to Evans, but figured if he'd taken this much time to get hold of Mickey, he'd only come looking for him if Mickey didn't call. Mickey would rather have it on his own terms.

'DC Evans speaking.'

'It's Mickey Taylor. What you after?'

'Thanks for calling,' said Evans, trying to keep his voice light. 'I need to talk to you about your Uncle Charlie.'

'I've got nothing to say to you about that cunt,' snapped Mickey.

'What if I told you he was dead?'

'So I'd heard.'

'Do you know how he died? Pretty nasty if you ask me.'

There was no reply. Mickey didn't know.

Mickey rubbed his forehead, scowled. 'Fine. I'm at the Cross Keys.'

'Couldn't you come down to the – '

'I'm at the Cross Keys,' repeated Mickey, and then hung up the phone. He turned to Fat Larry, the barman. 'DCI Evans will be down in a while.'

Larry started to say something, but Mickey cut him off. 'It's all right, he just wants a word with me.'

Evans climbed out of the cab, looked around. An old newspaper wrapped itself around his legs, the wind tugged at his coat. The street was a mess. The bloody dustbin men were on strike again, the black bags piled up on the pavement had been ripped open by the local foxes, and the rubbish had spilled out everywhere.

Evans pulled his collar up high, glanced nervously over his shoulder, pushed open the door of the Cross Keys.

Mickey looked up as the pub door opened and Evans shuffled in. Evans was in his mid-fifties, wearing a battered overcoat. Mickey thought he was a friendly looking bloke for a cop. He looked a bit like Colombo, but without the dodgy eye and the dirty old mac.

They nodded cautiously at each other as Evans approached the bar. Evans' arrival had cast a pall over the pub, sullen whispers and stares in his direction, the silence deafening. Strangers here were distinctly unwelcome. Evans could feel the distrust in the air, was keen to make this as quick as he could and get away.

Mickey nodded to a booth in the corner, grabbed his pint and strutted over to it. Two old men were sitting there, quietly sipping their pints while studying the Racing News. They looked up, saw Mickey approaching – in an instant they had grabbed their newspaper and their drinks and scuttled out of the way.

Mickey sat down heavily, gestured for Evans to do the same.

'Thanks for taking the trouble to contact me personally, Evans,' said Mickey, his voice quiet.

Mickey seemed mild mannered and self–effacing, but Evans wasn't fooled by it. He knew Mickey was probably the most dangerous man in the area. 'You're a hard man to find, Mickey' said Evans.

'Really,' Mickey replied, raising his eyebrows. He looked across the table at DC Evans, then peered into the beer glass, cupped in his big hands, swirling the drink around the sides, watching it as it settled back down at the bottom of the glass. Finally he took a sip, nodded at Evans. 'So what happened to that prick Charlie then? Shot? Knifed? What?'

Evans took a deep breath. 'You're not going to like hearing this.'

Mickey glared at him. 'The bastard's dead? Why should I care how he died?'

'Because he was buggered to death,' said Evans quickly.

Mickey looked up quickly, his glass halfway to his mouth. 'No way, you're having a fucking laugh with me ain't ya?' He furrowed his brows, still not sure. 'You can't be serious?'

Evans nodded his head. 'Serious as a heart attack.'

Mickey leaned back and laughed, his strong white teeth catching the light. 'Well fuck me!' He didn't know whether to laugh or cry. Charlie was a cunt, but he was family. Mickey suddenly glared back at Evans. Was he winding him up? Had he come to tell Mickey to see his reaction? Instantly Mickey closed off his emotions, his face cold, impassive. 'You're taking the piss ain't ya?' snarled Mickey. 'Charlie was a lot of things, but I'd wager ten years of your poxy wages that he wasn't a fucking queer.'

Evans shook his head. 'We think it was a revenge attack.'

'Revenge? For what and who?' snapped Mickey.

Again Evans shook his head. 'Not sure, but he had roughed up a lot of women in his time. Based on the information we have so far, we're looking for a couple, a man and woman in their early twenties, targeting abusers, men who think woman are their right. She lures and seduces them, takes them back to the room, then the man arrives, rapes and murders him.'

'Fuckin' hell!' Mickey sat lost in thought for some time. He felt that something was unspoken in the air, but he wasn't sure what it was. It was in DC Evans' eyes. He'd seen that look before, just couldn't place it. It served Charlie right, mind you, thought Mickey. He hated the cunt, he was a horrible prick just like Mickey's old man, Bobby. But still, finding out about the details of his uncle's death from the Old Bill, that wasn't right. Things were going on out there on the streets that he didn't know about, and that was a worry.

Mickey leaned forward, anger boiling up inside him. Someone was messing with the family! He glared at Evans, spat the words out at him. 'I hated that cunt,' he snarled, 'but that doesn't diminish the pain my family are gonna feel. And it's not a pain I want to discuss with you or anyone else from the police.' He took another mouthful of his drink.

'I appreciate that,' said Evans, trying to stay calm. 'I just wondered – '

Mickey sat back, laughed. 'I know a few of your men who'll be gutted he's dead – they've lost a nice little earner.'

Evans scowled.   'Are you saying there's corruption in the force, Taylor?'   He knew Mickey was right, but he couldn't sit there and allow this crook to insult the police.

Mickey winked at him. 'It depends what your definition of what corruption is, Evans.'   The smile disappeared instantly as Mickey leaned forwards. 'Just keep this out of the papers and low key, cause I don't want to start expressing my concern over the honesty of some of your officers, do I?'

Evans stood up, clicked his teeth, his anger evident.   He started to say something, but Mickey carried on talking. 'You're getting a kick out of this ain't ya? You've just come here to laugh at me and my situation. You don't give a fuck.   You're happy he's dead, I'm happy he's dead. One less prick for you to deal with. I reckon you've really enjoyed telling me this shit, sitting here gloating'.

Evans felt his face reddening. 'I didn't have to come here, Taylor, you know,' he grumbled. 'But in the case of serious accident or death most people are reassured by some sort of formal account, preferably from a senior officer,' he said dryly. He turned to go, and then paused. 'Honestly, I don't give a toss about who or what you are, but I do think, with the state of your uncle lying in the morgue…'   He ground to a halt, looked straight at Mickey. 'Do I look like I give a fuck?'

Evans turned and walked out the pub, the anger coursing through him. He was outside before he started to calm down, the chill wind on his face bringing him back to his senses. It wasn't smart talking like that to Mickey on his home turf, but the cocky bastard had got right up his nose – which, of course, was what he'd been trying to do.

Evans jammed his hands in his pockets, kicked at an empty beer can. He should have known better than to come out here by himself, let a jumped up little shit like Mickey Taylor wind him up.

He puffed out his cheeks and turned suddenly as his sixth sense warned him of a car slowing down behind him. Every copper's nightmare. Alone in the heart of enemy territory. Was it possible Mickey had set him up? He kept walking, fighting back the waves of panic.

'Evans!'

It was Mickey's voice. For a second Evans thought Mickey was about to shoot him.

'Evans! Can we talk?'

Evans turned warily. Mickey was driving the car, a Jag, his window open, seemingly unaware of Evans' fear.

Evans stopped, glanced around – no one else was about. Mickey climbed out of his car, seeming bigger than ever in a thick mohair coat. He was several inches taller than Evans, Mickey loomed over him. He used his height as a form of control, kept his voice low so that Evans had to lean closer to him.

Mickey looked at Evans' pale face. 'You all right, you're looking a bit peaky?'

'Yeah, yeah, I'm fine,' snapped Evans. 'What do you want?'

Mickey grinned. 'I had you scared, didn't I? You thought someone was coming for you?' Mickey moved closer, suddenly put his arm round Evans' shoulder and patted his back. 'Sorry mate, I didn't give it a thought. I saw you walking and wanted to apologise for my rudeness. You're only doing your job. I'm in a bit of shock that's all.'

If Evans was surprised by Mickey's change of heart he kept it to himself.

'You look like an intelligent man,' continued Mickey. 'We both want to find out who did this, right? So how about you help me and vice versa? Then we'll both be happy.'

Evans nodded, non-committal, waiting to see where Mickey was going with it.

'You keep this quiet and out of the papers - I don't want any journalists knocking on my door,' repeated Mickey. 'And take it easy wiv me muvver and sisters, they ain't gonna be able to handle this. They've had enough shit lately, they can do without all this.'

Evans nodded. 'I can do that.'

'Cheers Evans, appreciate that' added Mickey.

'None of them need to know all the gory details, it will destroy them.'

Evans looked up and down the quiet street, the rows of run down council houses with their peeling paintwork, tiny gardens. What must it be like to be the lord of this manor, wondered Evans, to be Mickey Taylor, the Big I Am?

'I know people will tell me if they know anything,' continued Mickey. 'I want the cunt who did this as much as you, Evans. When it's family, it's personal, right?'

Evans nodded. 'I'll try and keep a lid on it,' he said.

Mickey smiled. 'I don't think you're so bad, you know? My dad said was you was an honest man, that you kept your word.'

He released Evans from his grasp and they shook hands awkwardly.

Mickey climbed back into his car, grinned at Evans. 'Give you a lift?'

Evans smiled back. 'Think I'll walk.'

'Suit yourself'

Terri

Terri skittered along the landing of the block of flats, her heels clacking loudly on the bare concrete, rummaged in her bag for the spare key. Turning the key in the lock she slowly opened the door and peered in anxiously before stepping inside, breathing in the usual smell of Georgie's flat: bleach, disinfectant, Fairy Snow soap powder.

She was sure Georgie had OCD; he was obsessed with cleaning and washing his hands, a proper Mary Ann he was. And his entire flat was painted white, ceilings, walls, and doors, everything pristine, gleaming white. Terri thought it looked sterile, like a hospital. There was never anything lying around on the floor, no newspapers, no mess, no pictures on the wall, no ornaments, and no jackets hanging on the coat hooks. Everything was clean, stark white, sparse and unlived-in. Not like their house - since Georgie had moved out it was like a bomb had hit it. They had all got a bit lazy without Georgie around picking up behind them.

Terri reached for the light switch and flicked it on, but nothing happened; she tutted, the bulb must have gone or the electric had been cut off – but that was so unlike Georgie, he was so organised and in control, made sure everything was paid on time. As soon as a bill came in he paid it, hated owing anybody anything. If Georgie ever borrowed any money, he always paid it back down to the last penny.

Moving slowly along the small, dark hallway, Terri felt a strange cold tingle in her stomach. Georgie hadn't been seen or heard of for several days, which was also unlike him. He was always popping in and out of the house to check on Mum, and he never came empty handed. Always bringing Mum something, anything from a bunch of flowers to a bag of sugar. But Lizzie said she hadn't seen or heard a word from him in five days – that was why Terri had come round, Lizzie had asked her to go and check on him. Terri shivered. Something wasn't right, she could feel it.

The kitchen door was wide open. It was just as sterile as the hallway, nothing on the counters, just a white kettle. No tea, coffee or sugar canisters to be seen, no washing up in the sink, no overflowing bin, even his kitchen cupboards were stacked in order, tins, bottles, packets. His wardrobe was the same, everything had to be in order.

Nothing was out of place, but that was normal for Georgie. He had been the same when he was at home, before he moved out into his own flat, always on Mickey's case, telling him to get his arse into gear and tidy up and put things away after him. He told Mickey that he was a lazy bastard, told him off for leaving his clothes on the floor, not pulling the plug out the bath, not flushing the toilet – honestly. Georgie was worse than their mum, worse than anyone she knew, a proper nag when it came to being clean and tidy.

But Mickey never did anything about it – why would he? Georgie would have his moan and then clear up after you anyway. Georgie cleaned up after everyone. If you got up off the chair he would be behind you fluffing the cushion, before you finished your cup of tea he would have it out of your hand, washed up and put away. Sharon had even paid Georgie to clear up her side of the bedroom when they were younger, paid him to do her ironing and any other jobs she had to do indoors. Georgie liked ironing, said it was very therapeutic - he even ironed his socks and pants.

Terri walked past the wide-open bathroom door, everything again clean and white, nothing out, only a toilet roll on its holder, white fresh towels hung on the rail, no dirty washing on the floor, the toilet lid down. She took a few steps towards his bedroom – the door was open a crack. Terri peered inside – it was almost blinding, white bedspread, white curtains, white carpet, white wardrobe. Terri stopped, frowned. One of the wardrobe doors was half open, and hanging inside was a girl's black dress.

She peered at it, confusion furrowing her brow. Georgie was gay, all the family knew it, though it was never spoken about or discussed. They all just pushed under the carpet, preferred not to even think about it. But if Mickey had ever heard anyone say anything or take the piss he would have killed them. Georgie wasn't open about it in public – it was still pretty taboo in Dagenham – but he'd never hidden it from her. He didn't have to. Terri had always known Georgie was different. He wasn't into all the boys stuff. He was a bit of a loner, very quiet and liked his own company. He spent most of his time reading, he was so clever and intelligent, Georgie was definitely the brains of the family. He always helped Terri get ready before a night out. He would paint her finger nails for her, do her toes, blow dry and tong her hair for her. Georgie loved it, all the fussing about, appearance was very important to Georgie.

He had brilliant fashion sense too, always looked the bollocks. He didn't look queer or gay, he wasn't feminine in the way he walked or talked, he was a proper man, good looking, charming and respectful. He also liked cooking, was always knocking up different recipes for the family to try. What more could a girl want in a man? Georgie would have made a brilliant husband and dad, thought Terri, what a waste of a good man.

But as she stepped into his room she saw black stilettos next to his bed, a pair of French red knickers and a bra on the pillow. Mystified, Terri looked around the room, her eyes falling on more and more women's things. Make up and perfume on the dressing table, lipsticks of all different colours stacked neatly against the mirror. It looked like the cosmetics counter in Debenhams.

Terri was shocked. Fucking hell, Georgie had kept that quiet! He had some bird on the go! She wondered why he hadn't told her about this new girlfriend. He knew he could trust Terri with anything. Maybe this was why he didn't want anyone coming up the flat – he was probably confused, wasn't sure himself about his sexuality.

She walked further into his bedroom, opened the wardrobe door all the way – blimey, it was full of women's clothes! Dresses, suits, skirts, shoes. Had this mystery girlfriend moved in with him? She peered in the wardrobe, picked up a length of rope, some stockings, handcuffs, a wig. Fucking hell! He was into some kinky stuff! She felt herself blushing. No, not Georgie, he wasn't like that. He was a kind and gentle man. Not sadistic or dodgy in any way.

She walked out of his room towards the living room, more confused than ever.

'Georgie, it's me Terri!' she shouted. 'You in there?'

'Go away,' Georgie hollered back. 'I told you not to come here, to leave me alone.'

Hot tears stung her eyes. That didn't sound like the Georgie she knew – what was going on? Terri put a brave smile on her face. 'Come on Georgie, sort ya self out or we're going to be late for mum's big night out!' She forced a smile to her face. 'Chop Chop, Chinese Navy. Everyone's waiting for you, you know how impatient Mickey is, you don't wanna give him the hump do ya?'

'I've told you, go away, you aren't welcome here anymore!'

There was an edge to his voice that she didn't recognise. It made the hairs on the back of her neck stand up, scared Terri. That didn't sound like Georgie, not the Georgie she knew; he never raised his voice or said a bad thing about anyone. Something wasn't right, wasn't what it should be. What was going on with him, going on in his head?

To tell the truth, Terri had been worried about him since their dad died. He wasn't the same person. She couldn't remember the last time she saw him smile or even laugh. Georgie had become distant and detached, pulling himself away from everyone around him. He kept complaining of severe headaches and various pains, nothing specific. She got him to the doctor's, he had some tests done, they didn't find anything, but he kept waking at night crying and screaming with nightmares. Terri had tried everything she could to help him through his grief, but his emotions seemed awkward, false, like he was hiding something.

Was he grieving for his dad? Grief could affect people in so many different ways; Georgie seemed full of hopelessness and despair. Terri was no doctor, but she knew people reacted differently to the death of a family member, and, well, given Georgie's role in their dad's death, that would be enough to send anyone off their rocker. She had tried getting him to the doctor again but Georgie was having none of it, said he was fine, there was nothing wrong with him and to stop fussing about him.

Terri walked hesitantly towards the living room, a pained expression on her face, her eyes looking nervously around, stepped softly into the room. It was dark, she could just make out Georgie's silhouette, illuminated by a tiny streak of light sneaking through a small gap in the curtains. He was standing in front of the window with his back to her. 'Georgie?' she said softly.

There was a long silence. Finally she heard him exhale deeply, saw him move slightly. 'I told you not to come here,' he said in an angry tone, 'so just fuck off, go away!'

Terri stood still, frozen in shock, staggered, staring at Georgie. She didn't realise he had got this bad. This was far worse than she'd imagined. She peered into the darkness, but could see nothing. She took a deep breath, forced herself to speak slowly, calmly. 'Can you open the curtains please, let a bit of light in here?'

For a long time Georgie did nothing, then he suddenly turned and ripped the curtains open, flooding the room with bright, white light.

Georgie was still hidden, silhouetted by the bright light, but Terri could see the rest of the room. She turned around slowly, trying to take it all in. The walls were covered with mirrors of all different shapes and size, most of them smashed or cracked, with red lipstick – or was it blood? – scribbled and slashed across them. It took a second for it all to sink in, but as it did her body stiffened and she bit back a cry. She stood frozen to the spot, shaking with confusion and shock.

The words that had been scrawled on the walls were so hateful, so powerful, brought real fear to her – 'Die you cunt!', 'Rapist!', 'Child Molester!' Those she could almost deal with. It was the last few, scrawled in what looked like blood on one huge mirror, over and over again, that sent chills through her – 'Kill Charlie Taylor', 'Kill Charlie Taylor,' 'Kill Charlie Taylor '…

Terri swallowed; her rapid breathing was almost overwhelming her, she shook her head from side to side in horror and disbelief. 'No, no,' she murmured as it all clicked into place, all fitted together. Tears stung her eyes; she forced them back down, cleared her throat. Stunned, she managed to force some words out. 'Please tell me what the fuck's going on Georgie?'

But he stood with his back to her, still as a statue, saying nothing.

The need for words overwhelmed her. 'For God's sake, Georgie! Fucking talk to me!' she screamed at him. 'Don't just ignore me. Tell me what's going on! You owe me some kind of explanation!'

Suddenly she gasped. Terri knew what had happened. 'It's her, whoever this girl is you've been shagging! She killed Uncle Charlie, didn't she, that's what you're hiding, you're trying to protect her ain't ya?'

Georgie's silence filled the room.

'Fucking say something!' Terri screamed, her voice thick with fear.

His stillness was oppressive, his silence like a cloud of poisoned fumes creeping around her.

'Don't just ignore me!' she screamed. 'Don't pretend I'm not here and this is not happening. I can't believe you are covering up for her, Georgie, you could go to prison for this!'

The pain seared through her as she looked at all the girl's clothes lying around the floor. 'You've got to let us help you, Georgie.' Terri's bottom lip trembled. Her voice softened. 'Me and Mickey can get help. We'll get a good solicitor; Mickey can get it

all sorted, he will know what to do. Things will be
OK. I'm going to phone Mickey, get him - '

'No!' Georgie screamed, still facing the
window.

Terri jumped in shock, this wasn't the brother
she knew so well. 'For God's sake, Georgie,' she
pleaded. 'Turn round and look at me, talk to me! It's
about time you faced the truth, and stopped running
away from who you are!'

Finally Georgie moved, turning slowly
around to look straight into her eyes. 'My name is
Samantha,' he said in a soft, husky voice.

Terri stood still in shock, she felt an icy chill
crawl up her spine. Now she was really scared,
Georgie was frightening her.

He took a step towards her.

'Oh my God,' she whispered as she backed
away in panic. It wasn't her brother standing in front
of her. Everything was different, everything had
changed. The   sound of his voice, the colour of his
eyes, the way he stared at her, his posture, his facial
expressions, his body language. She was looking at
another person, a stranger. Where was her brother?
'You're really beginning to frighten me, Georgie,' she
whispered, her voice shaking.

'I've told you, my name is Samantha,' he
snapped, his voice cracked and vicious.

The fear froze in her eyes as he walked
towards her, his expression darkening.

'Oh my God!' Terri backed up, felt an overwhelming urge to escape him. She stumbled and tripped on something lying on the floor, and ended up on her backside. She was scared, more scared than she had ever been; Georgie looked evil, even worse than his dad had ever looked. She was looking at a different person.

'Please don't hurt me,' she begged, 'I only want to help you. I love you, Georgie.'

'Weren't you listening to me?' he snarled. 'I've told you my name is Samantha.'

He was close to her, 'You must go now.'

A step closer.

'Georgie, listen to me I can help you,' she whined.

He stood over her, his usually handsome face unbelievably scary. There was evil in his eyes, darkness, as he clenched his jaw muscles, flared his eyes. 'You're making me very angry,' he hissed. 'You're not listening to me are you? I've told you and told you, my name is not Georgie!'

'Oh my God, no.' She could feel the cold sweat trickling down her back. 'Please don't hurt me.' Georgie had never laid a hand on her, had always been so gentle with her, she'd never even heard him raise his voice. If he was ever angry, he didn't show it. Never in her life had she felt scared of Georgie, but at this moment he frightened the life out of her. Terri was shitting herself, and she didn't know how to handle this.

Dark anger flashed in his eyes, his expression unreadable. 'We don't need you anymore,' he said in a soft whisper as he stepped closer, loomed over her.

Terri scooted back, began throwing things at him, anything she could get hold of - an ashtray, a shoe, a tin of hair lacquer, a dress.

Georgie was right over her, his shadow covering her.

Terri cowered in the corner, curled up in a ball, all the fight washed out of her by his powerful presence. 'Someone, please help me,' she whimpered as he loomed over her . . .

Mickey

Mickey stopped outside Georgie's flat. The door was ajar – not good. Mickey eased his gun out of his pocket, stepped inside. 'Terri, Georgie, you in there?' The place smelt of bleach and disinfectant as usual, but there was no answer. The kitchen door on his right was wide open, but the room was empty, as was the bathroom. Mickey edged towards Georgie's bedroom. The door was shut. 'Anyone home?' he called.

Silence.

Mickey pushed the bedroom door open, slipped inside, gun ready. No one. His eyes took in the dresses, the make-up. Fucking hell, he thought, Georgie had kept that quite, the slippery bastard.

He came out the bedroom and moved slowly towards the living room. The door was open a little bit, so Mickey nudged the door with his foot and edged slowly into the room, the gun in front of him. Mickey couldn't believe what he saw as he walked in.

Terri was curled up in the foetal position in the corner of the room, quivering, eyes shut tight with fear, rocking backwards and forwards. Her hair stuck to her cheeks with snot and tears.

He took in the rest of the room, the bizarre mirrors covered in red scrawl.

He bent down next to her 'What the fuck happened, where's Georgie?'

Terri looked up at him, red eyed, stammered, 'Hhhhe's gone.' She started to cry again.

Mickey glared as he looked around, his strong jaw muscles working hard. 'Who did this? Georgie?'

Terri looked up at him, trying to find the words to explain what she'd seen, what had happened, but she couldn't speak, no words would come out of her mouth.

Mickey was already out of patience – he could tell something big was going down, had no time to tease it out of Terri. He reached down, grabbed Terri's hand. 'Come on girl, everything will be all right,' he said as he pulled her to her feet and wrapped his strong arms around her.

She fell against him, still weak from fear and shock, but somehow the strength and warmth of his body gave her strength.

'Where is he, Terri?'

Terri leaned into Mickey. Mickey would fix it,

Mickey would make it right – Mickey had always been there for Georgie, for all of them. Mickey was the strongest of them all, he could sort out anything. She forced herself upright, wiped the back of her hand across her face, smearing her mascara everywhere. 'He's gone to Billy Covey's,' she stuttered. 'Says he's going to kill him!'

As Mickey drove along the A13 towards Billy's house, Terri almost catatonic in the passenger seat beside him, he took in what Terri had told him.

Billy Covey was an old running mate of his uncle Charlie – could it really be true that Georgie had killed Charlie and was now on his way to dispense justice to Billy? He knew they were a pair of wicked fuckers, but what Georgie had told Terri was beyond that…

The old bill was flying around everywhere as they approached Billy's house. Shit! Was he too late? Mickey put his foot down and followed the blue lights and sirens, pulled up behind the police outside Bill Covey's house.

The armed police were already there, ready and waiting to go inside. Mickey turned to Terri. 'Stay in the car!' he told her. Not much chance of her doing anything else, he thought, she was fucking out of it.

Mickey jumped out of the car. Everyone in the street seemed to be at their front door or gate wondering what the fuck was going on. The roads had been sealed off it; it looked like a scene out of the Sweeney.

Mickey followed behind about eight armed officers as they raced towards the house. A copper tried to stop him, but DCI Evans saw him coming, stepped forward. 'It's all right,' he snapped. 'I'll vouch for him!'

He pulled Mickey aside. 'He's fucking flipped, Mickey, lost it!' Evans told him.

Mickey looked towards the house. 'Let me go talk to him.'

The armed response team stood impatiently by the doorway, waiting for the OK from Evans.

Evans took a deep breath, tried to marshal his thoughts. The last thing he wanted was bloodshed, and maybe, just maybe, Mickey could talk Georgie round. He nodded. 'OK. You follow them,' he nodded at the response team. 'Don't do anything until they've cleared the house, found where Georgie is. Got it?'

Mickey nodded.

'OK,' said Evans, 'let's go.'

The armed cops weren't messing. They kicked the front door in, raced straight inside, guns in front of them, Mickey at their heels. They checked each room as we went through, the living room, kitchen, then up the stairs to the bedrooms. Toilet empty, first bedroom empty, then finally, in the last room, the bedroom, they found Georgie and Billy.

It took Mickey a second to recognise his brother, wearing a dress, a wig, heavy make-up. Fuck me, thought Mickey, I never saw that coming!

Georgie had the crook of his left arm around Billy's neck, his arm jammed tight against Billy's throat. Something was rammed deep in his mouth, Billy was fighting for oxygen, gagging, couldn't breathe.

There was a gun was in Georgie's hand jammed hard into Billy's right temple.

Mickey took it all in at a glance. Georgie, a crazed expression in his face like he was ready to pull the trigger.

Mickey forced his way through the crowd of armed cops, all with their guns trained on his brother. 'All right, let me talk to him!'

The cops looked dubious. Evans came puffing up behind them, winded from the stairs, and took the situation in at a glance. He nodded to the cops. 'All right, give him some space.'

Slowly, reluctantly, the cops backed out of the room. Evans was last. He stared into Mickey's eyes. 'Five minutes, Mickey. That's all I can give you.'

Mickey nodded, turned back to Georgie as Evans retreated to the doorway.

Mickey couldn't believe what he was looking at. He felt like he was pissed, or high on something, it all seemed so unreal. Mickey and Georgie had been in some situations in their life but this was something else. He took a few deep breaths, trying to take it all in. How the fuck was he going to get them out of this one. 'Georgie,' he said gently.

'Go away!' Georgie shouted. His teeth were bared, he was snarling in anger. 'Fuck off, or I'll kill him!'

Mickey edged closer. 'Put the gun down, Georgie.'

Georgie looked up at Mickey for the first time, his unblinking eyes full of unsettling intensity. 'My name is Samantha,' he said calmly.

Mickey tried to keep his voice steady. 'Put the gun down, Samantha.' It felt weird just saying it, but he knew he had to play Georgie's game.

Georgie looked up at him with an almost childish, pouty expression. 'No!' he snapped. 'You don't know what he did to Georgie!'

Mickey looked at Billy's face. He was a pitiful looking cunt at the best of times, with stringy hair and bulging eyes. Right now he looked frightened enough to shit himself. 'Why don't you tell me, Samantha,' said Mickey softly. 'You want someone to know what Billy did to Georgie, right?'

Georgie looked up at him, and for a moment there was a glance of recognition between the brothers. Georgie nodded. 'Georgie was just a little boy,' he began. 'But Billy didn't care. He put Georgie in dresses, pushed him face down on the bed, his face into the pillow. Georgie could hardly breathe. He thought he was going to die, he wished he would die. Then Billy fucked him up the arse!'

Georgie glared at Billy, ground the barrel of the gun into his head, tearing the skin. 'Georgie was just a scared little boy, but Samantha is stronger than Georgie, he's going to make it right!'

Mickey's heart was pounding so hard he could feel it in his chest as he tried to figure out what to do. There were eight trigger-happy armed men waiting outside the door, and Georgie in a dress and full make-up with a gun to Billy's head. There are some things you can never be prepared for.

Billy stared up at Mickey, his face red, struggling to breathe, his eyes imploring Mickey. Mickey didn't give a toss about Billy – he was a nasty fucker, Mickey would happily kill him himself, but he didn't want to see Georgie go down for killing him. 'Don't do it,' he pleaded with Georgie. 'Billy's a piece of scum – you don't want to get banged up for him!'

Georgie's sad eyes looked up at Mickey. 'Sometimes Uncle Charlie was there too. He'd make Georgie suck his cock before he fucked him.' He turned his head away, the bitterness of the memories eating away at him. 'They told Georgie that if he breathed a word to anyone they'd kill you all – you, Terri, Sharon, Martin, mum… They said Georgie just needed to be a good boy and stay quiet and everyone would be fine.' He glared suddenly at Billy. 'This one used to laugh at Georgie, kick him, piss on him…' He ground the gun harder into Billy's head, the blood trickling down Billy's cheek. 'I'd like to shove this up his arse, pull the trigger!'

'Mickey? Clock's running.'

Mickey turned towards the door, nodded at Evans, and then directed his attention back to Georgie. He was shocked by what he saw. As he looked into Georgie's black eyes there was nothing – he was looking at a stranger with a familiar face.

'Do you know what else he did to Georgie?' he said suddenly. 'He's got a false eye. Remember he used to baby sit us when mum and dad went out? He would take his eye out put it in front of Georgie and say to him don't move, stay here, don't go anywhere, because I can see you all the time. If you're naughty and tell anyone our little secret I will know, I can see everything. I will come and get you and your brother and sisters.'

Georgie glared at the terrified Billy, his one good eye swivelling up to stare in fear at him. 'But I'm stronger than Georgie; he needs me to protect him, needs looking after.' He shoved the gun hard into Billy's ear, making him wince in pain.

'Don't do it!' gasped Mickey. 'We can help Georgie together'.

'You can't help Georgie,' came the cold reply. 'I'm the only one who's been there for him.'

'No!' protested Mickey. 'Let this cunt go, put the gun down!'

'No! Georgie would go to prison for what I have done, and I can't let that happen.' As he said it he put the gun to his own temple, still holding Billy tight around his neck.

Mickey could feel the situation slipping through his fingers. He fought desperately for the right words. 'Don't do it, Samantha!' he gasped. 'If you go, Georgie will have no one to look after him.'

Georgie looked up at him, curious. Mickey's words had unsettled him. 'I will keep him safe forever,' he said.

'Not if you're dead!' reasoned Mickey.

Georgie thought for a moment.

'Listen to me, Samantha,' begged Mickey. 'I swear to God I will get you and Georgie all the help I can,' he promised.

It was the wrong thing to say. 'You can't help him,' Georgie snapped back. 'I'm the only one.'

'I know all you want to do is to protect him,' argued Mickey.

'That's all I have ever done.'

'Right. But this isn't the way. Think about it, Samantha. If you kill yourself, you kill Georgie.'

Georgie seemed uncertain for a moment. Suddenly he seemed to make a decision. 'I have to kill Billy first,' he said calmly. He moved the gun from his own temple, pointed it back at Billy. It was the moment Mickey had been waiting for – as the gun moved towards Billy he threw himself forwards, crashed into Georgie and Billy, knocking the gun from Georgie's hand.

In an instant the police were in the room, swarming all over them, grabbing the gun, cuffing Georgie and dragging him to his feet.

Evans sighed, slapped Mickey on the back. 'You were only supposed to talk him around.'

Mickey shrugged. 'He's my brother. I did what I could to save his life.'

They looked around as Georgie was led out. He turned suddenly and glared at Mickey. 'You betrayed Georgie!' he snapped.

'I saved you!' countered Mickey, a hurt look in his eyes.

'That's my choice to make,' came the reply. 'Me and Georgie together!'

Mickey started to say something else, but Evans held him back. 'There's nothing you can do or say right now.'

Mickey nodded.

Two cops had helped Billy to his feet, pulled the gag from his mouth. He was gasping for breath, coughing.

'Get him out of here,' snapped Evans.

As the police led Billy past him, something inside Mickey snapped. He stepped quickly in front of him, and before the cops could react he nutted him hard, then smashed his knee into his balls. Billy crumpled, gurgling, to the floor, blood flowing from his nose.

Two cops grabbed Mickey, pulled him back.

Billy writhed on the floor, groaning. 'That's fucking assault, that is!' he spat out.

Evans shoved Mickey back out of the doorway. 'Go home, Mickey!'

Billy tried to climb to his feet, collapsed again, and vomited onto the faded carpet. 'I want him charged!' he screamed.

Evans looked down on him with disdain. 'I didn't see anything – you see anything, boys?'

The other cops shook their heads.

'Get this nasty prick out of here!' he snapped.

Mickey gave Evans a nod of acknowledgement, then hurried down the stairs, his mind racing, stomped outside, both hands jammed in his trouser pockets, his shoulders hunched. He was just so shocked, it couldn't be real.

He reached his car, stood in silence, gutted. Mickey had known more than his share of life's sadness, yet this affected him a way that he had not experienced before. Nothing could have prepared him for the actuality of it.

What had just happened with Georgie was the biggest blow in his life. They had been together 24/7. Georgie was his brother, his best mate, his confidante – but despite that, Mickey had not seen this coming.

Mickey churned it over and over again in his mind. Why? Why wasn't I there when he needed me? I should have seen it all, seen all the signs.

Georgie was the other half of Mickey, he felt like a part of him had died that day.

He leaned on the car, gazed down at Terri, still curled up in the passenger seat, her eyes glazed over with horror. How could Mickey explain this to the rest of them, to his mum?

A voice broke his attention. 'Georgie didn't kill Taylor. It was a separate person inside of him,' DCI Evans said quietly.

Mickey turned around. 'You think Georgie is still in there somewhere,' he wondered.

Evans shrugged. 'I don't know, I'm not a shrink. But Georgie has no idea he killed Charlie Taylor.'

Mickey closed his eyes, his face a rigid mask. When he finally glanced at Evans, although he was still finding it hard to believe the raw horrible truth, his face showed nothing of his thoughts. 'I should have seen the signs,' he said. 'I could have done something and helped him.' Mickey glared at Billy as he was shoved into the back of a police car. 'So Georgie the victim is taken away and the fucking child abusing cunt goes free?'

Evans shrugged. 'Sorry, you couldn't have done any more than you have, Mickey. Those demons look like they're chasing you, Mickey.'

Mickey stared into his eyes. 'No, Evans, I'm chasing the demons,' Mickey snarled, then turned, climbed silently into his car,

Terri looked up at him, said nothing. What was there to say? Sometimes there are no words, no clever quotes to say about what's happened. Sometimes the day just ends in silence.

Mickey

Mickey stood at the bar, Kenny, Joseph, Bernie, all the rest of the boys around him. The Cross Keys was jam packed, all pissed up singing and dancing, having a right laugh, helping Kenny celebrate his twenty-first birthday.

Every five minutes another cheer would go up, and glasses would be raised: 'To Kenny! Happy birthday mate!'

Or else: 'To Mickey! Hope it's healthy!'

Normally they would be at a nightclub, but Mickey had to stay close to home as Mandy was due to give birth to their first baby, it could happen at any time.

Mickey grinned. Mandy had the raving hump with him for going out at all, but he was only round the corner, he could be back indoors in five minutes. She was two days late – if she hadn't had the baby by next week they were going to take her in and induce her.

Mickey secretly hoped they had a boy – he wanted a son. He'd never told Mandy that, she would have done her nut. She said she didn't care what they had, a boy or a girl, it didn't make any difference as long as their baby was healthy. He told her if it was a girl she could choose the name, if it was a boy he was going to be called Tommy, no debate, that's what it would be. Tommy. He had no idea why, but he had always liked the sound of that for a boy. She could go on till the cows come home but if it was a boy, it was definitely going to be Tommy.

They were all in full voice, dancing and singing along to 'High Ho Silver Lining', everyone pissing themselves laughing. Mickey set his glass down and leaned on the bar. He'd had a few beers and felt good.

The kid collecting the glasses and bottles came up and gave him a nudge. 'Ere Mickey, there's a plain-clothed copper outside.' He glanced towards the door. 'He said he needs to have a word with ya, says it's serious. I didn't tell him you were in 'ere. I told him I would come in and have a look. He said his name was Evans.'

As soon as he heard Evans' name Mickey knew it was to do with Georgie. DC Evans, the bearer of bad tidings. Mickey was getting used to D C Evans' visits, it had been a regular occurrence down through the years - his best mate Stevie Blake, his dad, his uncle Charlie Taylor, now Georgie. Any time there was bad news, Evans was the one to deliver it. Mickey reached in his pocket, found a fiver and shoved it into the lad's hand. 'Cheers mate.'

He eased out past his friends, still drinking and singing, happy, oblivious, pushed open the door and stepped outside.

Evans was standing in the pool of yellow light under a lamp post, stamping his feet, his breath forming clouds around him. He looked up as Mickey appeared, stepped forward, offered his hand.

If Mickey had any doubts about what Evans might tell him, they were dispelled by the look on Evans' face as they shook hands.

Evans moved close to Mickey, their breath combining into a pale cloud under the harsh light. 'Mickey,' he began, 'I don't know how to say this, so I'll get it over with - Georgie tried to top himself.'

Mickey felt his guts turn over, felt sick inside. Georgie had tried to kill himself. A million thoughts, a thousand questions raced through Mickey's mind. 'No, no, not Georgie. Did he – where is he? I mean…' His words petered out.

'He's still alive,' said Evans calmly, 'he's unconscious but alive in the intensive care unit.'

Mickey tried to think clearly. Georgie had been in custody – how was this even possible?

Evans seemed to read his mind. 'He wasn't on suicide watch – he used his shirt to make a noose, tied it to a light fitting. It was only when the light ripped out of the wall that they even knew he'd done anything.'

Mickey staggered to the lamp post, leaned on it with one hand, suddenly began throwing up. Whether it was the sheer shock and horror or the need to clear his stomach, clear his mind, who knows. Three, four times, he vomited, emptying his guts. When he stood back up he felt sober, cold, the real Mickey Taylor. 'Where is he?'

Looking back, Mickey couldn't even remember how the fuck he got to the hospital – the boys must have sorted it for him. All he could think of was all the people he had to call. How the fuck was he going to tell his mum, Sharon, Terri, Martin? How could he even force out the words, 'Georgie tried to kill himself?' Then there was Frankie and Rosie, and Sheila and Johnnie in Ireland – the list of people he would have to phone would be endless. Mickey felt like he was dying inside, horrific thoughts and memories flooding his mind as he thought of what Georgie had tried to do.

When they finally made it to the hospital, Mickey ran into the intensive care unit, he couldn't get there fast enough. All he wanted to do was see his brother, touch him, hold him, and tell him that everything would be alright. There was a nurse in there when he arrived, Mickey had to wait outside, pacing, fuming, chewing ferociously at his fingernails, staring at the door every ten seconds, willing it to open.

Finally the nurse emerged, very prim in her uniform. 'You can go in now.'

Mickey was in the room before she'd finished speaking. He rushed towards the bed, stopped short – fuck! Was that really Georgie? There were tubes and wires everywhere, but the face – the real Georgie this time, no make-up or crap – that was unmistakably him. Despite his impatience, Mickey moved slowly towards the bed. What if he was dead already? Mickey glanced up at the monitor, showing a slow steady heartbeat, moved the final few feet to the bed.

Georgie was unconscious, but alive. That was a blessing.

Mickey tried to ignore the angry red welts around Georgie's neck, leaned over and touched his hair, kissed his forehead. It was the worst nightmare Mickey could ever imagine. He leaned on the bed. 'You silly, daft cunt,' Mickey said softly. 'What was you thinking of when you did this?'

Georgie breathed softly, his heartbeat still steady, no sign that he even knew Mickey was there.

He was sedated, that's what Evans had said.   But
surely something was getting through?

Mickey glanced down at Georgie's wrists,
strapped to the bed – just like in the movies, when
they had some crazy person strapped down.   Fucking
hell, Georgie, how the fuck has it come to this, he
thought?

He gently stroked Georgie's face.   No time for
recriminations, no time for doubts, just say what he
needs to hear…

'Come on, Georgie,' he whispered, his voice
strained, forced.   'You can't go, you silly bastard, I
need you.'

Mickey glanced around – he could hear voices
outside, saw a shadow against the opaque glass
window.   The others would be arriving, wanting to
see Georgie.

'Mum needs you,' he continued.   'I reckon
she's outside now, probably with Sharon, Terri and
Martin.   Auntie Rosie and Frankie, they'll be along.
And we've called Sheila and Johnnie in Ireland,
they'll be here tomorrow to see you with Kevin and
Danny.'

What was he saying?   It sounded more like
the guest list for a fucking wedding than something
to help save a dying brother!   But somehow he felt
the need to talk, to just keep rambling on, no matter
what nonsense came out.   'Everyone wants you to get
through this,' he told him, 'we are all here for ya,

Georgie. Even Tony and the boys from the Cross Keys are outside.'

Mickey fumbled for something else to say. A sudden memory flashed into his mind. He couldn't keep the smile from his face thinking about it. 'Do you remember that day me and you went up the court with Tony to get his licence for the pub, to get his name above the door. We all go strolling into court, Tony's standing there all suited and booted, looking very smart and respectable. We were cracking up when the judge says to him?'

'Mr Ebbs, how are you going to deal with the drink and drug problem?' And old Tony replies, well, your honour, I've knocked all that lark on the head now. I don't do drugs and drink now so it won't be a problem, your honour!' Mickey laughed, tried to sound happy. 'The look on the judge's face. We were pissing ourselves weren't we? He still got his licence though didn't he? Dozy as a bag of bollocks that geezer.'

Mickey wiped away a tear that was trying to form at the corner of his eye. No. Can't do that. They'll all be looking to him, he has to be strong, he has to be the one they lean on, the shoulder where they shed their tears. His own feelings would just have to wait. He sniffed back his tears. 'Listen, I've gotta go, Mum's outside, she wants to come in and see you. They will only let one of us in at a time, Georgie.'

He squeezed Georgie's hand tight.   'Mum needs you, Georgie, she won't be able to live without you, mate. How do you think Martin's gonna feel? You mean the world to that kid and he's been through enough already, so you've got to get through this. You're a Taylor for fuck's sake, you're strong, a survivor, don't give up. I need you how will I get on without you? You know what makes me smile, you know what winds me up, what gets to me and hits a nerve.'

He rested his hand on Georgie's head – it felt cool against his forehead. 'I'll always be here for you Georgie, always. You can't go and leave me, you can't.'

Just as Mickey released Georgie's hand, he felt a faint pressure, Georgie squeezing back – he looked quickly at the monitor. No changes, just the steady beep, beep. No matter, Mickey was certain that Georgie had squeezed his hand back, had heard Mickey talking to him. That was enough.

Mickey grinned. 'Atta boy! You gotta pull through this, you wanker! I want you to be the best man at my wedding, godfather to my baby - you're gonna be an uncle soon, right? Who else I am gonna have a pint with?'

He sighed, stepped away from the bed, looked back at his brother, a wash of memories threatening to drown him. Georgie was the clever one, the one with the brains in the family, blimey, he even passed his eleven plus! He was always reading and into books big time. You could have a conversation with Georgie about anything, anything, and he'd have the answer. And if he didn't, he would go to the library and look it up, or go and grab one of his encyclopaedias from the bedroom.

A right swat he was, but Mickey loved him, he was his brother, his best friend. They knew each other in a way nobody else did. Mickey often said to him, 'Georgie, you got the brains, I've got the good looks!'

Mind you, he wasn't a saint - Georgie liked a bet; he was always in the bookies, the Church Elms or Cross Keys. Martin sitting outside on the steps with a glass of lemonade and a packet of crisps. Martin loved it, running backwards and forwards for Georgie. In and out of the betting shop placing his bets and collecting his winnings for him. Georgie was always generous, if he had a good win on the horses or the dogs, he always treated everyone. Good as gold Georgie was, a good, decent bloke. He'd take his coat off his back for you if you needed it.

Mickey stepped away from the bed – he could hear voices outside, knew the family had arrived. He'd better go out, his mum and the others wanted to come in and see Georgie. He sniffed, took a deep breath, stepped outside into the corridor.

It was mayhem. They were all there, red eyed, anxious – his mum, his little brother Martin, his sisters, Terri and Sharon. Mickey hugged his mum first, tried to ignore her red-rimmed eyes – he didn't need to feed her anxiety. "Go on in, mum," he forced himself to say.

Lizzie looked at Mickey. Bit her lip. 'How is he?'

'They've got him sedated, but I swear he squeezed me hand when I was talking to him.'

As Lizzie pushed through the door Mickey realised how desperate that had sounded, like he was clutching at fucking straws. He forced a smile on his face and turned to his sisters. 'What a silly cunt!' he said. 'Always was one for the old melodrama! When I said I was better looking than him I didn't think he would take it this far!'

The hours dragged on – quick visits in to see Georgie when the nurses let them, endless cups of shitty coffee from them horrible foam cups, and regular breaks outside for a nicotine fix.

Mickey and Sharon stood under the eaves of the building, puffing away. It was raining, a steady veil of water running from the roof to splash in the gritty puddles at their feet.

Mickey stared out over the car park. Everything looked grey and miserable.

'Remember when Georgie bought his first greyhound?' said Sharon suddenly.

Mickey couldn't help but smile. 'I've seen staffies that could outrun that mutt!'

Georgie had brought the dog from a bloke he'd met at Romford. He fed him the best cuts of meat, had Martin take him out and run him, trained him, everything, but he finished dead last in every race! Romford, White City, Clacton – it didn't matter where he ran, he always finished dead last. They would go all around the dog tracks when he was racing, but 'Stride on Taylor' was never cut out to be a racer.

Georgie always said if he had a few bob he would buy a beautiful house in the country and build kennels for greyhounds and train and race them, and after they retired he would look after them and try to rehome them. A home for all the greyhounds. Soft as shit Georgie was.

But it was second time lucky when he bought Martin a greyhound - Georgie Boy they called that one. He was a good racer, even won a couple of races.

But win or lose, every Saturday they met up at Mum's house, had silly bets on the horses. The Grand National was always one of Georgie's favourite days, all sitting in front of the telly, cheering and shouting at the horses. It was like a public bar!

Through the night they all took it in turns going in to see Georgie, sitting with him, talking to him. Around four A.M., the doctor came round, said Georgie was stable. They all took a deep sigh of relief; there was some hope after all.

'You should all go home,' said the doc, 'get some rest and come back tomorrow morning.'

Mickey looked around. Not one of them moved! They weren't going anywhere. Mickey felt a surge of pride in his family. That was the Taylors. No one was going to leave Georgie alone, he needed them all to be close to him, by his side.

Mickey sat brooding, his heavy chin in his hands, tried to understand – Georgie's pain was overwhelming, he got that; he was in a bad way, sure, but why the fuck do what he did? Why didn't he come and talk to Mickey? Whatever was going on, Mickey would help him out.

Mickey was angry with Georgie for doing that to all of them. Much as he loved Georgie, he knew he would never completely forgive him for the pain he had caused the family.

He looked around. Everyone had the same expression as him – faces down, avoiding eye contact, each of them asking themselves the same question. 'Why? Why did he do it?'

And then there was the anger. All angry at themselves, all asking, 'how did I miss all the clues and signs'. All thinking, 'if only I ...' 'what if I ...' 'Why couldn't I help him? Why didn't I see it coming? I should have been there for him.'

Mickey closed his eyes. He was so tired. But every time he started to doze off, his mind filled with nightmares, flashbacks of his life, moments when Mickey could have done more for Georgie. Was he to blame?

Mickey glanced over at his mum's face. Lizzie sat stone faced, jaw tight, eyes staring straight ahead. Mickey knew she would never want to talk about it. She would certainly blame herself, for not being a good enough mother, for not protecting them better from Bobby, but what more could she have done? But she wouldn't see it that way, Mickey knew that.

Mickey sighed. Whatever happened, they were going to stick together, come through this. The Taylor family always pulled together as a family and stayed strong. The Taylor family may not have it all together, he thought, but together we have it all.

1972

Rampton High Security Psychiatric Hospital

As he walked through the door, Mickey breathed in a deep lungful of air. There was the unmistakable smell of hospital food and disinfectant, piss and vomit, fear and loathing, a blend that always depressed him. Mickey hated coming here, but it was something that had to be done, it was his responsibility, his duty.

He was met by Dr Peters, extending a perfectly manicured hand. 'Good Morning, Mr. Taylor.' They shook hands, Mickey enjoying the soft, cool feel of her skin.

'Morning Doc.' She always looked good, Mickey thought. She was in her early thirties, with a Diana Ross-like appeal, high cheek bones, a slightly superior look. Looking at her you would never think she was a doctor, let alone a shrink.

'How are you and the family?' Her voice was cool, measured, almost no hint of any accent that you could put your finger on.

'Yeah, I'm good thanks Doc, but the family aren't coping so well. All still in shock. Don't reckon me muvver will ever get over it.' He gave her a searching look. 'Any progress? '

Dr Taylor looked at him over the top of her gold-rimmed glasses, 'No, no change. The same as last week. As I said, I will telephone DC Evans immediately if there is any significant change in his condition.'

Mickey followed her down a long corridor, enjoying the way her white coat swished backwards and forward on her slim hips. She could treat him any time she wanted. He tore his eyes away from the doctor, looked around. He was in a place that was home to some of the most dangerous people in Britain. Some called it the Bleak Asylum, the place where mad monsters were banished and locked away forever.

As he walked through the echoing corridors alongside Dr Peters he could feel an air of tension and constant watchfulness. The continual jangling of keys held by each member of staff, another door to be unlocked, passed through and relocked every few yards. Mickey had heard that the hospital had over four thousand doors - he didn't doubt it. Every patient here was on twenty-four hour surveillance, eyes and ears were everywhere, on everyone, like a circle, with no end and no beginning.

The noise alone did his head in - men screaming and shouting, doors slamming, radios blaring. Mickey shivered and felt goose bumps on his arms. He remembered when he was a kid, his dad would torment his mum, telling her that she was mad, completely off her head, and that one day she would end up in a nut house. He'd sing to her, 'They're coming to take you away, ha ha, they're coming to take you away'. This was certainly the right bloody place.

Dr Peters ushered Mickey into her office; she followed, shut the door behind them and sat down at her desk. Opening the drawer she pulled out a hefty-looking file, began flicking through some paperwork, removed several sheets of notes, and placed them at the front of her file. Taking a pen from her pocket she scribbled a few notes.

Mickey wondered what she was writing down, putting on the records – what was she saying about her patient, her prisoner? Mickey stood by the doorway looking very boyish and vulnerable in contrast to his fearsome reputation, his eyes mostly fixed on Dr Peters long slim legs, exposed where she sat cross-legged at her desk.

There was the sudden sound of footsteps and two male orderlies appeared through another entrance, escorting a patient between them. They sat the patient opposite the doctor on a two-seater couch. She was dressed in pink satin pyjamas with matching fluffy slippers, looking relaxed and amiable. Her make- up was perfectly applied, her long nails painted in red matching the lipstick. Mickey found that he was holding his breath as her cool appraising eyes scanned him.

'How are you feeling today?' asked Dr Peters.

The woman crossed her legs, looked up from an inspection of her perfect fingernails. 'You tell me Doctor. You're the expert. How should I be feeling?' She shifted her position, re-crossing her legs, her fingers interlocked and resting on her knees, a challenging look on her face.

As Doctor Peters began to speak, the woman cut across her. 'Everyone in this place thinks they're going to be released,' she purred. She looked deep into the doctor's eyes. 'I'm not that naïve.'

Peters raised an eyebrow. 'You don't believe you are getting out?'

She leaned forward, smiled. 'Are you going to let me out, Dr Peters?'

'I'd like to talk about Georgie,' came the reply.

The woman looked bored, sat back, but the agitated way she swung her foot gave away her irritation, her edginess. 'You sound like a broken record Doctor. Why don't you change your tune?'

'You could help us find him.'

'No.'

'Why not? Is there something that you are hiding?' asked Dr Peters quietly.

'I'm not hiding anything.' The woman turned, looked towards the door where Mickey was standing, no expression on her face. 'I've been expecting you; I knew you would come again.'

Mickey straightened up, uncertain what to say.

'What do you want this time, Mickey?'

He cleared his throat, met her eyes. 'You know what I want.'

She looked directly at him. 'Tell me again, let me hear you say it.'

Mickey had to force the words out. 'I want to find Georgie.' He met her eyes, all the time knowing that they knew everything but said nothing.

'And I've told you time and time again, don't come here. You're wasting your time. How many times do you have to be told you're not needed anymore?' The unblinking eyes were filled with unsettling intensity. 'Just because you caught me, doesn't mean you'll get Georgie. You, the police, the doctors, the nurses, the psychiatrists, you're not nearly clever enough.'

Mickey could feel his frustration rising. 'It ain't about being clever, it's about doing the right thing,' he said quickly.

She lifted her head and searched his eyes. 'You had years to do the right thing, to look after Georgie when Charlie and Billy were abusing him. You weren't there. Now it's my turn.'

'But if only you - if only Georgie had -'

The woman cut him off. 'You want to find Georgie? You will never find Georgie. He's hiding, somewhere safe, and it's my job to protect him.' She stood up so quickly that Mickey thought for a moment that she was about to attack him, but she turned instead to the two orderlies. 'We're done here.'

She turned and headed towards the door, the orderlies side of her, stopped suddenly in the doorway and turned back to stare at Mickey. 'You talk about doing the right thing? I'm the only one here who is doing the right thing for Georgie.'

And with that she was gone, leaving Mickey alone with his doubts, his fears, his guilt.

It was another fourteen years before he saw Georgie again.

Part Two

Lizzie Taylor – December 1992

Lizzie sat quietly in her chair thinking about her life, her story, her journey - a journey she had started over sixty years ago. So much had changed, it felt like another time, another place.

Lizzie smiled to herself. If she put pen to paper and wrote her biography it would be a bestseller. The chapters full of the family's sordid goings on and dirty little secrets. A novel crammed with her memories of love, loyalty, friendship and intrigue, betrayal, treachery, violence, laughter and tears. A book to die for. Truth is stranger than fiction as the saying goes.

Lizzie shook her head. There had been too much change too fast, not just around her but in the world as a whole. It was scary how time passed so quickly - where had all those years gone?

She might be getting on a bit now, but she still had all her marbles. One thing age couldn't touch was her thoughts. There were some things that could never be forgotten, no matter how hard you tried. No one could take her memories away. For better or for worse, they would never fade.

Lizzie put her hand in her cardigan pocket, took out a packet of Benson and Hedges and lit a cigarette. She immediately started coughing and spluttering as her frail body shook. She'd had this rotten cough and cold for a few weeks now, just couldn't shift it. It had knocked her for six; everything seemed an effort lately. She felt like she didn't have any energy left. Her get up and go had definitely got up and gone.

She really hadn't been the same since she'd had pneumonia a couple of years ago. She'd been in hospital for weeks then. That place was so depressing, full of sick, old people, she felt like she didn't belong, just wanted to get home and back into her own bed. And once she was home, Lizzie told her kids there was no way she was going into any kind of residential or nursing home – the only way she'd be leaving this house again would be in a box.

But while she was in hospital the social services had fitted a stairlift and a walk-in shower, a proper bit of luxury. She'd had problems getting up and down the stairs for a while now as her breathing wasn't so good, she'd had a few dizzy spells, and a few falls, so it was all pretty welcome.

Now she had carers come in every day to wash, shower and dress her. Her daughters and granddaughters had said they would do all of her personal care, that she didn't need carers, they could do it for her, but Lizzie didn't want her children doing it. She had brought them into the world and cleaned and changed them, she didn't want or expect them to do it for her. Anyway, she would feel embarrassed; the thought of it horrified her. None of her children had ever seen her without any clothes on. She had to have a bit of pride and dignity left.

Anyway, they all did enough for her as it was, what with shopping, cooking, washing, cleaning, paying her bills. She didn't have to worry about anything, it was all taken care of, they waited on her hand and foot, nothing was too much. Still, there were times when she felt like a burden upon them, they all had their own families and lives to lead, but none of them ever moaned about it – well, not to her face anyway! Whatever she wanted, they did. Lizzie realised how lucky she was, she couldn't have managed on her own. She felt so sorry for old people who didn't have any family and were all alone.

When she got out of the hospital her grandchildren had bought her a big new TV, put it in her bedroom; the picture was perfect, like having her own cinema at home! She hadn't been downstairs for a long time, didn't need to. The toilet was upstairs, and everything else she needed was here in her bedroom. She missed cooking for herself, but apart from that she didn't mind. All of her family and friends had a front door key, so when anyone came round they would let themselves in then come on up to see her.

It was just as well. These days, the simplest of things, like getting up and down from her chair or getting in or out of bed, was hard work for her. She knew she was really getting old now the candles cost more than her birthday cake.

On the inside she was the same Lizzie, only the outside had changed. In the past her hair had been her crowning glory, a thick black mass of curls that cascaded past her shoulders. But the silver hairs had appeared over the years, and now her hair was almost all white. It wasn't as thick or as long as it used to be either, although she still had a little bit of a curl.

She sighed. Little by little the world was closing in. Her eyesight wasn't so good – she needed glasses now – and her hearing wasn't as good either. She was wheezy and breathless, but after smoking forty fags a day for most of her life what else did she expect? She wasn't doing badly for an old girl.

Lizzie took a puff of her fag with a shaky hand; she knew her family better than they knew themselves. She'd seen and heard the lies, the deceit, the misconceptions and the accusations. She wasn't mad or crazy like a few of them thought; she just knew too much. She had seen how judgement, blame and shame could destroy you. She'd seen the depths of the impressions we make on other's lives.

Lizzie chewed on her lip thoughtfully. We are all the authors of our own destiny, our own story, she thought, we interpret the past in our own ways. We can make it whatever we want it to be. A love story, a tragedy, a comedy, a thriller, a gripping drama. We can play the villain, the victim, the lover. It could make you laugh; it could make you cry.

She fiddled with her wedding and engagement rings, loose now on her scrawny hands. So why were the stories she told herself always sad, bitter, and disappointing? We look at ourselves, question ourselves and our lives, try to make sense of it all. It shouldn't be like this, she thought. This isn't how I imagined it would be. It's not what I expected it to be. Sadness washed over her as she thought of all the things that weren't meant to happen. She seemed to spend so much time going through all the shoulds, the shouldn'ts, the failures. Assessing it all, reliving all the pain, the suffering and the sorrow.

Lizzie picked up a glass of whiskey and took a sip of her nightcap. Life was a funny old thing. We chase around looking for something else, often forget what we already have.

She took another puff and began coughing again. She really should cut down on the fags. This cough was driving her mad, keeping her awake at night as well. She hadn't had a good night's sleep in a long time, despite the whisky to dull the edge. She put her drink down on her bedside table and looked around her bedroom. The walls were adorned with photos of the family, each picture telling its own story. She'd got a bit confused lately, but at the last count she had eight, ten, or was it twelve grandchildren? And now there was the first of the great-grandchildren. The number just kept growing.

Lizzie sighed deeply. She'd had her fair share of heartache and troubles, but nobody had ever said life was going to be easy. Many times she'd sat and cried, but in recent years, those times had been outweighed by the happy times. Life had been good to her, she was grateful for all she had. Despite her vicious bastard of a husband she had been blessed with a good family and she loved them all. She was proud of each and every one of them, whatever they did or didn't do. Lizzie tutted; she didn't like some of the things they'd done and she could tell you a few horror stories, but she still loved them. If it weren't for them she was sure she would never have lasted this long. Her family were her life, her love and her strength.

She smiled and glimpsed over at the photos. For a moment her face looked almost childlike. Her frowns and wrinkles disappeared and her cool blue eyes sparkled. She looked like the beautiful young Lizzie again.

She thought about the happy times, days when life was good. She could feel those moments inside of her, could recall them whenever she wanted.

Lizzie glanced at the beautiful statue of Jesus standing in the centre of her dressing table. It was surrounded by photos and Mass cards of those she had loved and lost. It was given to her years and years ago when she was a young girl; it had stayed by her side ever since. Whenever Lizzie was given a new photo they always said, 'This one's for the wall, we ain't ready to go on the dressing table with Jesus yet.' Cheeky sods!

Lizzie shivered. She didn't feel ready to keel over yet, but you never could tell. She often wondered who would be next. She took a puff of her cigarette, thinking of her old friend Maisie Miller. Seventy-five she was, mugged on her way home from Romford market. The bastards took her bag with her purse and pension in it, left her bruised and battered on the pavement. The poor thing was dead six weeks later. Lizzie was sure the shock of it had killed her. Maisie had been fit as a fiddle before that.

And it wasn't just out on the streets that things were like that. The local secondary schools were like war zones – some of them even had police monitoring the school entrances at the start and end of the school day. What a sad state the world had come to.

She picked up a photo of her husband, Bobby. He'd been dead for over twenty years now. No one ever really spoke about him, but she thought of him every day. Lizzie had fallen hopelessly in love with him when she was just a teenager. She knew life would change when she got married, but she could never ever have imagined the consequences and circumstances of marrying Bobby Taylor. For better or worse? Christ, Lizzie had definitely gotten the worst with Bobby.

Lizzie sat still and silent, her fingers gently stroking the image of his mysterious face. She rolled her eyes. What a silly, naïve, foolish girl she had been. How many years had she defended him, turned a blind eye to what he did, let him bully and abuse all of them. Christ, what a life…

She wiped a strand of long white hair from her forehead. Tears trembled in her eyes as she smiled, breathed in heavily. She was being a daft cow. Fancy getting all sentimental over Bobby. What was wrong with her? How could he still do this to her after so many years?

She fished in her pocket for her handkerchief, wiped her eyes and blew her nose. If her grandchildren only knew the half of it. Life certainly was a big lesson with many tests along the way. She put her cigarette out and then slowly and gradually eased herself up from her chair, her breathing shallow and rapid. She held tight to her walking frame, puffing and panting as she shuffled slowly towards her bedroom window. She pulled the net curtain back and leaned on the window ledge to take a look at the world going by, just as she had since she first moved to Dagenham, shortly after the war.

To start with it had seemed like a maze of identical streets and houses that all looked the same. When they first moved in, it was amazing - they had gas and electricity, running water, inside toilets, fitted baths and front and back gardens. It was luxury; they had been so lucky to get a new council house. They had lovely neighbours, and Lizzie would sit on the step and chat, everyone happy and content.

Dagenham, or Corned Beef City as some called it, earned its nickname because they said that that was all people there could afford to eat. It was true, they didn't have a lot of money, but everyone worked hard for what they had and the kids never went hungry. There was always dinner on the table. Everyone managed to make ends meet and get by somehow.

It was a struggle sometimes, mind you. Lizzie had lost count of how many times she had hidden from the Provident man because she had spent the money on dinners or the electric meter. They were all in the same boat and everyone looked after each other - as soon as he was spotted down the road, the word would go out, doors would shut and the curtains drawn.

The streets were safe to play in, too; you didn't need to worry about the kids. Lizzie loved the place - Dagenham in those days was a haven full of good people. Day in day out she had watched the families and children who lived close by grow up and have families of their own. Some had stayed in Dagenham; many had moved away. A couple of friends who lived nearby had even emigrated to Australia like her son Martin.

But all the locals, she knew their routines like clockwork; she didn't miss a trick. Lizzie knew when people were off to work, to school, to do the weekly shopping. She knew who was shagging who, what time they walked the dogs, when they went to the pubs and the clubs. She knew who would be in trouble on a Friday night for not coming home with their pay packet. There wasn't much that went on that Lizzie didn't know about.

For years she had watched Sooty the old tramp traipse along the streets, through all wind and weathers. All his worldly possessions were what he stood in - his worn out boots, a grubby black overcoat, a dirty woolly jumper, a flat cap on his head and a scarf wrapped around his neck. His trousers were tied at the waist with a piece of rope holding them up, their ripped hems dragged on the ground. He carried a wooden orange box and a faded grey itchy blanket with him wherever he roamed. The box was his chair. Passers-by would snigger and gloat at him with his long, matted beard, they saw nothing but worn out boots, dirt and grime, but Lizzie knew there was more to him, to his world, than just that.

Every day he strolled up and down the road at his own pace - time was his, no rush, no hurry. Some days Sooty walked along his road to anywhere with a look on his face that said the world was at his feet. He walked exultantly, no man his master, following his magic road to anywhere, taking his chances as they came. Other days he walked with his head bowed and eyes downcast, his shoulders slouched and tense, slowly dragging his feet, hunger, want and weariness etched on his face.

Then one day he never came back. Lizzie had wondered for weeks where his road had taken him – then one of the kids told her, he'd been found on a patch of wasteland just up the road, beaten to death. Who would do a thing like that to a harmless old tramp?

Lizzie loved her house. After Bobby died it became a happy place, always filled with family and good friends. Weekends were the highlight, they would have a good old sing-song and dance. Lizzie would get on the piano playing "The Hokey-Cokey", or "Knees up Mother Brown", and they'd all sing along to the old tunes. Happy times, happy days.

Sunday lunchtime, all the men went to the pub. When they came back at closing time - two o'clock - a lovely roast would be waiting for them. Lizzie always made sure the cupboards were full with plenty to go round.

Summer would find them all out in the back garden – the paddling pool and the barbecue always the first things out of the shed. Every year another baby would be sitting in the washing up bowl splishing and splashing and laughing with glee. There were water fights and chip butties, bread pudding and rock cakes, and the smiles and the beers seemed endless. Even now the weekends were still lively and full of family, Lizzie always had someone popping in and out.

Lizzie did miss going out, though. She missed walking up to the shops and having a look around, having a good old chinwag and catching up on all the gossip. She had a big family so there was always someone around to take her out in her wheelchair if she fancied it, but as much as she appreciated it, it just wasn't the same. Nothing was the same.

She didn't know anyone around her anymore. She used to know all of her neighbours and everyone up the street. There were the O'Riordans, the Bates, the Phillips, the Heaths, the Burrows; she could keep going, all the way up and down the street, both sides. She knew everyone.

But now, she didn't know a soul. Most of them had died or moved away. Now she had

Africans one side and an Indian family on the other side who shared her porch. The other side of them were some Muslims from Pakistan. Lizzie didn't mind any of them, they were all very polite, but they all kept themselves to themselves. They said hello to Lizzie if they saw her out with her kids or grandkids, but that was as far as it went. Not what she would call real neighbours. Not like the old days.

Even going up to the shops was different. What had happened to John Collier, Pollards, the fishmongers and the fruit and veg man on the corner? Now it was cab offices, estate agents, banks, funeral directors, halal butchers, Afro Caribbean fruit and veg stores, Chinese takeaways, Turkish kebab houses, and fried chicken or pizza places. Lots of them were open till eleven, twelve o'clock at night. Who would want to eat dinner then?

At least she had Tommy, her grandson. Tommy was a godsend, didn't mind taking her up the shops. He would chat away to her as he pushed her wheelchair, telling her about his latest pranks and misdemeanours. He was a right little sod, just like his father, Mickey, but he knew what he told Lizzie wouldn't go any further. Lizzie tutted, no wonder she didn't sleep very well at night. She used to think things got easier as your children got older and they grew up but it bloody well didn't. When you thought your kids were OK then it was your grandchildren you had to worry about.

She gazed out the window at the phone box across the road from her house. It used to be a meeting place for all the kids, a venue for their gatherings. They had congregated around that phone box day in, day out, through all weathers, winter and summer. In those days, few people even had a house phone, let alone these mobile phones that some of them had now. It was like an office in that phone booth. They would tell their friends what time to ring them, and it had to be on time as they had schedules to keep. There was always someone there answering the phone and taking messages. Then as they all grew from childhood to youth, their meetings became fewer. It seemed to Lizzie that almost overnight they had grown up and moved on.

Lizzie used to sit and watch the children playing hopscotch, rounders, off ground touch and knock-down-ginger. The little girls would be playing with their skipping ropes and the boys would be playing football in the street. Kids would be out in the streets at all hours, running around the streets or riding their bikes. Roller skating down Heathway Hill, swimming over at Leys, the local swimming pool, at old Dagenham Park on the swings, or over Matchstick Island feeding the ducks or having a go on the rowing boats.

Some weekends, if she had an extra couple of bob, she would round the kids up, get the train down to Victoria Park, and take them where she used to play as a child. If the ticket inspector got on the train, they would hide the little ones under the seat. They never did get caught bunking the fare.   Or they would all go to the Saturday morning pictures. They really were the good old days.

Most of the boys she knew had ended up on the production line or taking up apprenticeships at Fords. Lizzie would watch row after row of gleaming new Ford Anglia's, Cortina's and Corsair's go by her house.   And every night about nine o'clock, Ford would take the lid off the black furnace, and for a few minutes the whole sky would light up in a brilliant crimson, the colour slowly diminishing.   Ford had been the centre of everything about Dagenham. So many local businesses relied on Ford to make a living and the lads round about earned a fortune from the lorries coming in and out of Ford. Now it was all slowly dying...

You didn't see children playing in the streets anymore. Then, they would play out till late, walk for miles with no fear of being taken. Now kids stayed indoors, watched TV or movies on the VHS player – she didn't blame the parents, the streets were too dangerous nowadays with all the paedophiles about.

They were all so innocent then – they rode in cars with no seat belts or airbags, the kids used to fall asleep curled up on the back parcel shelf when they were little!   But now nobody seemed to walk anywhere; everyone seemed to have a car.

She remembered a few years ago when they used to have Tupperware and Avon parties – the other week the girls all came over for an Ann Summers party! Lizzie couldn't believe it! A couple of them dressed up in raunchy Basques and sexy lingerie, paraded around the living room, and they all had film star figures. Lots of them had even had boob jobs!

Lizzie couldn't understand it; some of them hadn't even had kids and were still young themselves, but everything was fake. Fake boobs, fake nails, fake eyelashes, fake designer clothes, fake jewellery, fake shoes and handbags, fake perfume, fake money. What happened to growing old gracefully?

Lizzie had thought that some of the underwear was romantic and chic, but the rest of it wasn't even worth putting on, and some looked like it would be a real job getting into it, let alone getting out of it. And the books! *'101 Triple X Sex Tricks', 'Explosive Sex'* and *'100 Red Hot and Rude Positions'.* Lizzie went red just thinking about it. Then there were all the different oils, lotions and potions and sex toys - she didn't have a clue what all those contraptions and gadgets were for and couldn't imagine getting any pleasure from them, they looked quite sadistic. It made her eyes water just looking at them – whips, chains, handcuffs, eggs, rings, jelly vibrators, rabbit vibrators and g-spot vibrators. She'd never even heard of the g-spot before.

If Mickey had seen and heard the way his daughters spoke in that room that night he would have gone mental and thrown a right wobbler. He would have called them all dirty sluts. She smirked; if the Old Bill had raided her place that night they would have thought it was a whore house.

Lizzie yawned. She felt tired; it had been a long and busy day. It had been like being at Piccadilly Circus today. She wasn't complaining, it had been a lovely day, with all the family celebrating the birth and homecoming of Lizzie's great grandchild. Terri had become a Nan, she was so happy, her eldest daughter Georgia had had her first baby. At eight weeks old, she was coming home from hospital, out of the incubator, all the tubes had been taken away. At last she could breathe on her own.

She was just amazing, born early at seven months and weighing just over two pounds, the same as a bag of sugar. The doctor's expectations hadn't been good, they hadn't had much confidence in her survival chances as she had complications with her heart and breathing. The nurses even called the hospital priest so she was christened straight away, but that little girl proved them wrong. She was strong, a fighter, a little survivor, a Taylor through and through.

It had brought tears of joy to Lizzie's eyes when she'd held her in her arms today. She was just perfect, one of God's little miracles. They'd named her Hope. It suited her perfectly.

She looked at her watch. She'd better go back over to her chair if she wanted to catch her soaps. EastEnders would be starting soon. Lizzie shuffled slowly over to her chair, puffing and panting as she went. She eased herself down and made herself comfortable while she waited for Tina, her carer, to come and get her ready for bed. Lizzie loved it when they came in of a night, they would sit and listen to Lizzie telling them stories about the good old days while she smoked her last fag of the night. They couldn't believe some of the things she told them. She was sure they thought she was joking and making it all up. Some days she would have them in fits of laughter, having a good old belly laugh with her tales.

She picked up the remote control and switched the television on. An enormous stream of light filled the room. Lizzie squinted, closing her eyes tight. 'Tina, is that you?'

No answer. She tensed, leaned forward.

'Switch that bleeding light off, love, it's too bright.'

No reply.

Lizzie's heart stopped; someone else was in the room, she wasn't alone. 'Tina?' Lizzie said, puzzled.

Rubbing her eyes, she strained to listen. There was no noise; it was so quiet and calm. Lizzie opened her eyes, blinking rapidly, turning towards the light. It was the most amazing thing she had ever seen. What on earth was going on? Why was she seeing all this? She must be dreaming, hallucinating.

She'd only had a couple of glasses of whiskey today, so she couldn't blame the drink. This couldn't be real, she was going mad. She rubbed her eyes again a couple of times then opened them wide, staring in awe at what was in front of her. The most beautiful being was slowly floating towards her. She stared harder, blinking.

No, it couldn't be. It wasn't possible, was it?

She took a deep, deep breath, and unspeakable joy filled her heart.

Georgie, her son, her beautiful, lost boy, was drifting towards her, surrounded by a bright light! His feet weren't touching the floor, they just seemed to blend into the air. She felt so happy – it had been so long since she had seen him and she had missed him so much. But at the same time, she wasn't surprised to see him. The demons from Bobby's past that had surfaced in the past few months had always led inexorably back to Georgie. She knew she would see him again, somehow, somewhere. The only real question had been when.

'Georgie, it's you,' she said, smiling.

He didn't answer, just moved closer and closer. The expression on his face was one of pure happiness and extreme love, his body illuminated by a white light, tinged with gold.

A growing sense of calm swelled within Lizzie's heart. 'Are you still watching out for Mickey?' she wondered.

A smile appears on Georgie's handsome face as he held out his hands to her. 'Come with me,' he said, but his mouth didn't move. She didn't hear what he said with her ears, but felt what he was saying. She heard him with her mind, body and soul.

'Georgie, I ain't going out now,' she told him. She felt suddenly and overwhelmingly tired. 'It's too bleedin' cold. I'm tired and I wanna go to bed. You deal with those creeps for me.'

Lizzie could feel the light enfolding her, encircling her. She felt confused, she knew she was here, but where was here? But she was calm, at ease, peaceful. The light was breathing her in, absorbing her. She was drifting towards the light, felt an overwhelming comfort, felt safe, free from fear. If Georgie was here, then everything would be fine, they couldn't hurt her family...

Lizzie turned and looked behind her. She was detached and floating above her body. She could see herself sitting in her chair, but she wasn't afraid - she felt a sense of freedom. A longing so powerful, yet so gentle. She was travelling to another realm, one of total and absolute peace.

Lizzie floated up through the light where there was no fear, no pain, no misunderstanding. She was enveloped by total bliss in an atmosphere of unconditional love and acceptance. In the distance, a horizon of glorious white light beckoned her forward. As the brilliance increased the all-encompassing rays stretched to meet her.

Time and existence were blending and melding, the past, the present and the future combining into this one moment. A sense of all-knowing enveloped her. Every part of her being was satisfied with a love beyond description. All her secrets could be released, all her fears calmed, all her questions answered.

She looked at Georgie with gratitude and wonder as she held out her hands to him. She felt herself becoming lighter each moment. She was wanted here but she wasn't needed here anymore. She had served her purpose. The family could take care of themselves without her. Lizzie found herself being held, cradled in his serene embrace, gently rocked and nurtured in his arms.

She felt the peace and comfort she had been searching for her entire life. It was all the love she had ever wanted, a love that heals and regenerates. She knew then that she was eternal, that she had always been, that she always would be, that she would never be lost.

She floated towards the centre of the light, lost in time and space.

Finally she was at peace, she was free.

Lizzie Taylor smiled and closed her eyes for the last time.

Tommy

Tommy sat in his car, rolled his shoulders. His body felt stiff and tense, his nerves tightly wound in anticipation of the day that lay ahead. His Nan's funeral. He couldn't stop thinking about her and the day she died, kept wondering if he had stayed there a bit longer that day, might he have been able to save her, do something?

Deep inside, Tommy felt that she knew she was going, knew she was dying. She had been acting a bit strange the last few weeks, saying some odd things about the family, and not all good things. That just wasn't like her. What she was saying to him didn't make any sense, although no one in the family would dare put her down, she had been there for all of them at one time or another, she never put herself first.   But looking back on things now, it all was making a bit more sense.   Still, the night she died would always be in Tommy's mind. The memory was clear as a bell . . .

Tommy settled Lizzie in her chair next to her bed, covered her lap and legs with her faux fur blanket. 'There ya go Nan, that will keep ya nice and warm. All sorted, Tina ya carer will be in soon.'

'Thanks Tommy,' she said as she leaned down to the side of her chair, reaching between her bed and her chair, where she kept her handbag. She fished around inside her bag and sat back in her chair, set two envelopes on her lap. She looked directly at Tommy. 'This is a very delicate matter, Tommy.' She held one of the envelopes in her hand. 'I trust you with this,' she said as she handed it over. 'Make sure Father Peter gets this, it's very important.'

Tommy looked at her puzzled.

'It's got a letter in there for your Dad and it's very important. I know it will be safe with Father Peter,' Lizzie explained.

Tommy looked at her, puzzled. 'You're not planning on going anywhere yet are ya?'

She smiled at him. 'No, not yet. I've got a few years left in me still. But I needed to get it sorted out just in case.'

Tommy started to say something, but she cut him off. 'Sssh, Tommy, listen to me for a change.'

Tommy snapped his mouth shut.

'My life has been a great big charade, Tommy. I'm tired of playing games.'

Tommy had to interrupt. 'Nan what's wrong? You're worrying me!' Oh my god, he thought, I hope she's not getting senile dementia or Alzheimer's.

'Don't worry, I've still got me marbles boy, there's nothing wrong with me.' She gave a tired smile. 'Just listen to me for a minute before you go and do what you need to do.'

Tommy nodded. 'OK, Nan.'

She lifted a tired hand, handed him an envelope.

Just in case? What did she mean? What had happened that she was keeping quiet about? Thought Tommy as he tucked the envelope in his back pocket. 'Sorted Nan, no problem,' he replied, looking at her with his penetrating blue eyes. 'I'll go and give it to Father Peter straight away.'

She handed him a second envelope. 'This one's for you. There's a note in there that tells you what to do when I'm gone.'

He scowled. 'Are you sure about this?'

'Course I'm bleedin' sure! Now take this and sod off before I change my mind!'

Tommy hesitated.

'Go on then!' She waved a frail arm at Tommy to usher him away. 'You ain't got time to be sitting here with me now, have ya?'

He leaned over, put his big strong arms around her and cuddled her close. 'Thanks Nan, I owe ya big time. I dunno what I'd do without ya.'

Choked, he pulled himself away from Lizzie. 'I'm going now Nan; I'll give you a ring tomorrow.'

She watched him walk away. 'Be careful, Tommy.'

He opened the bedroom door and looked back at her. Their eyes met. 'Come on, Nan! You know careful's not my style!'

She couldn't help but smile at his cheeky grin.

Tommy's face turned suddenly serious. 'I will never forget what you have done for me.' He gave a brief sombre smile. 'I love you, Nan.'

Lizzie nodded as tears sprung to her eyes. 'I know you do, Tommy, and I love you too. And Tommy?'

Tommy paused, his hand on the door handle.

'It will all turn out for the best, you'll see.'

He shut the bedroom door behind him and was gone.

Tommy sniffed and wiped his eyes with the back of his hand. He was going to miss that woman so much. She had been good to him, good to all of her grandchildren. Everyone in the family was gutted.

He had loved Lizzie so much, he would have done anything for her. Just about every day he would pop in and see her – he lived round the corner – so she knew he would be there in an instant if she phoned him and needed him for anything. And when he came he always brought her something -

some cake, a packet of fags, a magazine, the TV guide, some fruit, sweets or biscuits. He loved spoiling her in little ways, just seeing her smile made his day.

She would say to him 'You shouldn't do this Tommy, I've got enough stuff here to feed the Eighth Army.'

But sure enough, if he forgot to get something and didn't have anything in his hands when he arrived she would have a little moan. She loved it really. Any day he couldn't get by, he would phone her to make sure she was all right.

She cracked him up, nearly every time he saw her she'd say, 'You found yourself a decent girl yet?' She was always on at him, saying, 'Tommy, I wish you'd find yourself a nice girl and settle down. You'd make a good husband and dad.'

Tommy had no intention of getting married and settling down. He was always out and about doing whatever he wanted. He would say to her again and again, 'Nan, women are more hassle than they're worth, all they bring you are heartache and trouble. I've got you Nan, you're the only woman for me, and you cause me enough grief, don't ya?'

He loved winding her up. 'I've met them all Nan,' he said, 'Miss Right doesn't exist. I've met Miss Player, Miss Psycho, Miss Cheap, Miss Know-it-all, Miss Control Freak, Miss Stalker, Miss Married, and Miss Jealous...'

She'd tell him to hush, but he could tell she loved it when he joked with her.

'I don't need a woman to make me happy and put a smile on my face,' he continued. 'I can do what I want, I only have to worry about myself. No responsibility, no one to look after, and I can go to the pub when I want to . . . I ain't gonna be nagged at for not doing the washing up or leaving the toilet seat up. I've got no one to answer to, I can listen to what I want, watch what I want when I want. I don't have to get permission for nothing. Anyway, no decent girl would be able to put up with me; I drink too much, smoke too much and gamble too much!'

Lizzie would just look at him, tutt and shake her head, trying to hide her grin. 'One day, Tommy, one day.'

Tommy sighed, thought of the last night he'd seen her, the envelopes she had given him to give to the priest. He wondered what it was, what she needed to sort out. Mickey was going to want to see that last letter of hers, and when he did, the shit was going to hit the fan, big time.

Mickey

Two Weeks Later
Morning Of Funeral

Mickey sat on the edge of his bed staring down at the floor, a sad frown on his handsome face. He hadn't been able to sleep all night, so he was already up, washed, shaved and dressed, ready to face the day. In fact he hadn't had a decent night's kip since last week when he was called into the guvnor's office and given the bad news.

He had spent the night tossing and turning, then pacing up and down as best he could in his tiny cell, thinking and thinking, about the past, the present, the future – especially the future. What was going to happen now that Lizzie was gone, the glue that held the family together? Mickey stood up and stretched. He had to get himself together and liven up a bit, he would be leaving soon. Time for another ending, another farewell.

Mickey still felt numb and in shock, couldn't get to grips with it. He had lost a lot in his life, but nothing had hurt this much since Georgie had tried to top himself. He felt as if his world had caved in. Nothing would ever be the same again.

He walked over to the sink and splashed his face with cold water, studied himself in the small rectangular shaving mirror. Shape up! He was Mickey Taylor, not some mug. He pulled his shoulders back, stood tall, proud and fearless, pulled his black tie from his pocket, and took a step closer to the mirror.

'You're still a good looking fucker Mickey Taylor,' he said. It was true – he wasn't doing badly for forty.

Mickey was due for parole in two weeks – he would be a free man soon, had been sure he'd see his mum again soon. To lose her this close to the end of his sentence…well, he was choked that he hadn't had the chance to say goodbye.

He picked the paper up from his prison bed, smirked. He'd made front page news that morning.

'Dangerous' back in Dagenham

His eyes ran down the page, the grin not leaving his face.

Notorious Essex gangster Mickey Taylor, known locally as 'Dangerous', has been granted permission to attend his mother's funeral in Dagenham, Essex later today. Taylor is currently serving a fourteen year sentence for murder at Belmarsh Prison, where he is held as a maximum security Category B prisoner. His mother, Mrs Lizzie Taylor, known as The Dagenham Duchess, died peacefully in her sleep at home last week. A number of well-known celebrities and underworld associates of Taylor's are expected to attend the funeral service today.

During the 70s and 80s, Mickey Taylor ran one of the biggest crime operations in London since that of the Kray twins. This will be his first appearance in public since being sentenced. Michael Taylor was jailed in 1984 for the gangland double murder of Paul Miller and Daniel McCarthy, both of whom had long-time connections to the underworld. The crime is said to have had roots in a local blood feud going back nearly twenty years. Judge David Mitchum at the Old Bailey described Taylor as, "An unusually dangerous man".

Mickey scowled. They made him sound really dodgy, but he couldn't understand why. He would never harm women or children, or even Mr Ordinary off the street. He was a reasonable man and wasn't anywhere near as bad as they made out. As far as Mickey was concerned, it was simple – as long as you didn't take liberties with him or any of his family you'd have nothing to worry about. But whoever dared do him wrong would suffer the consequences.

Mickey knew certain people branded him a killer, but he was not some nutty psychopath. He didn't get a thrill out of killing someone just for the sake of it. Mickey wasn't a callous, cold-blooded bloke. He loved his family and his close friends. To each of these he gave his undying loyalty, and he expected the same in return. But if anyone broke that loyalty, then that was a sad moment, a very sad moment indeed, because then Mickey became their enemy.

That's what had happened with Miller and McCarthy. They'd all been part of the same world, knew the rules, and had operated their own business side by side. But then they'd got greedy, stitched Mickey up over a deal and made him look like a right mug. From that moment on their fate was sealed. You could take some money from Mickey, even take a bit of his business away, but once you touched his reputation, that was it. Mickey had learned very early in life that his reputation was everything – half the time it did his work for him without him even having to mess someone up.

Miller and McCarthy had known that, had known the risk they were running when they screwed him over, and they'd paid the price.

For Mickey, that was the way it was, loyalty and reputation meant everything, that was the way he did business, but he knew that things had changed while he had been inside. Loyalty today was determined by one thing, money. For many people, money was more important than friendship. In prison, Mickey had seen people fuck over their best mate for a pound. He soon discovered that inside, just like in real life, there were not many people out there you could give your word to, and there were way too many grasses.

When it came to retribution, Mickey had no conscience. He was a dangerous fucker who needed no seal of approval from anyone. Take him or leave him, Mickey wasn't fussed either way. He hadn't set out to get this reputation, it just happened. Situation and circumstance made Mickey's life what it was. His whole life had been a battle, one fight after another, and Mickey had had to learn early in life to use his fists to earn respect and survive. Some people have a way with words and can talk their way out of trouble; others manipulate or buy their way out. Mickey had a wicked punch, a jaw made of iron, and a ruthless need to come out on top. When it was time to put up or shut up, Mickey never came second to anyone.

When Mickey was sentenced for fourteen years, it didn't take him long to find out who his real mates were, who his enemies were, who stuck by him, who took advantage of his absence. And now it wouldn't be long before he was on the outside again, and those mugs who had taken liberties with him and his family, well, he would show them what loyalty and trust was all about. They would know he was out and back in Dagenham. He had a good memory, like a fucking elephant. Mickey never forgot a good turn, and he definitely didn't forget a bad one.

Mickey would have given his life for some of these people and he thought they would have done the same for him, but he'd learned otherwise – now it was their turn. They wouldn't be safe till one or other of them was dead and buried, and he didn't plan on it being him. Their day was coming, it had been a long wait, but it was going to be well worth it. He had his loyal friends out there, and Mickey knew exactly who they were.

There were two dirty scumbags in particular who were still out there who Mickey felt it was an affront were still living. Mickey didn't think they should still be alive, but they thought they were safe. They thought he didn't know how they were taking the piss, taking liberties while he was behind bars. They should be dead by now, but their day would come. They thought they had got away with it, but he'd simply been biding his time. As soon as he was out, Mickey would unleash every nasty form of pain he knew on them wasters.

Mickey had met some pricks in his life but these men were fucking cactus. Revenge was sweet, and as long as Mickey eventually got his revenge it didn't matter to him how long it took.

Of course, there were people out there waiting to do the same to him. Mickey had heard lots of rumours, it was on the grapevine that he was going to be taken out, killed, when he got released from prison. All Mickey could say to those geezers was they had better make sure they did the job properly, because if they didn't kill him cleanly first time, then they would pay.

Everyone had to die eventually, it was just a matter of when and where, sooner or later. Maybe his luck would run out one day, and if that happened, well so be it, no one lived forever.

Mickey grinned. One thing was for sure - he probably wouldn't die of natural causes! He turned as he heard the grille open, keys jangle and the door rattle. It was the prison officers coming to get him.

'You ready to go, Taylor?'

His face changed. He looked at them with a blank, brutal gaze. Of course he was ready.

He pulled the cuffs of his crisp, white shirtsleeves down, shook one sharply creased black trouser leg, then the other. Mickey followed the screws out of his cell, walking along the narrow landing towards reception. He had one officer in front, the other behind him. A few of his pals shouted out to him. 'Thinking of ya, mate.'

'Hope it all goes well.'

'Take it easy, Mickey.'

'All the best to you and the family.'

'Give 'em hell, Dangerous!'

Everyone in the prison knew who he was and what he was capable of, so most of the inmates avoided eye contact with him.

Mickey glanced to his left as someone emerged from a cell. It was Bernie Dale, a good mate. Bernie put his big hand on Mickey's shoulder and squeezed it.

'Mickey, I don't know what to say to ya, mate. I'm gutted for ya, your Mum was a lovely lady.'

Mickey put his hand out, they shook. 'There's nothing you can say.' Mickey turned, followed the guards. 'See ya later, Bernie.'

Mickey continued walking down the landing thinking about Bernie Dale. They knew each other from way back, from outside. Bernie had always been a loyal mate, always there when you needed him. He was a chatty, witty, intelligent man who could talk the hind leg off a donkey and had an opinion on absolutely everything. He was a bit of a comedian too, always wise-cracking, but you shouldn't let his funny jokes and wise cracks fool you. Behind his laughter there was a menacing character. When the shit hit the fan, Bernie would be there, covering your back. Mickey knew him like a brother, they went back a long time, he lived across the road from him growing up. They'd known each other since they were little kids, and had remained friends ever since.

Mickey grinned as he thought about Bernie's story, the story Bernie told everyone when he met them. Mickey had heard it so many times he could repeat it word for word, how he told it. Bernie said that Mickey had saved his life, and he would tell everyone the story of their time together in Wayland Prison. Mickey had never believed in fate up until then, but he did now.

A few years back, Mickey was shipped from Belmarsh Prison to Wayland Prison, where Bernie was finishing off a seven year stretch for demanding money with a gun. Bernie was always doing a course of some sort - you had to do some courses to be even considered for parole - and one day he came into Mickey's cell, a sheet of paper in his hand. 'Mickey, I've got a course for you to do,' he announced. 'It's called the Early Release Programme.'

'I'm up for anything that gets me out of this shit hole earlier,' Mickey replied.

Bernie nodded, a serious look on his face. 'Well, you know how hard up the prison is and how overcrowded it is? Well, some clever bastard has come up with this scheme. The prison management have decided to implement this new programme which makes all prisoners over the age of thirty five eligible for immediate release. So it makes you eligible, you're a fucking prison pensioner now!'

Mickey laughed. 'Fuck off you cheeky bastard. You're winding me up again.'

'No! Read this,' Bernie said, passing the paper towards Mickey.

'You read it to me,' said Mickey. 'You like the sound of your own voice.'

So Bernie did.

'The scheme will be known as **R.A.P.E** (Releasing Aged Prisoners Early),' he announced. 'Prisoners selected to be **RAPEd** can apply to the probation office for inclusion on the **S.H.A.F.T** programme (Self-Help After Release).'

Mickey grinned, shook his head. 'Where do you get this shit?'

Bernie grinned, continued. 'Prisons that have been **RAPEd** and **SHAFTed** will be reviewed periodically under the new **SCREW** scheme (Special Convicts Released Early Welfare). A prisoner may only be **RAPEd** once, **and SHAFTed** twice, but can be **SCREWed** as many times as the prison deems appropriate under the present prison service guidelines.'

'Did you write this?'

Bernie shook his head. 'I wish!' He continued. 'Prisoners **RAPEd** may have the additional benefit of receiving **A.I.D.S** (Additional Income for Dependents or Spouse). You may even receive **H.E.R.P.E.S.** (Half Earnings for Released Prisoners Early Severance). Applications are available at the wing office and will be transmitted by the P.O. Please note - prisoners who have **A.I.D.S** or **H.E.R.P.E.S** will no longer get **SHAFTed** or **SCREWed** by prison management.'

'That's fucking classic!' laughed Mickey.

'I'm not done yet,' Bernie told him. 'For those prisoners not eligible for the above, there is **S.H.I.T.** (Special High Intensity Training). All prisoners remaining in the system will receive as much **S.H.I.T.** as possible. The Prison Services Management always prides itself on the amount of **S.H.I.T.** it can give its inmates. Should you feel at any time that you do not receive enough **S.H.I.T.** Then please feel free to bring this to the attention of your personal officer or landing staff. They will make it their priority to give you as much **S.H.I.T.** as possible. Be assured, all our staff have been expertly trained to give you as much **S.H.I.T.** as you can handle.'

When they finished laughing, Bernie got around to the real reason he was visiting Mickey. He had been pestering Mickey for weeks about doing a first aid course with him. Mickey wasn't interested, kept putting him off – he'd left school with no qualifications, couldn't read or write properly. And besides, he didn't like the sight of blood or needles, and hospitals made him feel sick. He would have to be dying to go and see a doctor.

'Me do mouth to mouth?' he told Bernie. 'You have to be having a fucking laugh! You don't know what you could catch!'

But Bernie wouldn't give up, he was one of those people that once he got something in his head, that was that, he wouldn't stop going on and on, pestering Mickey to do the first aid course. Bernie was getting on Mickey's fucking nerves, doing his nut in, so in the end Mickey said yes, just so he would shut Bernie the fuck up and stop him going on and on about it.

And so, four weeks later Mickey had a first aid certificate, with his name on it and everything. Proper proud he was – he didn't think he had a chance of passing; he'd never had any kind of certificate or qualification before.

One of the screws brought it to him, in an envelope from the St Johns' Ambulance. He immediately jumped out of bed and hurried to Bernie's cell to show him.

'Ere, Bernie, you'll never guess what I got,' announced Mickey as he strode into Bernie's cell. Bernie was still curled up in bed. 'Come on, Bernie,' laughed Mickey. 'Get yer arse out the pit and take a look at this.'

Bernie didn't answer. He was still asleep – which was unusual, thought Mickey, he was always up, ready to get out the cell – or he was going fucking deaf.

Mickey looked at him, he didn't look right, looked strange. His face looked grey. Mickey raised his voice. 'Bernie? You getting up?'

Bernie finally opened his eyes, peered up at Mickey. 'Nah, I don't feel that clever.'

'Come on mate, a bit of fresh air will do ya good.' Mickey grinned, held up the envelope. 'And I got something to show ya!'

Bernie shook his head. 'Fuck off. I can't be arsed to move.'

Mickey was beginning to get impatient. 'Come on ya lazy cunt, get up!' Mickey threw his jeans and T-shirt at him. 'Get dressed.'

'OK, Mickey, hold ya horses.' Bernie slowly pushed himself up out of his bunk. He made it to his feet, then suddenly went down like a pile of shit in front of Mickey, flopping on the floor in a heap, his eyes rolling around in his head. Mickey pressed the panic button – he needed fucking help – then dropped down on his knees next to Bernie and shook his shoulder. 'Bernie, wake up! Answer me you dozy fucker!' But he wasn't responding.

Mickey looked around. Where was everyone? A few other inmates crowded the doorway, just looking. No one knew what to do.

Mickey knew he had to act quickly, do something fast. Then all of a sudden, he looked down at the envelope, still in his hand, and everything he'd learnt in the first aid course came flashing back. Instinctively he knew what he had to do.

He leaned over Bernie, took his pulse. Nothing. No breathing either. Fuck! He'd had a fucking heart attack!

Without thinking Mickey put the heel of his hands on the centre of Bernie's chest, began chest compressions hard and fast.

Fifteen he counted, then leaned over, checked again – still not breathing. Mickey pinched Bernie's nose shut, breathed into his mouth. The kiss of life.

Mickey had no idea how many times he repeated the cycle, it could have been ten or a hundred, then suddenly the paramedics were there, clearing everyone out of the cell.

Mickey stood on the landing, gasping, sweat pouring down his face, his hands shaking. People were clapping him on the back, telling him what a great job he'd done, but he just felt numb. Was Bernie still alive? Then suddenly they burst out, Bernie on a stretcher, hurried down the gangway towards the stairs.

Mickey raced after them.

'Is he still alive?' he shouted.

No reply.

Mickey pushed through the crowd that had gathered, leaned over the rail. The paramedics had reached the bottom of the stairs. 'Is he alive!?' he roared.

The paramedics stopped by the heavy iron doors, and one of them looked up as they waited for the screws to let them through. 'Yes, he's alive,' he said quietly.

A huge roar filled the prison. Mickey sagged back against the wall, grinned. Un-fucking-believable!

It was six weeks before they saw Bernie again. He had suffered a massive heart attack. If Mickey hadn't been there the morning when it happened Bernie would have died. Mickey had never believed in fate, but he did now.

When Bernie was released from the prison hospital he came strolling up to Mickey, shook his hand, gave him a huge bear hug. 'Thanks, Mickey, me ole mucker, you saved my life, he grinned. 'If it weren't for you, I would have been a gonner!'

After what happened to Bernie, Mickey realised how important your heart was, how important it was to look after yourself and your ticker. When he first got his life sentence, he'd let himself go a bit, eating too much crap, loads of chocolate and crisps, stuff that was no good for you, had put on over six stone. Sharon said he looked like Buster Bloodvessel from Bad Manners. His kids told him that he would be next to have a heart attack.

Now he realised he had to look after himself, his heart. Staying alive was his mission. There was no fucking way he was going to die inside! He knocked smoking on the head, cut down on the sweets and shit he used to eat, and got his fitness head on again. That's when the rigorous training started. He wanted to be fit, fast and alert. He wanted to live a long, healthy life. If you had a healthy heart, he believed, you had a healthy mind.

Mickey attacked the challenge of getting fit with the same intensity he attacked everything else - total commitment.   Even in the confines of his prison cell, he made himself do everything he could - press ups, squats, stretching, sit ups, burpees, running and jumping on the spot, anything he could think of.

He didn't have a fancy gym to go to, didn't have all the up to date equipment, so he kept it simple - self-will and motivation were his biggest tools.   Within a few months he felt like a new man, younger and healthier than he had since his early twenties. He felt better in body and mind, sharper in his thinking.

Most people thinking of getting fit, think of the money. Gym fees, new trainers, new tracksuit, and then buying the supplements and steroids that cost a fortune. What a rip off. Mickey didn't have any of that, yet he was stronger and fitter than he had ever been. He didn't know anyone who'd bought a fifty quid pair of trainers which made them run faster. It was all just mugging you off with the sales talk and advertising. Mickey didn't need the expensive running machines and rowing machines. Most people who had them indoors ended up using them as clothes horses.

The exercise gave him something to do to help pass the long prison days. Spending most of the day locked up in a cell left you with too many hours of thinking time, too much time for Mickey to analyse everything he'd done, what he'd got wrong, what he'd got right.

He needed to keep himself focused and busy, serve his time and get on with it.

It was hard work staying mentally sharp – the prison system destroys your thinking. They do everything for you, tell you what time to get up, when to you have breakfast, dinner, tea, when to go to bed – everything. Mickey soon realised it was up to him to keep his mind active and working while he was inside, banged up for hours in a small prison cell that he shit, ate, and slept in.

So Mickey knuckled down, got permission from the governor to use the gym for an hour a day. Then after his gym workouts he went back to his cell to finish off with crunches, pull ups and squat thrusts, spending every day in vigorous training. By the time of his mum's funeral, Mickey was at his peak of fitness; he hadn't had a smoke or any booze in years. When he finally got out, Dagenham would know he was back.

But despite everything he did, being inside still ate away at him. When he spoke to his mum, to Mandy, his kids, his sisters, Mickey just knew when things weren't right. He could tell by the tone of their voices, the pauses, if they didn't say they loved him or if they made an unusual comment, said something in a different way. And then he would go back to his cell and turn all the words around, make scenes up in his head. What was it that they were not telling him? What were they keeping quiet? What was going on that they didn't want Mickey to know about? Were they lying to him about something?

Mickey would turn an inch into a mile, that's the way his thoughts took him, his mind played tricks with him during those long periods of confinement. So he kept himself active and busy, that was all it was for him now, training, training, and training. What had happened to Bernie had made Mickey look at his life differently. They said things happened for a reason, and this was the pay-off. He was about to be released, and he was ready.

Mickey was led out of the prison, double handcuffed to a prison guard. The place was surrounded by police officers, security was tight. Mickey was quickly bundled into the back of a black car with a police escort.

He sat and stared out of the tinted window. There was so much noise, so many people rushing around everywhere. Newspaper reporters, television commentators, photographers. The click, click, click of the cameras, the flashing of the bulbs, everything moving so fast, madness and mayhem. It cracked him up; he'd heard it all before, *He's done this, he's done that, that's the one...*

Mickey didn't know what all the fuss was about.   He just sat between two officers, quiet, unmoving. He didn't want to talk, wasn't in the mood.

The prison gates opened and then he was on his way back to the place where his family had moved to over forty years ago. He couldn't believe how quickly the time had passed and how much had happened. Nothing seemed to make any sense. It hadn't really sunk in that his mum was dead. He'd thought that she'd be around forever. It all seemed so strange and unreal. He swallowed deeply; she would leave a big void in so many people's lives. Lizzie had been a simple and honest woman, full of wisdom. She always said to him, 'Mickey, no matter what happens, or how bad it seems today, life does go on and it will be better tomorrow.'

During this past week he had received over two hundred sympathy cards and letters. He was grateful to all those people who cared and took time out to write to him with their condolences. One of the letters was from one of his daughters. He had sat in his cell every night reading and re-reading it. One part made him feel he'd been kicked in the guts.

" 'A house is a brick, a home is a heart.' Nan's feels like a house, but its heart is missing. Dad, I miss her so much. What we are going to do without her?"

Prison could be a lonely place, and at the moment he read that, Mickey felt lonelier than he'd ever felt before. He realised how amazing Lizzie

39008 0 01147873

Taylor had been and he knew that he'd never meet another woman like her. He'd loved that woman more than anything in the world. No matter what happened, Lizzie had always stood by him.

She had visited him regularly until a couple of years ago when she got really ill with pneumonia; they all thought she was going to kick the bucket then. Since then she had been housebound and hardly ever got out. He'd missed her monthly visits.

But even then, every week, regular as clockwork on a Tuesday and Saturday, he'd receive a letter from her, filling him in on what was going on out there. He phoned her every morning at eight o'clock and every night before lock up. He spoke to her the night she died and she was fine, the same as always. They ended the phone call as they always did: 'Goodnight, Mickey, God bless, love you.'

'You too Mum, speak to you in the morning.'

'Please God,' she would always say.

'Bye Mum.'

'Bye.'

He never did hear her voice again ... He took a deep breath and cast his eyes up to the sky. God bless her.

Lizzie's house, number 38, or 'Nan's' as everyone called it, had been the centre of activity for decades. It was never empty; the place was always mobbed with different faces. Everyone went there to see Lizzie. It kept everyone together, kept them all in touch with each other. If you wanted to see anyone or find out how someone was, you just went to 'Nan's House'. One by one everyone would come through the door, Mickey's wife Mandy and their kids, his brothers and sisters with their children, aunts and uncles and cousins, mates and neighbours, everyone was welcome. There was always plenty of food and drink to go round. Lizzie didn't mind, she enjoyed the company. There was always someone with her so she was never lonely.

Weekends, especially during the summer, were the best. Lizzie would play the piano and have a good old sing-song. You name it, Lizzie played it. She was a brilliant pianist. She couldn't read music, she just played by ear. Her father had taught her how to play when she was a young girl.

It sounded like the Albert Hall in her front room sometimes. Music would blare out, all the old records playing. Everything - Nat King Cole, Johnny Cash, Frank Sinatra, the Beatles, Chas and Dave, Pink Floyd, the Jam, the Bee Gees, Madonna, Michael Jackson... Now where would everyone go? They'd drift away. It was the end of an era.

Even when Mickey got married and had his own place he still went back to his mum's with his mates after a night out. That's just the way it was. Mickey smiled to himself thinking of some of the good times he had with some of his old mates. There were many acquaintances, but the good friends you could count on one hand.

His best mates were Stevie Black, Mark Miles, Joseph Donnelly, Kenny Mason, and Bernie Dale. They went back years, friends since school. They had a long history between them. They were all very close, used to confide in each other on almost every subject. They knew each other inside out, all told each other the truth whether they liked it or not, never listened to any old bollocks, they told it as it was. They had some good times, some good laughs. What Mickey wouldn't give to have a night back with them all, a good old jolly up, go on a right bender with them. Mickey sighed, sadly it would never happen. There were only a few of them left. That too was fate. They had dropped off one by one; he loved them like they were his brothers. Mickey had lots of pals but these men were his real mates, proper friends.

It was hot and stuffy in the car and Mickey was getting fidgety. He undid his tie and loosened his collar. He was sweating like a pig and felt claustrophobic jammed in between the two screws. He needed a bit of space, some fresh air. He stared out of the window just thinking, reflecting on his life, Lizzie's life, wondering what she really thought of him, how they were as mother and son.

Mickey didn't have any time for regrets; he wished he could change some things, wished he had done some things differently, but there were no regrets but this one – that his mum had died while he was inside, just a few weeks before his release. In the end, he'd not been there for her...

Mickey glanced out of the window. It wasn't far to go before they reached the cemetery. He started looking around for familiar places, but they were all gone. To his surprise Mickey got a lump his throat, had to blink to keep his eyes clear. What had happened to the Dagenham he knew? He didn't recognise the place. All the landmarks were gone, the shops were different, nothing was the same. It was like the League of Nations. Most of the pubs and clubs had vanished or were closed. New flats – or apartments as they were now called – and new houses had appeared everywhere. Mickey was shocked at how much things had changed. This wasn't the place he left thirteen years ago.

Suddenly he caught himself. Silly bastard! Did he think it would all stay the same while he was inside? He grinned. No matter how much it had changed, it was still his territory, his manor, and he was ready to make his mark on it once more. He rebuttoned his shirt, straightened his tie, pulled a handkerchief from his pocket and wiped his brow. Even though this was his mum's funeral, this was the start of Mickey's return to Dagenham, and he had to be ready, on his game, look like he owned the place. People would be watching, and Mickey had to show them that he was back. Dagenham was Mickey's town, and he was ready to reclaim it.

Sharon Taylor

Sharon pulled up outside her mum's house in her red Mercedes. It was early, the street quiet, most people still tucked up in bed. Sharon wanted to be alone in the house for the last time, savour a few moments. She needed to spend a little bit of time on her own in her mum's house before everybody arrived and it was chock-a-block with people. That's how the house had always been – always lively and full of people coming and going. But after today, Sharon knew she never wanted to walk through that street door again, never wanted to set foot in this house again. She was done.

With her mum gone nothing would ever be the same again. Sharon was used to things being taken away from her, but as hard as it was sometimes, that was life and you have to be strong, get over it and move on. Hopefully after today all the horrors of the Taylor family would be put to rest, but she had a horrible feeling that they would soon rear their ugly head again. Sharon needed to be here and make sure everything was ready for today. There were still a few things she had to sort out, to finalise before the funeral. Everything had to be just so.

Sharon sighed heavily as she got out of the car. She wasn't looking forward to the day. A white van pulled up behind her; it was Gary Miles, the local florist delivering the flowers. She waved to him and he waved back. She knew his family well, they had used his granddad's flower shop up the road for donkey's years. The family could have bought shares in the company with the amount of flowers they had had off him over the years for weddings and funerals.

Sharon smiled to herself. Funny how all the local families were connected one way or another. When she was nineteen she shagged Gary's brother on the top of the 174 bus on their way home from Romford one night. And then Gary was the one who contacted Mickey and told him that Sharon was going mental over at the cemetery, freaking out on her dads grave. Bloody hell, she thought, it seems like yesterday, not like over twenty five years ago.

Sharon opened the gate and walked up the path as she had done so many times before. The front garden was already overflowing with wreaths and bouquets. She stopped in the porch and looked around her, up and down the road, across the street, the phone box over the road, the different houses where friends used to live. Momentarily she was unable to continue, unwilling to go into the empty house, then got herself moving, fumbled with the keys and finally managed to get the key in the lock. Her eyes were full of tears and she couldn't stop herself from shaking. She needed a drink.

She let herself into her mum's, shut the door behind her, took her coat off and hung it on the bannister - empty now but usually full of coats - then stood still at the bottom of the stairs, just listening. Silence. It just wasn't right; this house was never quiet. There was always some kind of commotion and activity going on.

She half expected to hear the telly blaring from Lizzie's bedroom. The times they had tried to get her to wear a hearing aid, but she wouldn't have it that she was going a bit mutton. She maintained there was nothing wrong with her hearing; she wasn't deaf, she just heard what she wanted to hear. 'Selective hearing' she called it, and she used it to her advantage whenever she could!

Sharon walked into the small kitchen and poured herself a gin and tonic. She knew it was early to be drinking but she didn't care, it was going to be a long, hard day and she needed a bit of Dutch courage.

She frowned, gazed out the window at the cold October morning, the early morning dew glistening on the grass, the birds sitting on the huge cherry tree at the back of the garden, the washing line empty.

Her full lips turned up in a smile. They had all played there as kids, brothers and sisters, cousins, nieces and nephews, friends in and out all the time. She closed her eyes remembering when she was a child, all the things Lizzie used to say and do. Her old-fashioned ways and sayings, sayings that Sharon knew off by heart. She could hear her mum's voice now, talking to her. She would stand there, hands on hips, tutting, puffing and blowing, shaking her head or wagging her finger.

What part of "no" don't you understand?
You think I'm a bank?
How many times do I have to tell you?
This is the last time, you know.
Why? Because I said so.
I want, never gets.
No one said life was fair.

Fucking hell, Sharon thought to herself, Lizzie got it right on that one.

And the next one was the best: 'Sharon, you can do what you want, have what you want when you leave home and you've got your own place, but not under my roof.'

Sharon did exactly that, she lived by it. She had done what she wanted to do, not what someone else expected from her or wanted her to do. She took no shit from anyone. Sharon swept her hands through her hair and stretched her aching back. She felt all the life had drained out of her since Lizzie had died.

Sharon had never given her mum any grandchildren, she couldn't have kids. The abortion she had years ago fucked her insides up. It was her dad's fault – Bobby Taylor's fault – she hated him, she was happy when he died; he had fucked her life up completely. It was his fault she was like she was, in this mess. Even dead he still managed to control her life, haunted her every day.

She hated him, hated him so much. He had been dead for twenty years but he still had a massive effect on her. Every time she thought about him and what he was, what he had done to her, the damage he had caused so many people, she hoped he was rotting in hell.

Her guts twisted. He might be long dead but every day he revisited her, came back and destroyed everything. Just when she had a bit of hope and something good was happening, then it all came crashing down again, taken away from her, all because of him. It was like he was still here, still watching her, still punishing her.

Sharon tried to turn her thoughts to happier times. She pictured Lizzie with a baby on her knee, one of her grandchildren, singing away to them. 'Daisy, Daisy, give me your answer do,' was a favourite she sang to the kids. 'Go to sleep my baby, close your pretty eyes,' was another. Sharon so wished that she could have had a baby of her own and given Lizzie a grandchild. It tore her apart every day. The one thing she had always wanted and couldn't have.

Sharon sighed heavily, wiped half-heartedly at the kitchen counters with a damp cloth. It was going to be a strange day. Everyone around her could show their sadness and sorrow. They weren't afraid to show their red-rimmed eyes, but Sharon just couldn't cry, just couldn't. Sharon threw the cloth in the sink, downed her drink, then turned and stomped up the stairs to her mum's bedroom.

From the top of her mum's wardrobe Sharon pulled down the old biscuit tin where Lizzie kept her savings and important papers in envelopes. She froze as she opened the tin – the money was gone, no envelopes. Fucking hell! Lizzie kept all sorts of bits and pieces in there, things like her pension book, rent card, medical card and passport, and of course her will.

Sharon didn't know why Lizzie had a passport, she had never left the country. Lizzie said she didn't want to fly, the thought of getting on an aeroplane frightened the life out of her, but she'd insisted on having one anyway. 'Just in case,' she had always said.

Sharon rummaged through the tin again. Maybe she'd moved her money somewhere else at the end? Sharon couldn't help but smile as she found some old green shield stamp books as well. How long had they been there? She took out the paperwork she needed and put the tin back. A life story in a tatty old biscuit tin.

Sharon sat in her mum's chair and closed her eyes, instantly was a little girl again, remembering the things Lizzie used to say to them all. She jumped up – no time for that. Not now. Not ever. She rummaged through the drawers of her mum's dressing table – still no money. She quickly searched around the rest of the bedroom. It definitely wasn't there.

Sharon picked up the phone, dialled quickly, and stood waiting, her bright red fingernails tapping furiously on the kitchen counter. 'Terri? How you doing?'

'Morning Shal.' Terri's voice sounded rough coming down the phone line. 'I feel like shit, how are you?'

'Same. How long you going be?

'I'll be five minutes'

'Have you been into Mum's room and moved the money from her tin?'

'No. What's the matter?'

Sharon sighed. 'Her money's gone, her will too. It's not in the old biscuit tin or in her black handbag that she kept down the side of the bed. The envelopes have gone. Are you sure you haven't seen them, moved them anywhere else?'

'They can't have gone, they must be there somewhere.'

Sharon's raised her voice. 'They're fucking gone, I tell you! I've fucking searched everywhere! I'm telling you, the money's not here!'

'All right, I believe you. I'll be there soon.'

Sharon said nothing.

'Don't mention it to anyone yet, Sharon. We can't have any more hassle, not today. We'll find it all. See you in a minute.'

Sharon searched the bedroom again like a woman possessed, pulling out drawers, emptying the wardrobe, searching under the bed, behind the curtains. Anywhere she could possibly think it might have been, where Lizzie might have hidden it. Sharon searched high and low but she knew she wasn't going to find it. Lizzie's money and will were gone.

Oh my God, thought Sharon, the shit is really going to hit the fan now. Let the fighting begin. She went downstairs and poured herself another drink. Thank fuck Lizzie kept a well-stocked booze cupboard – she was going to need it today.

Sharon was scared. There would be murders when this all came out. One thing you never did was steal from your own, especially from the woman who had given them life, given them hope, given them her love. She didn't know if she could handle any more grief. Lizzie had been putting money away for years -since way back when Bobby was alive. Christ knows how much she had managed to cram in her tins and envelopes. Sharon rolled her eyes. She knew who would get the blame, and she knew this would cause a war. There wouldn't be a Taylor family anymore, it would destroy them. She sat heavily in her mum's chair, rubbed her face. This was a nightmare, the opening for the past to creep back in and raise its ugly head. All the arguments and secrets that had been pushed under the carpet would come crawling back out. Then World War Three would begin.

Sharon could already hear it.   Money grabbing Sharon would be blamed. People thought she was a self-centred bitch, heartless and childless. She never babysat for anyone, couldn't get close to any of the children. They called Terri the saint, Sharon the sinner. But none of them knew, she'd never told them about her backstreet abortion years ago, how it had butchered her insides so she would always be childless.

She would have loved to hold her own baby in her arms, have something that was hers and no one could take away from her. That's why she couldn't get close to any of them, it was easier that way. Shut it out, not let even the tiniest thought of it creep into her brain. If they only knew she loved them all so much but she couldn't show it. She had learned a long time ago that as soon as her emotions got involved, that's when everything became fucked up.

She knew what they said about her, the dried up old spinster, not maternal in any way, shape or form. She knew that most of them thought she was strange, the odd one out. She could hear them muttering in those patronizing tones, but her secrets ran too deep. Only Lizzie knew the truth about Sharon, and now she was gone...

She could still remember the day she found out she wasn't Lizzie's daughter, could feel that moment every time she thought about it. Her legs had felt like jelly, she sat down quickly before they gave way. Fear ran through her, she was angry, furious. She wanted to scream, to shout – how could they keep this from her? As if they all hadn't been through enough as it was. Her face was ashen, she was in deep shock, her mouth dry; she stifled a sob, listened in horror as Lizzie told her the whole, gory story . . .

Her mother was Sadie Blake, Lizzie's sister, and her real dad was Alfie Blake, who murdered Sadie then committed suicide in Broadmoor a few years later. Lizzie had adopted Sharon when she was just six months old. Fuck!

What chance did she ever have in life really, with all these sick people with bad genes all around? She was going to be punished, forever, for something she hadn't even done.

'I hate you and all this family,' she had screamed at Lizzie when she had told her. 'You should have told me, not lied to me, misled me all my fucking life, about who I am and where I come from. I hate you and will never ever forgive you!' Lizzie said nothing, tried to hold her, but Sharon was having none of it.

'So that means Kevin and Danny are my real brothers? How could you split us all up, why didn't you keep us together?' demanded Sharon. Her mind raced. 'Why didn't Sheila want me as well? What was wrong with me that she didn't want me? Why did you split me up from my brothers?' So many questions, so much hurt.

Lizzie tried to explain that none of them could look after three extra kids. So they had decided it would be better for the boys to stay together, to grow up in Ireland, while Lizzie looked after Sharon.

Sharon just glared back at her for a moment. 'I hate you all!' she snarled again, then stormed out the house. She didn't know where she was going, she just kept on walking, the further away the better.

Sharon's world had been turned upside down yet again. When were all the lies and deceit going to stop? The whole family had lied to her, deceived her for her whole life. The whole family knew to keep it all hush, hush. The only one they didn't trust to know it was Sharon herself.

She turned it over in her mind again and again. There was so much she wanted to know, so much that she needed to know. Why me? Why did Lizzie adopt me? Why not keep them together as a family? Why did they split them up?

A feeling of not belonging overwhelmed her, a constant pounding in her head, she felt like it would explode. She felt like she was going mad. Her belly was in constant turmoil, she kept being sick, couldn't eat properly for weeks. Nights were the worst. She couldn't sleep, kept getting in and out of bed, drinking coffee, booze, crying for no reason, smoking non-stop, drinking again, popping painkillers. She felt like she wanted to die but nothing she did made it any better. Even fucking half the good looking blokes at the Room at The Top, her usual medicine, didn't seem to help. Sharon was in utter turmoil for months, the emptiness in her heart just wouldn't go away.

The truth was, however, that Sharon had always wondered if she had been adopted. She was fair-haired when everyone else was dark headed or red heads, but she was afraid to ask. Perhaps because she knew deep down that she was different from them, and even if it might be true, it was wrong of her to even think it. But she wasn't wrong.

Sharon had always felt different, always felt like an outcast. Sharon did this, Sharon did that, always seemed to be the one in trouble. Lizzie always made sure Terri was OK and got all her own way, little Miss Goody Two Shoes. Lizzie loved Terri more than her, Sharon was sure of it, she treated Sharon different from the others, she always had that feeling that she never really belonged.

Learning the truth had helped Sharon to resolve a lot of those mysteries. All those vague and confusing things she had heard in the past made sense now. She hated all the secrecy, there was so much she needed to know, but Lizzie had told her not to talk to the others about it. No need to rake over old coals now, she said.

But Sharon needed to know everything. She didn't recognise herself, felt like she had no self-identity. Since finding out she had been adopted she felt like she didn't belong in the world. She had been lied to for all these years, for eighteen years she had thought she was someone else.

The day Lizzie told her she was adopted, Sharon brought herself some acid from someone she knew and a large bottle of vodka, wound up at the cemetery, staring at Bobby's grave. Then she went berserk.

She stamped on his grave, kicked his headstone, scratched it with a stone, and desecrated it. She hated him, it was his fault. She pulled all the flowers up, destroyed it. Why was this happening to her, what had she ever done that was so bad, so wrong, to deserve this?

Sharon couldn't remember being arrested, handcuffed and taken to the police station, she couldn't remember seeing a doctor or being searched, having her fingerprints taken. Her mind was blank, she had no recollection of how she wound up in a cold, stinking police cell, lying on a hard concrete bench, dressed in a white paper overalls, no shoes on her feet.

How long had she been there? She didn't even know what day of the week it was. Her watch and all her jewellery were gone. Had she lost them, or did the police have them?

The cell was tiny, about two metres by two metres, a big metal door with four small windows above the door. Sharon lay on the bench reading the messages on the walls, the names and dates, the graffiti, even the telephone number for crime stoppers.

She was shivering and shaking from head to foot, her hands sticky and clammy. Suddenly she started balling her eyes out. She wanted to get out of here, go home to her mum. But Lizzie wasn't her mum was she? Not her real mum. Everything about her life was a lie. Sharon felt so alone, so lonely. She had no one, no one loved her, no one wanted her, no one cared about her. She wished she was dead.

At that moment she decided, fuck everyone else, look after yourself because no other fucker's going to. She had to be strong, stand on her own two feet. Be independent, don't ask or expect anything from anyone. She had no real family, she was on her own. Expect nothing from no one, they were going to be her watch words.

But first she just wanted to get out of the cell, get clean, sleep in her own bed. She hated it, felt bored, tired, pissed off, upset, humiliated, regretful, let down, disappointed, anxious, lost, lonely.

And suicidal.

Again.

So many different thoughts going through her head. She felt she had let herself down, let her family down. Sharon the waster had fucked up once again.

Trapped.

She counted the tiles on the walls.

She chewed her nails raw, paced up and down the cell.

Stared through the frosted windows, desperate to see something, anything else.

She was dying to pee, but all she had was a filthy chrome toilet in the corner, no toilet paper, and a camera watching you. It was so degrading and humiliating, she'd rather piss out in the street.

Finally she was led out of the cell to make her phone call. She sat and stared at the phone for a long time, her mind blank. She couldn't even remember her home phone number.

A policeman stood over her. "Well, you gonna make your bleeding call or not?"

That was the spark, the push she needed. She picked up the phone, dialled, the cop listening to her every word, the conversation being recorded.

She didn't know what to say, she was numb, just wanted to get out of there. Finally she managed to blurt out, "Get me out of here, Mickey!"

That was it. Then it was back to the cell.

She slumped back down on the bench, gradually piecing things back together. She'd been arrested and taken to Dagenham East Police Station, something to do with the cemetery. She didn't even remember going there.

It was only when Mickey picked her up, told her what the cops said, that fragments of what had happened started to seep back into her brain.

'Pigs said the cemetery warden called them, told them you were going ape shit over the old man's grave.'

Sharon frowned.

Images flashed across her mind.

Ripping up handfuls of wet grass.

Falling on her hands and knees and throwing up.

Fighting someone.

'Said you looked like you were tripping on something.'

The hallucinations, she remembered them getting too much for her, she couldn't handle them.

'When they tried to drag you way, you threw up, then finally passed out.'

Mickey glanced over at her. 'Rolling around in your own vomit, that's what they said. You still fucking stink.'

She licked her dry lips. Her throat felt parched. 'Did they interview me?' she croaked.

'For what it was worth.'

She had a vague memory of the small, dingy room, two police officers and three tapes, Christ knows what she said, then back to the cell.

'They were gonna press charges, but I got it sorted.'

She glanced at her brother. He was a vicious bastard, but where family was concerned, he always came through. You could rely on Mickey when the shit hit the fan. He'd be there, deal with it, and get you sorted.

The memory of what Lizzie had told her stabbed at her. Did Mickey know she wasn't really his sister? Would he have come and got her if he'd known? Would he have squared it away with the police?

'You're a crazy bitch when you're drunk,' said Mickey, a half smile on his face. 'You were abusing the police something rotten, having a go at anyone who came near you.'

She had a memory of shouting and screaming, just hysterical, out of control.

'When they tried to bring you in,' continued Mickey, warming to the story, 'you started picking up vases, statues, wind chimes anything she could get your bleeding hands on, throwing them at anyone who tried getting near you.'

Mickey suddenly laughed. 'Apparently you gave PC Jarvis a wicked right hander! I would have paid to see that! You called him a wrinkly old cunt who was well past his sell by date! Fuck, girl, it cost me a pretty penny to square that one away!' But judging by the smile on his face, it didn't seem that Mickey objected too much.

Sharon sat silent, stone faced, starting to remember - processing at the nick, taking her fingerprints, a mouth swab, her mug shot. Christ. They could have waited till she had done her hair and had a bit of make-up on.

He glanced over at her. 'What the fuck were you thinking?'

Silence.

'Christ, Shal, give me something. I've just got you out, probably saved you from serving time. I mean, hitting a police officer, even for me that takes a fair bit of palm greasing to get it to disappear!'

Sharon sighed. 'I wanted to be alone, think about stuff.'

'What stuff? What's going on? Has someone hurt you, fucked you about?' There was real concern and anger in his eyes. 'What is it, Shal, tell me and I'll sort it out.'

She took a deep breath. 'I bought meself a bottle of vodka and whiskey, she told him. She could never tell him about the couple of grams of acid, he would kill her and the bloke who sold it to her. Mickey hated drugs in any way shape or form. That would be the worst thing she could do in Mickey's eyes. 'I needed to go somewhere quiet, be by myself, I didn't want to see or speak to anyone.'

He was still staring at her with his hard eyes.

'So I walked to the cemetery, sat quiet next to dad's grave. It was really peaceful and calm over there. Beautiful it was.'

'And then the whiskey and vodka kicked in, right, you got out of your face?'

She nodded. "I should never have mixed my drinks. One minute it was all lovely, a rainbow, a sunny afternoon, the flowers all bright and beautiful, then suddenly I was in a dark, dark place. The colours gone. Only darkness.' She looked up, desperate for him to believe her. 'I'm never, ever drinking again Mickey.'

He snorted. 'Yeah right. Shal. I've heard that before.' He shook his head. 'You're off your fucking head, you are.'

She shivered, fell silent. What the fuck did he expect after what she had been through? But she couldn't tell him the rest, tell him the truth. Couldn't tell him what Bobby had done to her, couldn't tell him about the acid, couldn't tell him about the nightmare visions, about her dad climbing out his grave, his bones, his skeleton, coming to grab her. She knew it was him because of his eyes, those cold, vicious eyes. Then all around her there were dead people climbing from the coffins, snakes slithering between the bones, their heads bobbing in and out between the bones, spitting and hissing at her.

But the only skeleton with eyes was her dad, his twinkling eyes, glistening with pure evil.

Laughing eyes.

I'm going to get you eyes.

You've been a naughty girl eyes.

You're a dirty whore and I'm going to fuck you eyes...

She tried running but she was stuck, she couldn't move. The eyes were getting closer, and Sharon was screaming, shouting, flailing around, kicking out at anything that came near, her perception of the world gone, her senses confused and distorted.

Then suddenly she could hear Mickey calling her. Mickey would save her, Mickey had always been there for her. But when she turned and saw his face, his mouth was moving but she couldn't understand what he was saying. She tried to speak, but no words would come out of her mouth. And as she tried to reach him, his face began melting away, dripping like candle. It was like watching a horror film where she was the main character.

She had lost the ability to know the difference between reality and hallucination. She'd lost control of her body, of her mind. Everything and everyone was coming at her, the police were everywhere, asking her questions, she was popping in and out of reality.

A flash of the police station, the cops talking, but she was hearing only gibberish, seeing horrible things. She felt she couldn't breathe, they were all sucking her in, taking the very breath out of her.

'You all right?' Mickey was looking at her with concern. She had just seemed to blank out for a minute. 'Probably the drugs,' he said.

Sharon looked at him in fear - how did he know?

'They had to forcibly inject you with a sedative, just to calm you down,' he told her

Sharon leaned her head against the cold glass of the car window. He didn't know. Her secret was safe. She closed her eyes, wished she could just fall asleep forget, forget everything...

Mickey ushered her back indoors. Lizzie was waiting in the hallway, her arms held out. 'Come here, Sharon,' she said softly.

Sharon couldn't go close to her, hated her for lying to her, deceiving her. Lizzie didn't know anything, didn't know how Sharon felt, what she was feeling. Fuck, even Sharon didn't know how she was supposed to feel.

Sharon looked into Lizzie's eyes, could see the hurt and pain in her eyes. But Sharon didn't care, Lizzie deserved to feel bad, feel horrible, and feel just like Sharon did.

'Come here, Sharon,' she repeated. 'Let me hold you, try to explain.'

And at that moment Sharon broke. She couldn't do this by herself. She stumbled towards Lizzie, collapsed into her arms. She felt Lizzie's arms wrap around her, could smell that familiar scent of perfume and fags. They both sobbed in each other's arms.

Lizzie stroked her hair, spoke softly into her ear, barely more than a whisper. 'From the moment I held you in my arms I loved you. I felt the love straight away. I delivered you, you know, cut your cord, was there from your very first breath. I loved you then and I love you now. I have been dreading this day for years.' Her voice cracked, broke for a moment. Sharon felt her breathe deeply, steady herself.

'Please forgive me. I'm so sorry, I should have told you sooner, but I was frightened, frightened of losing you. I wanted to tell you, but I couldn't look into my little girl's eyes, into your sweet innocent face and tell you you're not mine.'

Lizzie held her closer. 'There was never a right time to put that burden onto those fragile shoulders of yours. Please, Sharon, don't hate me for not telling you. I thought it was for the best. We all did.'

Sharon stiffened. 'All did, who's all then? Everyone in the family, keeping quiet, everyone knowing but poor, stupid Sharon?'

'No! Just me and your dad, and Sheila, Johnny and Rosie. Your brothers and sister don't know.'

Sharon sniffed, somewhat placated. 'I don't ever want them to know, you hear me?'

Lizzie nodded. 'I don't love you any more or any less than Georgie, Mickey, Terri, Martin. I love you all the same. You know that, right?'

Sharon said nothing.

Lizzie sat her down in the kitchen, passed her a cup of tea, and closed the door so that they wouldn't be disturbed. She sipped at her own tea and gathered her thoughts. 'Maybe I was wrong for not telling you that your mother died, that she was murdered,' she began.

'No fucking kidding!'

'All the family were devastated, Sharon, all heartbroken after what happened to Sadie. She was my best friend as well as my sister. Nothing made any sense. Sadie's death affected us in so many ways. But I knew straight away that I wanted to protect you; I never wanted you to feel that you weren't a part of the family.'

Sharon stayed silent. She needed to listen, needed to understand.

'I could never find the right time to tell you. No time was ever the right time. I didn't want you to feel your family was a lie, because we are your family, you're my flesh and blood.'

Sharon understood exactly what Lizzie said to her - it all made sense. Christ, she would probably have done the same thing in Lizzie's shoes. But at the same time, the bitterness welled up inside of her, the hatred of Bobby, of all of them. She couldn't control herself. Sharon slammed her tea cup on the table. 'Didn't want me to feel it was a lie?' she snarled. 'My whole life has been a lie! I can't believe what I'm hearing, I hate you and all of this horrible family!'

And then she'd stormed out again. Christ, what Sharon wouldn't do to have that day back now, to not hurt Lizzie like that…

Sharon picked up a photo from Lizzie's dresser, it was her real mum and dad on their wedding day. Sadie looked beautiful, Alfie looked smart, he was a very handsome man. What had happened that it all went so wrong, that he murdered his own wife? That was one mystery they would never unravel.

Sharon looked at her mum more closely. She could see some similarities. Their eyes looked the same, the same shape, same colour. And the way she stood and cocked her head, a pose Sharon seemed to do as well.

She took a tissue from her handbag and wiped her face with her shaking hands. Sharon had tried to believe that all of this was behind her, all the secrets and lies. But she had a feeling that more of the deeply buried secrets of the Taylor family were about to come crawling out from under the carpet before this day was over.

Terri Taylor – Morning of Funeral

Terri turned onto the Heathway. She would be at her mum's house soon. She tried to relax, prepare herself for the day ahead. Simply being in the house without her mum there was going to be an ordeal, expecting any minute to hear her voice calling out, 'Terri, bring us a cup of tea, would you love?'

And when Terri would come up with a cuppa, Lizzie would be sat reading. Lizzie loved reading, and always had a book in her hand. She often said to Terri, 'Aeroplanes, boats and cars can take you anywhere in the world, but only a book takes you to a magical place, to wherever you want to be. And you ain't even got to leave your armchair!' Right now Terri wanted to be anywhere but where she was…

She usually got over to see her mum at least four times a week, whenever she could really. Mickey was in prison, Martin and Georgie were gone, so it was down to Terri and Sharon and the grandchildren. But they all lived close by, so Lizzie was never on her own. Still, some of them made a bigger fuss about it than others.

Like Sharon.

Even though she only lived round the corner she made it sound like she was Mother bloody Theresa, like she was the only one who did anything for Lizzie. But everyone helped, all the grandchildren as well, it wasn't just Sharon, but typical bloody Sharon, she had to make a song and dance about everything. Sharon the hard done by. Sharon left looking after Lizzie. Lizzie was her mum for fuck's sake! Sharon never stopped moaning about what she did for her, but she should be helping out of love, not looking at it as a burden or a big responsibility. It was strange how the roles had reversed, the kids looking after Lizzie, where once she had looked after all of them.

Terri pulled up outside her mum's, parked behind Sharon's car, still fighting back the tears. Sharon drove a nice looking Mercedes, always had lots of money. Whatever she did at the solicitor's office in London, she was making good money.

Terri sat quietly in her car for a minute. She could smell Lizzie, almost feel her presence, hear her whispering softly. She blinked her eyes, looked at the house. Everything looked the same; it was just as Lizzie had left it. Terri didn't want to change anything yet, it just seemed too soon. But after today they would have to start having a clear out, the council had given them three weeks to vacate the house.

They had all tried to coax Lizzie into buying her council house when Maggie Thatcher was in power pushing the right to buy scheme, but mum would have none of it, said she was working class through and through. A staunch Labour supporter she was. Her mum and Sharon had got into some heated debates between themselves on politics, the air would turn blue, especially when Sharon told her she had voted Conservative. Lizzie couldn't believe her daughter had voted for Maggie Thatcher, but Sharon was all about the money, getting a leg up, said she'd vote Conservative no matter what any of them said to her.

Clearing out a lifetime of memories, that was what Terri was dreading the most. It was all so final, that's when the reality of it all would hit her, throwing her mum's things away, getting rid of everything. It would all feel so sudden, so final, like death itself.

Terri got out of her car and gazed around her, taking it all in. Everything looked the same but nothing would ever be the same again. Life as the Taylors had all once known it had come to an end.

Sharon gave her a nod when she walked in. There was a coldness between them that was years in the making but seemed to get worse once Terri had her kids. 'I'll put the kettle on,' Sharon told Terri as she stepped into the kitchen. Over the past few days Sharon had been busy, emptying cupboards, shoving stuff into black plastic rubbish bags. It felt to Terri like she couldn't wait to get started. She was at it today, couldn't give it a rest even today.

Terri bit her lip. She didn't want to start arguing with her today, she could see that Sharon was on the drink already. She knew what that was like - she had been sober for ten years, had managed to stop it before it killed her, but she still craved it, especially at a time like this. Just one to take the edge off...but she also knew that one would become two, and before she knew it she would be hooked again.

Terri resolved not to say anything to Sharon, it wouldn't make any difference anyway. Sharon would only tell Terri to mind her own fucking business. Terri didn't need any more aggravation, any more arguing, any more fighting. She'd had enough of all that, she was worn out by it. She just wanted today to be over and done with.

Terri missed her Mum so much. You just expect your Mum to always be there. Terri wished her Mum was there right now to put her arms around her, talk to her, comfort her, help her understand what was going on in her head. Terri could always depend on her – Lizzie had always been there to hold her hand, put her arms around her when she was afraid. She had helped her mend her first broken heart, bandaged her wounds, dried her tears and wiped her snotty nose. She had stopped her falling apart, and had loved her without question, no matter what Terri did, even when she had been sectioned and sent to the psychiatric hospital at Warley. It was that fucker, Ricky, he was to blame. He ground her down, broke her spirit, her resistance, until one night she fought back...

Terri was curled up cosy on the sofa, blankets wrapped around her, watching a film on BBC. She loved a good film, especially horror films. Her all-time favourite was 'Psycho'; that or a good love story, they always made her cry. Shit, she even cried over Lassie or The Waltons!

She had her essentials close by on the coffee table: A glass of vodka and coke, cigarettes, matches, ashtray and the TV remote control, all within arms' reach so she didn't have to move an inch.

And then hidden behind the couch cushions was her bottle of vodka. She kept it there so that

Ricky, her boyfriend, didn't see it when he got in from the pub. He never stopped moaning about her drinking, that's why she hid it from him. She had bottles of vodka hidden all over her house, away from his preying eyes. And if he wasn't moaning about the booze he was moaning about her smoking, and if it wasn't moaning about any of those he would find something else to slag her off about. Everything that came out of his mouth was a put down, had a dig in it somewhere, and always aimed at Terri. It just came naturally to him.

Terri loved a Friday night at home on her own, no one around to put her down or judge her, no one to tell her what to do, just a few precious hours to be herself for a little while. The kids stayed at her Mum's most weekends, and Ricky would always be out with his mates.

Friday night was her night, she didn't moan to Ricky about him going out, she loved it, it gave her some peace and quiet for a while. He hardly ever got back before five in the morning, then he would just crash out when he came back, leaving her alone, meaning she could avoid having sex with him.

Terri hated sex, it didn't do anything for her. She just felt like a piece of meat, a toy, a whore, somewhere for him to stick his dick when he felt the need. She needed to have a good drink to even think about having sex with him, then she would just lie there and let him do whatever he wanted to do. She just wanted to get it over and done with as quick as possible.

Terri could never understand all the hype about sex. She thought that when people talked about how great their sex lives were, they were lying, making out it was as good as the books and films and magazines said it was to impress people. If it was really as good as people said, why didn't she feel it like the rest, why hadn't it happened to her?

But though she had always been different from everyone else, she had always wanted to feel this amazing feeling, she wanted the fireworks, the big bang. Was she missing something? She wasn't really sure - she didn't even like talking about sex, avoided the subject when she could. She would have felt embarrassed if she had said she didn't like it to her mates, so she always agreed and said it was fantastic.

Why was it just sex, sex, sex men thought about? She hated it and never got anything from it. Either she was doing something wrong or she just picked the wrong men. Sharon called her a fucking prude and that she should loosen up a bit.

Terri sat up suddenly as she heard the street door slam. Christ, was he home already? So much for a quiet Friday night.

The door opened behind her and she could feel his eyes looking her up and down. 'Look at the fucking state of you, pissed again,' he sneered.

She looked up at him. Somewhere, beneath that angry face, was the man she had fallen in love with. How long ago was that? How many insults, how many loveless fucks up the arse, how many sneering looks had passed since then?

'You're back early,' snapped Terri. 'Ya didn't pull tonight, so you thought you'd come back here and try ya luck with me?'

Ricky looked at her with undisguised contempt. 'You're off your head again, you are. There's no pleasing you. If I come back late I'm shagging someone else, if I come back early I didn't pull.' His cold eyes ran across her. 'You think I wanna come back and shag you? Look at the fucking state of you. You can't even be bothered to wash and get dressed properly, you're a fucking mess. You fucking stink like a pig.' He stood over her, warming to his topic. 'You are one fat, lazy cunt! All you do is sit on your big fat arse all day and get pissed!'

He suddenly snatched the glass out of her hand.

Terri looked up, eyes blazing. 'Give me my fucking drink back!'

'Fuck off! You're not having any more!' He slowly poured the drink out on the carpet.

'This is my house!' snapped Terri. 'I can do what I like!'

He stood over her, threatening, dominating, but she had grown up with men who would crush him like a bug. He didn't scare her. 'Who do you think you are, treating me like a fucking kid! My dad used to tell me what to do, but I ain't having that from you, you ain't my fucking Dad!'

He leered at her. 'Nah, but you wished I was though, don't ya?'

'Fuck off! I want another drink!'

'You ain't having no more!' And he turned and hurled her glass into the fireplace, where it smashed into a thousand pieces.

'Oh yes I am, and you ain't going to stop me!' Terri climbed to her feet, walked toward the kitchen door to get another drink.

As she reached the door, Ricky stepped in front of her, put his arm across the doorway so she couldn't go into the kitchen.

Their eyes met. 'This is my house! I can do what I like!' Terri always got brave and cocky with a drink inside her; she could take on the world.

But Ricky didn't move. 'You're pissed all the time, your kids are always with your mum because you're always out your face. They hate you as much as I do! You're a right fucking embarrassment, you are!'

'You're right!' Terri screamed back at him. 'They don't want to be here! You know why? Because you're here! They fucking hate you, always moaning about them and slagging them off!' She was fired up, the spittle flying from her mouth as she raged at him.

Ricky got right in her face. 'Don't fucking blame me for your kids not wanting to be here, it's because their mum's a dirty fucking alcoholic! The only thing you're worried about is where your next fucking drink's coming from! Every time I come near ya, you stink of booze and fags. Your breath smells like shit, I bet you ain't brushed your teeth for days, you never have a fucking bath, you fucking stink!'

Terri smiled in his face. 'You wanna know why I don't bath? So I smell, that way you won't want to come near me with that pathetic limp dick of yours!'

'As if I'd want to fuck you!'

'Don't kid yourself! When you don't score at the pub, this lazy, fat bitch is alright to fuck and abuse, isn't she?'

'You are one whore!' Ricky's arrogantly handsome face was sneering at her with pure disgust.

Terri gave him a haughty look, pulled her blouse open to show her breasts. 'You still wanna fuck this disgusting, fucking whore though, don't ya?'

Ricky couldn't take his eyes from her firm breasts.

Terri tried to push past him. 'Now move out of my fucking way and let me get a drink!'

His arm and his body blocked her path. 'No, you're not having no more!'

Terri looked up at him for a moment, then suddenly seemed to quit, stepped back. 'Fine, have it your way.'

She turned back towards the couch, then quickly grabbed the bottle of vodka from behind the couch cushions, unscrewed the top, took a big drink.

Ricky stared at her in disgust. 'Gimme that, you dozy fucking whore.'

Terri took another long pull. 'Or what?'

Ricky stepped in the room. 'Or I'll take it from you.'

She laughed a bitter mocking laugh. 'You're like my Dad, a fucking nasty bully.'

Ricky smirked, took a threatening step towards her, his eyes still on her breasts. 'Am I?'

Terri took another swig of vodka 'You stay away from me, or I'll . . . '

'You'll what? Go telling tales to Mickey?'

Terri looked at him, acid burning in her eyes. 'He'll fucking chew you up and spit you out!'

'You cunt!' Ricky's rage was terrifying. He strode across the room until they were face-to-face.

Terri didn't back off. Her drunken eyes stared back at him, filled with hatred. She took another gulp of her vodka, half pissed already, feeling cocky, indestructible. 'You think I'm your little fucking sex toy, click your fingers, supply on demand? You know what? You're worthless in bed, worthless Leave me fucking cold, you do!'

His cold eyes roamed over her, her face, her naked breasts. 'Course not. And you wanna know why? It's because I ain't your daddy!'

Terri stepped back as though she had been slapped.

'Don't you remember?' He smiled, seeing he had hit a nerve. And not just a nerve, but the most sensitive one of all. 'One night when you were pissed, out of your skull, you told me your shameful secret, the one you try and run away from. You pretend it never happened, but it's written all over you.'

Terri's eyes were filled with horror. 'No! No!' she screamed.

Ricky smirked. He'd saved this secret for a long time, and now he was going to enjoy using it, was going to drive the blade in as deep as he could. 'You loved what your daddy did to you, didn't you? Loved him coming in to your room and fucking you!'

Terri was fighting for breath, unable to think, unable to make him stop. 'Shut up, shut up,' she gasped.

'Good daddy, bad daddy, was that it?' He grinned, seeing the pain in her face. 'You loved your daddy the best didn't you? You enjoyed it, didn't you? He told you that you were special, that you had a little secret.'

She staggered back, trying to get away from him. 'Shut up! Shut up! Stop it, I'm not listening to you! Stop it!'

But every time she backed up, Ricky stepped forward. 'You wanted someone to stop it for you, wanted your mummy to come and hold your hand and stop it, right? But she didn't, did she? She let you down didn't she? Betrayed you, let your daddy fuck you instead of her!'

All Terri could see was his eyes, those cold, merciless eyes that bored into her. Just like her father's, just like Bobby when he climbed into bed, ripped her nightdress off her, pushed his boozy face into her neck as his hand fumbled between her legs…

Ricky kept up the attack. 'She let you take the punishment, didn't she? Your gutless shit of a mum who should have protected you. But she let you down, didn't she?'

Terri could see those cold eyes, feel his ruthless body pushing against her, stealing her innocence, her hope, her love…

Suddenly she cracked. With the neck of the vodka bottle gripped tight in her hand she smashed him in the face.

He staggered back, but she kept coming, kept hitting him, he shattered bottle smashing into his bleeding face again and again. She wanted those cold, evil eyes to go away. She wanted them to stop haunting her, stop searing their way into her soul.

Ricky stumbled back, fell to the floor, blood pumping from his neck.

Terri looked down at him, stunned, surprised by what she was seeing. She couldn't remember what had happened, simply fell to her knees, sobbing, sobbing.

The only thing that saved him, saved her from a charge of murder, was the neighbour - she had heard all the commotion, thought it sounded like it was getting out of hand, called the police.

Terri ended up in Warley psychiatric hospital. Ricky didn't die, she had just missed his jugular. Served the fucker right, he should never have lived, but he didn't press charges and she did eighteen months in Warley.

She was lucky. If things had turned out different she could have ended up doing time in Holloway, her children in care, but Lizzie took them in, looked after them.

And through it all her Mum had been there for her, always helped her, always told her everything would be alright, that it could all be worked out. She always seemed to find good in a bad situation.

And now she was gone, and Terri had lost the greatest gift of her life.

Tears filled her eyes. She blinked them away as she walked around the house. She must stop herself getting so emotional. She mustn't cry, because if she started she wouldn't be able to stop. She still couldn't believe that her Mum was dead and that she wouldn't see her again.

There was so much to do, although Sharon, Miss Organised, had already made all the funeral arrangements, the service, flowers, charity contributions, food, drink. You name it, she had it sorted. Not that Terri was complaining. Sharon had dealt with all of Lizzie's finances for years, collected her pension, paid her bills. Sharon was so organised and in control, but she had also always been about money, money, money. That was her God.

Terri hadn't even seen her cry since Lizzie had died, she wasn't showing any emotion in any way. Terri couldn't understand it; she couldn't stop herself crying, every time she thought about her Mum her eyes filled up with tears.

But Sharon? She was just being Sharon, acting just normal as if nothing had happened, like some kind of ostrich burying her head in the sand. Maybe she was still in shock and it hadn't sunk in that Lizzie was dead? thought Terri. They say people deal with grief in different ways, but Sharon seemed to be coping better than anyone else, and it made Terri feel uneasy.

Terri, on the other hand, couldn't deal with it at all, couldn't face it, and didn't want to believe Lizzie wasn't there anymore. She couldn't even make herself go and see Lizzie at the funeral home Although one part of her had wanted to go and see her for the last time, to talk to her, tell her how much she loved her, and tell her what a wonderful mum she was. She wanted to hold her hand and kiss her forehead. There was so much she wanted to tell her. But she just couldn't do it. Terri wanted to remember her as she was, alive and smiling, not a cold corpse in a coffin

She thought about Sharon as she sipped her tea. She was a strange one. She had never married or had any children, everyone called her the old spinster, Miss Havisham. Although she was her sister, to Terri she seemed bitter and twisted, had a massive chip on her shoulder. Even when they were growing up she didn't seem to like Terri, and nothing had changed as they got older. Sharon never had any time for Terri's kids, or any of her nieces and nephews for that matter. She would never babysit or take the kids out anywhere. In fact, she never seemed to have anything nice to say about anyone or anything. She was always on the defensive. And even now, with Lizzie having just died, she showed no emotion about anything, was cold as ice.

Sharon was adamant she never wanted any kids, she didn't feel maternal she said, she never was and never would be like that. Said she wasn't cut out for motherhood. The thought of changing shitty nappies and wiping arses just wasn't what she wanted. She would look at a baby and say, 'that's ugly, I'd be ashamed to take it out if it was mine! If I had to I'd put a bonnet on it!'

She could have settled down plenty of times, she had a choice of boyfriends and potential husbands - she was a real looker - but she would see a bloke for a couple of weeks then fuck them off. She'd broken more than her share of hearts. She had a great figure, nice tits, slim, had blokes falling at her feet, but she wasn't interested.

Take her or leave her, that was always Sharon's way, she didn't give a fuck. She always said she wanted to be single, use men and abuse them. She shagged who she wanted, when she wanted, she didn't care. She said she was good at it, she enjoyed it, so if you've got it, why not share it? You were only young once. Take her or leave her, she was only telling the truth, and if people took it as offense then that was their problem. If they didn't like her for what she was, then they could go fuck themselves, they weren't worth worrying about. Terri envied her in some ways - Sharon wasn't a worrier like Terri, she would never lose any sleep over anyone. Terri would love to have some of her apparent peace of mind for just a day.

Sharon was like their dad Bobby in many ways. She would find your weak spot and then go for the jugular. And just like their Dad, Sharon could be evil when she wanted to be.

Ever since she was little Terri had had a complex about her ears, hated them, thought they were big, they stuck out like an elephant and made her look uglier than she already was. She never wore her hair tied back because it made her ears stand out even more.

She remembered one day when Sharon kept calling her big ears. Eventually Terri had had enough of her taking the piss, putting her down, told her to stop. But Sharon just wouldn't give up - just like their dad - kept pushing and pushing, shitting on you from a great height.

Finally Terri snapped, screamed at her, 'Say it again, go on, I dare ya!'

'Or what, big ears?' taunted Sharon. She grinned at Terri. 'Do I look scared of you, Dumbo?'

Terri just saw red. She picked up her stiletto shoe, scragged Sharon by the throat, pushed her up against the bedroom wall, her stiletto shoe in her other hand, the heel close to Sharon's cheek.

'Fuck off, big ears!' snarled Sharon.

Terri lifted her arm high, brought it down, the heel of the shoe heading towards Sharon's cheek. At the last minute a big hand came from behind, grabbed her wrist, stopped the shoe inches from Sharon's face.

Mickey ripped the shoe from Terri's hand. 'Sort it out, girls!' he snapped. 'And Shal, stop being such a fucking bitch for once in your bleedin' life!'

Terri and Sharon had always been different, that was for sure. Sharon always said that Terri was the spoiled one and always got what she wanted, but for Terri it wasn't like that at all, it was always her, her, her, Sharon first and the rest could go fuck themselves. Sharon always had to be centre of attention. She would make sure you knew she was about, and if someone else was stealing her limelight then she would do anything to get noticed. She still got drunk regularly and shagged anything in trousers.

She said she was having the time of her life, but Terri knew her better than that, she could see the deep loneliness hiding behind her eyes – no matter how often Sharon got pissed, no matter how many good looking blokes she fucked, she could never fill the void in her life.

Terri sighed heavily as thoughts of the day and the future tumbled around inside her head. Lizzie had been a great nan to all of her grandchildren. She loved having them all round. She would always have someone on her knee, be changing a nappy or feeding someone. She would sit and go through all the nursery rhymes to them or getting on the piano and singing songs with them. Or she would read to them and tell them stories. She would play cards with them, show them cards tricks, play patience with them all, cards for coppers, or her favourite, the memory game. She would get a tray from the kitchen, put an assortment of different objects on it; a pencil sharpener, a tin opener, crayon, pen, box of matches, about twenty different things. Then they had to see who could remember the most of what was under the tea towel.

She smiled at the thought, but the pain didn't diminish. All Terri could think about was that she wouldn't be looking into her Mum's eyes again, her expression alert to whatever was happening in the family at that time. She let out another long sigh, feeling her memories crushing down on her. She was raking over her memories hoping to find the sort of inspiration that used to come from her mum's lips, but she had to face it, it would never happen. She should be grateful that they had had her for so long and that she didn't suffer any pain at the end. She was in a better place now, and with the ones she loved.

Terri blinked her long lashes. Who would hold the family together now? Terri wasn't strong enough, Sharon didn't give a fuck, Martin had sodded off to Australia and as for Georgie... That left Mickey.

Now there was a thought. He'd been gone for fourteen years, but he'd soon be back, stomping his mark all over the manor, paying off his debts, good and bad. She doubted he'd have time to look after the family. The world had changed so much while he'd been inside, Terri wasn't even sure if he would be able to deal with it all. No, with Lizzie gone the family would fall apart, crumble to pieces. Everyone would go their own way, get on with their lives.

She stood up. If Lizzie was here that's what she would tell her to do. She would tell her to stand up, brush yourself down and start again. So that's what she had to do…

She went upstairs to her mum's bedroom, somehow still expecting her to be sitting in her chair watching the television, reading a book or the paper, or doing the crossword, but the room was empty. Sharon was stomping around downstairs organizing something else, leaving Terri alone in her mum's room for a few minutes.

Terri remembered the nights when they were all little and they would all get into her bed with her, and she would read them bedtime stories until they all fell asleep. All the great English classics.

Terri sat in her mum's chair and closed her eyes; she could smell her, almost feel her presence. For a moment, Terri felt at peace. She opened her eyes; everything was just as Lizzie had left it. Terri stood up, went over to her mum's wardrobe and opened the doors. She felt her clothes, held them up to her face, smelt them. Her mum had always had a thing for coats, handbags and shoes. All her pairs of shoes had a matching handbag, and all the boxes were still stacked neatly in her wardrobe. Terri had taken after her mum with her love of coats, while Sharon was the one with a thing for handbags.

The times she had tried to get Lizzie to have a sort out and get rid of her old stuff, things she hadn't worn for years, but she never would part with anything. She would always say. 'I can't get rid of that, I might need that one day.' She was a bit of a hoarder.

Terri had been dreading today, and now the reality of it all was hitting her. Clearing out a lifetime of memories and throwing it all away. She couldn't do it. How could she be the one to throw her mum's stuff out? Just the thought of it made her feel sick.

Terri slumped down onto her mum's bed, shivering. She pulled the covers back and got into bed, covered herself with the blankets, drew her legs up to her chest, her arms wrapped around them.

She remembered cold winter nights when she would get herself a hot water bottle, and her mum would iron the sheets before they got into bed so it was nice and warm to climb into.

She felt weak with emotion, let her head sink down deep into the pillows feeling the devastation wash over her. She felt like a little girl again, only her mum wasn't there to put her arms around her and make it all better.

As Terri lay in her mum's bed, she could almost hear her mother talking to her, a story that

Lizzie had told her over and over again, but one she had never tired of hearing.

'You've heard this story a hundred times before, Terri,' protested Lizzie.

Terri smiled, pulled the bedclothes tighter around her. 'I know, mum.'

Lizzie smiled. 'All right. But when I'm finished, it's lights out and straight to sleep!'

Terri nodded sleepily.

'Back before the war, as long as I can remember, when September rolled around, me and the rest of the family would leave Poplar. We would join hundreds of other families streaming out of the city in a ragged procession on our way down to Kent. We'd all waited through the long, hot summer for the chance to get out of the city for a while. As the day got closer we would get more and more excited.'

'My Nan,' she looked at her daughter, 'you would have liked her, Terri, you are so like her in many ways. She had a beautiful voice, just like you.'

Terri smiled sleepily.

'Anyway, she would start putting bits and pieces aside weeks before we were due to leave; tins of food, old clothes, wellies. Every year it was the same ritual, a big adventure for us all to get away. It was our holiday, even though it was bleeding hard work.'

Lizzie took a sip of her tea and lit a cigarette. 'When the day finally came, all of us - me mum, dad, aunts and uncles, my sisters, Sadie, Sheila, even Rosie, though she was just a baby – we'd pack up all our possessions. Lord, we took everything; chairs, stools, food, kettles, even methylated spirit burners to boil water. It all went into the back of a lorry that my dad had borrowed from a friend of his who worked at Smithfield's. Once it was finally all packed up, we were on our way, to a little village in Kent for hop picking.'

Lizzie smiled at the happy memories. 'Every year we would stay at the same farm. Hop picking was hard work, but everyone was happy. And we kids were free to run and roam through the fields and the countryside. I'll never forget those days, waking up to dew on the grass, those wonderful country smells. Once all the work was done we children could go wherever we wanted, free in the countryside, scrumping for blackberries, plums, cherries, apples, pears, anything we could get our hands on.'

Lizzie closed her eyes, drew deeply on her cigarette. A blue cloud of smoke formed a halo around her. 'Most of the people who went hopping were from London - Bethnal Green, Bow, Whitechapel, Hoxton, Shoreditch and Hackney. Along the way we'd meet up with some of the gypsies, they had a seasonal path of work, too. Lots of people have bad things to say about the gypsies,' continued Lizzie, 'but we always got on with them.

Tough but fair my dad said they were. My dad got to know lots of travelling people over the years we were hopping, some of them are still friends of the family to this day.'

Lizzie stroked Terri's hair and continued. 'Not everyone travelled by road, mind you - lots of families took the train and were met by wagons. By the time everyone reached the farm, the atmosphere was electric! You could almost taste the anticipation in the air.'

Lizzie's voice became more and more animated as the childhood memories flooded back. 'Soon as we arrived, it was a mad dash, everyone scurrying around, making sure that the space where we were going to spend the next few weeks was fit to live in. We were all in long wooden huts, squeezed into a cubicle, sleeping under blankets on top of layers of straw. But let me tell you, at the end of a long day we were too tired to worry about beds or fancy things – we were too tired to do anything but sleep!'

Her face became more serious. 'Our days started at seven, damp and misty it was at that time, and all of us kids would shriek from the shock of the showers, ice cold they were! Not that it made much difference having a shower, mind you, within a few days our clothes were full of the smell of the hops, our hands too. I swear I could still sniff hops on the ends of my fingers, weeks after we returned to

London. But pretty quick the dew vanished, and the sun warmed everyone as we picked and chatted and laughed. The younger kids ran around while we worked, and the little ones lay in their prams in the shade.'

Lizzie glanced across. Terri's eyes were closed, her breathing slow and steady. She started to stand up, but Terri's eyes suddenly popped open. 'Don't stop!' she said sleepily.

Lizzie grinned. 'I swear you'll stay awake at your own funeral!'

Terri smiled, closed her eyes. Lizzie continued.

'Mid-morning someone went back to the huts and made tea, and then at midday a big pile of fresh sandwiches would appear as if by magic and we'd all dig in. If the morning had been a success, the kids would get the afternoon off, and we'd spend it running around the farm playing games.'

Lizzie smiled. 'It seemed magical, like everyone had a smile on their face; people were happy and content. Local shopkeepers came around each day with cakes, bread, groceries and cheese,' she told Terri, 'and at the close of the day the first songs would start up as we gathered around a big bonfire to cook our evening meal. In due course, some of the men would wander off to the nearest pub. I'd hear them returning hours later, stumbling into the huts. I remember lying awake sometimes, all around you could hear people sleeping, snoring, and snuffling. It was a comforting sound.'

Terri opened one eye, peered up at her mother. 'Tell me about Saturday nights,' she whispered, 'that's my favourite bit.'

Lizzie nodded. 'It was on Saturday night, after the week's work was over, that the real fun began. My dad – and most of the men, who had jobs - came down on a Friday and went back to London on a Sunday after dinner. So on the weekend, everyone would get together and sit around a huge open fire. Someone would play the piano accordion, and everyone else got to take their turn singing. But my favourite times were when the gypsies showed up – there was something wild and exciting about them, Terri, their music, their dancing. And of course the fights. There were some vicious bare-knuckle fighters. I suppose they have to learn to look after themselves from an early age. Big Frankie, your dad's mate, he was a bare knuckle champion when he was younger.'

Her voice fell low. 'I saw him fight one time. Wicked it was, stripped to the waist, him and this other big gypsy trading blows in a roped off area. They say there were over two thousand gypsies and travellers there that day. Blood and sweat sprayed off them, they just kept going at it till it seemed impossible that either man could still be standing.

But in the end, Frankie won the fight, became King of the Gypsies. It was talked about for years.'

She sighed. 'I asked him about it years later. "Lizzie," he said, in that soft voice of his, "it's a choice you make, to fight or not. It's all about honour, and you can walk away if you want to. The next day we shake hands and have a drink together. No malice.'"

Lizzie smiled. This time Terri was asleep.

She stood slowly, leaned over Terri, kissed her cheek, her breath no more than a whisper of love.

Terri sat up suddenly. It was almost as though something had touched her cheek, but when she looked around the room was empty. Her mum was gone. Lizzie was dead, and Terri had to find a way to survive without her. She jumped up out of the bed, looked around. Time to sort herself out, get herself together, face the day ahead.

Mandy

Mandy lay in bed, half-awake, just tossing and turning. It was always the same, she went to bed of a night trying to get to sleep thinking about all the things she tried hard to forget. She had been awake most of the night, thinking of Lizzie's funeral in the morning. All the kids were devastated, of course, but Tommy, she knew that something was on his mind; the way he had been acting lately, she knew it was something big, more than just his nan dying. He usually spoke to Mandy, told her what was going on good or bad, but this time he was unusually quiet.

She gazed at the ceiling, the shadow of the streetlights through the trees dancing as the wind and the rain battered at the window. She thought suddenly of her and Mickey. She was going to see him tomorrow at the funeral. She had sent him a new Italian black suit and tie and a pair of black shoes. He had to look the bollocks, his appearance meant everything to him. Her mind began to wander back over their life together. Fucking hell, where do you start?

She was just sixteen when she met him, and he was everything she wanted; good looking, great body, a few quid in his pocket. He was generous too, always bringing her little presents, took her to nice places, made her feel really special. He drove a decent car, a beautiful Triumph Stag, so she didn't have to worry about getting on the bus or trains as Mickey took her and picked her up from wherever she wanted to go. Mandy knew now that was all part of his control. She was young, Mickey was wild and romantic and she loved him. Everyone in the area looked up to him, everyone knew who he was, but it was his sense of humour that hooked her. He could always make her laugh. Mind you, looking back, he'd made her cry too at times, but even with his prison time, the tears had outweighed the laughter.

The response from her family when they found out who she was seeing was predictable. 'You'll have nothing but trouble,' her mum had said when Mandy announced that she was having his baby and getting married. She would never forget the look of shock and horror on her mum and dad's faces when they heard. And then there was the rest of the family poking their noses in, throwing in their two pennies worth.

But soon enough Mickey had them wrapped around his little finger, they thought the sun shone out of his arse. Right charmer he could be. He was always respectful to them, even though he swore like a trooper, which was a bit of a shock to them as they didn't swear at all. 'Bloody', 'sod', 'sugar' and 'fish' was the worst Mandy got from her parents, but they soon got used to it. Anyone would think Mickey suffered from Tourette's, there was always a 'fuck' and a 'cunt' in Mickey's vocabulary, that's just the way he was. He had always been a generous bloke and wasn't shy putting his hand in his pocket. When he had a bit of money he would go round to her mum and dad's and treat them to a few quid. Every year he paid for Mandy, her mum and dad and the kids to go on holiday.

Mickey would pop down and stay for a night or two, but he never stayed for long, he was always backwards and forwards. He had schedules to keep, he was always busy, busy, busy. Mandy soon learned never to ask him what he was up to - if he wanted to tell her he would. Whatever was going on, she just shut her eyes and ears to it. What she didn't know, she couldn't talk about.

Mandy was shocked when he proposed to her, it was hard to believe he wanted her as his wife, that he wanted that commitment. She realised now that marriage was a fantasy. Being a wife to Mickey Taylor just meant being a tedious but necessary ingredient in his life. My God! How young and naive she was then. She could see it all now, but it was a bit too late! The man falling at your feet, showering you with gifts and flowers. Taking you out to expensive restaurants, nice places. No noticeable defects, everything just perfect. Then he tells you you're the only one! No one has ever made him feel this way, he says, you're beautiful, everything a man could want. Out of all the women he has met in his life, he chooses you to propose to. You say yes, of course you do. You think you are the special one!

Then there was their wedding day. What a show that was! 'I do.' Those were the words that Mandy remembered, that they said to each other, face to face, looking into each other's eyes. At that point nothing else mattered, Mandy's mind was filled with wonderful thoughts. She was so happy, loved him so much, her knight in shining armour. She felt so lucky to be his wife. The future looked bright, she couldn't imagine anything coming between them. But within ten years Mickey was sentenced to life imprisonment.

At first, Mandy didn't know how she was going to survive without him. She was left with four kids, all aged between five and ten years old. But somehow she'd figured it out, the family had all pitched in, and now they'd been married nearly twenty four years.

That in itself was a surprise to a lot of people. 'You must be off your head.' That was the general opinion.   'Yeah, that will last about five minutes,' and 'you'll have a life of hell,' were others she'd heard.   But her mates saw it differently.   'I'm so jealous you got someone like him,' and 'who'd have thought Mickey Taylor and Mandy?'   That one had made her laugh.

But the one that had hurt was her lifelong friend Denise. Mandy would never forget the look on Denise's face. It spoke volumes. Without her saying a word, Mandy knew exactly what she thought of Mickey.   She only saw the bad side of Mickey, she didn't know him like Mandy did. It surprised Mandy, Mickey had never been mean to Denise. Sometimes she wondered if she fancied him and was trying to turn her off of Mickey, but Mandy knew in her heart that wasn't it. They got on well on the surface, but when Mandy told her the news about her and Mickey, Denise put her arms around her, gave her a big hug. 'I hope you're very happy, Mandy,' she said. 'If you're happy, I'm happy.' But her voice was flat, cold. She knew how much it hurt Denise to say it. And to be fair to her, Denise had always been there to pick her up when she was down, had stood by her through thick and thin.

Mandy didn't tell her everything that went on with Mickey as she knew exactly what she would say. In many ways, Denise was right, but it was hard to admit the truth even to Denise. Some things were best left unsaid. Mandy knew exactly what she should have done something years ago, but she never found the strength or the courage.

Denise and Mandy shared the same porch, had gone to the same nursery, infant, junior, and senior school together. They knew each other inside out.

Mandy smiled. Denise could write a very embarrassing biography on her!

But it had all come crashing down when Mickey had got arrested for murder. Mandy always half knew what he did, that he led a dodgy life, but she closed her mind to it. He was always ducking and diving, and everyone in the area knew that if it was anything to do with Mickey Taylor, it was illegal, immoral, or downright dangerous. That came with the territory if you married a Taylor, right? But murder? That was something else altogether, she'd never have imagined he was in that deep. Up until then he'd wangled his way out of the other charges that had come along, greased a palm here, done a favour there, but this one...

Mandy would always remember that fateful day when she found out Mickey had killed someone. Mickey had gone out on the Friday night, not come back till late Sunday. It wasn't unusual for him not to come home, but she'd stopped moaning ages ago because he took no notice. She had pulled him on it a few times when they were first married. She told him she felt like a single parent, but he simply turned up the wattage on his smile, said to her, 'I'm not like the rest of 'em, Mandy, you know that better than anyone. You know what I am and what I do.' He grinned. 'I notice you're not moaning when you're getting a new three piece suite, or designer clothes for you and the kids!' He wrapped his arm around her, kissed her on the cheek. 'You know whatever you want I give it to you, you've only got to ask, so give it a fucking rest!'

And if she pushed it he would say, 'You sound like me muvver, keep moaning and going on. You moan when I go out, so I say come with me, and what do you fucking say? I ain't got anything to wear! Fuck me, you're the one who's always out shopping!' Mandy felt as though she couldn't win whatever way she said.

That was Mickey through and through, a mixture of charm and threat, and she'd soon got used to it. Ultimately she didn't question him because she trusted him, she had to. The only person she didn't trust around Mickey was Miranda Solomon, a close friend of Sharon's.

Mandy thought that Miranda was a stuck up old tart who everyone knew had a thing for Mickey; she clearly reckoned that Mickey fancied her. Mandy sighed. Why wouldn't he? After four kids Mandy had got fat, while Miranda was skinny. Mandy was poor, Miranda rich. Mandy was ugly, Miranda pretty. Mandy smoked, Miranda didn't. Mandy was boring, Miranda was exciting. In short, Miranda was everything Mandy wasn't.

Miranda could have her choice of rich middle class men, they practically fell at her feet, but no, she wanted Mickey, fancied a bit of rough. Her bit of rough! Mandy hated her with a vengeance, the spoilt bitch! No one had ever said no to her, she always got what she wanted, but she wasn't getting her hands on Mickey! Mandy would kill to keep hold of Mickey!

Even when Miranda got married she was still the same, still chasing after Mickey. That didn't surprise Mandy, the bloke she married was thirty years older than her, a sugar daddy if ever Mandy had seen one. It would be a miracle if he could still get it up.

The old geezer died just before Mickey went to prison, Mickey even went to his funeral. Mandy didn't want him to go, she begged him not to go, but he went, told Mandy she ought to grow up and stop being so fucking paranoid.

So Miranda was always there, like a shadow over her and Mickey, a dark fucking cloud that wouldn't go away. She even wrote to Mickey in prison.

With Mickey coming home soon, Mandy was terrified that Miranda would be all over him again, and that this time he wouldn't resist. The years hadn't been kind to Mandy, what with working and looking after the kids, whereas Miranda still looked the bleeding same - it had taken a fair few thousand quid and several operations, of that Mandy was certain, but she still had the tits and the face of a twenty year old. If I was a bloke, thought Mandy bitterly, I'd want to do her.

They would be seeing Miranda Solomon today, at the funeral, and then she would stick around like shit to a blanket when Mickey came home.

Mandy frowned. She really didn't know how she felt about Mickey being released. It was the day that they had all waited for so long for, and half of her felt deliriously happy, but the other half of her was dreading it. Just thinking about it brought back all the memories of his arrest, the trial.

It was a Sunday, she had just got into the car with the kids to go over to her mum's. She switched the radio on in the car, singing along as she drove, when the ten o'clock news came on.

'A man has been shot dead at The Farmhouse public house in Dagenham. Police say they are pursuing some leads, but as yet no one has been arrested for the murder.'

That was all, no details, but Mandy suddenly felt sick, knew that somehow Mickey was involved, was either dead, or that it was him who had shot someone. She carried on driving to her mum's, when she walked in Mickey was standing there, looking calm, drinking a cup of tea, but she could see under the surface that all sorts of shit was going on. He didn't say anything, just nodded to her, but she couldn't help herself, she just fell into his arms and sobbed her heart out.

Mandy would always remember that fateful first day in court. She felt sick and her legs were trembling as she went into court number two at the Old Bailey. The Old Bailey for Christ's sake! It was the same feeling she got when Mickey was coming home after a night out on the piss. She didn't know what the outcome would be, good or bad.

She looked down at Mickey from the public gallery. He was sitting in the dock looking like a lawyer himself, dressed up to the nines in a suit and tie. He gazed up at her, gave a half-hearted smile. She smiled back and mouthed, 'I love you,' but right then, at that moment, she really questioned herself for the first time. Did she love really love Michael William Taylor, the man standing in front of a court charged with two counts of murder.

She looked at the nameless faces, six men and six women sitting in the jury box, the deciders of his fate. That was when it hit her how serious this was, that Mickey might not walk away with a smile on his face.

Three weeks the trial went on for. All Mickey's family and friends came every day to support him. Mandy was in turmoil; nobody tells you what's going to happen, where you should be, what is expected of you. She had these awful feelings of guilt and shame, was dreading bumping into people she knew. What would they think, what would they say? She knew all the old recriminations, all the old 'I told you so's,' would come out.

She couldn't get her head around it all, couldn't take it in. It was hard hearing all the stories going around, hearing the evidence in court. She was an emotional wreck, listening each day to the prosecution talk. The things they said about him, that wasn't the Mickey she knew, the man she loved, the man she had married. Who was this vicious, evil bastard they were talking about?

Mandy felt torn, she didn't know what to believe, didn't know how she felt about Mickey anymore. She felt like even if she had gone to the gym and started lifting weights, become Miss Universe, it could never come close to giving her the strength she was going to need when Mickey got his life sentence. There was simply nothing that could have prepared her for being a prison wife.

Mandy was left to deal with the kids, deal with their reactions, her family and friend's reactions – you name it, she had to deal with it and sort it out. She was shocked and traumatised herself, nothing made any sense. She was dealing with everyone else's feelings, had no time to deal with her own thoughts.

Her life as it was had gone. She was paranoid about what people thought of her and her family. She lied to some people, said he was working away or that they had split up. In the end she didn't know the truth from the lies in her own head, couldn't remember what she had told to whom. But the truth was it was all over the papers, so she couldn't really hide it, everyone knew, even if they didn't say anything to her.

She was also hurting so much for her children, she could feel their pain. How were they going to cope? She felt so alone, just wanted Mickey next to her, holding her with his strong arms, there for her when she needed him, looking after her, making her feel safe, the way he always had.

Even after all these years, she could still almost feel him sometimes, looking at her with those sparkling eyes, telling her everything would be alright. The last words he'd said before he went inside were still in her head. 'Don't worry about a thing, Mandy.' Yeah, right. Fourteen fucking years later and she was still worrying. Worrying about dealing with the kids now their Nan had died, worrying about all this shit with the missing money, worrying about the fact that in just a few weeks Mickey would be home. What would happen then?

So while part of her was happy, she couldn't wait to have him home again, she was frightened as well. She was so used to being on her own, she didn't know how she was going to deal with it all or how Mickey would deal with it.

Dagenham wasn't the place he had left behind fourteen years ago. Their lives would drastically change once again, and Mandy didn't know if that was a good thing or not.

For years she had worried that he might die in prison. Years of enduring the cold clinical prison visits, the security checks, searches that included everything, even her hair and mouth. Sniffer dogs, CCTV. It made her feel like a criminal, it was all so degrading.

The kids had suffered too. It had destroyed Tommy when his dad went to prison. He was doing well boxing but he'd lost heart in everything, he never got back into it, never went training, would go missing for days. Tommy and his dad would argue over the phone effing and blinding at each other, screaming and shouting. Then Mandy would get the stick from both of them, each slagging the other one off, and her caught in the middle.

Mickey didn't know half of what went on the outside to do with the family. He thought he did, of course, but it would all be a real shocker to him when he got home. He would be in the real world then.

For fourteen years she'd dealt with the abuse and the finger pointing, the nasty comments. People looked at her different, looked at the kids different, once Mickey was put away. The first few months were the worst – people she knew would cross the road when they saw her coming, because they didn't want to see her, couldn't look at her, they just judged. She certainly found out who her real friends were.

The kids got a lot of stick too, but lucky enough they could handle themselves, so a lot of kids wouldn't dare say a bad word against them. And it was the kids who kept her going, kept her strong, especially Tommy. They were hurting too, so she had to stay strong for them.

Mandy had learned to ignore it, if she didn't she would be fighting with someone every day. There were some horrible bitches about who thought their shit didn't stink, but over the years Mickey had been in prison she had learned who to avoid and who she could trust.

In many ways, it was like the whole family was serving a prison sentence; there were so many changes to deal with, so suddenly. It was like someone had died, but worse. When someone dies you can grieve, slowly come to terms with it, but when they are in prison, it's like a ghost hanging over everything. Mickey wouldn't be there for Christmas, birthdays, anniversaries, while Mandy had to face it all, deal with it all. And how was she going to keep a roof over their heads, feed and clothe the kids? Luckily, Mickey had left her with a bit of money that he had stashed away, and there was still some dribs and drabs of cash from his mates who had made money with Mickey in the past, but it was still tough.

Then there were the prison visits - he was so far away, over a four hour drive, what a nightmare every month.

In a way, their children lost both parents; their dad in prison for life, and a mum who was unpredictable in her moods and reactions, stressed and anxious. Mandy lost part of herself the day Mickey was sentenced. She was lucky she had a good family, her mum and dad only lived round the corner from her, they were there for her and the grandchildren no matter what. She didn't think she would have got through it all if it wasn't for her mum and dad.

Mandy found their relationship perplexing, but somehow the cold harsh reality was that she and Mickey managed to pull together and survive in a situation where most people would be bitter, would flounder. Mandy looked after the kids, worked full time, even found the time to study at home of an evening doing an open university course in Psychology. And through it all she spent as much time as she could with her children. It was all she could do, and day by day, month by month, year by year she got through it. But now Lizzie had died, and Mickey was coming home. Once again the Taylors had found a way to turn her life upside down.

She sat up, grabbed her dressing gown and wrapped it around her.   Lizzie's funeral was today.   Let the show begin ...

Mickey

The car was getting closer to the cemetery, only about ten minutes away now. Mickey was dreading it; the closer he got, the more the reality that his mum was dead was hitting him. No one wants to die, thought Mickey, but we all want to go to heaven. He wondered who would be the next to go. Life had taught him that there was no rhyme nor reason to it. Death was always lurking around, never seemed to take the person you expected.

His mind moved on to all the people who had died over the last few years. At times it seemed like everyone was popping their clogs, like barely a month went by when he didn't get bad news. He's died, she's died, she's got this, and he's got that.

Death.

It had recently claimed one of his closest mates, Mark. He shook his head, now he was gone only thirty six he was, died of bowel cancer. He left a wife and two children. He was a decent bloke, Mark, honest and down to earth. As kids they all got into a bit of bother, but Mark was the good one, he'd never got in trouble with the law, did everything by the book. Out of school he started in Ford, on the production line, worked his way up to management, made himself a good name in the trade union, even met Arthur Scargill and shook his hand. He was always on at Mickey to get a proper job, told him he could get him a job in Fords anytime, he just had to ask. Mickey just laughed. 'Mark, can you really see me clocking in and out, and being told what to do? I'd get the sack for chinning the foreman my first day!'

Mark had never been to prison, never been arrested, had never hurt a fly, but that didn't stop him dying first. Mickey remembered the day Mark told him that he had cancer, sitting across the table from him in the nick – they'd been talking about football, who was doing what in the manor, the usual stuff. Then suddenly Mark stopped, just stopped cold in the middle of what he was saying.

Mickey looked at him funny. He'd seemed a bit distracted, but nothing out of the ordinary – Mickey figured he'd had a tiff with his old lady, something like that. Mark stared at the floor for a moment, the grimy lino, then suddenly looked up at Mickey with his piercing blue eyes. 'I've got cancer,

Mickey,' he said softly. 'The doctors reckon I've got about six months if I'm lucky.'

Mickey couldn't believe it. Mark hadn't been ill, he kept himself in good shape – shit, and he still played football for Dagenham and Redbridge reserves. He didn't smoke, didn't do drugs. He liked a drink but nothing over the top, he knew when to say no and when he had had enough. He had always been the sensible one, had got Mickey out of trouble a few times.

Mickey stared at him open mouthed, finally managed to force out some words. 'You're shitting me, right?'

Mark shook his head. 'Bowel cancer,' he said.

Mickey's mind was in turmoil. 'What about Denise, the kids?'

Mark gazed out the window. 'I've got some life insurance. They'll get by.'

And that was it. What more could they say? Mark had already started his treatment, chemotherapy and radiotherapy, but he kept on coming to see Mickey as often as he could. Mickey had told him not to come, that it was getting too much for him, with all the travelling, but he didn't listen, kept on coming, regular as clockwork.

And the whole time he was ill he never moaned or grumbled about anything. He was always laughing and joking when he came to see Mickey, though he looked worse every time.

'Mickey, I'm a fighter, a survivor,' he said one time, 'I'm going to beat this, you see.' Mickey wished he could have believed him, but he could see it was never going to happen, every time he came he looked a step closer to death. Mickey had never believed in God, but he prayed for Mark, prayed he would get better, get back to the man he once was.

No chance. The cancer eating away at him.

The last time Mickey saw him, Mark's brother brought him to the nick. He'd told him it was what he wanted to do, insisted that he bring him. He shuffled into the visiting area, looking more dead than alive. Mickey could see the effort it took just to totter across to the table by the window where they always sat. He looked awful, his face drawn in, a deathly pale colour, the whites of his eyes had turned yellow. His hair was gone, and he'd lost so much weight.

Mark grinned. 'Fucking sucks, eh?' he said to Mickey as they hugged. Mickey held tight to him, but he could feel he was nothing but skin and bone.

Mickey didn't know what to say.

Mark slowly lowered himself into the chair, grimacing from the pain, the effort. His breathing sounded like an old man who smoked forty fags a day.

'What the fuck are you doing even coming up here, right now?' Mickey asked him. 'I told you not to come. You need to save your strength.'

Mark gave a sad smile, his once handsome face no more than a skeletal mask. 'For what?'

Mickey had no answer for that one, so they sat quiet for a while.

Mark finally forced some words out through his gasping breath. 'I know you can't do much from here, Mickey,' he panted, 'but you'll be out in a couple of years.'

Mickey nodded. 'Whatever, whatever you need.'

Mark looked into his eyes. 'Look out for Denise, the boys.'

'Of course, mate,' Mickey promised.

'Make sure they don't wind up as cheeky cunts like you,' gasped Mark.

Mickey stared at him for a second, and then burst out laughing.

A few days later Mark was dead.

When he got the news, Mickey sat alone in his cell, brooding. He felt so useless - he wanted to help Mark, but couldn't. He'd wanted to go home, get a gun and shoot Mark, make it quick and fast, no pain, no suffering. Christ, he thought, you wouldn't watch your dog suffer like that; it would be straight down to the vets, put them under. So why do we have to sit and watch people we love and care about suffer? A few days after Mark died, Mickey received a letter from him dated the week before. He knew it was from him when he saw it, he knew by his handwriting. He was gutted.

He tried not to think about that last time he'd seen Mark – as his brother half carried him towards the exit of the visiting room, Mickey heard Mark calling out to him, in a voice faint as a whisper. 'Mickey, Mickey'.

Mickey couldn't turn round and look at him; there were tears in his eyes, and he knew that if he turned and looked at Mark again he would lose it. He couldn't let Mark see that he was crying, couldn't let anyone inside see that. Mickey just kept walking, knew he would never see Mark again.

Mickey sighed. He was sweating, squeezed in between the two big coppers, but he wasn't going to give them the satisfaction of knowing that he was uncomfortable. After fourteen years inside he had learned how to endure pretty much anything – he certainly wasn't going to let anyone know that a couple of hours in the back of a cop car bothered him. At least he was out of the nick, seeing the outside world. He could hardly wait to actually step out of the car at the cemetery, on his turf. All eyes would be on him, all his family and friends would be there – or at least, those that were still alive…

Joseph Donnelly. Now that was another fucking sad story, another good man wasted. Joey had had a good start in life, he wasn't born into a life of crime like some of them. His mum and dad were hard working decent people who ran a pub in Becontree for donkey's years.   Four brothers and three sisters, but his mum and dad made sure all the kids were well dressed and always clean and tidy. They were comfortable, not hard done by like a lot of kids in the area.

Joey worked for Mickey on the doors of the clubs he ran, enjoyed his work, especially all the girls he got to meet.   Gorgeous models, singers, strippers, dancers, Joey had his taste of all of them.   He was a right slag, he didn't care who he fucked.

Unlike Mark, Joey got in trouble a few times, and always for the same thing, violence and fighting. But then he was a big fella, and working the doors of those places, people always had it in for him.   Every week there was some drunken idiot who thought it would be a laugh to take down the big geezer on the door.   And from time to time Joey was a bit overenthusiastic in dealing with them... but he'd never been charged with anything, he said he had been born lucky!

But a couple of years ago, something had changed, something had happened that Mickey had never been able to figure out.   If he'd been out there, out on the street, watching over his turf, Mickey would have sussed it out in a shot, nipped it in the bud. But stuck inside, he only ever got bits and pieces of what was going on, and almost always too late.

Mickey was almost certain that whatever had come up had something to do with both Joey and Kenny – at the same time they'd both stopped visiting him, after twelve years of showing up regularly, suddenly there were no more letters from them, no money sent in.

Mickey had put out feelers, had his people sniff around, but they always got the same response – Joey was busy at the pub he owned, while Kenny had moved out to Upminster and seemed to have severed his ties with everyone from the old days.

Mickey smelt a rat, had a feeling that it was something with roots buried deep in the past. Again, with him stuck inside, and Joey and Kenny staying clear of the nick, all he got was second hand reports, and they weren't good.

It all came to a head about six months ago when Joey was found hanging from a tree in the beer garden of his pub, right in the spot they all used to sit and have a pint. He'd tried to top himself, but the stupid bastard was so drugged up that the rope had slipped and he'd wound up half hanging, calling out for help.

It really stank to Mickey. Why would Joey do something like that? There was only one reason Mickey could think of – Joey had done something, but what? Had he opened his mouth when he was pissed and out of his face, said something to someone he shouldn't? Who did he piss off? Who did he stitch up that the consequences were that bad?

Lizzie always used to say, 'loose lips sink ships,' and she wasn't far wrong. Did Joey give out a bit of information that he shouldn't have?

And now when Mickey asked after him, he got the same reply. Joey had changed, he'd become a drunk, a coke head. That wasn't the Joey he knew!

He had always liked a good drink, it was normal for him being brought up in the pub game, having a pint to Joey was like anyone else having a cup of tea. But he always had it under control, he had a drink every day but you hardly ever saw him pissed.

But that had changed. Everyone said his personality had changed totally, he was becoming a fucking nuisance to everybody, he was a liar and a thief, poncing off everyone. He was borrowing money, running up big debts to people you didn't want to owe anything to.

His pub trade had gone down, he wanted to fight the world, and when he had a drink he turned into a nasty bastard, became a bully. Shit, Mickey knew all about that – when they were kids he had bullied Mickey for years, and it was only when Mickey finally stood up to Joey that Mickey had learned how to find his own place in the world. Mickey had Joey to thank for all of that - if he hadn't bullied Mickey, Mickey wouldn't be the man he was today.

By the time he tried to kill himself Joey was a different man, not the mate Mickey had known for thirty years. Drink had taken everything from him; his home, his wife, his kids, his job, his sanity, his dignity and his life. Drink and drugs were killing him, that's what everyone said, but Mickey knew there was more to it than that. It takes something – or someone – really rough to turn a man like Joey into what he had become. A drunken bum.

And that's what he was. Sharon said she'd run into him a few days before he tried to hang himself. He wasn't washing, wasn't shaving, she said, looked like a fucking bum living on the streets. He had lost a lot of weight too, looked drawn and grey, with that drinker's face - purple nose, blood shot eyes, yellow, dull looking skin. Sharon said she couldn't get away from him quick enough – he had the shakes, stank of piss.

What the fuck had gone wrong? Mickey would have to find out, but that was a job for another day. He sat up straight, adjusted his tie, pulled a hankie from his pocket and wiped the sweat from his brow. Today was his mother's funeral. Two weeks from now he was out, back on his home turf. Then he'd get some answers, or there would be fucking hell to pay. And Joey would be one of the first people he went to see...

As they got closer Mickey started looking around. He couldn't believe the amount of people that lined the streets. Then he spotted Miranda Solomon standing amongst the crowds. Fuck me, he thought, she still looks fucking good. She had always been tall, but looking at her in those high heels, she looked even taller. She walked like a supermodel, tall and erect, with a lovely pert bum, big tits.

Miranda had been friends with his sister Sharon ever since they met at school, a posh school out of Dagenham. They were so different from each other, but they had become best of friends, they just clicked. They had remained friends to this day.

Miranda had got Sharon a job in her dad's law firm in the city, and Sharon had worked her way up in the firm as PA for one of the top judges. Well that's what Sharon and Miranda told everyone, but Mickey knew exactly what Sharon's real job was. Sharon didn't know he knew her secret. But Mickey knew what she had been doing all these years, what she was up to, what she was.

Mickey couldn't suppress a grin as the car slowly slid past Miranda. Her face was full of all the expensive slap, she looked like she'd stepped off a catwalk, she'd always had class. There was something about her, a self-possessed quality, a natural aloofness. If she had any self-doubts, they were well hidden.

Mickey studied her face from behind the darkened glass of the car as the car crept towards the cemetery. She had aged well, but then she had the dosh. She could afford to look good with the amount of money she had. He'd bet every penny that he had that she'd had plastic surgery. Miranda would have had this lifted and that tucked, all that lark; whatever was available to make her look younger and different, Miranda had it done. She looked more like twenty-something than nearly forty.

Still, she had changed since Mickey had first met her, a long-legged beauty hanging around with Sharon. Her hair colour and style had changed; she had long blonde hair then, now it was dark brown; her eyes were naturally green, now she wore deep blue contact lenses. Her lips were a different shape and thicker, her nose was smaller. Every part of her body that could be worked on, she'd had it done. She'd had a boob job - or breast enhancement as they called it. Mickey grinned to himself. He wouldn't mind checking out her tits, giving them a squeeze. He was gagging for a shag, and Miranda would certainly fit the bill. He could feel himself getting harder just at the thought of her…

Then Mickey recalled the last time she'd spoken to him. She didn't sound so self-assured then. All she'd managed through her tears was a gasped, 'Thanks, Mickey,' down the crackly line at Pentonville Prison.

Mickey was on remand in Pentonville for handling stolen goods at that time. It was a real cesspit, a horrible place. Mickey was banged up with self-harmers, dirty smelly smack and crackheads, surrounded by paedophiles and rapists, the scum of the earth. The constant smell of piss, shit and sweat wafted deep into his nostrils. Suicides were happening all the time. Prison was a place with no pity or sympathy.

Every day at four o'clock he would ring home. There was no phone indoors in those days, they used the phone box directly across the road from their house. He knew the number off by heart, it had been like an office and meeting place for them since they were kids.

Sharon, his sister, answered the phone that day; he could tell by her voice that something wasn't right. He wondered what the fuck had happened, who was dead now. 'Mickey it's ... its Miranda, you remember her, don't ya?'

Of course he fucking remembered her, she had become a good mate of Sharon's and the family. If the truth be known he fancied the arse off her; she was a bit of all right. 'Course I fucking do,' he told Sharon. 'I've only been 'ere four weeks not four fucking years! Now tell me what the fuck's happened.'

Between Sharon's tears and hysteria she filled him in with all the gory details.

Mickey put the phone down, anger coursing through him. 'Cunts!' he spat.

'Fucking cunts!' He closed his eyes, trying to imagine the horror she'd gone through. Miranda didn't deserve that, no woman deserved that.

Two scumbags had broken into Miranda's house. As they ripped and ransacked through the place they soon realised it belonged to a judge. No one was in the house apart from Miranda, the judge's fifteen year old daughter, sound asleep upstairs in bed. The evil animals raped and beat her, this defenceless, terrified, innocent young girl, humiliated her in every possible way, left her bruised, bloody and unconscious on her bedroom floor.

But as luck would have it, these pieces of shit were so thick they left their fingerprints everywhere, were soon nicked. And now they had been sent to the last place of Earth they would want to be, if they only knew it. Pentonville.

Mickey was straight on it, wasted no time finding out who they were. They were both smelly heroin addicts with lank greasy hair and rotting brown teeth, looked like they hadn't had a bath in weeks.

Once he'd tracked them down, Mickey gave an evil smile of satisfaction. He'd made sure the news of what they had done got round the landing as fast as lightning. Some crimes needed more than the judicial system to put matters right. Some crimes could only be remedied by the kind of justice that was handed out in prison.

It was easy for Mickey to find volunteers. Not only was the crime despicable, but Mickey was the kind of person that other inmates wanted to please. Do someone like Mickey a favour and you would be protected for as long as you were inside.

Both of them went down the same night – the first was sitting watching television when someone came up behind him and poured boiling hot cooking oil over his head. You could smell his flesh frying. No one saw a thing.

The same night, another inmate got hold of a bottle of acid from the outside works department. The other fucker screamed with pain and horror as it was squirted over his face and neck, his skin smoking and smouldering. Again, no one saw a thing.

Mickey felt no remorse – they had got what they deserved. They were both carted off to hospital, barely alive.

The courts treated them much more leniently – they only received six years each. Where was the fucking justice in that? Mickey could receive the same for handling stolen goods. But they were both badly scarred for life. Justice.

The next time Mickey saw Miranda after that was at his dad's funeral. Miranda said something to him that day, words that turned out to be true. They say many a true word is spoken in jest.

Mickey had caught her eye when he saw her, and she smiled shyly at him. He nodded coolly as he made his way over to her.

'Mickey you look nice,' she said. 'You look like a real gangster.'

She blushed as Mickey opened his arms wide, 'Come 'ere girl.' He wrapped his strong arms around her delicate shoulders and the two of them embraced, holding each other for a long and tender moment.

They parted and he looked into her eyes. Her implacable stare told him how much she was hurt and damaged by those fuckers, how the pain would dominate her life. She was a different girl now.

'How ya doing Miranda?' he said finally.

She shrugged. 'Not so good. I'm just taking one day at a time - but I feel better now I've seen you, Mickey.'

Since the attack Mickey had made sure she wasn't on her own. He put her dad onto a geezer he knew with a security firm. They had a pukka alarm and security system fitted to their house. He also made sure she always got home safely after a night out at one of his clubs, had a couple of mates keep an eye on her to make sure she was safe.

Mickey knew that Miranda had a bit of a soft spot for him. It got to the point where she was practically stalking him – everywhere he went she seemed to turn up. Mandy got the hump with him every time Miranda showed up at one of his clubs or was round his mum's house, started really giving him grief over her.

The pair of them definitely didn't get on; Mandy said she was a stuck-up bitch, always hanging around his sister Sharon, that she was in love with him and she had told him that.

In the end Mickey had to put Miranda straight, had to be honest with her, told her they were from different sides of the street, it could never work. She had a fella, Charles Kingsley, and Mickey had a girlfriend as well. Of course, she told Mickey she wanted him not Charles, that she was just using Charles until Mickey wanted her. Mickey sighed. How do you put it gently to a girl you really like that is like a sister to you that it ain't ever gonna happen? He did fancy the arse off her, he wouldn't mind giving her a good seeing to, but things were serious with Mandy.

He pulled Miranda towards him, lowered his voice. 'Listen,' he told her, 'you know I will always be here for you, do anything for ya, help ya when you need it?'

She clutched at him, her face close to his. 'Is that a promise, Mickey?'

He nodded. 'Promise.'

She brushed her lips against his cheek. Just as he pulled away, she whispered frantically in his ear.

'You will need me, want me, love me one day, Mickey.'

Then she strutted away with that high class model walk of hers, leaving a trace of her perfume in the air.

Mickey shook his head. Fuck that, the girl was definitely off her head. Mickey didn't need any more hassles; he had enough things going on with his dad's murder. He didn't need a lovesick girl giving him jip. He really liked her, but as a mate, like a sister.

Out of the corner of his eye, he could see the way Mandy was looking at him; he could see she wasn't very happy. He strolled over to her, his usual cocky self. Despite turning Miranda down, it was nice to know that he still had what it takes. 'Alright Mand?'

Mandy glared at him. 'You fancy her, don't ya?'

Mickey did his best to look wounded, innocent. 'Fuck me, Mand, what's the matter with you. It's me dads fucking funeral, I'm talking to everyone and she's a mate for fuck's sake. I was only talking to her.'

Mandy immediately relented. 'Sorry, Mickey.'

He wrapped an arm around her shoulders. 'Don't ever doubt me,' he told her. 'I will always be honest with you. I want you, no one else, you're mine, you know that don't ya?'

She nodded as tears trembled in her eyes. 'Do you love me, Mickey?'

He pulled her into his arms. 'Course I do. I will never do nothing to hurt you, so don't ever question me again, understand?'

They pulled up outside the cemetery. Two police vans were waiting, and he spotted the plain clothes police mingling with the crowds. It was chocabloc, absolutely packed, everyone in black, heads down, tissues to bloodshot eyes.

Father Peter, the parish priest, was doing the service. Mickey felt choked just thinking about it. Two black feather-plumed pairs of horses appeared, exquisite, sleek and well-mannered, pulling an elegant Victorian glass carriage, mum in a beautiful oak casket, draped elegantly in a floral blanket of gardenias, lilies and orchids. Ten funeral cars filled with close family pulled up behind the hearse. Tears filled his eyes and he blinked rapidly, trying to pull himself together.

Mickey took a deep breath and sighed as he watched family and friends getting out of the funeral cars. Mickey was escorted out of the police car, his right hand cuffed to a prison guard.

Mickey Taylor, Dangerous, was back on his manor.

He held his shoulders back, locked his jaw tight and walked towards his family and friends with his head held high. This was the hardest day of his life, but it was also a special day and his mum was going to get the send-off she deserved. Mickey took a deep breath.

Showtime.

Sharon

Sharon looked in the mirror, touched up her make-up. She wanted to be anywhere in the world but here right now, but she had to go to her mother's funeral. Everyone would be there, all the friends, family, hangers-on, the press, the whole fucking nine yards. And as a part of the close family, there would be lots of eyes on Sharon.

What she wanted to do was hide away, stay here in her mum's old house forever and never come out, but there was no escaping it, she had to do it, for her mum, for Lizzie.

Her reflection stared back at her, her blue eyes cold showing no emotion. Everyone thought they knew Sharon, but none of them really knew her. Fuck them, she thought, as she emptied the large gin and tonic that she had set on the edge of sink. I really don't want to die with spinster on my death certificate. If only they all really knew the truth, knew why she was a spinster...

Miranda Solomon was the first person Sharon told that she was getting married.

The night David proposed to her, Sharon was so excited, she had to tell someone. She dialled Miranda's number, her hands shaking with excitement. Please be home, please be home, thought Sharon.

Miranda answered almost straight away - Sharon had barely said anything before Miranda said, 'I know by the way you are talking you are getting ready to tell me something. You can't be pregnant, so what is it?'

Sharon smiled to herself. 'Guess.'

Miranda laughed. 'I can't guess. Come on, Sharon, just tell me.' She paused. 'I hope it isn't bad news...'

Sharon felt suddenly coy. She had kept her relationship with David silent for so long, apart from Miranda she hadn't told a soul. 'No,' she said quickly, 'it's fucking good news for a change.'

Miranda thought for a moment. 'Don't tell me – that handsome brother of yours has realised what an idiot he's been all these years and wants to give me a right going over!'

Sharon laughed. Miranda had never given up hope that one day Mickey would want her. 'No, you silly cow,' she told her, 'and if Mandy ever heard you say that she would fucking kill you!'

The line fell silent, Miranda waiting.

Sharon took a deep breath. 'I'm getting married,' she said finally.

She could hear Miranda choke on her drink. 'You what?'

'I'm getting married'

Now Miranda was laughing. 'No! You're joking with me!'

Sharon found herself protesting. 'No, honestly I am.'

'You can't be!' came the startled reply.

'Well thanks very much.'

There was a long silence.

Finally Sharon spoke. 'Honestly, me and David are getting married – we've got the date and venue sorted, everything.'

She could hear Miranda sipping her drink. 'Fuck me, I am shocked.' Miranda took another slurp of her drink. 'Well congratulations Miss Havisham! Here's to Sharon and Dave.' Her voice sounded softer now, the laughter and teasing gone. 'I never thought I would see the day, Sharon, but I'm so happy for you.'

Sharon smiled. She'd told someone. It was real.

'You've kept this quiet, haven't you?' teased Miranda. 'I mean, I haven't even met him yet.'

Sharon grinned. 'Well my dearest, bestest friend ever, I wanted you to be the first to know.'

When she finally hung up the phone, Sharon was still smiling. Everything was just falling together.

She had met David through a pen pal advert in the paper, and they had been writing to each other for two years. He lived in Sussex, but they had so much in common, so many similarities, and like her he had been adopted as a baby.

Over their long phone conversations, their letters, their weekends away, David had helped Sharon come to terms with her own adoption.

She had gradually learnt to forgive her mum and accept that Lizzie had done it because she loved her, that she thought she was doing it for the right reasons. David helped her put her life into perspective, helped her to understand herself and finally start to like herself.

David had always known he was adopted, but his adoption parents had made him feel wanted, special, always told him he was their gift. His adoptive mother couldn't have children and his two sisters were also adopted. His parents had always been open with him, and always maintained that if he ever wanted to find his biological parents they would help and support him in any way they could and they would not resent or be offended if he choose to look for them.

They talked on the phone regularly, and though it was a long time before they met, there was an instant connection with them, a powerful emotional connection. They were open and honest with each other, and Sharon felt a breath of fresh air just having him in her life.

It was a year before they first met, and still Sharon waited before having sex – something she'd never done before. But when they did make love for the first time it was perfect, everything she'd ever hoped it would be. For the first time in her life Sharon was in love.

They were friends and lovers, and they both wanted the same things in life. Although her abortion years ago had left her unable to have children, David said that with new IVF treatments it would be possible for them to have children. Sharon felt giddy thinking about it – she could hold their baby in her arms, the baby she had craved for all her life, a son or daughter, it didn't matter. It would be hers and no one else's, hers, her little baby. She was so gloriously happy, she wanted to tell the world.

But despite that, Miranda was the only person she talked to about David. She didn't want to introduce him to the family yet, didn't want to scare him off. But she could picture the moment when she told Lizzie, the look on her mum's face. She would crack a big smile, say 'it's about bleeding time girl, you don't want to end up an old spinster!'

They met every time David came to London, in a quiet hotel near Liverpool Street. It was their place, and they always did the same thing – met in the lobby, went out for dinner, then went back to the hotel and made love. Sharon would have skipped dinner and gone straight to the room every time, but David insisted that they go out first, like a date, and she loved that, loved the respect he gave her.

Sharon lay back in his arms, pulled slowly on her cigarette, watched the smoke form a blue cloud above her. She could feel his heart still beating fast against her cheek, their sweat slowly drying in the cool air.

Sharon sat up, stubbed out her cigarette, and looked down at his kind, brown eyes. 'I need to tell you something,' she said softly.

He stroked her arm, smiled. 'As long as you don't get out of this bed any time soon, I don't mind what you tell me!' he laughed.

Sharon shook her head. 'No. It's about my family. If we're getting married and all, it's only fair you know what you're getting into.'

David gazed up at her, his eyes full of love. 'If you're anything to go by, I'm sure they're all delightful.'

Sharon gave a bitter laugh. 'If only.'

David's face turned serious. 'Whatever you need to tell me. It can't hurt what we have.'

She nodded her head. 'I know, but still...'

Here goes, she thought. 'I've got a big family,' she started. 'Three brothers and a sister.'

'Yes, you said.'

'But here's the thing,' continued Sharon. 'They've got a bit of a reputation around Dagenham.'

David's face clouded slightly. 'Taylor..' he said softly.

'Right. But my name's not just Taylor. We're THE Taylor's. Mickey Taylor – Dangerous they call him – he's my brother. And Bobby Taylor – may he rot in hell – he was my dad.'

Nothing could have prepared her for David's response. At the mention of Bobby Taylor his face blanched, then he turned suddenly, half fell out of the bed, crawled to the bathroom and began vomiting violently into the toilet.

Sharon jumped out of bed, wrapped a sheet around her, and hurried after him.

'David? David?'

He heaved again.

'What is it? Are you sick?'

He had his back to her, his head hanging over the toilet. There was a long silence before he finally whispered. 'I told you that I was adopted – what I didn't tell you was that Bobby Taylor was my father. You're my half-sister!'

Sharon's head span, she leaned against the doorframe, nausea engulfing her. How was it possible? What were the odds that of all the men in the world she could fall in love with, it would be with one of Bobby Taylor's bastard offspring? They all knew they were out there – rumour had it he'd had five of six kids with other women – but David? She would never be able to sort it out in her head, she was destroyed.

That night they clung to each other and sobbed in each other's arms. Sharon had lost the only man she had ever loved, and with it her last chance for happiness. When she left the hotel in the grey hours of early morning, her heart was closed, and Sharon the eternal spinster was born. Bobby Taylor had reached back from beyond the grave to destroy her happiness. Once more the family had taken everything from her, destroyed her.

She was still in her early twenties at the time, but she felt like it was the end of her life, that she had nothing good left in her life, that things would never improve for her. And so she finally gave into the inevitable, started using her one true talent. It was after that night that she went on the game . . .

The Funeral

Mickey fought to keep the smile from his face as the car doors opened and he stepped outside. Cameras flashed, a babble of voices washed over him: 'Mickey!'

'There's Mickey!'

'There he is…'

He stood up straight, tried to ignore the handcuffs, closed his eyes and let the soft rain caress his face. He would be out for real in a few weeks, but for now he wanted to savour this moment, his first taste of freedom in fourteen years.

One of the cops nudged him in the back. 'Get a bleeding move on, Taylor, we don't have all bloody day.'

Mickey opened his eyes, scanned the crowd. Apart from the press there were some familiar faces in the crowd, well-wishers and sightseers, all the usual crows that showed up at any kind of celebrity funeral.

Celebrity funeral – fuck, his mum wouldn't have liked that, but at least the police had had the decency to keep them all outside the cemetery – peering through the railings they were, like monkeys in the fucking zoo!

Mickey nodded to a few half familiar faces, turned and strode towards the crowd of family and friends waiting outside the chapel.

Terri was the first to greet him, that shy smile that still made him think of her as a little girl. Fuck, they had all grown up in one way or another. Then Sharon, and one by one all the others hugged him, held him, looked into his eyes. The Taylors. All of them there except Martin – well, what did you expect, the little fucker was in Australia, had been for over fifteen years. Couldn't blame him, better to be down there than banged up here like Mickey.

It was cool, quiet inside the chapel. Mickey's eyes went straight to the casket at the front of the church. Lizzie was inside there – that didn't feel right. How could his mum be dead? But then, does anyone ever really believe their mother is dead – mums are always there, that's what they do.

With Sharon and Terri on each side of him, Mickey made his way to the front pew – the cops at least had the decency to take his handcuffs off in the chapel, to wait by the doors. What the fuck did they think he was going to do, do a runner at his mum's funeral with just a couple of weeks left on his sentence?

Terri squeezed his arm. 'It'll be good to have you back, Mickey,' she whispered. 'Between you and me, there's a few things need straightening out.'

Mickey sighed. Just what he needed – to be pulled into the middle of a row between his sisters. Still, there was no way around it. He'd been the head of the family – even from inside the nick – and now, with his mum gone, even more was going to fall on him.

He stared straight ahead, thought about Terri's words: 'There's a few things need straightening out.' No fucking kidding. In the fourteen years he'd been gone all sorts of changes had come over the neighbourhood. Not just the immigrants, the closures at Ford, the deaths and births, but also the underworld that Mickey inhabited. Fourteen years ago, when he'd got sent down, he was the undisputed lord of the manor, Dagenham's big I Am, but now?

Well, he knew that he couldn't just waltz back in and act like he'd never been gone. There were new gangs, new rules, and people would be gunning for him.

But what else could he do? He'd never had an honest day's work in his life. He could hardly go get a job at Ford's, or start working down at the local Sainsbury's! That wasn't Mickey Taylor.

Still, he'd have to tread carefully, suss out the lie of the land, find out who was still on his side, who was looking to take him down. He'd be a target, that was for bloody certain – any two quid thug who got himself a piece of Mickey Taylor would have a real name for himself, and Mickey wasn't about to let that happen.

And drugs! He'd always hated drugs, but that was what it was all about now, that's where the big money was. Most of his old mates had got sucked up into it, told him they had no choice. We'll see about that, thought Mickey. If there's no other way to make some money, I'm not a fucking Taylor!

He looked around, was met by a flurry of nods, quiet greetings. Everyone looked familiar, but at the same time they all looked so old. Mickey turned back to the front, but couldn't look at the casket. He stared down at his shoes, polished so hard they reflected his own face back at him.

Do I look that old, thought Mickey? Is everyone else looking at me and thinking the same thing? Christ, look at Mickey Taylor, can you believe how old he looks? Ever since Bernie's heart attack, Mickey had taken good care of himself – when he looked in the mirror he saw the same good looking guy in his mid-20s that he'd been when he'd first got sent down, but in his heart of hearts he knew that he, like everyone else, was showing the years. Christ, what a waste, fourteen bloody years, that was a third of his life he'd spent inside.

As the organ slowly began to play, Mickey made a vow. Whatever happened, he wasn't going back inside.

He straightened his shoulders, looked up. This was Lizzie's time. They were going to send her off in a way that was fitting. The Queen of fucking Dagenham she'd been when she was alive, and the Queen of fucking Dagenham she would be today.

Martin

Martin stood outside the cemetery, puffed out his cheeks. How bloody typical. A Taylor funeral, and instead of being a quiet, dignified affair, it was a circus, a frenzy of police, press, and hangers-on.

Fifteen years ago he'd left the family, left Dagenham, left England, and now Martin was back. When he'd left he'd vowed he would never come back, but when Terri had called him, told him Lizzie had died, what else could he do? For all that he hated what his family represented, his mum was his mum, and she had never been a part of the mayhem and the murders and the madness.

Martin looked around – no one he really recognised. He pushed through the crowd to the gates. Jesus, there were even police there.

'Sorry, mate, this is a private funeral.'

Martin laughed to himself. He had been away a long time. 'I'm the son of the deceased,' he said quietly. The copper gave him a sharp look, turned to a heavy set man in his sixties who was standing behind him. 'You know this bloke?'

Frankie Priest looked at Martin. Suddenly recognition flooded over him. 'Well fuck me, if it isn't the prodigal!'

As the copper held the gates open, Frankie pulled him through, enveloped Martin in his huge arms. 'This is Martin Taylor,' he told the cop, 'Lizzie's youngest.'

The gates clanged shut behind them. Frankie finally released Martin from his bear hug. 'Well I never imagined to see you here today, that's for fucking certain!'

Martin nodded, fighting back a surge of emotions. 'Yeah, well I never figured it meself, but it's me mum…'

Frankie patted him on the back. 'You need to get on in there, they're about to start. I'll catch up with you after.'

Martin walked slowly towards the chapel, looking around at the grave stones in the soft autumn drizzle. He'd become so used to the bright glare of Sydney, he'd almost forgotten what a damp English day looked like. Still, it felt like the right weather for a funeral – bright sunshine would have somehow seemed wrong for saying your farewells to someone. but this, this soft, grey English light, this gentle rain that barely seemed to touch his cheeks, this was right for laying his mum in the ground.

Martin's footsteps slowed as he reached the chapel, and he found himself strangely reluctant to go inside. He glanced at his watch – five minutes until the service started. He knew he would have to face the family, but he wasn't quite ready yet. If he could slip in the back of the chapel and not have to talk to anyone until after the service he would be much happier.

The last time he'd seen them all it had been a far from happy experience. Mickey had been arrested and charged, Georgie was gone, everything seemed to be falling apart, and Martin knew he just had to get away. Some might call it a betrayal, but he'd reached a point where he just couldn't do it any more, couldn't be another violent, crooked member of the Taylor family.

Was it in your blood, or was it something you could choose for yourself? He knew what Mickey would say – Mickey was all about the family, the blood, being there for each other in times of need. Big fucking sentiments for a man who had spent the past fourteen years inside. The man who left his wife to raise their kids, his family to somehow muddle along without him.

Martin thought back to the last time he'd seen Mickey – visiting time, in that bleak room with the grey lino floor, the plastic chairs and tables, the bars on the windows, the screws with their uniforms and their scowls looking at everyone - prisoners and visitors alike - as though they were scum, the smell of piss and disinfectant hanging over everything.

'I'm leaving, Mickey,' Martin had said nervously.

Mickey glared at him, not understanding at first. 'What do you mean you're leaving?' he growled. 'You only just fucking arrived!'

'Not leaving here – leaving the country.'

Martin had never seen Mickey more shocked. He just stared at Martin for a moment, his brows creased together. 'Leaving the country? What kind of shit is that?' he said finally.

'I've got all my papers through, all approved,' said Martin, breathlessly. 'I'm immigrating to Australia.'

'Australia?' Mickey made it sound like a dirty word. 'What the fuck you want to go there for?'

'I've got to get away, Mickey.' He glanced around the dreary, oppressive room. 'I can't do this, can't be you.'

Mickey leaned across the table, grabbed his arm. 'You can't fuck off now – we need you. Mum needs you, Sharon and Terri need you...'

Martin tried to pull his arm free, but Mickey had it in a tight grip. 'I'm not like you,' said Martin softly. 'I thought I was, but I'm not...'

It was true. Growing up, Martin had idolised Mickey, wanted to be him. Mickey was so strong, so dynamic, larger than life with his huge fists, flash cars, easy charm.

Martin had followed Mickey into boxing, become really good, and little by little he'd been sucked into Mickey's criminal world. A delivery here, keeping an eye on someone there, it was easy money, exciting, and he got washed along in the wake of Dangerous, the notorious Mickey Taylor.

But there was always a side of it Martin struggled with – the raw, brutal violence. The first time he saw Mickey take someone apart he almost threw up. They were in a pub somewhere over Poplar way, having a quiet drink after a score, when some lairy geezer started getting up in Mickey's face. He strutted over to the bar, full of piss and beer, two of his mates at his shoulders. 'Ain't you Mickey Taylor?' he challenged.

Mickey looked up slowly. 'What if I am?'

Martin had been around Mickey long enough to know that voice, the icy calm that meant watch out, but the geezer didn't know Mickey, didn't know what he was dealing with.

'You may be the king of the manor over in Dagenham, but you ain't in Dagenham right now, are you?'

Mickey's cold eyes roamed across the bloke, quickly sized up him and his two mates. 'I'm just here enjoying a quiet drink,' Mickey replied softly.

The bloke looked over at Martin. 'And who's that? Your girlfriend?' He turned to his mates and laughed. 'Looks like Mickey Taylor's all luvved up with a little poof!'

Mickey wrapped his hand tightly around the handle of his beer glass, slid down off the bar stool. 'That's my kid brother.' He spat the words out. 'And you are going to apologise to him.'

The geezer grinned back at Mickey. 'Fuck off!'

Mickey reacted so suddenly that Martin didn't even have time to move – he just froze, his glass half way to his mouth.

Mickey's hand shot out, the beer glass held tight, smashed into the geezer's face, the glass shattering with the force of the blow.

The bloke fell backwards, blood spurting, but before he'd even hit the ground the broken beer glass had slammed into one of his mates' faces.

The third one tried to back away, but Mickey caught him with one of his huge hands, grabbed the bloke's bomber jacket and hauled him forwards into a vicious head butt that shattered his nose.

He crumpled to the floor beside his mates, all three of them groaning and bleeding.

Martin looked down in shock – the first bloke was screaming like a dying animal, a huge chunk of one cheek hanging half off.

Mickey threw down the broken remains of the beer mug, turned to Martin. 'Drink up, Marty. We're done with this shit hole.'

That was it. He threw a twenty pound note on the bar and strutted out, Martin scurrying along at his heels.

Nothing was ever the same after that. Martin continued working with Mickey, but his heart wasn't in it, he was always looking for a way out, a chance to escape – but with Mickey around, there was no chance, no way he could ever think about anything else, let alone do anything about it.

But it was shortly after Mickey was arrested that Martin realised that he just wasn't meant to be part of that world. It was a quiet night at the Cross Keys, Martin sitting having a quiet drink with a bird he was trying to pull, when Dave Bailey came up to him, clapped him on the back. 'Martin!' he crowed in his thick Scottish accent. 'Give my regards to Mickey next time you see him. Tell him that was justice and no fucking mistake!'

Martin was confused. 'What are you talking about?'

Dave grinned. 'Didn't you hear? Those animals what raped Miranda?'

'Yeah. They got put away.'

Dave shook his head. 'Yeah, but it's what Mickey done, that's what I call real justice.'

'What Mickey did?'

Dave grinned, warming to his story. 'You didn't hear? They wound up in Pentonville with

Mickey…' He sipped his drink, drawing out the story. 'Terrible accidents, don't you know? One of 'em wound up with a pot of boiling oil over his head, the other had an unfortunate accident with a face full of battery acid!' He grinned, downed his drink. 'Right fucking hero, your brother!'

After he'd gone, Martin sat quietly, thinking. What kind of man pours boiling oil over another, or squirts battery acid in his face? Was this the man Martin had admired? Was this the life Martin wanted? He resolved right there and then to get as far away from his family as he possibly could.

Martin checked his watch. The service was just starting. He climbed the three steps, pushed open the heavy wooden door and slipped inside just as the music started playing. It was going to be a long day, with a million questions to answer, but for now he could just stand quietly at the back of the chapel and think about his mum.

Mickey

Mickey closed his eyes. It was hot and stuffy in the back of the police car. 'Haven't you lot heard of air conditioning?' he grumbled.

'What, got spoiled in your cell have you?' chirped one of the cops.

'Yeah, but it's a right royal pain in the arse getting the pool man in to clean my Jacuzzi,' laughed Mickey. He leaned back, closed his eyes, felt like he could doze off. His mind had been everywhere today, all sorts of different thoughts racing through his head.

The funeral had been weird. He could hardly remember a thing about the service. Terri held tight to his arm most of the time, while Sharon stood on the other side of him, cold, aloof. Didn't she feel anything? That's what he'd thought – miserable, cold-hearted cow.

Then he'd caught a short glimpse behind the mask. As Lizzie's coffin slid forward to be cremated, he saw Sharon gulp, noticed the tightly clenched jaw, the single tear that rolled down her cheek. Yeah, she was feeling it all right, she just kept it all bottled up inside.

Then suddenly the music was playing again and it was all over. Everyone stood and waited while Mickey and his two sisters led them all outside – and fuck me twice sideways, there was Martin standing waiting for them, all grown up and come back from Australia. Suntanned and fit he looked. Whatever he was doing out there it obviously suited him.

Mickey wanted to talk to him, had a million questions for him, but the bloody coppers were already grabbing one arm each, trying to lead him away.

'Funeral's over,' they told him.

His hands still cuffed in front of him, Mickey pulled free from their grasp. 'This is my fucking brother!' he protested, 'I haven't seen him in fourteen years!'

'I don't care if it's the King of fucking Siam,' said one of the cops, 'your times up!'

As Mickey was dragged away, he shouted back at Martin. 'I'm out in two weeks. Will you still be here?'

Martin gave a soft nod of his head. 'I'll stick around until you're out.'

And that was it. Mickey's temporary freedom was over.

He turned to the cops either side of him, the ones who had dragged him away at the end. 'You really are a pair of cunts, you know that?'

One of them grinned. 'Thanks! That means a lot coming from a prick like you!'

'Will you autograph my dick?' enquired the other.

'Yeah, with my fucking boot!' snarled Mickey.

'Bet you see a lot of dicks inside don't you?' wondered the first cop.

'I see a lot of dicks in this car right now!' Mickey replied quickly.

The cops fell silent and Mickey settled back in the cramped seat. He could feel the sweat trickling down his back. He closed his eyes, and instantly an image flashed across his eyes of the day in court when he was sentenced to life imprisonment. Christ, the look of the faces of his family, especially his mum, Mandy, and the kids. The whole family shuddered when the judge sentenced him to twenty years.

Give them their due, they had all been behind him all the way, every day for three weeks they all got themselves to the Old Bailey. When he looked at them from the dock, they all had that funeral look, eyes downcast, and faces like a bunch of slapped arses. He wished he could say something to make them feel better, but his lawyer said right from the start that he could go down, it was really all about how long he'd serve, they were hoping for five to ten, maybe out in three or four years.

When the sentence had come down, it had changed everything for all of them. Twenty years – shit, his kids would be grown by the time he got out, and he'd be well over forty bloody years old – that was fucking ancient when you're only twenty seven. He knew right there and then that he had to keep his nose clean, do everything he could to make sure he got out as soon as possible.

But even with good behaviour – or at least, good enough that he'd never run foul of the authorities – he'd still served fourteen fucking years.

Mickey and Mandy had been married for over twenty four years now, and for two thirds of it he'd been banged up. Still, they were both determined to have a huge party when he got out, to celebrate their twenty fifth. Prison had taken a lot away from him, but not Mandy. She was a good girl, had stuck by him, never a question.

Mickey thought of the way she'd looked at the funeral. Time hadn't been kind to her - she had certainly piled on the pounds while he was away. Mickey thought of how beautiful she was when he met her, that look of defiance and mischief about her that had first attracted him, with her mahogany coloured hair, those dark eyes that twinkled with mischief. That spark had been worn down by the past fourteen years. But she was still his wife, and no matter what she looked like he would give her a good seeing to when he got out. Christ, Mickey felt himself getting horny just thinking about her.

For years he had dreamed of holding her in his arms and hearing her laugh again. Mickey had always thought she had a laugh that was so sexy. But it wasn't just her looks that had attracted him to her – she was a brave and clever girl, and she'd never stopped loving him, and that had to count for something.

Funny how tough times can make you or break you. Just before he was nicked they had been going through a rough time. She moaned constantly that Mickey was out all the time and never at home with her and the kids. Moaned that he was always down the pub or at one or other of the clubs. That was where I do my work, Mickey had protested, but she wouldn't hear it. You never take me out, she moaned, but when he offered to take her down the pub with him, she refused, saying she didn't have anything to wear. Nothing was good enough for her.

Typical bloody woman, thought Mickey. He had always tried to please Mandy, put a smile on her face, so when she moaned that he never bought her flowers any more or surprised her with little presents like he did when they were first dating, he started bringing more flowers and presents home. And what did Mandy say? 'What have you done wrong? What do you feel guilty about, because that's the only time you buy me anything.'

Fucking hell, with Mandy he couldn't do right for doing wrong. She had all the up to date gear in the house, the kids always had what they wanted. Mickey had always told her she could have what she wanted, all she had to do was ask. What more could she want?

Even when he was inside she had a holiday in Clacton every year with the kids. Fucking hell, she didn't realise how lucky she was. He knew blokes inside with him whose wives were out on the game because it was the only way they could survive when their men were inside. But despite everything he still did for them when he was inside, Mandy said she might as well be a single parent. He could never understand women; they were definitely from another planet.

Mickey thought about his kids, prayed that none of them ever ended up like him. Following his path only had three possible outcomes. One, spend most of your life in prison, banged up with self-harmers, dirty heroin addicts, and surrounded by paedophiles and rapists, the scum of the earth, the constant smells of piss, shit, and sweat wafting into your nostrils. Don't believe what anyone says, he thought, prison is hard. Suicides happened all the time. There was no pity or sympathy in prison.

The second possibility was that somebody jumps you one night and you end up in hospital, in the intensive care unit, wired up to a life support machine with the family standing around you, crying their eyes out because they don't know if you'll live or die.

And if you do miraculously recover, it won't be long before you wind up on path number three – dead on a mortuary slab with a bullet in your head after being found face down on some dark country lane.

But prison was all Mickey had now, and to survive he'd had to adapt. For lifers it's as good or as bad as you make it, and Mickey had to work hard to protect himself, stop himself being eaten away by it. He had to accept the reality of it all, because there was fuck all he could do about it. It was a matter of attitude. You have to be realistic, patient, endure it. Keep busy and keep sane, that's what had got him through, and that's what he had to do for the next two weeks.

A lot of the old timers say that's the most dangerous time, when you're about to be released. You feel like you're done, start counting the days, the hours, the minutes, and you let your guard down. Before you know it you've done something to piss off the screws and lost your parole, or worse still, got up the nose of some hard bastard who puts a shiv in your guts out of spite.

Mickey thought back to when he'd first arrived. He had enough mates who served time to know that one of the worst things about prison life was that unless you knew an inmate from the outside before you came in prison, or one of your mates in prison recommends a fellow prisoner to you, you can't trust anyone. There are about two hundred men on a prison wing, and you don't know what they are inside for. They put all sorts of cons together; grasses, nonces, child molesters and rapists, all on the same wing with everyone else. The scum bag screws use them as informants – as long as the prison officers get the information they want, they keep quiet about what these animals are banged up for. As soon as the inmates find out what these shitters were sentenced for, they are moved to segregation for their safety.

When you first get convicted they pack you off to a local prison – for Mickey that meant Brixton, Pentonville, Wormwood Scrubs or Wandsworth – and you're there until they decide where you're going to do your sentence. So a shop lifter, a joy rider or a tax dodger could be banged up with a rapist, a murderer, a paedophile, a psychopath. Nobody knew who was who and who had done what.

When Mickey was first sent to Brixton there was a young kid there, a first time offender, he'd been out on his birthday and had decided to drive home when he was stopped by the Old Bill. Silly bugger panicked because he had a few drinks, sped off in the motor knocking the copper over, and after a right old chase he ended up crashing into Woolworths.

Brixton was an intimidating place for anyone, but this boy must have been crapping himself. The screws banged him up with this big tall muscular man called Trojan, a pervert of the worst kind.

When the cell doors were opened up the next morning, the poor young kid was found naked, bound and gagged, curled up in the corner of the cell in a foetal position shivering compulsively. That dirty cunt Trojan had beat and raped him not once but throughout the night. That night must have been hell for the defenceless kid. His body was black and blue and covered with bite marks, he was in such a bad way, in such a state of shock he couldn't talk or walk. The other inmates gave Trojan a horrific beating, sliced him to pieces and left him for dead, but it still didn't make up for what had happened.

Mickey could never figure it out. Was it some kind of joke for the screws, did they think it was funny? Why put them together, where was the sense in that? Why put a joy rider with this piece of scum, a perverted serial rapist?

Both Trojan and the kid were taken to hospital, and though Mickey never saw either of them again, he heard that the boy never made it through his prison sentence. The poor little sod had hung himself. The kid's brain must have been tortured with images of what happened to him that night, he probably couldn't look at himself in the mirror or face any of his family and friends again. Mickey tried to imagine if that had been him – how could he look his mum in the eye again with memories of that happening to him?

The door of Mickey's cell clanged shut and he slumped down on the bed, his head in his hands. Two more weeks, just two more weeks he kept telling himself. It was going to be a bloody long two weeks!

Part Three

Mickey

Doors. Mickey had never thought much about them till he was put away, but when you're inside you think about them all the time.

The metal doors of the cell that slammed shut every night, sealing you in with your worst nightmares - Mickey would never forget the sound of those doors crashing closed. Or the doors with bars that separated every corridor   each and every one was covered by a CCTV camera, watching everything. The only way through was when the screws came along with their huge bunch of keys and let you through. Then there was the main door of the prison itself, the one he thought he'd never get through.

Mickey was always awake early in prison, part of the routine he had established to keep himself healthy and sane. But on the morning of his release he had been awake all night. He just couldn't sleep. He didn't know how he felt today. Relieved? Shocked? Excited? The realisation that this day had finally come, his release day, the day he had waited for so long, it all seemed so unreal. It really hadn't sunk in.

Mickey's commitment to the physical fitness regime that carried him through his prison sentence didn't change that day. His normal morning activities didn't change that morning. Push-ups and sit-ups in his cell, then a run around the yard, pounding the hard ground for the last time. Then back for a shower and breakfast. He couldn't stomach much that day, didn't feel hungry, felt a bit sick, but he was determined that nothing would change that morning. He keep to his normal morning activities, make sure nothing went wrong. He kept trying to get to grips with the notion that in a couple of hours he would be released, would be going home...

Mickey sat in his cell gathering his thoughts, wondering how it was going to feel walking out through those prisons gates, leaving the place that had housed him for fourteen years. He wondered if he would remember how to drive. Christ, would he have to take a driving test again? Mickey chuckled to himself, he didn't take his driving test himself the first time, his mate took the test for him, made out he was Mickey Taylor for an hour, passed first time. Mickey had taught himself to drive, was a good driver, but he certainly couldn't be arsed doing it the way driving instructors wanted him to.

He would have to get used to eating with stainless steel knives and forks again, eating from real plates, and it would be strange drinking from a proper glass, not plastic. He would be able to eat what he wanted, when he wanted, could wear decent clothes again, make his own choices, his own decisions. Prison provides a false sense of security. For years his life had been on a rigid schedule, he didn't have to think for himself, just had to follow orders.

The whole morning, Mickey felt as nervous as a cat in a kennel full of Pit Bulls. Suddenly prison seemed a dangerous place, he couldn't wait to get out, was scared that something would go wrong, that someone would exact a pay-back for something that Mickey had done. But it had all gone smoothly.

He sat in his cell, his stomach rumbling. No more prison slop, he'd grab something to eat as soon as he was out.

Then the screws made him wait around in his cell until they were good and ready, their last petty attempt to remind him that they were in charge.

Finally they came to get him.

As he walked along the landing of the wing, his pals shouted out their well wishes. Mickey strutted past, clutching his sports bag full of his possessions - letters, photos, a few clothes. The rest of the stuff - toiletries, some books, he'd given to his mates.

A prison officer escorted him to a secure part of the prison that the inmates didn't usually see for the processing, the form filling. It was all a blur, Mickey wasn't even paying attention, he was already thinking of the things he was going to do that day. A big meal – several probably – buy some new clobber, something sharp. Then a few beers with the boys, and his first real shag for years.

The prison officer walked him to the door, then suddenly it swung open and Mickey stepped outside into a crisp autumn day. He just stood for a moment, stared around at the trees, their leaves turning yellow, the tarmac, wet from overnight rain, the grass verge at the edge of the road. It was a scruffy place, but to Mickey it was more beautiful than the Gardens at Versailles – it was freedom. The blare of a car horn brought him out of his reverie. He walked across the grass and his legs turned to jelly. He thought he was going to end up on his arse, he felt wobbly, almost overcome by it all. It felt weird, a strange sensation ran through his body, it had been years since he had walked on grass.

A taxi driver was staring at him. "You Mickey Taylor?"

Mickey nodded. At the sound of his name his strength and certainty suddenly returned, he strode towards the taxi. He opened the door and clambered in, let out a deep sigh as he settled back against the seat.

"Where we going?"

"Home !" grinned Mickey.

And now Mickey stood and gazed at the front door of Lizzie's house. He knew the family would be waiting for him, but he hadn't told them exactly what time he was being released, didn't want them all waiting outside the prison for him. He'd had fourteen years of other people telling him what to do and when to do it. This morning he'd wanted to do things in his own sweet time and get himself together. Everyone had offered to pick him up but he didn't want that. He knew that had upset Mandy, she had wanted to come and get him and spend some time with him on her own before he was taken over by his family and friends. He tried explaining it to her, that he needed that little bit of time on his own, but she shouted and screamed at him, time on his fucking own, she said, she had spent the last fourteen years on her own. Yes, but not on the inside. So Mickey had already upset her and he wasn't even outside the prison gates yet. Fucking hell, welcome back to married life, he'd thought...

What would it be like being back in Lizzie's house knowing she was not there? In his mind she was in there waiting for him, a fag in one hand, a cup of tea in the other, nagging him to be careful. Or in the hallway pulling her coat on and fixing her hair, a quick spray of lacquer then on with her head scarf, before Mickey dropped her off for a night of bingo. How could she not be there?

Although if he'd been honest with himself, he'd been expecting her to go sooner rather than later. The last time he'd seen her, about a year or so ago, she hadn't looked good. She'd walked so slowly across the floor of the visiting room it had brought a lump to his throat, and when he'd hugged her she was nothing but skin and bone, like a tiny bird in his arms. She'd always been slim – had prided herself on it – but now there was nothing to her. Fucking hell, he thought to himself, the joys of getting old. There's something to look forward to.

But when she'd sat down opposite him there was still the same sparkle in her eyes, the same wit and sharp tongue when she spoke. Though she struggled for breath and coughed constantly. The start of the pneumonia that dragged her down and made her housebound.

'Mum, you shouldn't have come,' Mickey had chided her, but she'd given him a sharp look and he'd not gone on about it.

'I came because I wanted to, I needed to,' she rasped.

Mickey sat silent, waited for her to catch her breath, gently held her nicotine stained fingers.

'You've been away a long time,' she told him. 'I'm not blaming you, and you've somehow seen that Mandy and your kids were looked after…' Another long pause while she caught her breath. 'But there are things you've missed, things you would have dealt with if you'd been around.'

Fucking hell, thought Mickey, she came all the way out here to make me feel guilty. 'Don't you think I don't know it, mum? Taking care of Mandy, seeing the boys grow up – '

She cut him off. 'That's not what I'm talking about.'

'Then what?'

'Old business. Your dad's business.'

A scowl crossed Mickey's face. 'That cunt? I don't want any part of his business.'

'Sometimes you don't have a choice.'

Mickey looked at her curiously. She'd not spoken about Bobby since the day he died – at times it was as though he didn't exist. What had rattled her cage now? Her eyes looked troubled, she kept breaking off and gazing out of the window, thinking carefully each time she spoke.

'Your dad. He made lots of enemies.'

'No fucking kidding.' That was the understatement of the year, thought Mickey. It was virtually a day of celebration in Dagenham when people found out that Bobby Taylor was dead.

'I thought that all his old skeletons had gone to the grave with him,' she told Mickey, 'but one of them has been sniffing around again. The game's not over yet, son.'

Mickey scowled. 'Who? Mum, if someone's bothering you, I'll have them taken care of. You know I can do it, even from here. Just say the word.'

Lizzie nodded. 'I know you can, son.' She looked up and met Mickey's eyes. Her eyes looked tired, almost cloudy. 'It might be nothing,' she said softly, 'but I just wanted to give you a warning.'

'Who? Who is it mum?'

Lizzie shook her head. 'Probably just an old lady getting senile in her old age.'

But Mickey knew it was more than that. Whatever else Lizzie had been in her final years, she certainly wasn't senile.

But no matter how much he pressed her, she wouldn't say anything more. She turned on her their usual chat, updating him on what was going on at home. The antics of his children, who was moaning about what. Telling him everything except what he really wanted to know.

And in the weeks that followed, as her health deteriorated, he thought less and less about what she had said, felt inclined to believe that it was just an old lady getting twitchy in her twilight years.

And now he'd never seen her again. His last memory was of Lizzie walking slowly away, her back hunched as she leaned on a walking stick.

'See you next week, mum!' he'd called out.

'See you, love,' she threw back over her shoulder, then was wracked by a violent bout of coughing as she tottered out the door.

He should have known, should have realised that was the last time he could see her, but even if he had what could he have done? He'd hugged her, kissed her, and told her that he loved her. What more could a son do?

His eye caught a slight movement as the curtain twitched. Someone had seen him. It was game time. As Lizzie's front door opened Mandy came out first, then they all spilled out the front door, his family and good friends, all the people that mattered to him, everyone who had looked after him while he was inside.

Seeing Mandy reminded him of when he first saw her, her eyes, her smile, and knew she was the one for him. It had been a long, long time, and just the thought of her still did things to him, thinking about all the things they used to do. He wondered if she still felt the same way about him.

The others swarmed forwards, engulfed him, slapping his back, shaking his hand, arms around him. Mandy held back, and slowly everyone noticed, gave her some space as she walked slowly towards Mickey, tears rolling down her cheeks.

He looked at her in disbelief. He was finally coming home to her. He held his arms out wide, and Mandy collapsed into them, holding him like she was never going to let go. He felt a shiver down his spine just thinking about that moment, how great it felt, wondering how long this feeling was going to last. They eased away from each other, and Mickey took Mandy's hand. 'Come on,' he said, 'let's get inside.' Mickey strode up the garden path, chest puffed out, a cocky grin on his face. Mickey Taylor was back.

Martin

Mickey couldn't believe it at first when he saw that Martin was at the funeral. He'd been gone so long, with no contact that Mickey had virtually given him up for dead. But Terri, it seemed, had been in touch with him the whole time. Martin had wanted to keep it quiet from the rest of the family – Mickey couldn't really blame him for that – so he'd known about Lizzie's death the same day, and within hours had booked his flight to be there for the funeral.

Mickey just stared at him, couldn't believe he was seeing him again after so long. Part of Mickey wanted to smack him hard, right in the kisser, for leaving the family, but the other half of his mind knew that Martin had done the right thing. If he'd stayed he would only have wound up in jail like Mickey, or even dead, and he'd have done anything to avoid that.

'Mickey.'

'Martin.'

For a moment they stood and looked at each other, like two fighters sizing each other up before a fight. Mickey could feel all the others looking at them, waiting to see what Mickey said. Mickey would have time enough to talk to Martin in private later. This was a time of reconciliation, the family coming back together to honour Lizzie.

Mickey stepped forward, held his arms out. 'Fuck me, it's good to see you!'

As he held Martin, time seemed to wash away, it was almost like the old days, his younger brother not too proud to get a hug from Mickey when something was bothering him.

They just held each other, for twenty, thirty seconds, the rest of the family looking, no words necessary.

It was Martin who pulled away first, smiled at Mickey. 'Prison must have suited you!' he grinned. 'You look healthy as a horse.'

'You cheeky fucker!' replied Mickey. 'And what about you?' He couldn't find the words – Martin had been a kid the last time they'd seen him, now he was a man. It wasn't just that he had filled out, but there was a confidence and maturity in his face. 'No wonder you fucked off to Australia with towns with names like Mount Buggery, Cockburn and Tittybang,' laughed Mickey. 'You must eat raw kangaroo meat for breakfast from the look of you!'

It was true.   Martin was tanned, lean, with hardness to his face that Mickey barely recognised. And his clothes – sharp, fashionable, tasteful. Whatever Martin was doing, he was doing all right at it.

Mickey tugged at the sleeve of Martin's elegant suit. 'What the hell do you get up to over there? Robbing banks, like Ned Kelly?'

Martin grinned. 'I leave that to you.' His face turned serious, with a touch of pride in his look. 'I've got my own freight business. Run a fleet of lorries across the desert, between the big cities.'

'What do they call them, road trains, right?'

Martin nodded.

'A fleet you say? How many's a fleet?'

'Twenty seven.'

Mickey shook his head in disbelief. This was his little brother he was talking to.

'How the fuck did you manage that?'

'Started off as a truck driver, after a few years I managed to scrimp and save and buy my own truck, then built it up from there.' He looked around, saw everyone else looking at them – Sharon, Terri, Mandy, Lizzie's grandchildren, Aunt Sheila and Johnnie, Aunt Rosie. 'But they've all heard this already. Let's get you a cup of tea or something.'

Mickey stood in front of the fireplace, looked around at his family. Jesus, how long he'd dreamed of this. 'Fuck tea!' he said. 'You're having a laugh, right? If someone doesn't give me a scotch and coke soon there's going to be trouble!'

His words broke the ice. Terri grinned, grabbed a glass, a bottle of scotch.

Sharon headed for the kitchen. 'I'll get some ice.'

One by one they all got their drinks, turned their eyes back to Mickey. He was back home, back in his element. He rested one elbow on the mantelpiece, held his drink up, swirled the ice slowly round. Surrounded by his family and best friends, all the people who were important to him. He'd never seen anything that looked as good! 'Here's to mum!' he said.

'To mum!'

They all drank. Mickey drained his glass in one go, the cool liquid sweet as honey as it slid down his throat. 'Right, fix me another of these and then let's get down to business.'

With drinks refilled, they all turned their eyes to Tommy. He looked nervous, suddenly the centre of attention for the whole family. 'Nan gave me something,' he said, almost apologetically. 'The last time I saw her.' He looked around at all the expectant faces. 'I think she knew, you know...' His voice trailed off.

Mickey stood close to him. 'What did she give you, son?'

Tommy reached in his pocket. 'There's a few things, but she said this was real important, that I was to read this to all of you, that you should all know about it.' He pulled out a couple of sheets of paper.

Mickey could see they were covered with Lizzie's spidery handwriting.

Tommy took a deep breath. 'Right. This is what she wrote…'

'This story goes back a long way – a couple of months before Bobby's death. In those days he used to hang around a bit with two blokes from the East End – Tommy Wolfson and Derrick Cooper. Real old time crooks they were, both had served time, both would skin their grandmothers for a fiver. But every now and then Bobby would have a job for them. He always said he wouldn't trust them as far as he could throw them, but he used them because they got the job done, however dirty it was. But this one time, they came to him, said they had a big job, a jewellers in the East End, would Bobby do it with them? Bobby checked it out, reckoned it seemed legit, so he agreed. I don't know what happened, but Bobby said it all went tits up, they all got away, but they didn't get much for their troubles…'

The Jag crawled down the narrow side street, Bobby Taylor at the wheel. There was no need to slow as they passed the jewellery shop, they were already moving at walking pace in the heavy traffic. Bobby turned his head, scanned the shop. It was quiet – a couple huddled under their umbrellas were peering in the window, but no one was inside. A bored shop assistant polished a glass counter.

'You can park round the corner,' said Wolfson. He was a slim Irishman with a mop of thick red hair, an angular face.

Bobby nodded, turned left up an alleyway, eased the car into a parking space.

Cooper rummaged in a bag, handed them both stockings, gloves. 'You sure you can handle the safe?'

Bobby nodded as he rolled the stocking up and tugged it onto the top of his head. 'The manager will open it, trust me.'

Cooper glared at Bobby with his dark eyes. 'All right then. Me and Tommy will clear out the cases up front.'

Bobby turned round, stared at the two of them. 'But don't be greedy – wait till I give the signal. Just keep watch until I tell you I've got the safe open, otherwise you'll set off the alarms.'

Wolfson and Cooper nodded impatiently. 'Yeah, yeah, we got it,' snapped Cooper. 'We're not fucking amateurs, you know!'

Bobby's look suggested that he thought otherwise, but he said nothing. He pulled the car keys out, dropped them on the floor of the car. He didn't want to be fumbling in his pocket for them when they got back, but around here your car would probably be gone in five minutes if you left it with the keys in the ignition. 'Let's go.'

Bobby was the first through the door, the stocking distorting his handsome features, spreading his nose further across his face than any fist had ever managed. 'Down on the fucking floor!' he yelled as the door slammed open, his gun pointing from one shop assistant to the other.

They were both kids – teenage girls – and not likely to give any trouble.

Bobby didn't give them a second glance as he strode across the floor, kicked open the door to the small back office, left Wolfson and Cooper to manage the front of the shop.

The manager look up, startled, as Bobby stormed in. He was small, in his sixties, with wisps of white hair clinging to the sides of his head. His hand started to slide towards the desk – Bobby grabbed him, picked him up by his shirt front, and threw him down in the corner of the office.

'Let's not try anything silly, all right? No alarms.'

The manager looked up, eyes full of fear, as Bobby crouched down in front of him.

'Now you know, and I know, that you got a big shipment of uncut diamonds in from Rotterdam this morning.'

The surprised look in the manager's eyes told Bobby all he needed to know.

'People talk, word gets around. Get over it.'

Bobby peered around the gloomy office, saw the safe in the far corner. He looked back at the manager. 'Got a wife? Kids?'

The manager nodded.

'What's your wife's name?'

The manager licked his lips, forced the word out. 'Sylvie.'

'Nice name.' Bobby nodded over towards the safe. 'So here's how it works. You open the safe. I get the diamonds. You claim it on your insurance, Sylvie gets to see you again. Do we have an agreement?'

The manager's eyes wandered to the safe then back again to Bobby.

Suddenly the gun was shoved in his face, jammed up against his cheek. 'The alternative is that you say no, I blow your brains all across that wall, and Sylvie gets to be a rich widow fucking anyone she wants.'

The manager stared at the gun, almost cross eyed it was so close to him, nodded weakly.

Bobby grinned, an evil grimace beneath his stocking mask. 'Attaboy. Let's go.' He hauled him to his feet, shoved him towards the safe. 'Chop, chop. We don't have all day.'

Wolfson stood over the two shop assistants, leering down at them. 'Wouldn't mind me a piece of these two,' he smirked.

Cooper glared at him. 'Keep your dick in your trousers and your mind on the fucking job.' Cooper was the more edgy of the two, glancing around nervously the whole time, constantly looking back towards the office. 'Isn't he done yet?'

Wolfson glanced at Cooper, then returned his gaze to the girl at his feet, her short skirt showing a good looking pair of legs. 'Just relax – he'll be out in a moment.'

'Well I just wish he'd hurry – '

Both of them froze as a passer-by stopped and peered in the shop window.

Wolfson glared at Cooper. 'Did you lock the fucking door?'

'Yes. I mean, I don't know...'

They both stared at the front door – the sign facing them still said "Closed" – to passers-by, it would read "Open".

The man stared long and hard at something in the window, then turned and pushed open the shop door.

'Fuck!'

He looked around in surprise as he entered, saw the two robbers behind the counters, their faces distorted by their masks.

'Oh my!' was all he said. He stared back and forth between them for a second, then turned and rushed out of the shop.

The gunshot hit him when he was half way out the door, slammed into his back. He crashed into the glass door, stumbled out into the street.

'Fuck!'

The two crooks stared at each other for a second, then raced out from behind the counter towards the door.

As they did so, the girl Wolfson had been eyeing reached up from the floor, pushed a button under the counter. Immediately, a bell rang, loud, insistent, over and over again.

The man they had shot tumbled out into the street, fell at the feet of two pedestrians, a pool of blood forming beneath him. A woman screamed, stared in horror at the body.

Wolfson and Cooper froze in the doorway.

'Now what?' gasped Cooper.

Wolfson shoved him into the street. 'The car. We'll meet him at the car!'

Bobby leaned over the manager's shoulder, calm as ever.

The manager span the dial and the door clicked open.

Bobby smiled, shoved him out the way, he was just about to look inside the safe when the gunshot went off. He let out a deep moan of annoyance. 'Fucking amateurs!'

He bent down, peered into the safe – there was a small, dark blue velvet bag on the top shelf, a neat pile of cash beside it. Bobby grabbed the cash, shoved it inside his jacket, then picked up the bag, shook it next to his ear, grinned. 'This it?'

The manager nodded.

'How much?'

'Two million, more or less.'

Bobby looked impressed.

Suddenly the alarm bell sounded. Calmly, Bobby opened the bag, tipped the contents into the palm of his hand. A pile of large, uncut diamonds gleamed in the dim light. 'Nice!' He slid them back into the bag, closed the bag and shoved it into the pocket of his trousers. 'Back door?'

The manager nodded to a dark corridor.

Without another word, or a glance back, Bobby hurried down the corridor, past a bucket and mop, a small bathroom. There was a fire door at the far end – without breaking stride Bobby kicked the metal push bar and the door swung open.

The gloomy light of the alleyway seemed bright after the dark corridor. Bobby glanced around – no one was there. He ripped the stocking off his head, shoved it in his pocket, started down the alleyway towards the car, a grin on his face. Just as he reached the end of the alleyway he stopped.

'Fucking wankers,' he muttered to himself.

He looked around. The alleyway was narrow, the fag end of all the shops and businesses, lined with overflowing rubbish bins, piles of broken down cardboard boxes. The rear of one shop had tape across the door, the unmistakable signs of a fire inside – blackened door, broken windows, the post box overflowing with junk mail.

Bobby paused, looked around one more time, then hurriedly pulled out the junk mail, shoved the small bag of diamonds in the bottom of the mail box, crammed the mail back in on top. With a last look around to make sure no one had seen him, he turned and jogged back to the car.

Bobby slammed the door of the Jag, scrambled round on the floor for the keys. 'What the fuck did you two cunts do?' he demanded as he started the car.

'Cooper forgot to lock the fucking door!' snarled Wolfson.

Bobby shook his head in irritation, slammed the car into first gear, roared away.

The other two leaned forward, faces eager, full of greed and excitement and fear. 'So did you get them?'

Bobby shook his head. 'No. The old cunt was slow as Christmas.'

'Jesus fucking Christ!'

Wolfson glared at him. 'You said you could get him to open it.'

'And you cunts were supposed to secure the front of the shop!' Bobby reached inside his jacket, pulled out the bundle of cash, and lobbed it into the back.

Wolfson caught it, looked suspiciously at Bobby. 'Where'd you get that?'

'The old bastard was counting his money when I came in.'

Still Wolfson looked suspicious.

Bobby glanced back at him in the rear view mirror, turned onto Holborn, their car blending into the busy London traffic. 'But if you don't want it, chuck it up here.'

Wolfson flicked through it. It was several thousand pounds. He glanced at Cooper, sitting beside him looking confused. 'No, we'll take it,' he said slowly.

Bobby scowled at him. 'You got something to say?'

Wolfson said nothing.

'What? You think I got the diamonds and aren't giving them to you?'

'I'm just wondering, is all,' said Wolfson softly.

Bobby slammed on the brakes, the car screeching to a halt. The black cab behind them almost rear-ended them. The cabbie pulled around them, leaning on his horn and cursing. 'Fucking idiot!'

Bobby turned around in his seat, eye-balled Wolfson. 'You think I got the diamonds and then stiffed you? Is that it? Then let's do it right now!'

He threw the door open, climbed out the car.

Wolfson opened the rear door, stood up slowly.

'Come on, fucking search me right here!'

Bobby peeled off his jacket, threw it at Wolfson, reached into his trouser pockets, pulled them out so they stuck out. 'Go on. Fucking search me!'

Cars pulled around them, a pedestrian stopped and stared.

Wolfson scowled. 'Not here!'

The wail of police sirens could be heard approaching.

'Yeah, right here, right now!' snarled Bobby, 'or never fucking mention it again!'

Wolfson sighed, patted Bobby's jacket, then threw it back at him with a nervous smile. 'OK, OK. I'm sorry.'

Bobby eye-balled him for a moment longer, then climbed back in the car.

As they moved forwards again, two police cars raced past them heading towards Hatton Garden.

Bobby glanced in the rear view mirror one last time. 'Don't you ever fucking question me again!'

Tommy took a deep breath, continued reading Lizzie's letter.

'I never really thought anything about it until a few weeks ago, when Wolfson and Cooper suddenly showed up. They reckoned Bobby DID get the goods, but then stitched them up over it. They said they had tracked the manager of the shop down, roughed him up, and he stuck to his story, that Bobby got the diamonds. I told them I had no idea, it was twenty years ago, and they could see that I wasn't living the life of Reilly on a million pounds worth of stolen diamonds, so that was it. But I kept my ears open, and started putting two and two together, asked around about those two. It seems they were very interested in Kenny and Joey. Of course, Joey's become a drunk and Kenny's disappeared to Upminster, but I think there's something to it, and the word is that they'll be looking for Mickey when he returns. I know you know nothing about this, Mickey, but I just wanted you to know – Wolfson and Cooper are still out there, they think someone in this family's got something of theirs, and they won't stop until they find it.

We all thought that the day we laid Bobby in the ground all the horrors would die. I suppose he's laughing now, seeing how he's still screwing us all up.

I love you all,
Mum XX'

Tommy slowly folded the letter, held it out to Mickey. 'Sorry to be the one bringing bad news.'

Mickey took the letter, looked at it thoughtfully for a moment before slipping it into his pocket. 'Not your fault, son,' he said. 'I'm proud that she trusted you enough to give you this.'

'I remember that night!' said Martin suddenly.

All eyes turned towards him.

'What the hell you talking about?' demanded Mickey.

'I haven't thought about it in years, but it just came back to me as Tommy was talking. Me and Georgie were in our room, wide awake when we should have been sleeping, when we heard dad come in…

Georgie crept to the top of the stairs, Martin at his heels. A floorboard creaked, and Georgie turned quickly, his finger to his lips. 'Keep quiet. If dad hears us you know he'll give us a beating!'

The boys knew they should be in bed, knew that Bobby would be mad if he found them wandering around and spying on him, but they just couldn't resist – you never knew what he'd be up to. Sometimes he brought some of his dodgy friends' home, one time they'd seen him sitting playing with a gun.

It was late – really late – and Bobby was taking care to be quiet for once, but something had disturbed Martin and he'd been awake in an instant, listening. He heard Bobby come in, the door close, then silence.

He glanced over at the clock – it was almost three o'clock. He tried to get back to sleep, but he was too awake. Then he noticed Georgie sitting up, his thick hair tousled, his brown eyes gleaming in the dark.

'What was that?'

'Dad coming in,' hissed Martin. 'Wanna go see what he's up to?'

Georgie nodded, slid his feet into his slippers as he climbed out of bed.

They crept out onto the landing and down the first couple of stairs. As long as they didn't go too far down the stairs, they were pretty much invisible from below, and could peer into the living room.

Georgie sat down on the stairs, Martin peering over his shoulder.

'What's he doing,' hissed Martin impatiently. He couldn't see past Georgie.

'Hush! He's just sitting,' Georgie told him.

Martin squeezed up closer behind Georgie. He could smell his aftershave, the warmth coming off his body. He liked being close to Georgie. Mickey was definitely the tougher of his brothers, but Georgie made you feel safe, loved.

He was right. Bobby was just sitting, staring at his hands, the stub of a cigarette dangling from the corner of his mouth.

Suddenly he looked up, as though he'd heard something, and for a moment Martin thought he'd seen them – his heart stopped. Bobby had a wicked temper, and Martin had lost count of the number of beatings he'd had – there were times when his body was black and blue from Bobby's abuse.

But Bobby was not looking at Georgie and Martin, his gaze was off in the distance somewhere.

He suddenly dug in his pocket, pulled out a small, dark velvet bag. Martin peered past Georgie. 'What's that?'

Georgie said nothing.

Bobby looked thoughtfully at the bag, then gently tugged the strings to open it, tipped the contents out into one of his huge hands. Martin had to fight to suppress a gasp as the diamonds sparkled in the light. 'What are those?' he squeaked.

Before Georgie could reply, Bobby froze, looked up towards them, then quickly dropped the gems back into the bag, stood up, headed towards the mantelpiece.

'What's he doing?'

Georgie put his fingers to his lips. 'Quiet!'

Mickey looked at Martin. 'So you definitely saw the diamonds, but you never actually saw where he put them?'

Martin nodded. 'But I swear, Georgie saw.'

Mickey's eyes narrowed. 'Georgie saw?'

'I'm sure of it. He never said, but I always knew he'd seen. There was something about him, that little smirk he had when he knew something you didn't.'

Mickey sighed. 'Well if Georgie knows, he'll carry that secret with him to the grave.'

Martin looked puzzled. 'Why wouldn't he tell you?'

Mickey looked towards his sisters. 'You haven't told him?'

'I know he's locked up,' said Martin.

Terri shook her head. 'Sorry, I should have told you more. But you were so bleeding far away, it didn't seem right to burden you with all the gory details...' Her face looked sad. 'You'd escaped, got away. I didn't want you feeling guilty, like you had to come back or something.'

Martin furrowed his brows. 'What's the matter with Georgie? What haven't you told me?'

The other three looked at each other, said nothing. Finally Mickey spoke. 'Why don't we take you to see him? I need to go visit him now that I'm out.'

'You can't just tell me?'

'There are some things you have to see for yourself,' replied Mickey firmly. 'But first I need to go see Kenny, see what he can tell me about this nonsense.'

Tommy caught his dad's eye.   'There's a couple of other things,' he said, 'from Nan.'

'Go on then.'

'She said they were for you. Private, like.'

Mickey looked at the family, their expectant faces. 'All right. We'll do it later, this evening.'

Tommy looked uncomfortable. He'd held onto these secrets for too long already, but he nodded. You didn't argue with Mickey once he'd made a decision.

Mickey and Kenny

Just being behind the wheel of a car put a smile on Mickey's face. It was the simple things he'd missed when he was inside – waking up when you want to, getting in the car and going for a drive, wandering down to the local newsagents to pick up a paper.

But there was a downside too that Mickey had a hard time admitting even to himself – at times he felt overwhelmed. Not only had everything changed, but there were also too many choices to make. What to eat, what to wear, what to do. In prison everything is done for you, no one asks you what you want, you just do what you're told, eat what they give you, get up when the bell rings, go to bed at lights out. In some ways it's a lot easier than real life.

The first night he was home he had almost frozen when Mandy had asked him what he wanted for dinner. She started rattling off choices, all the things he used to like – lasagne, scampi, a bit of Indian take-away – then suddenly she'd seen his face. She was a smart girl that one, knew when to push and when to back off.

'Tell you what,' she said with a smile. 'Why don't I just do you some steak and chips? That was always one of your favourites.'

Mickey gave a grateful smile, turned back to the TV. 'That will be great, thanks love...'

And then he'd had to chat with Tommy. The other papers Tommy had were his mum's will - no surprises there - and a hand-written agreement between his dad and Big Frankie, the gypsy. Apparently they shared ownership of a piece of land off the A12 in Stratford. Of much more interest to Mickey was the big envelope full of cash that Tommy gave him.

He'd known that his mum was putting away some of the cash that came in from his businesses - she'd been doing it long before Bobby died, and had continued to do so once Mickey was inside - but the surprise was how much she had in there.

When Mickey counted it out - rolls and bundles of fifties - he found that she had managed to save over eighty grand. For someone just released from the nick it was a tidy sum, enough to take the pressure off for quite a while.

Mickey grinned as he pictured it - his mum with all that money, then checked his speedo. He was doing over eighty, enjoying the sheer pleasure of speed, but there was no point in getting nicked his second day out of prison. He slowed down, thought about Kenny. He hadn't called first, felt it was better to turn up unexpected – he liked the element of surprise, especially if there was something a bit dodgy going on.

And anyway, Kenny had always been a bit of a strange one. He lived across the road from Mickey when they were kids. Kenny was an only child, adopted at six months old, always got what he wanted, his mum never said 'No' to him, he was spoilt rotten, her gift she called him.

Kenny never said anything to his mum about where he'd come from when she was alive, but when his mum and dad died he wanted to find out who his real mum and dad were, just to find out more about himself, his history, who he was. He said he couldn't do that to his parents while they were alive, he would feel like he was betraying them.

His mum had told him that all she knew was that was his mum came from London and his dad was an American who'd fucked off back to the USA and left her with the baby. No wonder Kenny hated the Americans and held a big grudge against them. He was always slagging them off, the people, the country, the films, the president, he hated anything to do with America.

When his adoptive mum and dad died they left him the house, he got a nice few quid, decided to up sticks and move away, ended up in a big, beautiful house in Upminster. Mandy was well jealous when they moved, all she went on about was buying their council house, doing it up and moving. But with Mickey inside, it wasn't possible. Anyway, he didn't want to move, Dagenham was where he wanted to be, it was his home, his turf.

Kenny always acted the hard man, and could take care of himself if he had to, but behind Kenny's toughness there was a real gentleness, he was a very polite, quiet man. He and Mickey had been really close when they were younger, Mickey was the best man when Kenny got married, Mickey and Mandy were godparents to Caroline, the oldest of Kenny's kids, and Kenny and Collette were Godparents to Tommy. That had caused a right old ruckus, Mickey and Mandy had rowed about who the godparents should be. She said they should keep it to family, Mickey said that Kenny was part of his fucking family. In the end Tommy had two lots of godparents so Mandy could choose the other ones.

Before Mickey was banged up, the four of them went out together all the time. Mandy and Colette got on really well, and the kids were round about the same age so they had a lot in common.

They would go out for a meal or down the pub, even had a few good caravan holidays down in Clacton with them and the kids.

Mickey thought about the night Kenny's daughter Caroline was born. Mickey picked Kenny up outside Upney hospital. He came out of the hospital, his face was beaming, he looked like he had just won the pools.

They gave each other a huge bear hug, Kenny grinning like a maniac. 'Mickey I can't believe I'm a dad,' he said as they climbed into Mickey's Jag. 'You should see her, she's beautiful. I had her in my arms, she's so tiny I was scared I was gonna hurt her. Perfect she is.'

At that time Mandy was pregnant, and Mickey was shit scared about what it would be like to be a dad for the first time.

Kenny grinned at him. 'You wait, it will be happening to you soon. I can't explain the feeling but it's…' His eyes filled with tears of happiness. 'It's fucking amazing'.

Kenny started talking about the details of the birth, but Mickey started to feel a bit queasy. He wasn't into all that side of it. 'All right, mate,' he said quickly, 'I don't need to hear all the gory details.'

Then suddenly, out of the blue, Kenny started bawling like a baby.

Mickey pulled over to the side of the road 'What the fuck's wrong?' Mickey stared at him.

'There's nothing wrong with Collette or the baby, is there? Something you didn't tell me?'

Kenny shook his head, wiped his nose on his sleeve. 'No, no, it's me with the fucking problem.'

'Alright,' said Mickey, wondering what the fuck this was all about. 'Calm down a bit and stop crying, then tell me what's so fucking bad.'

Kenny looked up, met his eyes. 'The second I saw her, the second I held her in my arms, I loved her.'

'Yeah, yeah, so you said. So why all the blubbering?'

'What I can't understand, is that woman who gave birth to me, my mum, how could she give me away, how could she abandon me? Why didn't she love me? What's wrong with me, Mickey? What's so bad about me that she didn't want me or love me?'

Mickey didn't know what to say to him, felt choked for him. He took a deep breath. 'Enough of that old bollocks. There's nothing wrong with you, it's her who had the problem. But you need to forget about her right now, think about you. You've just become a dad. So put that smile back on your face, we're going to go wet the baby's head. Right?'

Kenny nodded as Mickey pulled back into traffic. 'I could do with a drink,' he admitted.

'More than one, I hope,' laughed Mickey.

He switched the radio on – they were playing 'Sweet Caroline.'

They both began singing along:

'Sweet Caroline, hands, touching hands, reaching out, touching you, sweet Caroline.'

Kenny suddenly smiled. 'That's what I'm going to call her. Caroline!'

And they did, their little girl became Caroline.

Mickey drove through Upminster, looking around. He could see why Kenny had moved there, why Mandy wanted to. It was a different class. Big flash houses, big flash cars, and long, wide roads. Fuck, some of the gardens were as big as old Dagenham Park!

It was a proper posh place, all very nice and clean. No rubbish flying around the streets, no overflowing bins. No kids hanging around on the corners of the streets, no vandalism or graffiti anywhere. No traffic, no sirens or Old Bill, no noise or chaos, just peace and quiet.

Mickey pulled up outside Kenny's house, behind Colette's Mercedes. She used it to run the kids to and from school and to all their after school clubs. She always said to Mickey that she felt like their cab service – all she needed was a hat and she could be their personal chauffer. Parked next to it was Kenny's BMW. They're doing all right, thought Mickey.

Mickey got out of his car, glad to stretch his legs, walked up the driveway. He reached for the doorbell then paused – the door was open a couple of inches. Strange.

Mickey paused for a second, then slowly pushed the door open.

'Kenny?' His voice echoed through the large house. 'Kenny? Collette? It's Mickey. Mickey Taylor.'

There was no reply.

'Bet you didn't expect to see me turning up at your door, did you?'

Silence.

An uneasy feeling settled over Mickey.

He pushed the front door wide open. 'Kenny? It's me, Mickey,' he repeated as he stepped inside.

There was no one to be seen.

The hallway was highly polished parquet flooring, elegant cream coloured walls, a large glass light fitting overhead.

Mickey tiptoed forwards, all senses on high alert, paused by the living room door, took a deep breath, then pushed the door open.

It took a moment for it to register. Mickey's eyes could see it, but his brain wasn't having it.

Kenny was lying dead on the floor, his chest blown apart, blood and guts splattered on the walls, and all over his cream shag pile carpet.

Behind him was Collette, sitting upright in one of the expensive leather armchairs, her throat sliced open, blood soaking her chest. There was an electrical cord tied around her, holding her to the chair, gaffer tape around her ankles, and a cluster of cigarette burns on her face. She'd been tortured before she died.

Mickey sank to his knees. He couldn't move. What the fuck had happened?

He took a few deep breaths trying to calm himself. He had to get a grip, take it easy. Who had done this? And what the fuck was he going to do about it?

Mickey felt the bile rise in his throat as he stared into Kenny's cold dead eyes. He fought it back down as the icy self-control that was Mickey's trademark kicked in.

Mickey's car was parked up outside, if that got reported and traced back to him, the murder squad would have him in straight away. This was a fucking nightmare!

Mickey stood up quickly, looked down at Kenny for the last time. He was back in control now.

Kenny was dead, there wasn't anything Mickey could do for him. But he would find out who did this, and why, and he would lay those fuckers in the ground.

Mickey turned on his heel and strode out the house. He paused in the doorway to wipe the door where his hand had touched it, then walked back to his car, casual as could be, thankful for how quiet the neighbourhood was.

So much for a few days to relax and adjust to being back outside. Mickey was right back into the thick of it, up to his neck.

Georgie

Martin looked thoughtfully at Mickey. 'Why didn't you tell me this before?'

'When? Replied Mickey without taking his eyes off the road. 'At the funeral? On a fucking postcard to Australia from Parkhurst?'

Driving through the leafy lanes of Nottinghamshire, it seemed incongruous to think that they would soon be in one of the most notorious high security psychiatric hospitals in Britain.

Martin gazed at the trees flashing past. 'So you haven't seen him since you were, you know, inside?'

This time Mickey did glance over. 'We make a great pair, eh? Me banged up for murder, Georgie in a nut house for fucking Charlie Taylor to death?'

'So we have no idea what state he's in, whether he'll even recognise us?'

Mickey nodded, slowed the car down as the long, high fence of Rampton opened up into a pair of metal gates. 'We'll soon find out.'

'This is fucking disconcerting!' growled Mickey under his breath as they were escorted through another locked door. 'I've only just got out of somewhere like this!'

The institutional battleship grey doors, magnolia walls, echoing voices in the distance, the constant slamming of doors. Mickey's skin was crawling as they were taken to the interview room. 'He doesn't get many visitors,' the orderly told them as he led them down the drab corridor. 'Doctor's not sure how he'll react, especially after the last lot.' He held open the door to the visiting room, Mickey and Martin followed him inside.

There had been some attempt made to make the room less institutional - cheap armchairs in a cheery bright blue material. Some dodgy paintings of flowers and birds on the walls, a small plastic vase of fake flowers, but there was no disguising the bars on the windows. Even a cursory glance around the room showed that there was nothing there that could be used as a weapon, no glass, nothing breakable.

The orderly pointed to a couple of chairs. 'Make yourselves comfortable, I'll bring him in.'

Mickey watched nervously as the orderly locked the door behind them, unlocked a door at the far end of the room, and disappeared. He glanced up.

Cameras in the corners of the room covered every angle.

Martin dropped down into one of the chairs, looked comfortable, relaxed, but Mickey paced nervously, gazed out the window at the damp grass. 'Leave the talking to me,' he ordered. 'I know the way Georgie's mind works.'

Martin glanced up at him. 'He went fucking psycho, Mickey! You really think you know how he thinks?'

Mickey span around. 'I don't know! But I did know Georgie…' His words trailed off as the door behind them slowly opened. Two orderlies appeared, but Mickey barely noticed them. It was the woman between them that he had his eyes on.

She was dressed to a T, make-up, hair, everything. Georgie. Samantha. Samantha. Georgie. Just the way Mickey last remembered her.

He could see Martin starting to react, confused, even though he had explained that Georgie was hidden behind this façade, this persona. Before Mickey could speak, Samantha had scanned the room, sized them both up.

'Michael Taylor, as I live and breathe!' she gasped.

'Samantha.'

Samantha gazed into his eyes. It was disconcerting - Georgie's unmistakable brown eyes, hidden inside this other person.

'So they finally let you out?' she said softly.

'I did my time.'

Samantha spun around, her eyes examining Martin. For a second Martin caught a glimpse of recognition, surprise in Samantha's eyes. 'Oh my,' she said softly, dropping into a chair opposite him. 'I didn't expect to see you.'

Mickey watched curiously. It was Mickey who had mostly dealt with Georgie when he had first come to Rampton - Lizzie couldn't bear to see what he had become, Sharon was never going to be the one to visit him, and Terri struggled with it. But Martin - Martin hadn't seen him like this, it was a total shock to him. He just knew, remembered the old Georgie, up the betting shop and down the pub with his mates.

Samantha looked flustered. 'When did you - I mean, I thought you were...'

Martin glanced up at Mickey, unsure what to say.

Mickey dropped down into the chair next to her. 'Martin got back a couple of weeks ago. He came back for...' Mickey found the words difficult to say. A part of him still struggled to accept that his mum was dead. He forced the words out. 'For mum's funeral.'

Samantha's eyes slowly turned to Mickey. Incomprehension passed across her face. She looked between Mickey and Martin, then stood slowly, her hand to her mouth, stumbled to the window.

Mickey climbed to his feet, followed Samantha, stopped just behind her. 'I'm sorry, I didn't know of a good way to tell you.'

Samantha was still facing the window. Suddenly she turned, moved quickly towards Mickey. The orderlies stepped forward, alert, ready to intervene, but Samantha simply threw her arms around Mickey's neck, buried her face into his shoulder, sobbed. 'Oh, Mickey!' was all she said.

Mickey held his brother tight as he cried on his shoulder. For a moment it was Georgie, it was his brother, he could feel that connection, that presence, that part of him that had been missing for so long. Maybe, just maybe, thought Mickey, as he held tight to Georgie, this would be the thing that would break through the barrier? The thing that would break through the visage of Samantha that Georgie had built up to protect himself?

Then just as quickly the hope was gone. Georgie straightened up and was instantly Samantha once again. The husky voice, the poise - a quick dab of the eyes on her sleeve, and she was back in control. 'Thank you for coming to let us know,' she said, her voice brittle, forced. Then she turned on her heel and headed back towards the door.

'Georgie!'

Samantha ignored Mickey, kept on walking 'We're done here,' she told the orderlies.

Mickey gazed at her back in frustration, bit his lip, forced the words out. 'Samantha, please!'

She had reached the door, paused, and looked back at Mickey with those cold, appraising eyes that he had come to hate.

'There was something else I wanted to talk to you about.'

She shrugged dismissively, gestured to the orderlies to unlock the door.

'There were some blokes, they came and bothered mum, gave her a hard time. '

The orderlies had unlocked the door.

'That's not right,' pleaded Mickey. 'I want to find them. I need you to tell me if -'

Samantha paused in the doorway, looked back at Mickey. 'They came sniffing around here, looking for Georgie.'

'When?' Mickey couldn't keep the hope out of his voice.

Samantha glanced at the orderlies for an answer.

'About six weeks ago,' one of the orderlies told Mickey.

The other chuckled quietly. 'Our Samantha here sent them away with a flea in their ear!'

'And a scratch down the face of the one of them - Irish prick he was, kept pushing Samantha. She showed him, didn't you, love?'

Samantha gave a cool smile. 'He was quite ungentlemanly, wouldn't take no for an answer. That's one thing I can't tolerate.'

'What did they ask you about?' asked Mickey eagerly.

Samantha's eyes were still on him, that amused, half mocking smile playing at the corners of her mouth. 'I can read you like a book, Mickey.'

Mickey licked his lips, glanced at Martin, then back at Samantha. 'Did you tell them anything?'

Samantha shrugged. 'I don't know anything.'

'And Georgie?'

Again the smile. 'You're going to have to do better than that, Mickey.' And with that she turned on her heel and sauntered out of the room.

'Wait!' Mickey burst forward, towards the door.

The orderly held out his hand. 'You can't go that way, mate!'

'Samantha!'

The orderly shook his head. 'No point, mate. Once she's made up her mind, she ain't going to change it for anyone.'

The heavy door closed with a soft click, leaving Mickey and Martin alone.

Martin let out a deep sigh. 'Well that was fucking weird!'

Mickey said nothing, jammed his hands deep in the pockets of his coat, thoughtful, angry, confused.

The remaining orderly led them towards the door, glanced back and forth between the two of them. 'You should be happy you caught him on one of his good days.'

Martin gave him a sharp glance. 'What are his bad days like?'

The orderly shook his head as he opened the door, guided them out into the long corridor. 'Believe me, you don't want to know!'

Joey

Joey shuffled along the pavement, hands shoved in his pockets. Another day, another struggle to get drunk, get high, get hold of anything that would dull the pain. He hated the way people looked at him as he stumbled past them. He knew what they were thinking – druggie, bum, tosser. He deserved it. He'd been sleeping rough for so long that he couldn't even remember the last time he'd had a shower, brushed his hair, and cleaned his teeth. He knew he must stink, look a right old sight, but he couldn't smell himself any more, and most of his teeth were gone, so what was there to brush anyway?

He spotted a half-finished cigarette butt on the pavement, scrambled to grab it before anyone stepped on it, heard – and ignored – the curses of a couple of pedestrians as he got under their feet.

Joey didn't care. A half a cigarette meant a couple of minutes of escape, a couple of minutes to focus on the pure pleasure of drawing the nicotine in. Then holding it in his lungs as long as possible, then slowly, slowly letting it out. Thinking of nothing but the sheer pleasure of the smoke. It wasn't booze, it wasn't drugs, but it was something...

His trophy gripped tight in his hand he shuffled down a quiet side street. He wedged himself in between a stack of rubbish bins behind a Chinese restaurant. He set the stump of the cigarette between his lips and lit it with his disposable lighter, just about the only thing he owned.

As he drew in the smoke he relaxed, closed his eyes. Once he'd enjoyed the cigarette he'd rummage through the bins, find something to eat, maybe something he could sell for a few quid, enough for a bottle of booze. He wasn't fussy what he drank, anything would do – you drink enough of it, fast enough, you can find oblivion.

He was desperate for a hit, it had been a few days, but he was out of cash, out of credit. He'd have to break into somewhere and find some cash or something he could fence, he was getting desperate. But for now there was just the cigarette, the smoke flowing in and out of his lungs, five minutes of peace.

'Fuck me! Would you look at the state of you?'

Joey opened his eyes, peered up. The light was in his eyes, he couldn't see who was talking to him. He peered into the glare, saw only a large figure in a dark overcoat leaning over him, face hidden.

'Fuck off!' he snarled.   He was pissed off.   The intruder had disturbed him, ruined the only few minutes of peace he might enjoy that day.

But the intruder didn't leave – instead he crouched down, peered into Joey's face. 'I can't fucking believe it,' he muttered.   'What the fuck happened to you, Joey?'

Joey looked closer at the face - the voice was strangely familiar. 'Dangerous?' How could that be? But it sure as hell sounded like Mickey, looked like him. 'I thought you was inside?' coughed Joey.

'I was. Now I'm back out – and doing a lot better than you by the look of it.'   Mickey wasn't getting any closer than he needed to.   Even from a few feet away Joey smelt awful.

Joey smiled, revealing a row of blackened broken teeth. 'When did they let you out?'

'Last week.'

Joey nodded slowly, suddenly brightened. 'You don't have anything on you, do you? You know, a drop of booze or something?'   He licked his lips, peered anxiously up at Mickey.

Mickey sighed.   He'd been warned that Joey was in a right old state, but nothing could have prepared him for this. 'No, I don't have anything on me, Joey, and from the looks of you, it's the last thing you fucking need.'

Still Joey peered up at him.   'You couldn't lend me a few quid, could you?   I'm a bit short right now…'

'Lend you?' Mickey couldn't keep the edge out of his voice. 'You mean give you some dosh so you can get high?'

'Ahh, Mickey, don't be too hard on me, you don't know what it's like.'

Mickey glared at him, felt like gagging from the smell. 'I can see exactly what it's like,' he replied. 'Who did you talk to Joey? What the fuck happened?'

Joey's face snapped shut. He scowled, looked down at his stained trousers. 'If you're not going to help me, just fuck off and leave me alone!'

'I'm not going anywhere Joey. I need to know what the fuck happened!'

Joey said nothing, stared down at his filthy, cracked hands.

'They killed Kenny,' said Mickey softly. 'Shot him at close range with a shotgun, blew half his chest off. And Colleen too. Tortured her, then sliced her throat wide open.'

Still Joey said nothing, but his breathing quickened as the memories flooded over him. A single tear rolled down his cheek.

'I need to know if it's Cooper and Wolfson, need to know what the fuck is going on – they'll be coming after me next,' continued Mickey, 'and I need to be ready for the cunts.'

'I didn't want to tell them nothing, Mickey,' Joey gasped suddenly. 'But they made me. They came to the pub one night, just as I was closing, I was by myself. They must have been watching me for a while, knew when to catch me alone…'

'Gentlemen, it's time to leave' said Joey impatiently. The three strangers had been drinking quietly for the past hour or so. He'd asked them to leave several times, but they kept on drinking. They carried on talking quietly among themselves. Now they were the last ones in the pub.

Joey wasn't worried – two of them were older, in their sixties, and the third one, well, he was a big bloke and he looked a bit suspect, Joey had him figured as a poof. And anyway, Joey had a baseball bat and a shotgun under the counter, both within easy reach. In twenty years of running the pub he'd never had any trouble that he couldn't sort out for himself, no one he couldn't get out the door when push came to shove.

But these three had really pushed it, and now Joey was growing impatient. 'All right,' he told them. 'Out!'

And that's when one of the old fuckers suddenly pulled a gun. One minute Joey was getting ready to throw the cunts out, the next he was staring down the barrel of a handgun.

Still, he didn't panic. If they wanted to rob him, that was their funeral. Plenty of regulars had seen them in there that evening, they'd track them down soon enough, and then the bastards would pay.

'Do you really think this is such a good idea?' said Joey. 'Half the fucking pub has seen you.'

But the old bastard with the cold eyes just stared at him. There was something disconcerting about him, he had the cold eyes of a fucking psycho, like a shark, or a crocodile, some big predator that killed without even thinking about it. For the first time Joey felt a shiver of fear. 'It doesn't matter who's seen us, Joey,' he said softly, 'because you're not going to tell anyone we came to visit.' He had a lilting, Irish accent. 'So why don't you get your hands away from that shotgun and come on out from behind the bar?'

Joey had been edging closer to the shotgun, but seeing the look in the old geezer's eyes, he knew that he would shoot Joey as soon as look at him.

Joey put his hands on the bar. 'OK, OK, no need to get lairy about it.'

'And give us the keys,' commanded the Irish geezer.

Joey edged out from behind the bar, set the keys on the table. The other old guy hurried over and locked the doors. The big poof said nothing, just smiled at Joey.

'What the fuck are you looking at?' snarled Joey.

The geezer just kept on smiling.

'Why don't we all just take a deep breath?' said the Irish bloke with the gun. 'We just want to ask you a few questions, Joey.'

'Who the fuck are you?'

'I'm Tommy Wolfson,' replied the bloke with the gun, 'and this is Derrick Cooper.' He nodded towards the other old guy. 'We're old friends of Bobby Taylor.' Wolfson gave a cold smile. 'And him,' he gestured towards the big poof, 'we just call him Clemence.'

Joey waited, wondering what two old mates of Bobby Taylor might want with him. But at the same time he had a growing feeling of unease spreading out from his gut.

All of a sudden the three of them moved closer – the gun was shoved into Joey's gut, and Wolfson's cold eyes stared at him from close up. 'We need to ask you some questions, and you will answer them.' Clemence's strong hands grabbed Joey's arms from behind, there was the ripping sound of gaffer tape, and his wrists were bound tight together. He was shoved down into a chair, Clemence behind him, one big hand resting lightly on his shoulder.

'You've been shooting your mouth off, Joey, about a little job you did for Bobby Taylor when you were a lad.'

Cold sweat broke out on Joey's brow. He'd kept that secret for years. Bobby Taylor had been dead for almost twenty years now. Then when his name came up in conversation in the bar a few weeks ago, well, what could it hurt to tell that old story about how he and Kenny had done a few jobs for Bobby back in the day?

'I knew Bobby,' bluffed Joey. 'What of it?'

'Everyone knew Bobby,' said Wolfson. 'But you did some jobs for him. One job in particular…'

Joey knew exactly what they were talking about. It was out of the ordinary at the time – Bobby had given them five hundred each to retrieve a little bag from an old letter box up in Hatton Garden. He'd told them not to look in the bag, but five hundred quid for a pick-up was a lot of money, and the bag was so small, so tempting… He could still remember the wide eyed wonder as he and Kenny had peered at the diamonds.

'I've no idea what you're talking about,' Joey told him.

Wolfson just smiled. 'Of course you don't. That's why we brought Clemence, to help jog your memory.'

Joey looked uneasily at the big man. He didn't look tough, but you never knew.

'Don't worry, Clemence isn't going to beat you. That's not his stock in trade.'

Without warning they grabbed Joey, manhandled him across one of the tables, face down. Wolfson and Cooper held him down while Clemence stood behind Joey, ripped his trousers and pants down.

Joey's face was pressed against the table, his view blocked by Cooper's body, but he knew what was coming next, knew it even before the excruciating pain seared through his body as Clemence thrust into him.

As Joey struggled, tried to choke back the screams that were trying to burst out of him, Wolfson leaned over, his face close to Joey's. 'Yes, Clemence has an entirely different skill set. And as you can tell, he's a very big boy.'

Joey looked up at Mickey, his face covered in tears. 'He buggered the shit out of me, Mickey. I don't know how long it lasted, but he just did it over and over again. You know I'd never grass on anyone, but I had to tell them, Mickey, I had to. It was the only way to make him stop.'

Mickey nodded slowly. Now he knew why Joey had gone downhill so fast, what had destroyed him – and he also knew that he couldn't tell a soul. Staring into Joey's eyes he could see the last remains of the friend he'd once known, lurking deep within the shattered shell that cowered before him.

'We need to get you straightened out,' said Mickey softly. 'Get you cleaned up, into rehab.'

Joey shook his head violently. 'No way. No fucking way, Mickey. I don't want to get clean. The only time that memory doesn't haunt me is when I'm drunk or high. You can't take that away from me.'

Mickey shook his head. 'What can I do, Joey? I've got to do something.'

Joey held up a shaking hand, made the shape of a gun, turned and pointed it at his own forehead, pulled the imaginary trigger.

Mickey took a step back, shook his head, shocked. 'No, I can't do that. There's got to be another way that we can –'

Joey cut him off. 'I know you're always tooled up, Mickey. Do it right now, please!'

Mickey rocked back on his heels, stood up, and rubbed his forehead. 'Jesus, Joey, you don't know what you're fucking asking.'

Joey looked up at him, his tortured eyes searching Mickey's face. 'I know exactly what I'm asking,' he said softly.

Mickey paced backwards and forwards in front of him. Joey couldn't ask this, they'd known each other for their whole fucking lives! How could he do this to him?

'Mickey?'

Mickey stopped, looked down at Joey.

'The fucker, Clemence. He's got AIDS. I've got AIDS.'

Mickey froze.

'I've not got long either way. Either the booze and drugs will kill me, or the AIDS will kill me, or some thugs will beat me to death for sport. You'll just be ending the suffering for me.' He forced his ragged breath out. 'Please?'

Still Mickey said nothing, but the weight of his gun, usually such a reassuring feeling against his chest, now pressed heavy, a physical presence calling to him, demanding to be answered.

'I know you don't owe me Mickey – I grassed you to those cunts – but you're the only person who can help me out of this, give me some peace.'

Mickey stopped, looked up and down the alleyway.   It was early morning, the restaurant wouldn't open for a couple more hours. No one had passed them the whole time he and Joey had been talking. If he was going to do it...

With one smooth motion Mickey reached inside his coat, grabbed the gun, aimed it at Joey, his hand unwavering, the barrel pointed directly between his eyes.

Joey's gaze never flinched as he stared up at Mickey. 'Thanks, mate,' he whispered.

Mickey softly caressed the trigger, then gently squeezed it.

The bang echoed in his ears, and Joey's grateful face lingered in his mind for hours afterwards.

Mickey

Mickey had to go somewhere, do something. He couldn't go home, couldn't face his family. He spent the day wandering from one boozer to another, sitting, thinking, horrified by what he'd done, unsure what his next move should be. For the first time in his life he felt in over his head, was second guessing himself. Eventually, around eight o'clock that night, he wound up at the Epping Forest Country Club.

He knew Miranda and her mates would be there, knew he should stay away, but he'd reached a point where he just couldn't fight it any longer. Everything in his life seemed fucked up, he just needed a friendly face, someone who wouldn't judge him, wouldn't question him. And ever since the funeral, wherever he was, whatever he was doing, he found himself thinking about her. And every time he thought about her his heart raced and his body tingled.

Sure enough, half way through the night, Miranda showed up with a few of her posh mates. Just by looking at them you could tell they were from money, a different class. It was something in the way they moved, the way they looked, they had class written all over them.

Mickey sat quietly in the corner, watching Miranda, trying not to stare. He didn't want her catching him, not yet at least. She looked sensational, dressed to please as usual - a short, figure hugging skirt that showed off her long legs, and a black blouse, the top two buttons open, that allowed anyone who wanted to catch an eyeful. It didn't take long before some local blokes came sniffing around, buying drinks, making excuses to lean forward and gaze down the front of her blouse.

At first Miranda was acting cool, not very interested, but then she spotted Mickey. He gave her a wave, but didn't come over, and suddenly she was all over one of the blokes. He was looking at her like a love sick puppy, and she started really playing up to him, giving it the old come on, leaning forward, pouting, and brushing her hand across his chest.

When the bloke disappeared to the gents, Miranda came over to where Mickey was sitting. 'Why didn't you come over and say hello?' Her voice was challenging.

Mickey shrugged. 'You looked like you had plenty of company.'

Miranda gave him a sideways look. 'Not the company I want.'

Mickey ignored her comment. Simply seeing her had got him heated up, the last thing he wanted to do was give her encouragement. 'Who's that bloke you can't keep your hands off?' he asked.

Miranda grinned. 'That's Josh. He loves me dearly.' She took a sip of her drink, looked up at Mickey through her long eyelashes. 'Jealous are you, Mickey?'

He laughed. 'Jealous, me? No, but you're making yourself look like a proper slag the way you're giving it to him.'

Miranda looked him straight in the eyes. 'Come on, Mickey! Admit it! The truth is you want me.'

He started to argue, but she cut him off, slid close to him. He could smell her perfume, wanted to push her way but couldn't. 'You know what I'm saying is true,' she purred, 'you just don't have the bollocks to admit it.' She leaned over, kissed him lightly on the lips and ran her hand up his leg. 'Fourteen years without sex? You must be so horny,' she cooed, then turned and skipped back to the bar to rejoin her friends, knowing his eyes were all over her.

Mickey sat brooding, trying not to look at her, but unable to help himself. Fuck it! He hated it when a bloody woman was right like that! He did fancy her something rotten, she did something to him that no other woman had ever done, not even Mandy. Sex with Mandy was OK, but that was all it had ever been, OK. And since he'd got out of prison, when he did it with Mandy it was Miranda he was imagining, Miranda he was fantasizing about, Miranda naked beneath him, Miranda sucking him off...

The dickhead of a bloke she was coming on to was loving it, couldn't keep his hands off her. Mickey watched, his agitation and his passion rising as the bloke slid a hand onto her knee, right up her thigh. Mickey looked away, sipped at his pint. What she did was her business he told himself.

Right!

He looked back just as the bloke grabbed her tits, gave them a big squeeze.

That was the final straw. Before he even realised what he was doing, Mickey was out of his seat, striding across the floor towards them.

He grabbed Miranda by the arm, pulled her away from Josh. 'You're fucking coming with me!' he ordered.

Miranda's eyes blazed in triumph as she felt Mickey's hand on her arm, but the bloke, Josh, wasn't letting her go that easily. 'Oy! She's with me!' he protested, squaring up to Mickey. He was a big bloke, but Mickey sized him up in an instant. No real bottle, no real threat, just a bit of bluster.

Calling it a fight wouldn't even do it justice. The geezer took a step towards Mickey, then Bam!

One smack in the face and he was down, out cold on the floor, blood flowing from his nose. Before the bouncers had even noticed anything was going on, Mickey and Miranda were halfway towards the door. 'I'm taking you home, Miranda,' Mickey told her.

Miranda glanced at Josh out cold on the floor, then back at her friends. 'I thought you'd never say that!' she laughed as she tottered along next to Mickey, heels clacking. She gazed at Mickey with puppy dog eyes, partly love struck, partly out of her face.

The cold night air cooled Mickey's anger. He turned to Miranda. 'You really showed yourself up in there with that geezer. You looked like a right slag. I thought you had more respect for yourself, Miranda.'

They had reached Mickey's car. He unlocked the door, held it open for her.

Miranda stood very still, looked Mickey straight in the eye. 'Respect? I have no respect for myself, Mickey. You should know that better than anyone.' And then she burst into tears, sobbing. 'You don't like me, do you? You think I'm dirty and disgusting. You hate me, don't you Mickey?'

Mickey looked at her for a second, then reached out and took her into his arms. He didn't know what to say or do. Fuck sake, why did she have to start crying? He didn't mean it the way she thought. She clung tight to him, put her head on his shoulder.

Mickey tried not to smell her perfume, tried not to feel the soft warmth of her body against him, but he could feel himself getting hard just from holding her.

'Don't be fucking silly,' he said softly. Their eyes met and locked together, he felt he couldn't breathe. He thought she looked more beautiful than ever. 'You know I think the world of you. You're part of the family. I'll always be here for you, look after you. Nothing bad will happen to you again.' The words just spilled out, words he had never meant to say. He directed her towards the car. 'Come on, in you get.'

She slipped into the car seat, Mickey's eyes unable to resist staring at her smooth thighs as her skirt rode up. Jesus Christ, thought Mickey, why did she have to be wearing black stockings?

Mickey closed the door, walked slowly round to the driver's door, telling himself, just get in the car, drive her home, leave her there. That's all you have to do. Life is complicated enough already without adding more grief.

He dropped into his seat, glanced across at her. She was still sitting exactly as he had left her, staring straight ahead, her skirt still exposing her thighs, the tops of her stockings. He dragged his eyes away.

'Come on, stop crying,' he said. 'I didn't mean it like that. It's just you just made yourself look really cheap in there and you ain't cheap, you've got class. You've got everything, Miranda, everything a bloke could ever want.'

Finally she looked over at him. 'Do you promise you will always be here for me, Mickey?'

He could feel her eyes boring into him, as though she could read his lust, his confusion. 'Yes,' he said softly.

'Say it then.'

'I promise.'

She nodded. 'That's good.'

Mickey let out a deep breath. 'Right, get your seatbelt on and let's get you home.'

But still she didn't move.

Mickey forced a laugh. 'Am I going to have to do everything for you?'

'I hope so!' she sighed.

He leaned across her to put her seat belt on, got another scent of her perfume - Chanel no 5. He knew the smell, it was one that always got his motor running. He clicked her seatbelt, started to sit back, then suddenly she took him by surprise - her arms wrapped around his neck and she pulled him urgently towards her, kissing him hard on his lips, her tongue pointing and darting.

A shiver of pleasure went through him as she kissed him. He could taste the whiskey on her tongue, found that despite himself he was responding, he couldn't fight it, he held her tight, returning the kiss with a passion he hadn't felt for almost twenty years. He knew he should break the embrace but he didn't have the strength or the inclination, he was caught up in this moment of passion.

Then suddenly he pulled away, sat back, trying to gain control of the situation.

Miranda gave him a look. 'What's wrong?'

'I can't do this.' Mickey. said. 'I've known you too long, I'm married -'

Miranda cut him off. '- And you want me like you've never wanted anyone in your life.'

Mickey looked at her, still breathing hard. 'Let's get you home.'

'And then?'

Mickey said nothing, cranked the car, and fixed his eyes on the road, pulled out of the car park.

Miranda had a smile on her face like the Cheshire Cat. She slipped her shoes off, slid back in the seat, her skirt riding up even higher, revealing her black lace panties. She saw Mickey's eyes dart towards her legs then back to the road. 'You like that, do you?' she said in a husky voice.

Mickey said nothing.

Miranda reclined the seat, she was almost half lying down. 'I was counting on you to take care of me,' she said, her eyes never leaving Mickey. She slid her hand up her leg, then between her legs. She began to gently stroke herself through her panties, moaning softly with pleasure.

Mickey couldn't tear his eyes from her, was having trouble driving. 'That's enough, you've got to stop that!' he croaked.

Miranda responded by stroking faster, moaning louder, arching her back.

Mickey could feel that he was as hard as he had ever been, wanted nothing more than to fuck her right there and then in the car. He licked his lips, tried desperately to keep at least one eye on the road. 'I can't do this,' he groaned.

Miranda met his eyes. 'You don't have to - pull over into that car park.'

Mickey followed her gaze - an empty supermarket car park. Without even consciously making the decision he wrenched the wheel, raced to the far side of the car park, pulled up into the shadows.

Before he had even parked the car she was all over him. She pushed him back in his seat, her tongue darting in and out of his mouth, her hands all over him. 'You just lie back and let me do the work!' she ordered, and to his surprise, Mickey did.

He was shocked at her boldness, but it turned him on. He had never let a woman take control like this before - but then again, he had never met a woman like Miranda before.

She leaned across him, grabbed the handle and reclined his seat. As he dropped back, almost flat, she grabbed both sides of his shirt, ripped it open. Her hot mouth covered his face in kisses, slid down his neck, down across his chest. At the same time her hands were fumbling with his trousers, ripping open the button, unzipping. Suddenly her cool hands were on his cock.

For just a moment he felt the cool touch of her fingers, then he felt her hair tickling his thighs, her tongue tickling his balls, every inch of his skin tingling. It felt so good he didn't want her to stop. Then that sensation was replaced by pure heat as her mouth enveloped him.

Mickey groaned in pleasure as she sucked on him. He grabbed her dark hair and thrust up against her mouth, pushing down on her head, going as deep in her mouth as she could take him. She was sucking harder and faster, like a woman possessed. There was no way he could last long, he'd gone so long without sex, and he came in a hot, thrusting torrent, an explosion that forced a low moan from him.

It was one of the best blow jobs he had ever had, she knew what to do with her mouth and tongue. But rather than finishing him, the first climax seemed only to engorge him further.

Miranda sat up, smiling. 'Do you like the way I suck your cock?' She had a wicked look on her face.

'That was the best,' admitted Mickey.

'The best you've ever had?'

'Yeah, the best,' he sighed.

She ripped her own blouse open, slipped her bra straps off her shoulders to reveal her perfect breasts. She was undeniably gorgeous. Mickey had fantasised about Miranda many times, but she looked even better than he had imagined. He couldn't keep his hands off her breasts, gently pushed her tits together, tonguing her nipples simultaneously.

Miranda squeaked in delight as he kissed, licked, nibbled, sucked hard on her nipples. She hitched her skirt up, slipped her silk panties to one side. 'Payback time,' she whispered as she pushed him down in his seat.

He slid his mouth down to her hairless pussy, began blowing it softly.

'I want your tongue inside me!' she ordered. Grabbing his head and thrusting her hips against him, she forced his tongue deep inside her, began moving her hips faster and faster, moaning and groaning while he licked her. Mickey could barely breathe, felt almost overwhelmed by her as she came with a deep shuddering gasp.

But still she wasn't done. She quickly moved herself up on top of Mickey, slowly lowered herself onto his cock. Mickey gasped as she slid down onto him. She was wet and ready, no friction, just sheer pleasure as she rode up and down on his lap. Her breasts in his face, her hands grabbing the back of his head, pulling him in closer. He kissed her hard, more hungry and heated as his hands explored her body.

Harder and harder she thrust. She was so tight and warm, Mickey had never felt a woman so urgent. He wasn't aware of anything; he lost all sense of time and place, just the feel of her warmth and the tightness he felt inside her. She ground herself against him, pulled him closer to her, her fingers sliding over his skin, his heart beating faster, the excitement, her nearness, her touch, feeling sensations unlike anything he had ever felt before.

She satisfied his every need, teased him, getting him nearly there and then stopping, making him wait until he begged her for more, begged her not to stop.

Finally she grabbed the hair at the back of his head with both of her hands, unable to contain herself any longer. Yes, yes!' she said in an awed tone as she started to climax, drove herself against him harder and harder.

Mickey listened to her moans and groans as he ground her hips against him, gasping, digging her nails in him, telling him how much she loved him.

Mickey felt himself reaching another climax. Miranda could feel it too, she thrust harder and faster. Her face screwed up with pleasure, until they both climaxed with a huge gasp.

Finally she stopped, slipped down and lay on his shoulder. He cradled her in his arms. Mickey could smell the sex as she lay half on top of him, found himself wanting her again, wanting to taste her, know her, own her. Wanting to have her over and over again. Until he knew every line, every crease, every square inch of her. She tasted and smelled unlike anyone else. Just the thought of it made him start to get hard again.

Miranda turned her head slightly, smiled, her lips slightly parted to show her perfectly white teeth. He kissed her very, very slowly.

She pulled away looked into his eyes. 'Again?'

Mickey laughed as she traced gentle lines on his chest with her fingertips. He felt better than he had in years, happier, more fulfilled. Christ, why had he waited so long, denied himself for all these years? She seemed to have a power over him, all he wanted was more.

Miranda slid down and took him in her mouth again, but Mickey stopped her. 'What's wrong?' She looked up at him.

'Not here. Not now.'

Miranda sat up, gazed into his eyes.

'Then where? When?'

Mickey grinned. He wanted her badly. Sex with Miranda was beyond anything he had ever known, she took him to new heights and back again. 'Like I said earlier. We really need to get you home!'

Miranda

Mickey looked around Miranda's flat as she led him into her bedroom.   Everything was designer, quality, reeked of money. He could get used to living like this…

Miranda pulled him to her, kissed him hard, then just as quickly broke away. 'You get comfortable. I'll be back in just a moment.'

She turned and strutted into the en-suite bathroom, Mickey's hungry eyes following her all the way. Christ, they already done it twice and he still wanted her again.   He looked at the bed, at the maroon silk sheets, the soft pillows, then quickly tore off his shirt, pulled off his trousers and pants, then slid between the sheets. Her smell was all over the bed, he felt himself getting hard again just smelling her…

Miranda locked the door behind her, opened the cabinet and took out a makeup bag, rummaged inside and came up with a tiny bag of cocaine. She carefully tipped some onto the black marble counter top, packed it into a line, sniffed it up with practiced ease, first the left, then the right.

She straightened up, blinked at the bright lights as she looked up. Wow, she needed that, she felt better already. Then she quickly hid it away, cleaned up the evidence - it would be best if Mickey didn't find out about her addiction, not knowing how he would react.

Miranda stripped down naked, looked at herself in the mirror. She'd spent a lot of money and a lot of time and sweat keeping her body like it was, and it had finally paid off! She looked slim, tanned, her skin smooth, breasts full and firm. She couldn't keep the smile from her face. Mickey Taylor! The man she had always wanted, in her flat, in her bed! She was going to do everything she could to keep him there, use every trick in the book. She would do anything for him. Anything!

She stepped into the shower and quickly rinsed her body, then turned her attention to her makeup. She needed a bit of blusher, another coat of lipstick, but didn't need any mascara – she'd put false eyelashes on earlier. They looked like spider's legs, but Miranda liked them. She thought they gave her eyes a sexy look.

For a moment she thought about going back out to him as she was, naked, letting him feast his eyes on her body, but quickly decided against it - he'd have plenty of time to see her naked. Let him work for it a bit first!

She opened up a tall cupboard, pulled out a black basque with a zipped front opening, a figure-hugging PVC outfit that made her look like Miss Whiplash.

Fishnet stockings, thigh-high boots and studded leather cuffs completed the outfit.

She looked at her reflection, surprised at her own boldness, yet totally exhilarated. She already had him in her power, had no intention of letting him go. Miranda had learned very early in life that if you want something, there was always a price to pay, that you don't get anything for nothing in this world. She had got Mickey in her bed, where she knew she had the power. Sex was a very powerful tool, and she intended to use her looks and her skills to get him completely hooked. Let's see how Mandy competed with that!

She ran her fingers through her hair, turned and twisted, adjusting herself until she was finally satisfied. Mickey would be blown away when he saw her all done up like this. A quick dab of her favourite perfume and she was done.

Mickey lay in Miranda's bed, gazing at the ceiling. He felt contented, happier than he had in years, relaxed and comfortable from their sex, but ready for more. Christ, after twenty years of fancying each other, it had been like a dam breaking - and it wasn't over yet! He closed his eyes, a satisfied grin on his face.

A sudden flash of Joey's face appeared in his mind. He sat up with a start. Those pleading eyes, looking up at him like a dog, begging Mickey to kill him. Is that all he was, a killer? Putting people out of their misery, friends, enemies, anyone who came across him, Mickey just killed them, was that it?

He rubbed his face, tried to put the image out of his mind. His eyes wandered round the room, taking in Miranda's stuff - a half open wardrobe full of clothes, a silk blouse thrown across a chair, a dressing table with a mirror, cluttered with make-up, odd bits of jewellery.

That was better, think about Miranda, think about her tanned skin, the rise of her breasts, her dark nipples growing hard as his tongue flicked back and forth across them...

He lay back down. Christ, what a woman. He'd had plenty of women - too many to remember, all sizes, all colours, all sexual preferences - but he'd never had one who could turn him on like that. She seemed to read his mind, know what he wanted, know when to take control, when to let him be in charge.

Mickey closed his eyes, thought of how she had forced herself on him, forced him to eat her soft, shaven pussy. He'd never let a woman force herself on him like that, but he would have stayed there forever if she'd told him to. He began to get hard again, ready for her to emerge from the bathroom, wondering what it would be like this time.

Then just like before, an image of Joey burst into his mind. Joey dead. Joey with his brains blown out, the way Mickey had left him. Mickey hadn't wanted to look at him again, didn't want to remember him that way, but he couldn't get the image out of his mind. In fact the only time all day he had stopped thinking about it was when he was with Miranda.

'I hope it's me you're thinking about?'

Mickey looked up, and all other thoughts were chased from his mind at the sight of Miranda, her breasts swelling out of her basque, her long legs clad in black stockings and high boots. She strutted into the bedroom, peered at the outline of his body beneath the thin silk sheet.

'I'm disappointed,' she purred, 'you didn't stay up for me!'

Mickey grinned self-consciously. 'Sorry, a lot on my mind.'

Miranda stood over him, shook her head. 'No, right now, there's just one thing on your mind.'

Mickey wolf whistled as his eyes travelled greedily up and down her gorgeous body, his dick instantly hardening. God he wanted her so badly. She affected him in a way he couldn't explain. Miranda had done something to him, he wanted and needed her more than anything in the world. She had a hypnotic power over him, he had never felt like this about anyone or anything in his life.

She smiled, seeing him begin to grow beneath the covers. 'That's better.'

With a quick motion she pulled the covers back, looked at his naked body. 'I've got some wicked surprises for you,' she told him, 'I'm going to do things to you that you've only dreamt of. All of your deepest fantasies will come true tonight; you'll be begging me for more and more.' She stood at the side of the bed looking down on him, her hands on her hips, her lips pouting seductively. 'What do you want me to do to you?'

Before he could reply she knelt on the floor beside the bed, reached out and stroked his cock. 'I can be nice, or I can be naughty, whatever you want.'

Mickey rolled onto on his side, thrust his cock towards her open mouth. 'I want you to be very, very naughty,' he croaked. Her smooth mouth began to suck him. He felt the spasms running through his body. He reached out to grab her hair and push himself even deeper into her mouth, but she was too quick for him. She danced away from his outstretched hands, jumped on the bed and straddled him, their eyes locked together. 'You're mine, Mickey Taylor,' she told him, pinning his hands to the bed by the side of his head.

With one quick move, he reversed the situation, had her trapped underneath him. He grinned, full of a desire that he had repressed for so long. 'I don't think so. What I think is that you're my prisoner now. I can do whatever I want to you.'

She gazed up at him, her eyes filled with love and want. 'Do you know how long I have been waiting to hear you say that?'

It was light when Mickey woke up. He lay very still for a while, not wanting to disturb Miranda, just gazing at her exposed shoulder as she lay sleeping beside him. Finally he rolled over, eased out of bed, stepped quietly out of the bedroom.

He found his way to the kitchen, opened the fridge and grabbed a carton of orange juice, stood stark naked drinking straight from the carton. Christ, he could barely remember half of what they had done last night, but what he did remember, fucking hell! He had never experienced anything like it.

He glanced up at the clock. Shit! It was past seven. Mandy would be doing her nut, going mental. She'd probably phoned all his mates and sent a search party out for him!

He picked up the phone and dialled home.

Mandy answered, a terse, 'hello?'

'It's me.'

'Where the fuck are you?' she snapped back at him.

Mickey felt his anger rising. 'What are you, a fucking copper? Don't fucking question me again,' he warned.

'What whore's bed have you been in?' Mandy said icily.

She was right and she was wrong, thought Mickey. Bed, yes. Whore, no. 'For fuck's sake, Mandy, I'm at a mate's place. I've got a lot going on, shit you wouldn't fucking believe. I had a bit too much to drink last night, crashed out. That's the end of it.'

'You think I don't know where you are?'

'Oh, for fuck's sake Mand, give it a rest!'

Out of the corner of his eye he saw Miranda wander into the kitchen. She was wearing a piece of silk nothing that revealed far more than it hid. 'I'll be home soon,' he told her, knowing it was a lie even as he said it.

'Fuck off, I don't want you home, stay with your little whore,' she snarled. 'I wish you were still in prison!' And she slammed down the phone.

Mickey stared at the phone for a moment, then set it carefully on the counter, fighting to control his anger. Things were getting seriously fucked up.

Miranda moved beside him, gently kissed his cheek. 'I'm sorry - and I'm not sorry.'

Mickey met her sparkling eyes. 'Yeah, me too.'

She kissed him passionately. The kiss sent shivers running through him, but he needed to clear his head. 'Not now, I need to think.'

Miranda smiled at him. 'Not in the mood?'

'Right.'

She reached out, stroked his naked cock. It was already hard. 'Someone thinks otherwise.'

Mickey sighed. 'I know, but...'

She dropped to her knees in front of him, began covering his belly with soft languid kisses. Her fingers reaching up and circling his nipples, tracing the contours of his chest, while her tongue darted in and out of his belly button.

He tried to stop her, but knew he couldn't, was powerless to resist as she closed her mouth around him, and began sucking hard.

It was all Mickey could do to stop from groaning as the tip of her tongue circled his cock, sending tingling vibes shooting through his body. She was biting, sucking, tasting, exploring, her hands reaching round to cradle his backside, pulling him into her mouth with urgent thrusts.

He wanted to stop her, wanted to figure out what the fuck he was going to do, but he couldn't, he was intoxicated, just being around her was enough to drive reason from his mind.

He grabbed the back of her head, began meeting the urgent movement of her head with thrusts of his own, her mouth driving him crazy as she sucked and teased. It didn't take long before he exploded in a hot torrent, gasping and moaning with pure pleasure.

Miranda waited until he was completely sated, then looked up at him, a mischievous look on her face. 'I thought you weren't in the mood?'

'Yeah, well you have a way of getting me in the mood.'

'What, you mean like this?' She began to flick at his soft cock with her tongue, but he pulled away, tried to take control of the situation.

'We can't keep doing this,' he told her. 'I'm married.'

She climbed slowly to her feet, met his gaze. 'You don't love her. Get a divorce.'

Mickey sighed. 'It's not as easy as that.'

Miranda smiled, reached out and began stroking his chest. 'I'll make it easy.'

Mickey could feel the passion rising again. 'No... I ....I can't...'

She slipped her arms around his waist, began softly kissing him, forcing him to be quiet.

Mickey responded to her kiss, couldn't keep his hands from exploring her beautiful body, feeling her smooth skin through the diaphanous silk chemise she was wearing.

She pushed him back, pinned him up against the cold steel of the fridge, kissing him hard on the mouth. He closed his eyes, inhaling her perfume, his hands exploring her more frantically, grinding himself against her soft body.

Suddenly he wrapped his strong arms around her, lifted her like a child and carried her into the bedroom. Miranda closed her eyes, instantly felt as though she was sixteen again, in Mickey's arms, no pain, and no bad memories to torture her at night. She felt safe with Mickey, she was always safe with Mickey. And she was going to keep him.

Her soft eyes were on him as he gently lay her on the bed, began covering her face in kisses, her forehead her nose, her chin.

Between each of her kisses she whispered to him, 'I love you, I will always love you, Mickey, nothing can ever change that,' over and over again.

He gazed down at her, her dark hair across the pillow, her skin smooth and soft, then slid down, gently pulled the chemise up from beneath her, peeled it off to reveal her naked body.

He thought she looked more beautiful than ever. Mickey had slept with many women but no one had ever made him feel the way she did. He knelt down by the side of the bed next to her, ran his fingers across the tips of her breasts, touching her softly, stroking her nipples until she sighed and made little moaning noises, then dropped his head, let his tongue move slowly from nipple to nipple.

She grabbed his head, her fingers tangled in his short hair, shoved his head downwards. 'I want to feel your tongue deep inside me again,' she sighed, but Mickey was in control now.

'Not yet,' he teased, sliding down the length of the bed to her feet. He began licking and sucking her toes. Miranda moaned in ecstasy and expectation, squirming, rubbing her thighs together as he slowly ran his tongue up to her ankles, her calves, finally her thighs.

Miranda's body tingled as his hands and tongue explored her body. She was in ecstasy as she lay on her back watching his handsome face devour her. She could feel his soft stubble against her thighs, his tongue searching, seeking, and tracing a line up the inside of her thigh towards her soft, shaved pussy. He paused, so close, yet so far away. She could feel his breath on her, but he still hadn't touched her with his tongue.

Miranda could stand it no more, she suddenly grabbed his head, thrust her hips downwards, forced her hot pussy onto his waiting mouth, groaned in ecstasy as his tongue dived into her.

Her hips began moving in rhythm, wanting him even deeper inside her, hungry for the pleasure he could give her, watching him licking her, his tongue inside her, feeling her urgent need.

Mickey's tongue darted in and out, kissing, sucking, exploring, breathing in the smell of her, gliding over her, devouring her, relishing the taste of her.

She wrapped her long slim legs around his neck, ground her hips against his face, feeling the heat rise, the feeling build until it spilled out with a long groan.

She unlocked her legs, lay back, pulled urgently at Mickey's shoulders. 'I want to feel you inside me, Mickey,' she gasped.

Mickey needed no second invitation. He climbed on top of her, slipped easily inside her, sending another wave surging through her.

Mickey thrust himself against her strong body, his face contorted with effort, with passion.

'Hmmmm, that's so good,' she cried. 'Come on, harder, faster, I want to feel you really deep inside me.'

He thrust deeper and deeper, lost in the pleasure, making love, fast and passionately.

Miranda was laughing, crying, the surge of emotions almost overwhelming her as she felt him reaching a climax. 'Oh, Mickey, that feels so good,' she gasped, 'you inside me.'

She was squirming beneath him as he thrust deeper and deeper, circling his hips, the feeling so intense, utterly lost inside her.

'Tell me when you're going to come,' she said urgently, 'I want to climax together.'

Harder and faster he thrust, over and over, again and again his fingers sliding over her skin, his teeth biting at her shoulder, nothing existing for either of them but the moment, the passion, the heat.

Mickey had no need to tell her when he was about to come, she could feel it, his body pulsing and shaking, moaning, then suddenly stiffening as he could take it no longer.

She met his surge, thrust against him, the two of them exploding together, then collapsing in a heap of sweaty limbs.

Mickey rolled off, laid his head on her shoulder, and gently rested a hand on her breast.

Miranda stroked his hair. 'I love you, Mickey,' she said softly.

Mickey could feel her heart hammering inside her ribs, knew that he should not respond, shouldn't encourage her, and should say anything but the words that spilled unbidden from his mouth. 'I love you too…'

Miranda smiled triumphantly, let out a deep sigh.

She had him.

Martin

Martin leaned on the mantelpiece at Lizzie's house, sipped his scotch. How many times had he stood in this room and talked with Mickey, listened to his stories, then did what Mickey told him to do? Strange how even now this was where they met, this was the centre of the family, the one place they were all on neutral ground. And this was the place where Martin was going to defy Mickey.

Martin swilled his drink around in his glass. Mickey had returned a few minutes ago, and Martin could see straightaway that he had bad news. His face was set, hard, his eyes cold. He poured himself a stiff drink, downed it in one go, then excused himself to go wash his face.

Mickey had already told him that Kenny was dead, and now he had been to see Joey. Was he dead too? Martin had fond memories of Joey – he was a big bloke, looked out for Martin when he had first started getting himself into trouble. With Joey working as a bouncer at the club Mickey owned, Martin knew he always had some back-up if things turned sticky. Not that Martin couldn't take care of himself, but still, a little support was always helpful...

But Sharon said Joey had really let himself go, he'd changed, become a filthy crack-head living on the streets. Martin couldn't imagine that.

Martin drained his glass, set it down on the mantelpiece among Lizzie's collection of knickknacks – ceramic dogs, a snow globe of the Eiffel Tower and a painted plate from the Queen's Silver Jubilee.

'Looks like you need a refill.' Mickey strode back into the room, forced a smile on his face as he grabbed Martin's glass from the mantelpiece and turned towards the drinks cupboard.

Martin looked at his brother as he fixed their drinks. He was solid, still had his boxer's build, still moved with power and authority, but there was something different, something that had changed since his time inside. Whereas before Mickey had done everything with a carefree abandon, knowing that he was the Big Man, now he was no longer untouchable, and he knew it.

The air of absolute certainty had gone, replaced by a degree of caution. This was a more calculating Mickey, someone who thought a little before he acted, who knew that he was vulnerable.

He'd been nabbed, served time, come through the fire of prison, and emerged sharper, more calculating. If anything, thought Martin, as his brother turned around and handed him his drink, Mickey was even more dangerous now than before he'd served time. So much for rehabilitation.

'Get that down ya,' said Mickey as he slurped at his own drink.

'Thought you'd be back yesterday,' said Martin. 'Did you have trouble finding Joey? I had Mandy calling every hour last night to see if you'd turned up.'

Mickey nodded, his eyes dark, revealing nothing. 'Yeah, I found him.'

That in itself says something, thought Martin. No emotion. Nothing. 'And?'

'Those cunts got to him – Wolfson and Cooper – had some big queer bloke rape the crap out of him until he spilled the beans.'

'Fuck! About the diamonds?'

Again Mickey nodded. His big shoulders sagged. 'And Georgie's the only one who knows where they are.'

'So you'll go back up to Rampton, see if you can get anything out of Georgie?'

Another nod, Mickey's face still cold, impassive.

He's hiding something, thought Martin. 'What will you do if you find them, the diamonds? Give them to Wolfson and Cooper?'

The look that Mickey shot Martin was pure Dangerous. 'Fuck no. I intend to find those saucy bastards and kill them.'

'Two thirds of those diamonds are theirs by rights,' Martin pointed out.

Mickey's eyes flashed dangerously at him. Some real emotion at last. 'Were. But they've crossed the line. If they'd come to me at the start, maybe I might have worked something out with them. But they crossed the line. They fucked with the family. Came to the house and threatened mum, killed Kenny and Colleen, fucked Joey up.' The muscles in his shoulders tightened, his eyes narrowed. 'No. Those fuckers are going down.'

Martin sipped his drink, tried to remain impassive. He couldn't get wrapped up in this, couldn't allow those old feelings to cloud his judgement. Martin could certainly take care of himself, had dealt with his share of hard men in Australia while building his company, but this was different. Mickey operated in a different way, at a different level. These people tortured and murdered, talked about killing like normal people talked about washing the car, just something else that you had to do. He took a deep breath. 'But you don't even have the diamonds, don't know where they are, and I don't fancy your chances of getting anything out of Georgie. Why don't you go and talk to Wolfson and Cooper, tell them that?'

Mickey gave Martin a look of pure venom. 'Deal with those cunts? Is that what you're suggesting? After what they've done?'

'I dunno,' began Martin, 'I just thought – '

'Didn't you hear what I just told you, Marty? They killed Kenny. They tortured and killed Colleen. And Joey – fuck me, the state of him...'

'Where is he?'

Mickey said nothing. His grip tightened on his glass, his eyes gazing off into nowhere. Suddenly he lifted the glass, drained it, hurled it down onto the stone hearth of the fire, the pieces smashing and showering the room. 'Those cunts have challenged the family,' he snarled. 'They've stepped on my fucking toes in the most provocative way possible! If I let this go, that's it, it will be over for me! Every fucking Johnny-come-lately will know that Mickey fucking Taylor has lost it, is slowing down, is fair game. How long do you think I'll last if word of that gets around?'

Martin said nothing. He knew Mickey was right.

'I'll get the word out, see if I can track down where those bastards are hiding,' continued Mickey. 'They had their chance, now it's my turn.'

Martin looked at his brother, recognised the look. He knew there was no reasoning with Mickey, no changing his mind. He had to say his piece now, before it was too late to turn back. 'I can't – I won't – be a part of it Mickey,' he blurted out. 'That was why

I left in the first place. I can't get dragged back into it.'

Mickey said nothing, and for a moment Martin thought he was going to explode, challenge Martin, and shout at him. Then suddenly he stepped close, threw an arm round Martin's shoulders, drew him in close. Martin could smell the scotch and coke on his breath. 'I know, I get it,' he said quietly. 'And I wouldn't want you to become a part of this. You've found your own life, made good. I'm pleased.'

He let Martin go, looked down at the shattered glass spread across the floor. 'I'll have to clean that up,' he said quietly, turning towards the doorway.

'And the diamonds?'

Mickey paused, answered without turning around. 'I'll have to go have another word with Georgie . . .'

Mickey

Mickey strolled into the Cross Keys, the collar of his coat pulled up against the cold wind. The pub had a lively lunchtime trade going, people eating, drinking, chatting, but even after all these years, when Mickey Taylor walked in the door, heads turned, conversations stopped. People knew who he was.

There were a few calls of 'All right, Mickey,' and 'Welcome back, mate,' as he strode to the bar.

The owner, Barry, was old school Dagenham, had known Mickey since he was a kid running in and out with Bobby's betting slips. In his late seventies now, Barry had a huge belly, a stained white apron straining to contain it, but the eyes that shone out of his ruddy face were still sharp, still took in everything that went on in the place.

'Mickey fucking Taylor! Welcome back, son! 'He wheezed. He'd been diagnosed with cancer several times - throat, lungs, God knows where else, but each time he pulled through, each time he kept on smoking his John Player Blacks. He reached back behind himself, grabbed a bottle of Pernod, and had a glass poured and waiting before Mickey had even settled on his stool.

Mickey grinned as he saw the drink on the bar. 'You don't forget much, do you Bazza?'

Barry smiled, coughed into the back of his hand. 'Not for my regulars.'

'It's been a while since I was a regular,' mused Mickey.

'You'll always be a regular here,' Barry told him. He set the bottle down next to Mickey. 'Help yourself.'

As Barry waddled to the far end of the bar to serve another customer, Mickey looked around. Not much had changed in the Cross Keys - there were a couple more machines with flashing lights standing against the wall, and the music was a bit louder than Mickey remembered, but most of it was the same. The same old geezers in the corner poring over the Sporting Life, some teenagers drinking too fast and talking too loud, a couple of Dagenham slappers sipping their wine and hoping someone would notice them. Fuck me, he thought, and here I was worrying that everything had changed.

A couple of blokes stopped by, shook Mickey's hand, welcomed him back, but he was buggered if he could put a name to their faces. That was one thing that had changed - Mickey had prided himself that he never forgot a name, always knew who everyone was, but after fourteen years...

'So is this just a social call?'

Mickey turned around, found Barry looking at him questioningly.

Mickey sipped his drink, looked round the bar. 'Yes and no.'

Barry nodded. 'We've missed you, Mickey. Whole fucking area's gone to pot while you were away. Drugs everywhere, and you don't know who to trust - the coloureds and the Pakis all run their own game, people from all over the fucking shop coming in and doing business. It's getting so a white geezer can hardly make an honest living.' He paused, grinned at Mickey. 'Or a dishonest one!'

Mickey laughed. 'Yeah, things have changed a bit, haven't they?'

'There's not many of your old gang still around, Mickey.'

Mickey nodded.

'I heard about Kenny,' continued Barry. 'Fucking tragic that was.'

Mickey's jaw hardened. He turned slowly back to face Barry. 'That wasn't right, Bazza. He was one of us.'

Barry nodded. A customer waved to him from the far end of the bar but Barry ignored him.

'I need some information,' Mickey continued. 'Someone who's got their nose to the ground - knows what's what and who's who.'

'And can keep their mouth shut?'

Mickey nodded.

'Remember Jimmy MacDonald?'

'Old MacDonald? The Scottish geezer with the red hair?'

'Yeah.'

'He was all right, he was,' laughed Mickey. 'For a Jock!'

Barry nodded across the bar towards a slim, red haired lad sitting in the corner, sipping a pint and half reading the Sun. 'That's his boy, Gus.'

Mickey eyed the boy - he had intelligent eyes, an alert expression.

'He's had a couple of scrapes, but he mostly keeps his nose clean. And he's an absolute fucking gold mine of information. You want to find out what's happening in the manor, you won't do better.'

Mickey nodded, refilled his glass. 'Thanks, Bazza.'

Mickey made his way across the pub, found Gus looking up at him with pale eyes, a quizzical look.

Mickey lowered himself onto the bench beside Gus, said nothing. He wanted to see how the lad reacted, if he had nerves. He picked up Gus's paper, began to read.

Gus didn't stir, sat patiently beside Mickey, took a couple of tiny sips from his beer. Although he had been in the pub since before Mickey arrived, his glass was still three quarters full. He clearly knew how to make a pint last, look natural, blend in. That was good.

Finally Mickey set the paper back down on the table, turned to look at the lad. 'I knew your dad.'

'My mum said you helped her out a bit after he died.'

Mickey nodded. 'He was all right, was your dad, even if he was a fucking Jock.'

Gus said nothing, just kept his pale eyes fixed on Mickey.

'You can do some work for me, earn yourself a few quid.'

It wasn't a request, and Gus understood that.

'I'm told you have your nose to the ground, and that you know when to keep your mouth shut.'

Still Gus said nothing.

Mickey grinned at him. 'Like now, right?'

The kid laughed, nodded. 'Yeah, like now!'

'You do me right,' said Mickey, 'and we can have a very profitable relationship.' He looked around the pub. 'But after today, we can't meet - at least, not in public like this. People can't know that you talk to me. They rumble that, you become worthless - or worse still, a target. Understand?'

Gus nodded.

'Come by me mum's house tonight and we'll arrange the details.'

Again Gus nodded.

'So here's your first task, your test if you like. I'm looking for two geezers, old school crooks, used to live in Poplar, but they work over this way from time to time.'

Gus's demeanour changed, he was suddenly all business. 'Names?'

'Tommy Wolfson and Derrick Cooper. Wolfson's an Irish git, had red hair like you, though I wouldn't know if he's still got any left. Cooper was an ugly little cunt, reminded me of a rat.'

Gus nodded. 'That's it?'

'That's it. Find them for me and I'll make it well worth your while.' Mickey emptied his glass, stood up, and raised his voice slightly so that people could hear if they had an inclination. 'Nice to meet you, son. Say hi to your mum for me, let me know if she ever needs anything.'

Gus played right along. 'Thanks, Mister Taylor, it was nice meeting you.'

Mickey turned and strode out the pub, trying hard to keep the grin from his face. That was more like it. Back in the game, just like the old days. If only he didn't have to go see Georgie again...

Mandy

Mandy leaned heavily on the kitchen counter, looked up at the grimy ceiling. She could hear Mickey moving around upstairs, getting ready to go out again. He said he was going to see Georgie, but after the last few days, she didn't know what to believe. She had waited so long for him to get out of prison, had dreamed about it, fantasised about it, but now it had actually happened, now he was out, it was turning into a nightmare.

The first night had been everything she had hoped for - just the two of them, snuggling up on the couch, Mickey eating steak and chips, a bit of telly, and then they'd done it.

Mandy almost blushed, just thinking about it. She had been as hungry as him for sex - fourteen years without a shag is a fucking long time! Mickey had been all over her. Tearing her clothes off, burying his face in her soft breasts, doing it on the couch. Then the two of them up the stairs like two love sick teenagers, ready to do it all over again in their bed.

But afterwards, as she'd lain wide awake, staring at the ceiling, listening to Mickey sleeping soundly beside her, the fears had started to kick in.

She slipped naked out of the bed, looked at herself in the mirror. Jesus Christ, what had happened to her? Her tits sagged half way to her waist, she had a pot belly, and her thighs were like two wobbly sacks, meeting in the middle and spilling out on either side like giant white saddlebags. Thank Christ she couldn't see her arse, it must be the size of a double decker bus!

When Mickey was inside, none of that seemed to matter. She'd been so busy taking care of the kids, trying to keep it together without her man that she'd never even thought about her weight, what she looked like. And so, little by little, year by year, the pounds had crept on. Who had time to exercise, think about what they were eating, when there were kids to feed, a house to clean, a job to go to?

The result, fourteen years later, was what she saw before her. She glanced over at Mickey, sprawled out on his front, just the edge of the sheet across his back. His body still looked great, looked pretty much the same as it had when she'd first met him. He was muscular, no excess body fat, still an attractive, sexy man. What woman wouldn't want him? Mandy shivered, grabbed her robe from the end of the bed, hurried into the bathroom.

Over the next few days, the doubts that had crept into Mandy's mind began to surface more and more. They'd had sex again the next night, but it was perfunctory, a quick shag before turning out the lights, with none of the passion or heat that had marked Mickey's first night home. And since then? Nothing. Mickey was busy sorting out his businesses, getting himself re-established in the manor, and had barely even glanced at Mandy.

She'd tried dressing herself up a bit the other day, put on some make-up, a bit of perfume, a top that showed off her tits, but it hadn't made any difference. Mickey went out early, came home late, then just crashed out in the bed and went straight to sleep. And then the other night he hadn't come home at all . . .

Mandy ran a cloth across the kitchen counters, but her mind wasn't on what she was doing. She'd always been a strong minded woman - she'd had to be to get through the past fourteen years - wasn't the kind to sit back and do nothing. If something was bothering her, she'd get it out in the open, deal with it, even if it meant having a big row about it. But Mickey, he was a hard man to argue with. She knew he'd never hit her, nothing like that, but he had such a powerful way about him, he was so confident, so sure of himself, she never wanted to get into it with him. But given the choice between letting it fester and dealing with it head on...

Mickey looked up as he heard Mandy come into the room. 'All right, Mand?'

She looked around the room, finally turned her eyes to Mickey. He was dressed up sharp, designer suit, flash tie, she could smell his aftershave from across the room. 'You look nice. Going somewhere?'

Mickey glanced at her in the mirror as he tied his tie. 'I told you, I'm going up to Rampton to see Georgie again.'

'Right.' Her tone was sharp, sarcastic. 'I'm sure Georgie will appreciate you dressing up so nicely for him.'

Mickey finished his tie, lifted his jacket off the back of a chair, slipped his arms in to it. 'If you've got something to say, say it, Mand. I've got a lot on my mind.'

'I know that look, Mickey, what it means when you dress up like that, splash on the old aftershave.'

'It means I like to look good when I go out.' He straightened his cuffs, glanced at her again as he smoothed a hand across his hair. 'Something you might try doing once in a while.'

There it was. She could feel it building. She'd wanted a row, and here it was. 'What the fuck is that supposed to mean?' she snarled.

Mickey stayed calm, tried not to rise to the bait. 'You know exactly what it means,' he said quietly.

Mandy put her hands on her hips, gave him a look simply loaded with attitude. 'No, I don't. Why don't you fucking enlighten me?'

Mickey sighed. 'I really don't want to get into this right now, Mand.' He turned to face her. 'I've got loads to do, and -'

'Who gives a fuck what you want?'

Mickey rubbed his hand across his face. 'You really want to do this, right now?'

'Right now.'

'Fine.' He took a deep breath. 'Look at you,' he began. 'You must weigh thirteen stone, you dress like a slob, you've let yourself go. You complain that I'm out all the time, why the fuck would I want to come home to you right now?'

Mandy's eyes blazed. 'You arrogant fucking prick! You leave me to deal with the house and kids for fourteen fucking years. Then have the nerve to come home and complain that I don't look like a fucking runway model anymore!'

Mickey shook his head. 'I don't have time for this!'

He moved towards the door, but Mandy blocked his path. 'And then you come home smelling of some other woman's cunt!?'

Mickey tried to push past her, but she moved in front of him, caught the look on his face.

'You are, aren't you? You're screwing some other woman! You've not come near me since the second night you were back!'

'I've got to go!' Mickey pushed past her, hurried down the stairs, Mandy right behind him.

'You're not even going to deny it, are you?'

Mickey grabbed his car keys off the hall table, threw his overcoat over his arm.

Suddenly everything fell into place for Mandy. 'It's her, isn't it? Miranda?'

Mickey paused, one hand on the front door handle. 'How the fuck do you come to that conclusion?'

Mandy's eyes were full of fury. 'Because she's not been sniffing around you. I know that dirty bitch, she's drawn to you like a moth to a flame. The only reason she wouldn't be sniffing around was if she already had her claws into you!'

Mickey opened the door.

'Answer me, Mickey! At least have the fucking balls to give me a straight answer. Are you fucking Miranda Solomon?'

Mickey paused, turned back to look at Mandy. His eyes ran up and down her, took in her messy hair, the baggy sweats and oversized sweater she wore. 'And if I was, who would blame me. I mean, look at the fucking state of you! Who the hell would want to shag something that looked like that?'

Their eyes met for a moment. 'If you think this is the end of this, you are so fucking wrong, Mickey Taylor,' Mandy hissed. 'Now fuck off, before I throw up just at the sight of you!'

Mandy slammed the door on him, stood staring at it for a moment, then slumped to the floor, sobbing. Mickey hadn't needed to say anything - the look in his eyes was enough. He found her disgusting, didn't want any part of her, and was doing it with Miranda fucking Solomon.

Mandy leaned against the wall. So be it. If he wanted to go crawling off to Miranda, if he wanted to stick his dick in her, let him. But Mandy swore one thing to herself. As long as Mickey was with Miranda, she would make his life as miserable as possible...

Georgie

Samantha smiled as she walked into the room, saw Mickey standing by the window. 'So here we are again.'

Mickey glanced over, trying to control his thoughts, his mind in turmoil after the last few days - Kenny, Joey, Miranda, Mandy... 'You look nice,' he said.

Samantha smiled. 'I do, don't I?'

The orderlies stationed themselves by the door, one each side, eyes fixed on Samantha. When Mickey arrived they had warned him that Georgie had been acting up, encouraging the come-ons of the male patients, then beating them up when they got too fresh.

'I hear you've been having fun since I last saw you?'

A guilty smile flashed across Samantha's face. 'They were asking for it,' she replied quickly.

'And you were the one to give it to them!'

Samantha looked up at Mickey curiously as he paced back and forth in front of her. 'Something on your mind?'

Mickey sat suddenly beside her. 'You know what's on my mind. Those geezers are fucking with the family, and I won't stand for that.'

'Same old Mickey.'

Mickey met Samantha's eyes, Georgie's eyes. 'Yeah, same old Mickey.' He sighed. 'We like to think we change, but we don't. Remember when that bloke, what was his name? Malcolm, some poncy name like that, remember when he kept hitting on our Terri on her way from home from school?'

'You wanted to beat the shit out of him.'

'Well, she said he'd grabbed her dragged into the park and started trying to kiss her and stuff.' Mickey grinned. 'But you had a different idea, something much more devious.'

Samantha laughed at the memory. 'He got what he deserved.'

Mickey grinned. 'I can still see his face when we left him in the middle of the street, stark, bollock naked.'

'He never bothered Terri again.'

'No fucking kidding!'

Again their eyes met, and again Mickey saw that flash of his brother hiding inside, there, always there, but just out of reach. He sighed, rubbed his face. 'Joey's dead,' he said suddenly. He glanced up as Samantha turned away - she didn't want him to see her reaction. 'The fuckers had some big ponce fuck the life out of him to try and get him to talk, but what could he tell them? He found the diamonds, like Bobby told him to, gave them to Bobby. That's where the trail ends.'

Samantha was staring straight ahead, no sign of emotion on her face, but Mickey could see how tight her strong jaw was, how hard she was fighting to keep her emotions in check.

'Right fucking state he was in when I found him, hooked on booze and smack, living rough, dying of AIDS...'

Still Samantha said nothing.

Mickey leaned in close, his voice a whisper. 'I put him out of his misery, Samantha. I had to. You'd do it if it was your dog, wouldn't let them suffer like that...' His voice was cracked, hoarse. 'He begged me to. What else could I do?'

He sat up straight, gazed towards the window, the damp grass outside, the high metal fence in the distance.

They sat like that in silence for what seemed like forever.

Finally Mickey heard Samantha stir next to him.

'That was the right thing to do,' she murmured.

Mickey nodded, eyes still fixed on the horizon.

'He was a mate,' she added. 'You've always looked after your mates, Mickey.'

Mickey sighed. 'I'm not doing a very good job right now. They're all fucking dying and I can't do a fucking thing about it.'

'You can't think like that,' said Samantha softly, 'can't ever regret what you did. It will drive you crazy.'

Mickey turned suddenly and met Samantha's deep brown eyes.

'Do you ever regret what you done?' he asked.

Samantha shrugged. 'Why should I? They got what they deserved.'

'What about Georgie, did he get what he deserved,' wondered Mickey.

Samantha's face softened. 'Georgie was special.'

Mickey could feel that he was getting closer, that the part of Samantha/Georgie that he wanted to talk to was just below the surface. 'If he's so special, why don't you tell me how to find him?' There was an urgency, a pleading in his words.

'Because he's in a better place now, Mickey.' Samantha smiled gently, as though thinking of a loved one, a child maybe. 'Georgie is in a safe place, where no one can hurt him.'

'I'm not sure that's a choice for you to make,' Mickey replied quickly.

Samantha fixed her eyes on Mickey. 'You knew Georgie better than anyone. Tell me I'm wrong, come on, tell me.'

There was a silence in the room; Mickey was unusually lost for words, a sense of hopelessness fell over him.

'Anyway, why are you so bothered,' said Samantha, her voice suddenly challenging. 'Why do you care so much about Georgie? '

Mickey's eyes flared. 'Why am I so fucking bothered? Why do I fucking care? You know why. He was my fucking best mate, my brother. I miss him, and I want him back.'

Samantha stared back at him. 'You're trying to soften me up, trying to wear me down so that you can get what you want.'

'No,' replied Mickey firmly, 'I'm waiting for you to do the right thing.'

It was Samantha's turn to get emotional. 'I did the right thing!' she snapped back.

They both stood up at the same time. In a split second they were face to face. The two orderlies were instantly beside them, but Mickey held out a hand to stop them. 'It's all right.'

Samantha took a deep breath, brought herself back under control. 'Tell me something, Mickey. How long you will keep visiting me here?'

'Until I find Georgie.'

Samantha turned away, her ghostly smile flickering across her face. 'Well, Mickey, you will be waiting a very long time.'

Mickey felt a wave of despair wash over him. He was getting nowhere. 'Is there nothing I can do?'

The helplessness in his voice seemed to strike a chord in Samantha. At the last moment she turned, gave Mickey a half smile. 'You have to have a little faith, Mickey. Jesus will provide.'

Mickey and Miranda

Mickey pulled up outside Miranda's apartment, turned off the motor, sat for a moment just thinking. What was he doing? He should be going home, patching things up with Mandy.

Right! Patch up what? They'd been apart for fourteen years, and now he'd come back to someone he barely knew, who moaned at him all the time and left him cold. He could barely stand to look at her, avoided seeing her naked, certainly didn't want to have sex with her. She was always complaining and nagging about something, was never happy. He gave her everything she asked for, everything she wanted, but she still wasn't pleased, it wasn't enough.

And the problems with their sex life were nothing new - their sex life had been non-existent for a couple of years before he was banged up. Every time he fancied a bit she made excuses, shying away from him. She loved him enough to look past his criminal activities and enjoy the spoils, but when it suited her - like now - she could be a complete bitch.

And then there was Miranda. She'd been right all along, he'd always fancied her, had been fantasizing about having sex with her for years, and now that he finally had... Even Mickey would admit that there was more to life than sex, but after fourteen years without it. What with all the shit that was going on since he'd been released, he needed something, something to make him happy, to make him feel good about himself. Miranda did all that to him. She had left a mark on him, and every time he thought of her or saw her his heart skipped a beat. He felt like a love struck teenager, knew that anywhere she went he would follow. Thoughts of her filled his mind, consumed him. Even when he closed his eyes he could still see her silhouette.

He pulled the keys out of the ignition, opened the car door. Miranda was what he wanted, Miranda made him happy, and he was going to take whatever she offered, enjoy every minute of it, and let the future take care of itself.

Even just opening the front door to her apartment he felt himself getting horny. What would she be wearing? What would they do? Whereas with Mandy sex had been something you did on a Saturday night, in the dark, under the covers, with

Miranda it could be any time, any place, any position... He dropped his keys on the hall table, pulled off his coat. 'It's me!

There was no reply.

Mickey grinned, stepped into the living room, and looked around. No sign of Miranda - but he knew she was home, her car was outside, the scent of her perfume was in the air. There was no sign of her in the kitchen either - that meant there was really only one place she would be...

Mickey slowly opened the bedroom door. The bedside lights were on, casting a soft glow over the room, over Miranda, lying in the bed waiting for him, on her back, her knees up, her body hidden beneath the dark, silk sheet.

'You're late,' she said seductively, her voice dripping with honey.

'Yeah, I'm sorry, I -'

She cut him off. 'You are a very naughty boy, Mickey, disobedient and disrespectful, and now you have to pay the price.'

Mickey couldn't keep the grin off his face. 'And what's the price?'

Miranda slowly pulled the sheet, up over her knees, until her upper body was covered, but her legs, her lower half were exposed. She wore nothing but a pair of black, lace topped stockings.

'God, you're gorgeous,' he sighed, his greedy eyes going straight to her smooth pussy as she reached down, gently stroked her lips with her fingertips.

'You have to make it up to me,' she purred. 'Over and over again.'

Mickey moved towards the bed. Christmas had definitely come early this year!

'Stop! You do exactly what I tell you, when I tell you. You understand me?'

Mickey licked his lips, unable to tear his eyes away from her fingers as she gently stroked herself. He nodded his agreement.

'Strip!' She commanded.

Mickey needed no second invitation - he ripped his clothes off, threw them on the floor. Within seconds he was naked.

'Now, on your hands and knees and crawl up the bed towards me.'

Mickey did as he was told, crawled up towards her naked body, those softly stroking fingers.

'Don't touch me yet,' she told him.

He stopped, no more than a foot away from her, staring at her beautifully shaved pussy as she caressed it with her fingers.

'I want your tongue inside me, as deep as it will go,' she commanded him.

As he moved forwards she reached out and grabbed his hair, thrust his face into her pussy, began grinding her hips against his face.

'Oh, yes, that's it!' she moaned. It was clear that she had been waiting for him for a while, thinking and planning, getting herself excited, so it didn't take long for her to climax for the first time, a long shuddering squeal that shook her whole body.

She held him tight as the orgasm rippled through her body, then released his hair, lay back with a sigh. 'Not a bad start,' she told him, suddenly sitting up, a wicked grin on her face, 'but you're not done yet!'

Mickey grinned. 'No shit!'

'Lie down! On your back!' she ordered.

Mickey did as he was told, rolled over and lay flat on his back, looking up. Miranda's eyes took in his muscular body, impressive hard on.

She turned around and straddled him, trapped his arms beneath her legs, her wet pussy rubbing against his chest. She slid backwards and forwards, reached back and grabbed his stiff cock, began slowly stroking it up and down. 'You have a bit more work to do before this fella gets what she wants,' she told Mickey.

Mickey's eyes feasted on her beautiful body, she looked incredible in the soft light, her stomach flat, breasts firm, dark nipples sticking out. She saw where his eyes were going, leaned over so that her breasts hung just above his face.

He reached up with his mouth, searching, questing with his tongue as she leaned slightly closer, allowing him to kiss and suck her nipples, then closer still as he opened his mouth wide and sucked her breast into his mouth, relishing the taste of her. She ran her fingers through his hair, and Mickey could feel himself falling further and further under her spell.

'Do you love me, Mickey,' she said suddenly.

'Yes!' he gasped, looking up at her, dreamy eyed.

'Say it.'

Mickey pulled an arm free from under her leg, reached up to caress her face, he tilted her chin so that he could kiss her. 'I love you, Miranda,' he whispered.

'Say it again.'

'I love you.'

Nothing else existed for him, just Miranda's body, his hand teasing her hard nipple, her soft moans, her pussy rubbing against his stomach. No cares, no worries, no Georgie or Mandy, no Wolfson or Cooper, no Joey or Kenny.

She suddenly sat up, smiled at him through her long dark lashes. 'You've got me all soaking wet,' she teased, 'and you need to do something about it.' She lifted her hips, moved forward until her body was directly over his face, her pussy lips just inches from him. 'It's time for your tongue to show me how much you love me.'

Again Mickey lifted his head, his tongue stretching, trying to reach her, taste her.

Miranda smiled. 'You want it, don't you? Want to taste me, eat me?'

Mickey nodded, transfixed, unable to speak.

'You want to bury your tongue deep inside me?' She smiled. 'I want that too!' With a deep sigh Miranda lowered herself upon him, his tongue driving up into her, almost smothering him, began grinding back and forth, lost in her own world of private pleasure.

'God you've got a wicked tongue,' she moaned, her hips moving faster as she rubbed her pussy against his face. She grabbed his hair, pushed down harder against his mouth. 'Yes, yes!'

Mickey had never done anything like this before. When he and his mates talked in the pub about the girls they'd had, the things they had done, most of them considered giving a woman oral sex to be soft, unmanly. They were more than happy to get a blow job, but going down on a woman? Well, that wasn't for them.

Mickey had done it a few times before, but never for long, always under his own terms, when he wanted to. Certainly not like this, not with the woman on top of him, using him as a toy, using his tongue to satisfy her needs, grinding herself against his face.

And yet, with Miranda, he would have been content to stay there forever. The smell of her, the taste of her, the feel of her. Her occupying his total attention, nothing to concern him, no decisions to make. Nothing but Miranda and her beautiful body pressing down on him.

Faster and faster she rubbed against him, her eyes closed, her body writhing, her fingers still locked into his hair to ensure that he did exactly what she wanted.   Suddenly her body stiffened, every muscle taut, then with a loud scream she collapsed against him, slid down next to him to hold him tight.

'Oh God!' she gasped.

'I take it you liked that?'

She nuzzled in against his chest, reached a hand down to stroke his stiff cock. 'I didn't hear you complaining?'

Mickey grinned. 'I wasn't exactly in a position to do much talking!'

'Good thing too!' She started stroking him faster, up and down, up and down. 'And I guess you're thinking it's your turn now?'

'Turn about is fair play.'

'And what exactly might you want?'

Mickey ran his hands through her thick dark hair, gently pushed her head downwards. 'You know exactly what I want!'

The surge of ecstasy that swept through his body as she enveloped him in her warm mouth almost made him come straight away, but he controlled himself, lay back. He wanted to enjoy this, enjoy every minute he could, make it last as long as possible.

As her mouth slid up and down on him he closed his eyes, let out a deep sigh, knew that he would never be able to let her go...

Mickey and Mandy

Mickey opened the front door, stepped inside, listened. All he wanted to do was get in, grab some stuff, and get back out. No fuss, no rows, no nonsense. Mandy was usually at work at this time of the day, although her hours varied a bit from week to week.

The house was quiet, no radio blaring from the kitchen. He relaxed, stepped towards the stairs, froze as he heard her voice.

'I was wondering when you would show up!' Heavy footsteps, then she appeared in the living room doorway, frumpy and frowsy in a tatty dressing gown, her hair mussed up, a scowl on her face. She'd obviously been sleeping on the couch, waiting for him to come home.

'Look at the fucking state of you!' sneered Mickey. He hadn't meant to say it, hadn't wanted any drama, but it just came out. So much for no fuss...

Mandy stepped forward, right up close to him, sniffed. 'I can smell her fucking perfume!' She sniffed some more. 'And her cunt!'

Mickey looked down at her, tried to recall what he had once felt, but there was nothing there. 'Leave it out, Mand,' he muttered, tried to push past her, but she stepped to the side, blocked his way.

He sighed, trying to keep his cool. 'Don't do this, not now. There's all kind of shit going down that you don't know about -'

' - I reckon the only thing going down is Miranda Solomon, on you!' she screamed.

'I don't have time for this!' He shoved past her, raced up the stairs two at a time, heading for his bedroom. Grab a suitcase, get his stuff packed, get out of there. He could hear her heavy footsteps labouring up the stairs behind him.

Mickey threw open his bedroom door, stopped cold.

'Didn't expect that, did ya?' she cackled.

It took Mickey a moment to take it all in. All his stuff, all his clothes, everything, were spread around the bedroom. But to call them clothes . . . Mandy had shredded them all, every last suit, jacket, tie, shirt, the whole lot had been hacked and sliced to pieces, then hurled on the floor. It was a mess, a complete and utter fucking mess. He stood, frozen, taking it all in, could hear her behind him.

'You were out fucking Miranda, I was at home, bored,' she said in a cold voice. 'Seemed like a good way to kill the time.'

Mickey didn't even bother turning around to look at her. He didn't want to see her, didn't want to talk to her, just wanted to get the fuck out. He'd have to buy himself some new clobber - not that he minded, most of it was pretty old anyway. He stepped through the mess, grabbed a few personal items that she had forgotten to trash - some cufflinks, his toilet bag, an antique watch that he kept in the drawer beside the bed, turned to go.

Mandy was standing right behind him, a strange look on her face, and a pair of scissors still in her hand. He ran his cold, hard eyes over her. 'I'll leave the rest of this lot for you,' he said. 'Maybe you can practice your cutting skills while I'm fucking Miranda!'

He cast his eyes around the room one more time, knowing that he would never be back, then turned to go.

A sudden movement out of the corner of his eye caught his attention, but he still barely dodged aside as Mandy came at him with the scissors. Her first lunge skimmed his ribs, slicing through his shirt and drawing blood, her second narrowly missed his arm.

Mickey stumbled back, his feet tangling in the mess of shredded clothes on the floor, hit his leg on the frame of the bed, landed flat on his back on top of the bed.

Mandy was on him in a flash, her legs straddling him, the scissors rising high to flash down towards his neck.

He turned his head to the side, just avoided the blow, then managed to grab her arm and wrestle it upwards as she prepared for another slashing blow at his face. His strong fingers wrapped around her wrist, stopped her, the scissors hovering just above his face.

Her other arm darted out, her broken nails trying to claw at his face. With his right hand he grabbed her wrist, held her in place above him, her arms straining to break free, to slash him, hurt him, kill him if she could. Her wild eyes stared down at him. 'You fucking bastard, I'll kill you!' she screamed.

Mickey wrenched on her wrist, and with a scream of pain she dropped the scissors. They landed on the edge of the bed, slid harmlessly to the floor.

With a thrust of his powerful body Mickey flipped her over, reversed the position so that she was lying flat on her back, he was on top, pinning beneath him.

Her face contorted with rage as she struggled to throw him off, but he was too heavy, too strong.

'Mandy! Enough!' he shouted.

She struggled and squirmed, trying desperately to free her arms. 'You bastard, you fucking, fucking bastard!'

Then as suddenly as it had appeared, her rage collapsed, her arms went limp, she burst into tears.

Mickey kept a firm grip on her wrists as her arms flopped back onto the bed, prepared for a trick. But it was no trick, all the fight had gone out of her. Eyes closed, she sobbed, her bottom lip trembling. 'I knew it, I always fucking knew it,' she sniffed. 'Sooner or later, that fucking woman was going to get her claws into you.'

Mickey didn't know what to do, didn't know what to say. Mandy had changed - and not for the better. She had been worn down by the years of taking care of the family while he was inside, and it showed everywhere - her tired, puffy face, her flabby body, her bitter, defeated mind. It was Mickey's fault, he knew that, accepted it. But he also knew that he no longer loved the woman that she had become, and with the children grown up, there was nothing to keep them together.

Even if his thing with Miranda turned out to be a passing moment, he could see no way he would ever want to come back home to Mandy, no scenario under which he would ever be happy with her again. Even if he came home, he would always be looking for the next escape, the next attractive piece of skirt, the next woman who could get his motor running. And Mandy would know it, would always be looking out for it, suspicious every time he was out, nagging every time he came back.

He slowly released her wrists, ready in case she tried to attack him again, but it was no act. Eyes closed, she lay sobbing on the bed.

Mickey climbed slowly to his feet, glanced down at his ribs. She had nicked him with the scissors and the blood had stained his white shirt, a trickle that ran down across his stomach to his waist. Nothing bad, no stitches needed. Just one more shirt he needed to buy.

He stepped back, searching for the right words. 'I'm sorry, Mand.'

No response. She just lay on the bed, sobbing gently, hadn't moved since he released her wrists and stood up.

'I'll take care of you, you know that.'

He looked around the room at all his shredded clothes. Christ, it was going to cost him a bit to replace all of these. He moved towards the wardrobe. He kept a box of cash on the top shelf, right at the back. He had never let her see him use it, see where he kept it. He prayed that it was still there... He rummaged back past the old sweaters he hadn't worn in twenty years, finally wrapped his fingers round the old shoe box. He gave a deep sigh of relief as he pulled it out.

Thank Christ for that! He could tell just from the weight that the money was still there. He pulled it out, checked it quickly. Close to thirty grand. There was also an old shooter in there, a Browning he'd had for donkey's years. He never used it for big jobs - anything he actually shot someone with was always wiped off and ditched in the river - but it was still better off in his hands than Mandy's.

'So that's where you kept it!'

He turned, found her staring at him, wiping at her puffy eyes with the corner of the sheet.

'I would have fucking shot you if I'd found it!'

He looked at her, his eyes gradually softening. She looked so sad, pathetic. 'No you wouldn't.'

Mandy slowly shook her head. 'You're right, I wouldn't.'

Mickey checked the safety catch was on, then shoved the gun down the back of his trousers. He glanced around the room. 'I need to go shopping.'

'No fucking kidding!'

They both laughed, a painful shared reminder of what they had once had. Mickey counted out five grand, tossed it on the bed towards her. 'Try and make it last. I don't exactly have a full time job right now.'

She looked at the money for a moment, lying on the bed beside her, and for a second he thought she was going to throw it back at him, or tear it to shreds, but then she reached out a hand, picked up the money, set it in her lap.   'When will I see you again?'

Mickey shrugged.   'I'll be around, check in on you from time to time.'

She nodded sadly, looked up and met his eyes. 'We had a good run, Mickey.'

Mickey met her sad gaze.   'Yeah, we had a good run, girl.'

Without another word he turned and marched out.

Sharon

Another night, another client. Sharon had been on the game too long to feel anything about her work - it was what she did, it paid well, and it beat the fuck out of working in an office or at the supermarket like a lot of her mates.

She knew she was getting to the end of her working life in this game, and had been putting money aside for years to support herself when the flow of customers started to dry up. She was a realist - she turned forty in a few months, and though she had looked after herself, she couldn't compete with the dewy eyes and soft skin of the teenagers and twenty year olds out there. Her stock in trade had become a bit of domination, a bit of bondage. Blokes of all ages liked an older woman, done up to the nines in stockings, high heels, a leather or PVC basque, telling them what to do.

It suited Sharon - she had always liked to be in control of any situation, whether it be family, friends, or in the bedroom, so she had taken to it like a duck to water.

With some girls who did the domination thing it was an act, but there was a side of Sharon that enjoyed it - she'd been fucked over by enough men in her life that the opportunity to have one obey her every whim was a bit of a turn on.

She did with them whatever they wanted and paid for - forcing them to strip, lick her shoes, sometimes a bit of a spanking if they liked that, and then teasing and tempting them until they could stand it no more. It was amazing what you could get a man to do if he knew he was going to get his rocks off in the end!

She looked in the mirror, touched up her make-up. Thank God for make-up, she thought! With a good quality cover up to hide the crow's feet that were starting to spread around her eyes and her body held tight in the basque, she still looked pretty good.

And once she started peeling off her silky robe, revealed her boobs spilling out of her top, her pussy visible at the open crotch, well, no bloke was looking at her crow's feet!

She checked her watch. Five minutes till showtime. She was seeing a new client tonight, an older bloke the agency had said, he had heard about her from a mate and asked for her by name. She preferred it when clients came via a recommendation, it usually meant that they knew what to expect, had an idea what they would get, and were less likely to take liberties.

You could never completely eliminate the dodgy ones, it was part of the job, but they were few and far between. The agency did background checks these days, they were pretty good at weeding out the dangerous ones. But it still happened from time to time. Some bloke decided that he didn't want Sharon to be in charge, he wanted to set the agenda. He started pushing her around, or gave her a quick slap. Usually she sorted them out right away, but occasionally some vicious bastard would slip through the net, give her some really rough treatment.

Just because they were paying for it, some blokes thought they could do whatever they wanted, that she was their personal sex toy to use, abuse and throw away when they were done.

If it turned ugly, she had learned to go with the flow. Blokes like that liked it if you fought back, it wound them up, and they knew they were hurting you, so they just did more.

Most times they would slap her around a bit, arse fuck her, something like that where they felt they were in control, where they felt like they were raping her, making her do something she didn't want to do.

Fat fucking chance, she had done just about everything sexual it was possible to do over the past twenty years, so the chance of some bloke actually surprising Sharon was pretty slim.

The ring of the doorbell echoed through her stylish apartment. Sharon gave a last touch of perfume to her neck, her full cleavage, tied her silk robe around her, and headed for the door.

The punter was a small man, receding grey hair, a mild manner, a soft Irish brogue. She guessed he was around sixty.

He looked her up and down, smiled as she let him in. 'I can see I've come to the right place?'

Sharon took his coat, led him into the living room. The sumptuous couches encouraged you to settle back, relax. Soft jazz music was playing in the background. Candles dotted the room.

Sharon settled herself down on the couch, her silk robe falling open to show her stocking clad legs, indicated that the man should sit next to her.

He glanced at her legs, gave another shy smile as he carefully hitched his trouser legs and sat down. His eyes wandered round the room, took in the expensive flock wallpaper, the tasteful oil paintings. 'Business must be good?'

Sharon smiled. 'Satisfied clients are the best recommendation.'

He nodded, still not really looking at her. A shy one. Sharon kept the smile from her face as she thought of what a soft piece of putty he was going to be in her powerful hands. 'So what do I call you?'

He turned quickly, ran his piercing green eyes down her body. 'Thomas. You can call me Thomas.'

'OK, Thomas,' she began, 'why don't we start by getting you more comfortable.'

He wore an old fashioned tweed jacket, a tie from the 1960s, his shirt buttoned tight.

Sharon leaned over, gently stroked his cheek with her long red fingernails. 'One of us has done this many times before,' she purred, 'while one of us looks a little nervous and uncertain.'

Thomas nodded. 'This is all a bit new to me.'

'Then let me tell you what to do,' Sharon continued. 'Exactly what to do. Agreed?'

Again Thomas nodded.

Sharon smiled. 'So now we know the ground rules, shall we begin?' She untied her silk robe, allowed it to fall open, revealing her milky thighs, the black leather basque, her full breasts. She moved closer, blowing softly in his ear, her arm wrapping around his shoulder to pull him closer to her, forcing his head down into her cleavage. 'Why don't you start by saying hello to my girls?' she whispered.

Thomas buried his face in her cleavage, his soft lips and tongue kissing her gently. Give him a minute to enjoy that, thought Sharon, get him warmed up, then pull the rug from under him, show him who was the boss...

The suddenness with which he sat up caught her completely by surprise, the top of his head crashing into her jaw, rocking her head back, making her bite her tongue.

She fell back against the sofa, tasted blood, momentarily stunned. Any thought that it was an accident was swiftly dismissed as the man leaned over her, grabbed her by the throat, and punched her hard in the face.

Sharon had suffered at the hands of some clients before, but nothing as savage, as swift, as premeditated as this.

Her eyes were streaming tears as she clutched at her broken nose, the blood flowing through her fingers. Through the fog she could vaguely see the man standing over her. He ripped his tie off, was suddenly on top of her, pinning her down. She felt weak, dizzy, wanted to throw up.

He grabbed the tie, wrapped it around her neck, and pulled it tight. The rough fabric bit into her skin, the pressure closing off her breathing. Her hands went to her neck, scrabbled to get a grip, loosen the tie, but he was too strong, she was already stunned and weak, the tie was just too tight.

Sharon gasped, tried to suck in some air, but nothing was getting through. She squirmed, thrashed with her arms, but he had her tight, and she was already weakening.

She could feel the end approaching. A fog covered her eyes, she could barely make out the man's features through the haze, but what she could see was strangely impassive. He didn't seem excited, turned-on, in any way affected by what he was doing as he squeezed the life out of her.

Little by little she could feel the life drain out of her. What a way to go, she thought. Then a strange thought crossed her mind. I wonder if he'll fuck me once I'm dead. She almost started to smile, then suddenly was gasping and coughing, sucking in air in great rasping lungful's as he released the tie.

Sharon coughed and spluttered, each breath hurt, but at the same time each breath brought precious life flowing back into her body.

She blinked, looked up at the man.

He wasn't even breathing hard, still looked at her with the same slightly quizzical expression he'd worn when he first walked in the door. 'So,' he said softly. 'I think we have established the new ground rules, don't you?'

Sharon nodded weakly. Just play along. Let him have his jollies, stick his dick wherever he wanted, do whatever it takes to get out alive. She'd never felt more desperate to simply survive, her life had never seemed more precious to her. 'What do you want?' she gasped.

The man moved with sudden swiftness, jumping off of her, rolling her off the sofa to land hard on her expensive Moroccan rug, swiftly tying her hands behind her back with the tie. She didn't struggle, didn't resist. This was OK, he was probably going to fuck her up the arse then clear off. That was fine with Sharon...

He stood up, turned and headed towards the hallway. 'You just stay there, there's a good girl.'

She could hear his footsteps on the parquet tiles of the hallway. He stopped a moment, then turned and headed back towards her.

'I have something I wanted to show you,' he said, crouching down next to her. He held an A4 manila envelope. 'Do you know what it took to get these?' he said reproachfully. 'It's expensive for good work like this.'

He reached in the envelope, pulled out a small stack of photographs, began showing them to Sharon one by one, giving her time to take each one in. Sharon on her knees blowing some guy, Sharon across the arm of her sofa taking it up the arse...on and on, everything that she did for a living in beautiful, crisp, clear black and white.

She looked up at him, for a moment couldn't keep her natural Taylor defiance out of her voice. 'So? I'm not ashamed. That's what I do.'

Wolfson nodded slowly, glanced at the pictures, stopping on one even more depraved than the others. It showed Sharon kneeling between three guys, one dick in each hand and one in her mouth. 'That's a particular favourite of mine,' he laughed. 'Good coordination required, I would imagine?'

She remembered that night, it was a stag night, there had been five of them in total, and she had done just about everything it was possible to do in the course of the evening. She'd barely been able to walk by the time they were done, but a grand for a night's work wasn't to be sneezed at.

'So here's the thing, Sharon,' he said softly. 'I don't believe that your friends and family know what you do for a living...'

A shiver of fear ran through Sharon. Only Miranda knew what she did. Everyone else thought she worked in an office. If they ever found out, if they ever saw those photos, she could never face them again. She could not let that happen. 'What do you want?' She forced the words out through her dry, cracked throat.

'Now we come to it.' He slid the photos back into the envelope, set it on the floor by Sharon's head. 'Our little deal.'

'I've got money, I can get you -'

He reached out suddenly, slammed her face against the floor, ground her cheek into the rug. 'I don't want money, you fucking whore! I want your cunt of a brother!'

The sudden change of his demeanour, of the subject, flummoxed her for a minute. 'My brother?'

'Mickey. Mickey fucking Taylor. Remember him?'

'What do you -'

He cut her off. 'The bastard owes me. An old score I need to settle.'

Sharon looked up at his cold face. 'What do you need me for?' she croaked.

'He's a canny bastard,' he told her, 'hard to get alone. Always has his mates around him at the pub, or when he's out and about. But there's times he disappears. He covers his tracks well, but he's going somewhere, to some whore's place, something like that.'

Sharon's mind instantly jumped - she knew exactly where Mickey was going. Miranda hadn't been able to contain her excitement, had had to tell someone, had revealed all to Sharon in a breathless phone call.

Sharon tried to fake indifference. 'How the fuck would I know where he goes? I've only seen him once since he got out. He didn't tell me anything.'

The man looked at her carefully. 'You are in a particularly vulnerable position right now...' He ran a hand up her stockinged thigh, rested it with his fingertips just brushing her pussy lips.

'You don't frighten me!' blustered Sharon. 'I doubt you can think of anything that some cock sucker hasn't already tried.'

The man said nothing, just reached in his jacket pocket, pulled out a switch blade. The knife flicked open before her eyes, and Sharon found that she couldn't tear her eyes from it. 'I should frighten you,' he said softly. 'I am prepared to do anything - absolutely anything - to get you to tell me about your brother's habits, where he goes, what he does.'

'I don't know!' protested Sharon. But this time there was an edge of fear in her voice.

The blade suddenly flashed. Sharon flinched, but it was just her silk robe he sliced, cutting it in two, slicing off the sleeves, pulling it all free from beneath her prone body.

His movements were quick, sudden. He grabbed a handful of robe, crammed it in her mouth, took one of the sliced sleeves and tied it tight around her head. 'There. Now you won't disturb the neighbours with your screaming.'

Another quick movement and he flipped her over onto her back, tied one of her ankles to the heavy coffee table, the other to one of the feet of the couch, her legs wide apart.

Sharon had never felt more vulnerable in her life as she stared up at him, eyes wide, horrified, unable to resist watching his every move. 'Right about now you are probably thinking that there is something that you would like to tell me, but I think it's best if you see the way I work first, so that when you do decide to speak, I can be sure you are telling the truth.' He spoke in calm measured tones, a contrast to Sharon's increasingly frantic state.

With Sharon secured, he stood up, walked slowly across to the ornate stone fireplace, where a gas fire nestled.

'Everyone has their own preferred methods of inflicting pain,' he explained to her, turning on the fire. The blue flames burst into light, casting a soft glow over his face. 'Me? I find heat is always very effective.'

He turned his back to her, held the tip of the blade into the flame, watched as it slowly heated up, turned red.

Sharon began to struggle as he stood up and turned back towards her, but she was bound too tight, and there was no mercy in his eyes. He squatted down next to her, held the red hot blade between her thighs, so close that she could feel the heat on her pussy. 'We could start there,' he said, 'but then we'd have nothing for you to anticipate, no incentive for me to stop.'

Another quick movement and the blade sliced through one of the shoulder straps of her basque. Her breast spilled out, full and lush, the nipple soft, pink.

Sharon started to squirm, but he knelt down, straddled her, and slowly lowered the hot blade towards her breast. Still she squirmed, but it made no difference, she was unable to move.

The pain seared through her as he pressed the hot blade to her breast, she could smell the burning flesh, wanted to scream as she writhed, twisted, anything, anything to just make it stop...

Then just as suddenly he lifted the blade back up, grabbed her jaw with his strong hand. 'Next time I burn your nipple off, then the third time...well, you know what happens then.' He stared into Sharon's petrified eyes, gave it all a moment to sink in. 'So. Are you ready to talk?'

Despite his firm grip, she managed to nod vigorously.

'Good girl.'

More quick movement and the gag was pulled from her mouth. She gasped for breath, sucking in the cool air.

'So?'

'He's got a girl, her name's Miranda!' She blurted it out, couldn't tell him quickly enough.

The man gave a satisfied smile. 'Thank you. And you know her address?'

'She lives out towards Hornchurch,' gasped Sharon. 'Maple Crescent, number 7.'

Another brief smile. 'See, it wasn't that hard, was it?'

Sharon gazed up at him, desperate to please, as always, hoping she had done enough to stay alive, make him stop the pain. 'Will you let me go now?'

He looked down at her. 'Now that's a bit of a problem.   Because if I let you go now, you'll be straight on the phone, calling Mickey, calling this Miranda girl, telling them I'm coming over for a visit.'

'No I won't, honest.   You've still got the pictures!' she said desperately.   'If I said anything, you could, you know, show them to people!'

He still sat on top of her, pressing her against the floor. 'Indeed I could.'   He looked down at the angry red burn on her breast.   'Does that hurt?'

Sharon said nothing, unsure where this was going.   He suddenly leaned over, pressed his mouth to her breast, sucked hard, his tongue rubbing back and forth across the burnt spot.   She fought to not cry, not give him the pleasure of seeing how much he was hurting her.

After a moment he sat up, gently jostled both her breasts.   'Do you know how long it's been since I had a prime piece of meat like you?'

Sharon said nothing.

He grabbed the cloth, shoved it back into her mouth, stood up and unzipped his pants.   'It would be almost rude to leave here without enjoying your services, wouldn't it?'

He dropped his pants to the ground, knelt down between her legs, then with a sudden jerk thrust himself inside her.

Sharon's eyes remained fixed on the ceiling, tears streaming down her cheeks as he thrust himself against her, again and again. If she ever got free, she told herself, she would tell Mickey to hunt this bastard down and cut his fucking balls off!

Mickey and Georgie

Mickey was finding it harder and harder to drag himself up to Rampton - it was a long old drive, Martin didn't want to come with him, and he himself was beginning to think it was a colossal waste of fucking time. But at the same time, when he was talking to Samantha he kept getting tantalising glimpses of Georgie. It was just enough to encourage him to believe that Georgie was still hiding in there somewhere, and that maybe, maybe, if Mickey was patient, was clever, he might eventually find out where the diamonds were.

It was late afternoon when he arrived, the low sun casting long, flickering shadows of the trees across the road as he approached the hospital.   He was tense, his hands gripping the wheel so tight that his knuckles were white. It was the doors, the bars, the smell of the place that got to him. It was too reminiscent of being inside, too soon for him.

Everything was taking its toll, Martin was heading back to Australia later tonight, Mandy had gone psycho on him. All he needed now was one of his fucking sisters or kids to kick off and he would lose it himself.

He breathed deeply, forced himself to calm down as the high fences appeared along the side of the road. He needed to be totally in control, on top of his game, if he had any hope of getting anything out of Samantha. Take it slow, be calm, forget about everything except his brother, Georgie, trapped inside there and wanting to get out, wanting to talk to Mickey.

Samantha was her usual immaculate, composed self, in a form fitting red dress, high heels, nails to match. If he were honest with himself, Mickey felt almost intimidated by her. Georgie had always been the smart one, with a sharp mind that seemed to be two steps ahead of everyone else, and Samantha seemed to have enhanced that aspect of Georgie's mind. Mickey always felt that Samantha was totally in control of their conversations, had a plan, and knew what Mickey would say even before he said it. But not this time. This time Mickey was going to go on the offensive, see if he could ruffle her feathers a bit, break through the veneer to what lay underneath.

'Back so soon?' she said coolly as she settled herself into a chair.

'You would have liked the funeral,' said Mickey standing above her, looking down.

Samantha crossed and uncrossed her legs, buying herself a moment. 'Funerals bore me,' she said. 'I've been to too many in my time.'

'But mum? Our mum? You should have been there.'

She said nothing.

'Sharon and Terri had to do all the planning, chose the music, the flowers, all that stuff. You would have been brilliant at all that. But neither of us was there to help out, were we? Neither of us saw her before she died.'

There! Mickey saw it, a tiny twitch at the corner of her eye.

'I couldn't have done anything about that, of course. Once I got my sentence, well, that was it, banged up until they decided I'd been a good boy and could go home. But you, you. You've served long enough for killing Charlie. If you decide to stop hiding, to let Georgie come out and face the light of day... Well, you could do any time you want, couldn't you?'

Samantha squirmed in her chair. 'It's not that easy,' she whispered.

Mickey leaned in close. 'Sorry love, can you say that again? Didn't hear you.'

Samantha looked up at him, eyes blazing. 'I said it's not that easy!'

Mickey sneered at her. 'Says you!'

'What does that mean?'

Mickey dropped into the chair beside her. 'I don't doubt that when you started this you had Georgie's best interests in mind. What was done to him, what he went through... ain't no kid should have to suffer like that.' Mickey shook his head. 'Fuck, none of us should have had to put up with what that sick fucker did to us. And then you, you had the double dose, what with the beatings at home and then Charlie and Bill Covey giving it to you as well...'

He glanced at her face. It was a mask, nothing showing, but she was whispering something to herself, over and over again. Mickey leaned in closer.

'Jesus will provide, Jesus will provide, Jesus will provide...'

'You going to go all religious on me now?'

Louder now: 'Jesus will provide, Jesus will provide, Jesus will provide.'

'Come on Samantha, let Georgie out, let me talk to him, let him tell me what I know he wants to say.'

And finally shouting: 'Jesus will provide! Jesus will provide! Jesus will provide!'

Samantha suddenly stood up, stared at Mickey wild-eyed. 'Don't you fucking get it?' she snarled. 'Jesus will provide!'

The orderlies stepped forward, ready.

'What I want, what you want,' she continued. 'Jesus will provide!'

Mickey was shocked, silent. The voice that was speaking to him now wasn't Samantha, that cultivated husky voice he'd been hearing on all his previous visits - it was Georgie, unmistakably Georgie! He finally managed to force the word out, the word he'd been desperate to say. 'Georgie?'

And then Georgie looked back at him. Despite the make-up, despite the wig, it was Georgie who was looking back into Mickey's eyes. He grabbed Mickey's collar, pulled him close, hissed at him. 'Don't you get it? Jesus will provide!'

And just like that he was gone, turning on his high heels and strutting back towards the exit, leaving Mickey standing stunned, confused, torn between hope and despair.

Mickey and Wolfson

It wasn't until he was on the motorway, driving back home, that Mickey suddenly started to laugh. That cunning bastard! He'd known all along where the diamonds were - Georgie had known - but he couldn't find a way to tell Mickey, not with Samantha as his gatekeeper. She was keeping him safe, yes, but also stopping him from reaching out to Mickey, telling his brother what he needed to know.

Fuck! Thought Mickey, the human brain works in devious fucking ways! The fact that Samantha existed at all, that she served to protect his brother, was a mind fuck enough. But then you got into the whole idea of Georgie being in there somewhere, hidden behind this front he had created, and finding it impossible to break out. And then finally, the fact that somehow, through all of that, Georgie had managed to communicate with Mickey in a way that Samantha wouldn't suspect, wouldn't understand. A total mind fuck indeed!

Mickey checked his watch. He'd not been at the hospital very long in the end, he still had enough time to drop by Miranda's for a quickie and   then make it back home. Just in time to deliver his bombshell, before Martin buggered off back to Australia.

He settled back in the seat, enjoying the feel of the warm air on his face, thinking about Miranda, the sort of welcome she always gave him, then turning his thoughts to Martin, Terri and Sharon. Christ were they going to be surprised. He was pretty sure they all thought that he was on a wild goose chase with his visits to Georgie. Especially after Martin had come along himself and seen what he was like. But now, against all the odds, Georgie had come through, had told him what he needed to know. He couldn't wait to see the looks on their faces.

He pulled up outside Miranda's. He liked being here, it was a classy neighbourhood, quiet, you could leave your car unlocked overnight and still expect to find it where you'd left it in the morning.

He grinned as he climbed out of his car. Who would have thought that the diamonds were right under their noses the whole time? All those years they'd been staring right at them, they'd all taken the mick out of his mum for the crap she kept around the house, little knowing what was hiding there.

Did she know? Mickey wondered. Was that why she'd been so specific in her will? Or was it just Bobby being clever, knowing that was one thing she'd never throw away, no matter how much she hated his guts?

He locked his car, turned towards the house. The lights were on, Miranda would probably be wearing something exciting, ready and waiting for him...

'Mickey fuckin' Taylor, as I live and breathe. What a lovely surprise.'

Mickey cursed himself. How could he be so stupid, so fucking inattentive? 'Hello Wolfson.' Even after all these years he recognised him – he'd aged, like all of them, but he still had that weasely face that Mickey remembered from when he was younger. Mickey knew without turning around that Cooper would be behind him.

'We need to have a little chat,' said Wolfson in his soft Irish burr.

'What – like your little chats with Kenny and Joey?' Mickey couldn't keep the edge out of his voice when he said it. He sensed Cooper close behind him before he felt the gun jabbed in his back.

'We can bring Clemence along if you'd like,' sneered Cooper. 'But you probably enjoy taking it up the jacksy after your time inside.'

Mickey started to turn towards him, but Cooper jammed the gun tighter into his back, grabbed his shoulder with the other hand. 'Let's go somewhere more private for this little chat, shall we?'

Mickey glanced towards the house. If he threw Cooper off, shouted –

'Don't even think about it, Mickey,' purred Wolfson. 'By the time your girlfriend made it out the front door, you'd be lying on the pavement with your liver spread half way across Hornchurch, and we'd be long gone.'

Mickey sighed, relaxed. They were right. He'd have to go with them now, wait for his chance. And when it came...

Mickey was bundled into the back of Wolfson's car, Cooper right next to him, the gun still jammed into Mickey's side. Wolfson climbed into the driver's seat, turned around and threw a black bag at him. 'Stick this over your head,' he told Mickey. Mickey glanced at the bag, knew he had no choice. He slipped the bag over his head, was immediately plunged into utter darkness.

'Hands behind your back!' ordered Wolfson. Mickey leaned forward, heard the rip of tape then felt as Cooper wrapped his wrists in gaffer tape.

With Mickey secure, the car started, moved forwards.

'They'll come after you!' snarled Mickey.

Wolfson's voice carried to him from the front seat. 'I think you overestimate your influence around here, Mickey,' he said. 'Twenty years ago, maybe. But now? Half of Dagenham doesn't even know who you are. The other half don't give a fuck.' Mickey heard the click of a lighter, the sound of Wolfson taking a deep drag on his cigarette. 'No, I'm afraid you are on your own here, boy.'

'I don't know where the diamonds are. You know that, don't you?'

'I know that's what you'll want us to believe,' replied Wolfson.

Hot breath increasing the feeling of claustrophobia each time he exhaled.

'The trouble is, Mickey,' continued Wolfson, 'you're not exactly what I would call a reliable witness. You've done time, you're a crook, you'll say whatever comes to mind if you think it will help you.'

The car pulled to a halt. 'That's why we have to make sure you're telling the truth.'

Mickey settled back against the seat. 'Do what you fucking want,' he growled. 'You'll get nothing out of me.'

A short laugh came from Cooper, sitting beside Mickey. 'That's what your mate Joey said.' Mickey felt Cooper lean in close to him, felt his face against Mickey's ear as he whispered to him. 'But then Joey discovered that the problem wasn't what we got out of him, but what we put in him!'

Without warning, Mickey smashed the side of his head into Cooper's face in a sideways head butt. He felt Cooper's nose and lips crushed against his head, heard a grunt of pain.

'Fuck! The fucker head butted me!'

Wolfson laughed. 'I told you to be careful around him.'

'Cunt!'

Mickey was ready for the blow, but it still forced a gasp from him as Cooper clubbed him across the head with the butt of the gun, once, twice, three times, sending Mickey slumping against the car door.

'Enough!'

Wolfson's shout from the front of the car stopped the onslaught.

Mickey's head was reeling, his world spinning. He felt a wave of nausea rising up in his throat, tried to fight it back, but the pain was too intense - he suddenly vomited inside the bag, felt it splatter across his face, run down his shirt.

'Oh, fucking charming!' snapped Cooper. 'Is that something else they taught you inside?'

Mickey lay against the side of the car, fought for control. These fuckers were not going to defeat him, he would not give them the pleasure of seeing him crack. 'Why don't you untie my wrists and I'll show you a few things I learned inside.'

Cooper's fist slammed into Mickey's kidney, causing him to grunt in pain once again. 'You little fucker. By the time we're finished with you, you'll be begging to be back in prison with some big geezer making you his bitch.'

The car stopped, and Mickey heard the driver's door open.

Then suddenly the passenger door opened and Mickey tumbled out, landing hard on the wet pavement. The hood slipped off his head as he fell forwards, but Cooper quickly grabbed it, yanked it tight over Mickey's head.

'Come on,' ordered Wolfson, 'let's get him inside before anyone sees us.'

Strong arms grabbed him, hauled him to his feet, half dragged him inside. Mickey fought to control himself as he was dragged up a narrow flight of stairs, fought against the feeling that with no one to help, no one even knowing where he was, he might never make it out of there alive.

Martin paced back and forth in front of the fireplace, he looked as his watch for the one hundredth time. 'Where the fuck is he? He knows I have to leave for the airport by ten o'clock.'

Terri sat nursing a cup of tea, watched Martin. She was going to miss him. He'd keep in touch, probably be much more regular with his phone calls now that they had all seen each other again, but it wouldn't be the same.

'He'll be here soon enough,' she said. 'Mickey's always on time, prides himself on it,' she reminded Martin.

'Which is why I'm wondering where the hell he is!' Another glance at his watch. 'Visiting time finished at six, even if he had trouble with the traffic he should have been here by nine. It's almost quarter to ten.'

Terri sighed. 'And where the bloody hell is Sharon?'

Mickey peered out through blurry eyes. One of the problems with the life he'd led was that he could take a beating. Any normal man would have passed out a long time ago, but Mickey was still conscious. Still looking up at Wolfson and Cooper through half closed eyes, still spitting insults out at them through busted, bloody lips. 'Is that the worst you can fucking do?' he snarled.

Cooper stood over him, his arms tired, hands aching from the blows he'd given Mickey. He pulled his fist back, smashed it once again into Mickey's face, cursed as the pain shot through his hand and up his arm.

'Enough!'

Wolfson peered at Mickey's battered face. 'He's an old style hard man. It's going to take more than that for him to talk'

Cooper flexed his aching hand, slowly began to unwrap the cloth strips he'd tied around his knuckles to protect them.

Mickey was a mess – one eye was completely closed, the other swollen half shut, his nose splattered across his face, several teeth missing. He peered up at Cooper through his one working eye, watched as he unwrapped his hand and gazed at his swollen knuckles.

'Looks like my face beat the shit out of your hands,' he gasped.

Wolfson gave him an admiring glance as Cooper ran his aching hands under the cold water tap.

They were in a small flat above a shop, somewhere in Poplar. Mickey looked around – the place was a shit hole. Old, dirty linoleum on the floor, a kitchen full of dirty dishes and old Chinese take-away boxes, three cheap plastic chairs. Mickey was strapped to one of them with about half a roll of tape. Wolfson sat in another chair, legs crossed, one foot swinging as he lit another cigarette. 'You're making this harder than it needs to be, Mickey,' he sighed. 'So far we haven't done anything that will leave any permanent damage, but if you don't start cooperating, we'll have to get nasty.'

Cooper stood with his hands under the cold water tap. 'Told you we should have brought Clemence with us.'

Wolfson shook his head. 'No. There's no need to get that nasty. Mickey's one of us, aren't you, son?'

Mickey shook his head. 'Don't think so. Last time I checked I wasn't a cock-sucking paddy.'

Wolfson sighed. 'You're determined to make this difficult, aren't you?'

Mickey met his gaze. 'What can I tell you? Like I said a hundred times, Georgie is the only one who ever knew where Bobby put those diamonds, and like you've seen, he's been out of his gourd in Rampton Hospital for twenty years. I've spent the last three weeks trying to get some sense out of him, but it's like talking to Alice in fucking Wonderland.'

Wolfson shook his head. 'You're going to have to do better than that, Mickey.'

He stood up, moved closer to Mickey, leaned down and whispered in his ear. 'The thing is, before I came over here, I was in the IRA for a few years, back during the Troubles.' He gently stroked Mickey's hair back off his face. 'In those days, we often needed to get information out of people who were less than cooperative.' He took a drag on his cigarette, held it up and admired it for a second, then slowly ground it out in one of the open cuts on Mickey's cheek. Mickey didn't even flinch, just stared straight up at Wolfson.

Wolfson smiled. 'I haven't done this for a while, not a real, full blown torture session, but you know what? I think I'm going to enjoy it.'

He crouched down beside the chair, pulled a knife from his pocket and flicked the blade open, then turned back towards Cooper. 'Shove something in his mouth. We don't want his screams disturbing anyone.'

Cooper picked up the bloody strips of cloth from the kitchen table, tried to shove them in Mickey's mouth.

Mickey clamped his jaw shut, glared defiantly up at Cooper.

Wolfson smiled once more. 'You've got to love his consistent defiance,' he purred. He suddenly reached in Mickey's lap, grasped his testicles, squeezed hard. As Mickey gasped in pain, Cooper shoved the cloth into Mickey's mouth, half gagging him.

'Better,' said Wolfson. 'You'd better add a bit of tape to keep it in.'

Cooper grabbed the tape from the table, tore off a strip and wrapped it across Mickey's face.

'Now we're ready,' said Wolfson. He gently slid the knife across Mickey's upper arm, cut through the sleeve of Mickey's jacket and shirt, then ripped them off close to his shoulder, leaving them dangling from his wrist, his arm exposed.

'The thing is, there are all sorts of different types of pain,' he explained. 'One of the most interesting is the pain you get from burns.'

He stood up, walked over to the cooker. There was a stack of dirty plates piled up on it. With one sweep of his hand he swept them onto the floor, where they smashed, scattering the pieces everywhere.

'Oi!' protested Cooper. 'This is my fucking place you're smashing up!'

Wolfson replied without turning around. 'When we get those diamonds you can move into a mansion – even hire a maid to keep it clean.'

Cooper grinned. 'I like the sound of that. Think she'll give me a good going over too?'

Wolfson turned on the front hob, picked up a dirty knife from the counter, held the blade in the flame. 'With your charm, how could she refuse?'

Mickey watched as Wolfson patiently waited for the blade to get hot. Mickey knew he was tough – he'd faced enough men down in his time, taken his share of beatings – but this was something else. Everyone had a breaking point somewhere, and if Wolfson was as good as Mickey suspected, sooner rather than later Mickey would be crying like a baby and telling him where the diamonds were. And that meant he'd go to the house. Go to the house where Martin and Sharon and Terri were waiting. And when he took the diamonds he wouldn't want to leave any witnesses alive…

Wolfson turned around, the blade of the knife glowing red. 'Perfect.' He stood beside Mickey, slowly lowered the knife towards Mickey's exposed flesh. 'Let's begin, shall we? Wouldn't want the blade getting cold.'

The pain seared through Mickey's brain and the smell of burnt flesh filled the room. Don't tell them anything, Mickey told himself as the waves of shock and pain washed over his body. Don't tell them anything...

'This is fucking ridiculous!' snapped Martin. He glanced at his watch, although he already knew the time. 'I've got to go or I'll miss my bloody flight!'

Terri nodded slowly. She had hoped desperately that he would stay, that Mickey would come back and tell them all where the diamonds were, and Martin would stay, not go back home to Australia, but she knew that it was a fantasy.

He had a life in Australia, a business, a girl, everything. Here he only had his family, and let's face it, they were the sort of family you'd want to get away from if you could.

Terri envied him. It sounded wonderful – she'd got Martin to tell her all about it. His flat in Sydney overlooking the beach, trips to the Outback to see kangaroos, lazy Sundays where they sat on the balcony drinking beer and having a bar-b-que. Not like England where as soon as you lit the barbie it started to rain!

She slowly stood up. She had promised to drive Martin to the airport. 'I'll get my stuff,' Terri said to Martin, 'then we'll get going.'

As she stepped out into the hallway she saw a shadow in the glass of the front door. For a moment she thought it was Mickey, but there was something wrong, it wasn't big enough to be Mickey. The doorbell rang, and Terri heard Martin's voice. 'About fucking time!"

Terri opened the door, heard Martin hurrying into the hallway behind her.

'What do you want?'

Terri recognised Stewie, he was one of the regulars at the Church Elms. In his mid-60s, he lived just around the corner, had known the family for years.

Stewie was breathless. He swept a wisp of silver hair out of his eyes. 'It's Dangerous.'

Something in his voice set Terri's nerves jangling. Martin pushed past her.

'What? Have you seen him?'

Stewie nodded. 'I was with some mates, over in Poplar at the King's Head.' He paused, caught his breath. 'Anyway, we were just coming out, heading down to the Indian, when I saw these two geezers bundling someone out of a car and into a doorway.'

'And?' Martin already knew what Stewie was going to say, but had to hear it from him.

'So as the geezer fell out of the car, well he had one of them black bags on his head, like in the films. Anyways, as he fell out of the car, the bag fell off – it was Mickey!' His eyes bulged, still amazed by what he'd seen.

'What. You mean someone has kidnapped Mickey or something?'

Stewie nodded. 'I swear it on my mother's – '

'Yeah, yeah, your mother,' snapped Martin. 'It was definitely Mickey?'

Again Stewie nodded.

'And the blokes who were with him. Do you know them?'

'I only saw one, but I'd recognise him anywhere.' He gulped for breath. 'It was that Irish prick, Wolfson.'

Martin cursed, turned to Terri. 'Give me your car keys.'

'What are you going to – '

'Your keys – give me your fucking keys!'

Terri grabbed her car keys off the hall table, clasped them tight in her hand. 'Martin! You don't need to do this. We should call the police.'

Martin slowly shook his head. 'This isn't a police matter, Tel. Someone's messing with the family. I need to deal with it.'

Terri looked up, met Martin's eyes. There was a determination there she recognised, a bull headedness that all the Taylors had. He'd made his

mind up, he wasn't going to be dissuaded. She
shoved her keys into Martin's hand. 'Bring him back,
Martin.'

Martin gave her a quick kiss on the cheek,
hurried out the door, dragging Stewie along with him.
'You know where this place is, where you saw them
taking Mickey?'

'Yeah, yeah, I know it.'

'In the car!'

Mickey's eyes flashed open, and for a minute
he didn't know where he was. It took him a second
to focus, his vision was blurry – he was in a skanky
looking kitchen, it seemed vaguely familiar. A
second cup of water in his face brought him right
back to the present, to Wolfson's cold eyes staring at
him.

'Don't go passing out on me, Mickey. You
can't talk to me if you're out cold.'

The throbbing in Mickey's arm reminded him
of exactly where he was, what was happening.
Wolfson reached out, grabbed Mickey's arm and
squeezed the burnt flesh. Mickey grimaced, rolled
his head, unable to get away from the pain.

'Ah, that's better. Now you remember where
we are.' Wolfson looked over at Cooper. 'Heat it up
again, would you?'

Mickey couldn't help it, his eyes flashed over
to where Cooper stood, by the cooker, the blade of
the knife thrust into the flames.

'Or if you prefer, you could talk to us,' said Wolfson. His voice sounded calm, reasonable, but Mickey could hear the underlying tension. Wolfson was getting angry, frustrated at his inability to break Mickey down.

'We should cut his fucking bollocks off!' suggested Cooper. 'That would loosen his fucking tongue!'

Wolfson looked down at Mickey. 'What do you think about that, Mickey? How do you think this knife would feel on your balls?' He reached out, took the knife from Cooper, the blade once more glowing red. 'Or would you like to talk?'

Mickey stared into Wolfson's cold eyes. He knew that Wolfson wouldn't stop, would just keep on inflicting more and more pain on him until he either talked or died. And right now Mickey just wanted the pain to stop – his arm was on fire where Wolfson had burned him over and over again. The smell of his own burning flesh was in his nostrils, sweet and acrid all at once. He had to get a respite from the pain. He slowly nodded his head.

'You want to talk?' said Wolfson.

Again Mickey nodded.

'Good boy.' He handed the knife back to Cooper, who set it down on the kitchen counter. 'I told you he would come around eventually.'

Wolfson leaned over Mickey, grabbed one end of the gaffer tape, ripped it from his face, then pulled the soggy mass of cloth from his mouth.

Mickey gasped as the cloth was removed, gulped in several deep breaths of cold air.

Wolfson's eyes never left him. 'So. The diamonds?'

Mickey started to speak, forced his voice into a raspy wheeze, then began choking. 'Water', he gasped.

Wolfson nodded impatiently to Cooper. 'Get him a glass of water.'

Wolfson grabbed a dirty coffee cup from the counter, threw the dregs in the sink, filled it quickly from the tap, and held it out for Mickey.

Mickey leaned forwards, gulped at the murky liquid, spilling half of it down his chest. It was the sweetest drink he had ever tasted, sliding down his parched throat.

'Enough!' Wolfson jerked Cooper back out the way, stood in front of Mickey, his hands on his hips. 'Now, tell me where those fucking diamonds are before things get really unpleasant.'

Mickey nodded. 'Georgie was the only one who saw what Bobby did,' he gasped. 'But he's been out of his fucking skull for years, so I had to take my time, work towards it, tease it out of him.'

Wolfson leaned forwards. 'But he knew?'

Mickey nodded. 'Yeah, the crazy fucker knew all along.'

'And?'

'He kept rambling on about Jesus. He used to be very religious – probably because he fucked a priest when he was younger.'

Wolfson was getting impatient. 'Do I look like I care about your brother's sordid fucking love life?'

'I'm getting there,' Mickey reassured him. 'So he keeps banging on about Jesus, and God, and the devil and all that shit, and finally I realised what he was trying to tell me.'

Wolfson licked his lips, glanced at Cooper. This was it. Finally, after twenty years, they were going to get their reward.

'What he was trying to tell me was...' Mickey paused for effect. 'Go to fucking hell!'

There was a moment's silence as Wolfson took in what Mickey had said. Then he exploded. 'You miserable fucking cunt!' he roared. He grabbed Mickey's shirt front, began shaking him, screaming in his face. 'You bastard, I'm going to cut your balls off and shove them in your mouth, then I'm going over to your house, killing everyone there, and tearing the place apart until I find those fucking diamonds!' He turned back towards Cooper. 'Give me that fucking knife!'

As Cooper reached for the knife, the door exploded open, crashing against the wall, and Martin stood framed in the doorway.

Cooper turned, the knife in his hand, but he was way too slow. Martin had been a boxer – a really, fucking good boxer – and no old geezer was going to stop him.

Before Cooper could even bring the knife up, Martin grabbed his wrist, slammed it down on the counter. Cooper screamed in pain, stumbled forwards, and was met by Martin's knee rising up to crush his nose.

He collapsed backwards on the floor, blood pumping from his face.

When Martin stormed in, Wolfson had reacted quickly, calmly. He drew a gun from his jacket pocket, aimed it at Martin.

As Martin looked up from Cooper's writhing body he found himself staring straight down the dark barrel. 'You're all as stupid and impulsive as your fucking father,' sneered Wolfson. He looked at Mickey. 'Time to choose, Mickey. Do I shoot your brother, or do you tell me where the diamonds are?'

Mickey glanced over at Martin.

'Don't tell him,' yelled Martin. 'He'll kill us both as soon as you tell him!'

'Don't pretend to be clever, son,' Wolfson snapped, glaring at Martin.

It was all Mickey needed – Wolfson distracted for a second. With every ounce of strength he had left, Mickey hurled himself sideways, toppling the chair over at Wolfson's feet.

Wolfson couldn't help himself – as Mickey landed at his feet he stumbled backwards, the gun no longer pointing at Martin.

Martin needed no second invitation. He grabbed the large knife that Cooper had dropped on the counter, lunged forwards, caught Wolfson in the arm as he brought the gun back up. The knife sliced into his arm and he dropped the gun, instinctively grabbing his bleeding arm with the other hand.

He was defenceless as Martin crashed a left hook into his face, crumpled in a heap, the gun skittering away across the floor.

Martin jumped over Wolfson's fallen body, picked up the gun, span around to survey the damage.

Cooper was still groaning and gurgling, holding his crushed nose. Wolfson sat up, blood flowing from his arm, began to stand up then thought better of it as he saw the gun in Martin's hand.

Martin moved quickly over to Mickey, slipped the gun in his jacket pocket, then sliced the tape binding Mickey to the chair.

Mickey pulled his arms free, rose slowly, his balance uncertain at first. He looked down at his arm, covered in cuts and burns, then turned to Cooper, lying on the floor behind him. Mickey stood over Cooper, who peered up through his bloody fingers.

'I never touched you,' pleaded Cooper. 'You've seen Wolfson, what he's like…'

Mickey looked down at him with disdain. 'I seem to recall you wanted to cut my bollocks off!'

Before Cooper could say anything, Mickey lifted his size eleven boot, stamped down on Cooper's groin with sickening force. There was an animal like squeal as Cooper grabbed his crotch, curled up in a ball on his side, vomited on the dirty lino.

Martin watched as Mickey turned back to Wolfson.

Wolfson gave a rueful grin. 'No hard feelings, eh, Mickey? You would have done the same.'

Mickey walked slowly towards where Wolfson sat on the ground, clutching his bleeding arm. 'Yeah, you're probably right,' he said quietly. Then once more his boot lashed out, catching Wolfson in the face and sending him crashing back into the wall. Two, three times more he kicked him with brutal intensity, breaking several ribs as Wolfson tried to curl up and protect himself.

Mickey turned to Martin. 'Gimme the gun.'

Martin shook his head. 'No.'

Mickey glared at him. 'We can't leave them alive, they'll come after us. Gimme the fucking gun!'

Martin looked down at the gun in his hand. 'I know.' He looked up and met Mickey's eyes. 'You know, I spent years running away from you, trying not to be like you.'

'And you did a fucking good job of it. So thanks for saving me, and now fuck off and let me finish this.'

Martin ignored him. 'But deep down,' he said, 'I always knew I'd come back, knew I'd wind up being a part of your world.'

Mickey shook his head. 'It doesn't have to be this way. You've done what you had to, so walk away, let me clean up this mess.'

Martin looked at Mickey, sadness in his face. Finally he gave a bitter smile. 'I guess it was inevitable,' he said finally.

Mickey took a step towards him. 'Martin, give me the gun!'

Martin shook his head.

'Why the fuck not!'

'Coz I'm a Taylor, and coz these two cunts fucked with the family!' Before Mickey could stop him Martin turned on Cooper. Bang! Bang! The gun was deafening in the tiny flat.

Wolfson started to try and rise, a groan escaping his lips as the pain from his ribs grabbed at him.

Martin stomped over to him, stood directly above him. 'You knew my dad, knew all of us growing up. You should have been smart enough to remember one simple thing!'

Wolfson looked up at him, met Martin's cold, unblinking eyes.

'Don't ever fuck with the Taylors!'

Both shots hit Wolfson between the eyes, slamming his head back against the wall.

As Mickey watched, Martin calmly grabbed a filthy tea towel, wiped the handle of the gun clean, then holding the barrel in the tea towel to avoid any further prints, he slipped it into Wolfson's dead fingers.

Martin looked up, found Mickey staring at him in admiration. 'Fuck me! And I thought you'd not learned anything from us!'

As Martin started to reply, Mickey swayed slightly. Martin wrapped a strong arm around him, guided him towards the door. 'Learned from you? Don't flatter yourself. Everything l learned comes from films!'

He paused in the doorway, looked back. 'Let's see what the Old Bill makes of that little mess!'

Diamond Geezer

Mickey climbed wearily out of Terri's car, fighting to ignore the screaming pain coming from his arm. Martin hurried round, offered him a hand, but Mickey brushed him away. After all he'd been through, he was determined to stand on his own two feet.

Martin led the way up the path, reached up to unlock the front door, but it was open before he could get there, Terri framed in the doorway, her wide eyes gazing out into the darkness. As she saw Mickey her face fell. 'Oh shit!'

She ushered them both inside, her eyes showing her pain at the state of Mickey, but knowing that the last thing he wanted was a thousand questions. She'd been around Mickey long enough to know that when he came back worse for wear – even in a state like this – he didn't want a fuss, just the space to recover.

Mickey walked into the living room, a little unsteady on his feet.

Sharon looked up, her eyes bleary. 'Did you kill the bastard?'

Mickey looked at her, concerned. Her face had been busted up badly, she looked really rough. 'Are you all right?'

'Just answer the fucking question! Is that Irish prick dead?'

Mickey slowly nodded.

'And did he suffer first?'

Martin followed Mickey into the room. 'I think Mickey broke half his ribs first.'

Sharon slumped back into her chair, sucked down the remains of her drink. 'That's good.'

Mickey staggered forward, slumped into a chair.

Terri was all business – she was used to dealing with her kids, knew that when someone was hurt, you just got on with it, didn't make a fuss. 'Martin, fix your brother a drink, I'll get the first aid box.'

As Martin headed for the drinks cabinet, Terri hurried into the kitchen, opened the cupboard over the sink, pulled down the battered white tin with the first aid stuff in it. Jesus, she thought, how many times have I seen mum reach for this first aid kit?

Visions of Lizzie swamped her mind – sitting at the kitchen table, the trusty white first aid kit open, applying some Savlon or a plaster to the latest cut or scrape the boys had come home with.

Mickey was the most regular recipient of Lizzie's ministrations. He'd sit there, eyes staring straight ahead, pretending it didn't hurt while Lizzie cleaned him up, patched him up, and cheered him up. And always, after the treatment was over, there'd be a treat from Lizzie's little tin.

Terri stopped in the doorway. It couldn't still be there, could it?

Even though she knew Mickey was waiting, Terri had to look. She turned back, rummaged in the back of the cupboard – and there it was, at the back as always, the battered old Cadbury's tin. Terri lifted it down – there was still something in it. Grinning, she headed back to the living room, the first aid kit in one hand, Lizzie's tin of treats in the other.

Mickey looked like shit, every one of his forty two years showing in his battered, bleeding face. He was slumped back in the armchair, eyes closed, one arm clutching a tall glass, the other – the injured one – resting lightly in his lap.

He looked up as Terri knelt down in front of him, forced a smile to his face. 'All right, girl?' he said softly.

Terri dropped Lizzie's tin of treats into his lap.
'Here. Help yourself.'

When he saw the tin, Mickey couldn't help
but grin. 'Fuck me! Where did you find that?'

'In the cupboard, where it always used to be.'

Mickey gazed at the tin then at Terri. 'A
rotten mother you are – you're supposed to just give
me one treat, not the whole bloody tin!'

She smiled up at him, gently lifted his arm,
and winced as she saw the scorched flesh. 'It looks
like you've earned it tonight.'

Mickey raised his glass. 'This will do me for
now.'

Terri nodded, wondered where to start.
Mickey really needed to be in the hospital.

As if sensing her thoughts, he leaned forward,
held his arm out. 'Just do what you can.'

'It's going to hurt,' she said softly.

'Not as bad as it did when that cunt was
doing it.'

Terri nodded, began gently cleaning the mess
that was Mickey's arm.

Mickey closed his eyes, gritted his teeth.

Martin stood by the fireplace, watching
quietly. He'd not only missed his flight, he had the
feeling he'd made a decision – he wasn't going back.
Despite how fucked up everything had been, despite
the shit he'd got into, he realised he missed all of this.

Missed home, missed the lousy weather, missed his family.

He'd be able to sell his business in Australia easily enough. Several of the bigger trucking companies had been sniffing around for a couple of years, wanting to buy him out. They would trip over themselves to snap his business up.

What had swayed him, changed him? It was Mickey – the strong one, the head of the family, the Big I Am. Martin had seen him at his most vulnerable, had seen him on the verge of death, and in that instant had realised that he loved his brother more than anyone else in the world. If Mickey was killed while he, Martin, was on the other side of the world, sitting in the sun or relaxing at the beach, he would never forgive himself.

'So where the fuck are those diamonds?' Sharon had suddenly come awake, peered around at the other three through her red rimmed eyes. 'I mean, that's what the fuck this whole fucking fiasco has been about, isn't it? They've tortured me, tortured Mickey half to death. Is there any pay-off?'

Terri looked at her sister with barely concealed contempt. 'Your brother's half fucking dead, and all you care about is the money?'

Sharon sneered back at her. 'Don't tell me you haven't thought about it too? I see you scrimping and saving to feed those four fucking whelps of yours.'

Mickey leaned forwards, glared at both of them. 'Enough!' He shook his head, looked at his arm. Terri had cleaned him up, was just finishing up bandaging. 'Thanks, love.'

'You'll need to get it checked properly,' she said as he stood up.

Mickey nodded, forced a smile to his face as he stood in front of Martin. 'Listen, I'm sorry you got dragged – '

'Fuck off!' laughed Martin. 'I chose to come back for the funeral, chose to stay for a few weeks after, chose to come save your sorry arse tonight.'

This time Mickey's smile was genuine. 'I'm glad you're here.'

Martin's cheeky grin lit up his face. 'I'll bet you are! But don't expect me to get in the habit of bailing you out!'

Mickey felt a warm glow surge through him. It was good having all four of them back together again. It felt right, things the way they should be. If only Georgie were here... He turned and faced his sisters. 'So I guess we all want to know about these fucking diamonds, eh?'

Sharon sat up and leaned forwards, fixed her eyes on Mickey. 'Yeah, we could all do with a few bob, right, Tel?'

Terri sat primly in the chair that Mickey had vacated. 'I'm just happy that those bastards that roughed up you and Mickey aren't going to be coming after us anymore.'

'They won't bother us again,' said Martin.

'How can you be sure?'

Mickey and Martin exchanged a glance.

Terri caught the look, understood in an instant what it meant. 'Oh,' she said quietly.

Mickey looked at each of them in turn. Martin looked indifferent – he had plenty of money back in Oz, the diamonds would make no difference to him. His interest was simply in seeing the end to the mystery, finding out what it was he had killed two men for, other than family pride and protection.

Terri still looked shocked by the realization that Mickey and Martin had killed the men that had threatened them. She knew it happened, certainly knew that Bobby, their brutal father, had killed several men, but it had never occurred to her that it could happen now, or that Martin would be involved. She thought those days were over, were behind them all. But then another voice spoke to her, a bitter, realistic voice. With this family, it said, you really think that kind of shit ever really ends?

Then Mickey's eyes fell on Sharon. Pissed as a skunk. She'd always been a sloppy drunk, and it wasn't getting any better as she aged. Her hair was a mess, lipstick smeared, her pale eyes stared at him with undisguised greed. Of all of them, Sharon had always been the one who hungered for money.

However much she had, she wanted more, whatever you gave her as a present, she was always thinking about the price tag. Always comparing it with what everyone else had got, making the calculation to see if she had come out on top. And she was also the one who pissed away money the fastest, the one who always seemed to need more. But on the other hand, Wolfson had paid her a visit today, and though she'd given Mickey away, she'd still had the determination to free herself after he left, to come to the house and try and warn them. She may be a drunk, he thought, but she was still a Taylor.

Sharon met his eyes, as though she knew what he was thinking. She licked her lips, stared at Mickey. 'Come on then, don't fucking keep us waiting. That cunt raped and tortured me. The least I can do is get something out of it!'

Mickey sighed. 'You lot can't imagine what it has been like talking to Georgie these past few weeks. His mind wanders all over the place. Half the time I think he's completely bonkers, half the time I think he's the sanest, smartest geezer I've ever met and he's winding me up.'

'So what the fuck did he tell you?' Sharon was growing impatient, but Mickey was going to tell them his story in his own way.

'He seemed to go back and forth at the drop of a hat, but the one thing he kept coming back to was God.'

'Jesus! Save us from fucking religious nuts!' moaned Sharon.

'He knew what I wanted. No matter how I tried to skirt around the subject, I could always tell that he knew.' Mickey glanced at Martin. 'Seems like Wolfson and Cooper had been to see him, on the sly like.' Mickey laughed. 'Good luck with that! I'll bet they left tearing their fucking hair out!'

He looked at his empty glass, handed it to Martin. 'Do us a favour and fill that up – the pain killers are wearing off.'

As Martin filled the glass, Mickey continued talking. 'I always thought all Georgie's religious talk was just that – he'd always been a bit of a Jesus freak, and I figured what with going off his rocker and all, he'd become a complete and utter religious nutter.'

He paused as Martin handed him his drink, took a long sip, then set the drink on the mantelpiece. He turned and walked out the living room and upstairs to his mums bedroom. Within minutes he was back downstairs with their mums statue of Jesus in his hand. 'Today, it suddenly twigged. He was telling me in his own fucked up way.'

'Telling you what?' Sharon could barely contain herself.

'He kept saying the same phrase, over and over, with this weird look in his eyes.'

'What?' gasped Sharon. 'What was the phrase?'

Mickey smiled. 'Jesus will provide.'

Terri frowned. 'Jesus will provide? What does that mean?'

Mickey glanced at Terri, then back at the statue. 'Mum, I know you're up there looking down right now – please forgive me.' And so saying he dropped the statue of Jesus down onto the stone hearth.

Terri gasped in shock as it smashed into a thousand pieces, shards of plaster flying across the room to lose themselves in the thick carpet. 'Mickey! That was mum's...' Her voice trailed off.

There, on the hearth, lay a small, dark blue velvet bag.

Sharon started forward from her chair, fell to her hands and knees.

Martin moved quickly, easily, picked the bag up, held it out in front of him. 'What have we here?' he said quietly. The others all gazed at him as he gently loosened the strings on the bag. 'Hold your hand out, Mickey,' he said.

Mickey opened one of his big hands, palm up, and Martin tipped the bag upside down into the palm of his hand.

They all gasped as the gems spilled out, sparkling in the light, lay in a pile in Mickey's big hand.

'Fuck my old boots!' exclaimed Mickey.

'Are they real?' wondered Terri.

Sharon climbed to her feet, leaned on Mickey's shoulder to gaze at them. 'After what everyone has gone through to find these? They had fucking better be!'

Mickey snapped his hand shut, and the light that had reflected on all their faces vanished instantly. 'These don't exist,' he said in a low growl. 'You've never seen them, know nothing about them. If anyone asks, the whole thing was a hoax, a fairy story from twenty years ago that amounted to nothing more. Got it?'

They all looked at him. Sharon scowled. 'How come you get to decide?'

Mickey glared right back. 'Because I've just about died to get these things, because I'm the one holding them, and because I'm the head of this fucking family, and you will do what I say!' His voice grew louder and louder with each word, until it filled the room. As he fell silent, nothing could be heard but his heavy breathing.

Sharon met his gaze for a brief second, then looked down. 'OK,' she mumbled.

'None of you are used to dealing with this type of situation, where you suddenly have a load of cash, cash you can't explain,' continued Mickey. 'If you go flashing the money around, shooting your mouth off, you'll have the Old Bill breathing down your neck – or worse.'

He turned to Martin. 'Gimme the bag.'

Martin handed him the bag, and Mickey trickled the gems back inside, pulled the string tight, dropped it in his trouser pocket. 'Here's how this works. I'll have to find someone to fence this lot, someone I can trust. It's a lot of cash for anyone to come up with, so it might take a while. You won't know when I do it or where I do it, so don't ask. Agreed?'

They all nodded.

'Once I have the cash, I'll split it five ways, five equal shares. I'll hold Georgie's for when he's released.'

Sharon licked her lips, her eyes fixed on Mickey.

'I'll give you the money little by little, over the next five years.'

'What!' squawked Sharon. 'Who the fuck gave you the right to – '

'Shut it!' The command in Mickey's voice froze her into silence. 'This is not a fucking discussion, this is the way it is. Agreed?'

Terri and Martin nodded. 'Agreed.'

'Sharon?'

Sharon said nothing, chewed her lip. Finally she looked up at Mickey. 'What if I get caught a bit short, need an advance or something?'

'No.'

'But Mickey…' she whined.

'In or out?'

Sharon gave a deep sigh. 'Agreed. And fuck you!' She turned away from Mickey, grabbed her glass from the side table, and filled it with several measures of vodka.

Mickey looked at each of them in turn, then slowly nodded. 'It's settled then.' He picked up his glass from the mantelpiece, held it up. The others all raised their glasses. 'Here's to Georgie, for coming through when we needed him.'

They all drank.

'And here's to mum and Jesus for guarding this so well for so long.'

Again they all drank.

'And here's to Bobby fucking Taylor, may he rot in hell.' Mickey grinned. 'I'll bet he's turning in his fucking grave at the thought of us all getting our hands on these diamonds!'

He drained his glass, looked around at the others. 'Now if you'll all excuse me, I've had a long, hard fucking day, and I'm going to bed!'

The End

Other Books by Sandra Prior

Dangerous – published 2012

www.SandraPrior.co.uk

http://www.facebook.com/sandrapriorauthor

http://twitter.com/Sandra_Prior

About the Author Sandra Prior

It's a little ironic that Sandra Prior created her first novel around a kingpin named Bobby Taylor. After all, Sandra's life isn't anything like Bobby's!

Sandra grew up happy and healthy with four sisters, a brother, and parents who lived in the same Dagenham home for more than half a century. She describes her childhood as "sunny and safe", living in a place where you could play for hours and wander the streets with your friends, without any fears

Today, Sandra lives in Clacton with her partner, her youngest son, and her dog— who, she notes, was kind enough to "let" her write *Diamond Geezer* in between their walks on the beach.

Unlike other writers, Sandra took a different path to get where she is today. Her books aren't the result of years of schooling and formal writing training. In fact, while she was raising her young children, Sandra took evening classes to complete her English and math qualifications (as she puts it, "I didn't do what I should have at school."). After that, she studied Sociology through the Open University which led to her heading off to the University of East London — where she earned a degree in Cultural Studies.

By 1998, Sandra was a business owner — the owner of

a domiciliary care agency, to be exact. It didn't take long for her to learn the value of hard work, passion, and communication, along with the importance of balancing her business commitments with her family commitments. Years later, she would add one more thing to the mix — by balancing her business responsibilities and her family life with her writing duties.

And speaking of writing...

For years, Sandra dreamed of writing a book. Alas, like so many of us, her dream sat in the back of her mind collecting dust. After all, she had a demanding career and a busy family life. How can you add writing a book to all of that?! For years, she told herself that there wasn't enough time, that she wasn't organised enough to pull it off, and that it was a nice thought — but not something that you actually go out and DO.

But then, one day, Sandra's life completely changed when she flipped through the pages of a magazine and read about a man named Anthony Robbins and something called "life coaching". She went to one of Robbins' London seminars and actually managed to walk across a 15-foot bed of burning coals!

From there, she decided that if she was going to make the most of her life, she would have to "keep walking"...

That's when she decided to make her writing real, instead of just a fantasy that lived deep in her mind. Sandra sat down and began working on *Dangerous* – with just Stevie Wonder, Bob Marley, Barry White, Rod Stewart, and the like to keep her company.

Through the laughter, the tears, the shouting, and the frustration, Sandra was able to realise her dream and finish *Dangerous*. Oh sure, there were times when she didn't think she was going to make it. On more than one occasion, she considered tossing the half-finished manuscript right in the bin and calling the whole thing off. So, when she finally got to write the words "The End" on her very first novel, it was a huge accomplishment and, in a way, almost an even bigger relief!

However, *Dangerous'* ending was really just the beginning...

Today, she is the proud author of *Diamond Geezer*, the second book devoted to the Taylor family. While she still spends time running her business, Sandra has replaced all of those long hours with just a couple of trips to the office every month. Most of the time, she handles everything over the phone or through email. That way, she has plenty of time to write!

So, what's next in the writing department?

Sandra will soon start working on the third book in the Taylor trilogy. She is already brimming with ideas as to where the Taylors wind up! She still dreams of seeing her name on the *New York Times'* bestseller list, but in the meantime, she wants to write one new novel every year.

And, of course, Sandra has her own family to keep her company as she comes up with new adventures for the Taylor family. She's madly in love with her four children and her four grandchildren.

When she's not writing, Sandra loves spending time at the beach (with and without the dog!). She enjoys everything from walking along the rocks to enjoying a beach snowfall in the winter. She's also a big fan of the theatre and, of course, reading! In fact, Sandra credits fellow British author Martina Cole as her "inspiration" for getting into the crime-writing business.

www.SandraPrior.co.uk

http://www.facebook.com/sandrapriorauthor

http://twitter.com/Sandra_Prior